D1685160

*The
Hidden
Girl*

Also by Lucinda Riley

Hothouse Flower
The Girl on the Cliff
The Light Behind the Window
The Midnight Rose
The Italian Girl
The Angel Tree
The Olive Tree
The Love Letter
The Butterfly Room
The Murders at Fleat House

The Seven Sisters Series
The Seven Sisters
The Storm Sister
The Shadow Sister
The Pearl Sister
The Moon Sister
The Sun Sister
The Missing Sister

By Lucinda Riley and Harry Whittaker

Grace and the Christmas Angel
Bill and the Dream Angel
Rosie and the Friendship Angel
Alfie and the Angel of Lost Things
Atlas: The Story of Pa Salt

The Hidden Girl

LUCINDA RILEY

writing as Lucinda Edmonds

PAN BOOKS

Previously published as *Hidden Beauty*

This revised and updated edition first published 2024 by Macmillan

This paperback edition published 2025 by Pan Books
an imprint of Pan Macmillan
The Smithson, 6 Briset Street, London EC1M 5NR
EU representative: Macmillan Publishers Ireland Ltd, 1st Floor,
The Liffey Trust Centre, 117–126 Sheriff Street Upper,
Dublin 1, D01 YC43
Associated companies throughout the world
www.panmacmillan.com

ISBN 978-1-0350-4796-3

Copyright © Lucinda Riley 2024

The right of Lucinda Riley to be identified as the
author of this work has been asserted by her in accordance
with the Copyright, Designs and Patents Act 1988.

All rights reserved. No part of this publication may be reproduced,
stored in a retrieval system, or transmitted, in any form, or by any means
(electronic, mechanical, photocopying, recording or otherwise)
without the prior written permission of the publisher.

Pan Macmillan does not have any control over, or any responsibility for,
any author or third-party websites referred to in or on this book.

1 3 5 7 9 8 6 4 2

A CIP catalogue record for this book is available from the British Library.

Typeset in Sabon LT Std by Palimpsest Book Production Ltd, Falkirk, Stirlingshire
Printed and bound by CPI Group (UK) Ltd, Croydon, CR0 4YY

This book is sold subject to the condition that it shall not, by way of
trade or otherwise, be lent, hired out, or otherwise circulated without
the publisher's prior consent in any form of binding or cover other than
that in which it is published and without a similar condition including
this condition being imposed on the subsequent purchaser.

Visit **www.panmacmillan.com** to read more about all our books
and to buy them. You will also find features, author interviews and
news of any author events, and you can sign up for e-newsletters
so that you're always first to hear about our new releases.

Foreword

Dear Reader,

Thank you for picking up this Lucinda Riley novel. I'm Lucinda's son, Harry Whittaker. If you know my name, it will no doubt be from *Atlas: The Story of Pa Salt*, the conclusion to Mum's Seven Sisters series, which became my responsibility after her death in 2021.

I wanted to explain how *The Hidden Girl* has come to be published in 2024. To do so, I must provide a potted history of Mum's work, so I hope you'll indulge me.

From 1993 to 2000, Mum wrote eight novels under the name Lucinda Edmonds. Her career was seemingly cut short by a book called *Seeing Double*. The fictional plot suggested that there was an illegitimate member of the British Royal Family. The recent death of Princess Diana and subsequent monarchical turmoil meant bookshops deemed the project too much of a risk. Consequently, Lucinda Edmonds orders were cancelled, and her contract was voided by her publishers.

Between 2000 and 2008, Mum wrote three novels, all of which went unpublished. Then, in 2010, she had a breakthrough. Her first book as Lucinda Riley – *Hothouse Flower* – hit the shelves. Under this new name, she went on to become one of the world's most successful writers of female fiction, having sold sixty million books at the time of writing. Alongside her brand-new novels, Mum rewrote three 'Edmonds' books: *Aria* (which became *The Italian Girl*), *Not Quite an Angel* (which became *The Angel Tree*) and the aforementioned *Seeing Double* (which became *The Love Letter*). As for the three unpublished novels, all have now been released with great success.

This brings me on to *The Hidden Girl*. It was originally published in 1993 under the title *Hidden Beauty*, and was the second novel Mum penned, aged twenty-six. She often spoke of how proud she was of the story, and it was her intention to reintroduce it to the world. Sadly, she never had the opportunity.

When I read it for the first time, I was enormously impressed. In these pages, you will discover thwarted ambition, forbidden love, revenge and murder . . . culminating in a fatal, forgotten prophecy from the past. It struck me that the manuscript contained so much of what Lucinda would bring to the fore in her later work – glamorous locales, the meaning of family and the ability of love to transcend generations. But, as ever, she does not shy away from difficult realities such as depression, alcoholism and sexual violence against women.

There's no doubt that Lucinda has always been one of the world's best storytellers, but her authorial voice naturally matured over her thirty-year career. She conducted extensive work on her three previous rewrites, changing plots, adding characters and amending her style. Consequently, I have undertaken the role here, refreshing and updating the text, helping to turn the 'Edmonds' into a 'Riley'.

The process has been challenging. Naturally, I wanted to keep the original work as intact as possible, but it was my responsibility to modernise perspectives and sensibilities without ripping the heart out of the novel. The world has changed a great deal in thirty years, and internet commentary seems to grow more vicious by the day. I hope I have managed to walk the tightrope successfully, and done Mum justice. I must stress that she was highly familiar with the world you are about to be immersed in. Her early life was spent as an actor and model, and I am certain that parts of this book were based on personal experiences.

As Lucinda's readers will be aware, Mum often chose to structure her fiction around real historical events, quite often to tell lesser-known stories from those periods. The Seven Sisters series captures the tensions of the World Wars, the conflict between Britain and Ireland, the American civil rights movement, plus the challenges faced by Aboriginal Australians and the Roma people of Spain. In *The Hidden Girl*, Lucinda portrays the horrors of the Treblinka extermination camp in occupied Poland during the Second World War. The topic was clearly important to her, as it will no doubt be to all compassionate and engaged citizens. She would be hopeful that the fictional events portrayed in this novel might encourage wider reading around the Holocaust.

And so, *The Hidden Girl* is hidden no more. To Lucinda's returning readers, Mum is waiting for you like an old friend, ready to pull you into the past and waltz you across the globe. As for new readers, welcome! I'm thrilled you have decided to choose to spend some time with Lucinda Riley.

Harry Whittaker, 2024

Prologue

The old woman stared at Leah, then smiled, her face creasing into a thousand wrinkles. Leah thought that she must be at least a hundred and fifty years old. All the children at her junior school said she was a witch and they howled like banshees as they passed her near-derelict cottage on their way home through the village after school. To the adults, she was old Megan, who took in injured birds and used herbal concoctions to mend their broken wings. Some said she was mad, others that she had the gift of healing and strange psychic powers.

Leah's mother felt sorry for her.

'Poor old biddy,' she'd say, 'all alone in that damp, dirty cottage.' Then she'd tell Leah to collect a few eggs from the hen-shed and take them round to Megan.

Leah's heart always beat with fear when she knocked on the crumbling door. Usually, Megan would open it slowly, peer round and grab the eggs out of Leah's hand with a nod. The door would close and Leah would run as fast as she could back home.

But today, when she had knocked, the door had opened much wider so that Leah could see behind Megan and into the dark recesses of the cottage.

Megan was still staring at her.

1

'I . . . I . . . Mum thought you might like some eggs.' Leah proffered the box and watched the long, bony fingers close around it.

'Thank you.'

Leah was surprised at the gentle tone. Megan certainly didn't sound like a witch.

'Why don't you come in?'

'Well, I . . .'

Already an arm had closed around Leah's shoulder and was propelling her inside.

'I can't stay long. Mum'll wonder where I've got to.'

'You can tell her you were having tea with Megan the witch,' she chuckled. 'Sit yourself down over there. I'm about to brew up.' Megan pointed to one of the battered armchairs placed on either side of a small, empty fireplace.

Leah sat nervously, her hands clasped under her legs. She looked around the cramped kitchen. On every wall, there were shelves filled with old coffee jars full of strange-coloured potions. Megan pulled a jar down, opened it and put two teaspoons of yellow powder into an ancient stainless-steel teapot. She added water from the kettle, placed it on a tray along with two cups and set the tray down on a table in front of Leah. Slowly, Megan lowered herself into the other armchair.

'Will you pour, dear?'

Leah nodded, leaned forward and poured the steaming liquid into the two chipped china cups. She sniffed. The liquid had a strange, acrid smell.

'It's all right, I'm not trying to poison you. Here, I'll sip mine first and you can see if I die. It's only dandelion tea. It'll do you good.' She took the cup in both hands and drank. 'Try some.'

Leah tentatively put the cup to her lips, trying to breathe through her mouth, the pungent aroma too much for her. She sipped, and swallowed without tasting.

'There now, that wasn't too bad, was it?'

Leah shook her head and put the cup down on the table. She fidgeted in her chair as Megan drained her cup.

'Thank you for the tea. It was very nice. I really must be going. Mum'll start to—'

'I've watched you pass here every day. You're going to have extraordinary beauty when you're older. It's already starting to show itself.'

Leah blushed as Megan's piercing green eyes scanned her from top to toe.

'It may not be the blessing the world thinks it is. Take care.' Megan frowned, then reached across the table. Leah shuddered as the bony fingers locked in a claw-like grip around her hand. Panic rose inside her.

'Yes, but I . . . I must go home.'

Megan's eyes were staring far beyond Leah, and her body was taut. 'There is evil, I can feel it. You must be on your guard.' Megan's voice was rising. Leah was paralysed with fear. The grip around her hand tightened.

'Unnatural things . . . evil things . . . never mess with nature, you upset the pattern. Poor soul . . . he is lost . . . doomed . . . He will come back to find you on the moors . . . and you will return of your own free will. You can't alter destiny . . . you must beware him.'

Suddenly, the grip around Leah's hand slackened and Megan crumpled back into her chair, her eyes closed. Leah jumped to her feet and ran to the front door and out into the street. She did not stop running until she reached the hen-shed at the back of the small terraced house where she lived with her parents. She opened the latch and slumped down onto the floor, causing the hens to scatter.

Leah leaned her head back against the wooden wall and allowed her breathing to slow.

The villagers were right. Megan was mad. What had she said about Leah taking care? It was scary. She was eleven years old and she didn't understand. She wanted her mother, but couldn't tell her what had happened. Her mum would think she had made it up and say that it wasn't nice to spread nasty rumours about a poor, helpless old lady.

Leah stood up and slowly made her way to the back door. The secure smell of home calmed her as she stepped into the warm kitchen.

'Hello, Leah, just in time for tea. Sit yourself down.' Doreen Thompson turned and smiled, then a frown of concern crossed her brow. 'Why, Leah, whatever is wrong? You're as white as a ghost.'

'Nothing, Mum. I'm fine. I've just got a tummy-ache, that's all.'

'Growing pains, most likely. Try and put some food inside you and I'm sure you'll feel better.'

Leah crossed to her mother and hugged her tight.

'Now, what's all this about?'

'I . . . I love you, Mum.' Leah nestled into the comforting arms and felt much better.

But the following week, when her mother asked her to take the eggs round as usual to Megan, she adamantly refused.

Megan died six months later and Leah was glad.

Part One

June 1976 to October 1977

1

Rose Delancey dropped her fine sable brush into the jar of turpentine. She put down her palette on the paint-spattered workbench and sank into the threadbare armchair, pushing her heavy titian hair away from her face. She picked up the photograph from which she had been working and compared it with the completed painting resting on the easel in front of her.

The likeness was excellent, although she found it difficult to distinguish between one sleek mare and the next. However, while she was trying to gather a collection of work to show at the London gallery, paintings like this paid the bills.

The work had been commissioned by a wealthy local farmer who owned three racehorses. Ondine, the chestnut mare staring soulfully at Rose from the painting, was number two. The farmer was paying her five hundred pounds for each painting. This would allow her to replace the roof of the rambling stone farmhouse where she and her children lived. It wouldn't stretch to solving the deteriorating damp problem, or make any headway into the dry rot and woodworm, but it was a start.

Rose was banking on the exhibition. If she could sell just a few of her paintings, it would make all the difference to her mounting debts. The constant promises to the bank manager were wearing thin and Rose knew she was treading a very fine line.

But it was a long time since she had shown – almost twenty years. People may have forgotten her since those heady days when she was adored by critics and public alike. Rose had been young, beautiful and immensely gifted . . . but then it had all gone wrong, and she had left the bright lights of London to live in seclusion here, in Sawood, on the rolling moors of Yorkshire.

Yes, the exhibition in April next year was certainly a gamble, but it had to pay off.

Rose stood up and manoeuvred her large frame expertly through the clutter of her small studio. She stared out of the picture window at the serenity beyond. The view never ceased to fill her with peace and was the main reason she had bought the farmhouse. It was perched on top of a hill, with an un-interrupted view of the valley below. The sliver of silver water known as Leeming Reservoir far beneath contrasted well with the thorough greenness of its surroundings. She'd hate to lose this view, but she knew that if the exhibition failed, the farm-house would have to be sold.

'Damn! Damn! Damn!' Rose slammed her fist down on the solid grey stone of the windowsill.

Of course, there was another option. There always had been another option, but it was one she had resisted taking for nigh on twenty years.

Rose thought of her brother, David, with his penthouse in New York, country residence in Gloucestershire, a villa on an exclusive island in the Caribbean and the oceangoing yacht moored somewhere along the Amalfi Coast. Many were the nights, when she had listened to the drip-dripping of water into the metal saucepan placed to the right of her bed, that she had thought of asking him for help. She would far rather face eviction than ask him for money. Things had gone too wrong, too long ago.

Rose had not seen her brother for many years, only keeping track of his meteoric rise in the corridors of power through newspaper articles. Most recently, she had read of the death of his wife eight months before, which had left him widowed with a boy of sixteen.

Then, a week ago, she had received a telegram.

Dear Rose stop I have severe business commitments for the next two months stop my son Brett is out of boarding school on the twentieth of June stop I don't want to leave him alone stop still mourning the death of his mother stop could he come to you stop country air do him good stop pick him up end August stop David.

The arrival of the telegram had prevented Rose from entering her studio for five days. She had taken long walks over the moors, trying to reason why David was doing this.

Well, there was little to be done. David had presented her with a *fait accompli*. The boy was coming, probably a spoiled brat with airs and graces who would not take kindly to staying in a crumbling farmhouse with nothing to do save watch the grass grow.

She wondered how her own children would feel about the arrival of a previously unknown cousin. Rose had to work out a way of explaining the sudden appearance of not only Brett, but also an uncle who was probably one of the richest men in the world.

Miles, her tall, handsome twenty-year-old, would nod and accept it without question, whereas fifteen-year-old Miranda . . . Rose felt the usual twinge of guilt as she thought of her difficult adopted daughter.

Rose worried that it was due to her that Miranda was such a handful. She was spoiled, rude and fought with Rose about everything. Rose had always aimed to show her as much love

9

as Miles, but Miranda seemed to feel that she could never compete with the bond between mother and son, flesh and blood.

Rose had tried so hard to love Miranda, to do her best. But instead of Miranda helping to bring a family atmosphere into the house, Rose found that she only created tension. The mixture of guilt and lack of communication between mother and daughter meant that, at best, they tolerated each other.

Rose knew how impressed Miranda would be by Brett's arrival and his father's amazing wealth. No doubt she would flirt. She was a very pretty girl with a long line of broken hearts behind her already. Rose wished that she wasn't so . . . obvious. Her body was already well developed and she made no attempt to conceal it. She made the most of her stunning blonde hair. Rose had given up forbidding the bright red lipstick and the short skirts, as Miranda would sulk for days and the atmosphere in the house lasted as long.

She checked her watch. Miranda would be arriving home from school shortly and Miles was on his way from Leeds, where his university term had just ended. She'd asked Mrs Thompson to lay on a special spread for tea.

Rose would join them and announce the impending arrival of her nephew as though it was the most natural thing in the world for her brother's child to stay with them during the holidays.

Rose steeled herself. She had a part to play. For none of them must ever know . . .

2

'Leah, how do you fancy coming to help me up at the big house today? Mrs Delancey has a guest coming to stay tomorrow and I have to get one of those upstairs rooms ready and give it a good clean. Thank goodness it's summer. If we open some of the windows, it should clear the room of that awful damp smell.' Doreen Thompson wrinkled her nose.

'Of course I'll come,' said Leah, studying her mother. Doreen had thick brown hair worn in a sensible, short style. The recent demi-wave meant that the curls were far too tight on her forehead and at the nape of her neck. Years of hard work and worry had kept her statuesque figure slim, but had added too many lines to the thirty-seven-year-old face.

'Good. That's settled then. Go and put on your oldest jeans, Leah. It'll be filthy dirty in that room. And be quick about it. I want to leave as soon as I've prepared your dad's lunch.'

Leah needed no further bidding. She raced up the stairs, opened the door to her shoebox of a room and scrabbled in the bottom of her wardrobe for a pair of tatty, ancient jeans. She found an old sweatshirt and pulled it on, then sat on the end of her bed so she could see in the mirror to plait her waist-length, mahogany-coloured locks. With the heavy braid hanging down her back, Leah looked younger than her fifteen years, but as she stood up, the mirror reflected the gently

11

developing contours of a much more mature girl. She had always been tall for her age, taking after Doreen, but in the past year she seemed to have shot up, and was a good head and shoulders above the other girls in her class. Her mother was always on about her growing out of her strength, which made Leah feel a bit like a sunflower, and urging her to eat more to fill out her skinny frame.

Leah found her trainers under the bed and quickly tied them, anxious to get up to the big house. She loved it when her mother took her there. The farmhouse had so much space, compared to the confined two-up, two-down that she lived in. And Mrs Delancey fascinated her. She was so different to anyone else Leah knew, and she thought how lucky Miranda was to have her as a mother. Not that she didn't love her own mother, but with her father to look after and having to work all day, Mum would sometimes get bad-tempered and shout. Leah knew it was only because she got tired, and she tried to help her with the chores as much as she could.

She could only vaguely remember her father when he could walk. He'd been stricken with rheumatoid arthritis when she was four and had spent the past eleven years confined to a wheelchair. He had left his hard, manual job at the woollen mill and her mother had gone to work as housekeeper for Mrs Delancey to bring in some pennies. In all that time, she had never heard her father complain, and knew that he felt only guilt for the way his wife had to care for him and earn them a living.

Leah loved her father dearly and spent as much time as she could keeping him company.

She ran downstairs and knocked on the door of the front room. When her father had become sick, the sitting room had been turned into her parents' bedroom, and a shower and toilet had been installed by the council in the walk-in pantry just off the kitchen.

'Come in.'

She opened the door. Mr Thompson was sitting in his usual spot, by the window. The brown eyes that Leah had inherited lit up as he saw his daughter.

'Hello, pet. Come and give your dad a kiss.'

Leah did so. 'I'm going to the big house with Mum to help her.'

'Right, lass. I'll see you later then. Enjoy yourself.'

'I will. Mum's bringing in your sandwiches.'

'Lovely. Bye, pet.'

Leah closed the door and went into the kitchen, where her mother was covering a plate of Spam sandwiches with grease-proof paper.

'I'll pop these in to your dad and we'll be off, Leah,' she said.

It was a two-mile walk from Oxenhope up to the tiny hamlet of Sawood where Mrs Delancey's farmhouse sat on top of the hill. Mrs Thompson usually cycled, but today, as Leah was with her, they walked briskly away from the village and up the hill towards the moors.

The sun was shining in the bright blue sky, and the day was warm and balmy. Nonetheless, Leah had slung her anorak over her shoulder in preparation for the walk back later, knowing that the temperature on the moors could drop suddenly.

'I think we're in for a scorcher this year,' Doreen commented. 'Mrs Delancey told me it's her nephew that's coming to stay. I didn't know she had one.'

'How old is he?'

'In his teens. It'll mean Mrs Delancey has a houseful, what with Miles home from university and Miranda breaking up from school. And her in the middle of getting this exhibition organised.'

There was a pause. 'Can I ask a question, Mum?' Leah asked.

'Of course,' her mother replied.

'What . . . what do you think of Miles?'

Mrs Thompson stopped and stared at Leah. 'I like him, of course. I've helped bring him up, haven't I? Why do you ask such a silly question?'

'Oh, no reason,' said Leah, seeing the fiercely protective look on her mother's face.

'Now, if you were talking about that little madam of a sister, well, some of those things she wears . . . It's not decent for a girl her age.'

Leah was rather in awe of the daring outfits Miranda wore and she looked on with admiration as the boys flocked round Miranda at Greenhead Grammar School, where the two girls were in the same year. Leah sometimes saw Miranda heading for Cliffe Castle Park after school with a group of the boys from the year above her. She wondered how Miranda managed to look so pretty and grown up in the dull, regulation uniform, when Leah's own only served to accentuate her lankiness. Although only a month younger than Miranda, Leah felt like a child beside her.

'I know you say that Mrs Delancey has no money, but Miranda always has new clothes. And they do live in that big house.'

Mrs Thompson nodded knowingly. 'It's all on a scale, Leah. Now, take our family, for example. We don't have two ha'pennies to rub together, same as Mrs Delancey says she doesn't. But she used to be rich, really rich. So, compared to that, she thinks she's poor. Do you understand?'

'I think so.'

'Miranda complains if she can't buy a new outfit to go to a party. You complain if there's no food on the table for tea.'

'Why isn't she rich any more?'

Her mother gestured vaguely. 'Well, I don't know what she did with all her money, but she only started painting again a couple of years ago, so she probably didn't sell anything for a long while. Now, enough of this chatter. Hurry your step, lass, or we'll be late.'

Mrs Thompson opened the back door of the farmhouse, which led directly into the kitchen. The room alone was larger than the entire downstairs of Leah's house.

Miranda, attired in a bright pink satin dressing gown and furry mules to match, was sitting eating breakfast at the long scrubbed-pine table, her blonde hair catching the sun's rays.

'Hello, Doreen, you've arrived just in time to make me more toast!'

'Well, you can sing for it today, young miss. I've got my work cut out preparing that room for your mother's guest.'

'Then I'm sure Leah wouldn't mind, would you, darling?' drawled Miranda.

Leah glanced at her mother, who was preparing to retort, and quickly said, 'Of course I don't mind. You go up, Mum, and I'll join you in a minute.'

Mrs Thompson frowned, then shrugged her shoulders and disappeared out of the kitchen. Leah popped a couple of slices of bread into the toaster.

'You grow every time I see you.' Miranda appraised her slowly. 'Do you diet? You're very thin.'

'Oh no, Mum calls me the gannet. I'd lick the plate if she'd let me.'

'Lucky old you. I just have to look at cream and I put on pounds,' said Miranda mournfully.

'But you have a lovely figure. All the boys in our year say so.' Leah jumped as the toast popped up behind her.

'Use the low-fat spread, and only a thin layer of marmalade.

15

What else do the boys say about me, then?' asked Miranda nonchalantly.

Leah blushed. 'Well, they say they think you're . . . very pretty.'

'Do you think I'm pretty, Leah?'

'Oh, yes, very. I . . . I like your clothes.' Leah put the plate of toast in front of Miranda. 'Do you want another cup of tea?'

Miranda nodded. 'Well, you should tell my dear mama you like my clothes. She goes mad if my hemline's above my ankles! She's such a prude. Why don't you pour yourself some tea and keep me company while I eat this?'

Leah hesitated. 'I'd better not. I've got to go upstairs and help Mum.'

'Suit yourself. If you have time later, come to my bedroom and I'll show you the new outfit I bought last Saturday.'

'I'd love to. See you later, Miranda.'

'Sure.'

Leah went up two flights of creaking stairs and found her mother vigorously shaking a threadbare rug in the wide corridor.

'I was just coming to find you. I need help turning the mattress. It's got mould on one of the corners. I've lit the fire in the grate to try and dry the room out a bit.'

Leah followed her into the large bedroom and took one end of the heavy double mattress.

'Right, lift it onto its side . . . that's right. I hope you won't make a habit of letting that madam downstairs treat you like a servant. Give an inch and she'll take a mile. Next time, you say no, lass. It's not your job to fetch and carry for her.'

'I'm sorry, Mum. She's so grown up, isn't she?'

Doreen Thompson caught the admiration in her daughter's eyes.

'Aye, that she is, and no role model for you, miss.' Doreen exhaled and placed her hands on her hips. 'Now, that looks better. We won't put the sheets on it till the last moment. That'll give it time to dry out, and with any luck the poor soul will just about avoid pneumonia tonight.' Her gaze fell to the window. 'There's some glass cleaner in that box. Give those filthy panes a good scrub, will you, pet?'

Leah nodded and took the bottle to the leaded window. She ran a finger through the dust on the pane, dislodging a small spider from its web.

'I'm going downstairs to get the hoover.'

Mrs Thompson went out of the room and Leah set to work on the dirty glass, smearing the liquid and scrubbing until the cloth was black. When she had cleaned four small square panes, she peered out. The sun was still shining and the moors were bathed in light. The view was magnificent, reaching down into the valley, where she could see the chimney-tops of Oxenhope village on the other side of the reservoir.

Leah noticed a figure perched on top of a hillock, perhaps a quarter of a mile away from the house. He was sitting with his arms around his knees, staring down into the valley below him. Leah recognised the thick, black hair. It was Miles.

Miles frightened her. He never smiled, he never said hello; he just . . . stared at her. When he was home, he seemed to spend hours alone on the moors. Only occasionally would she see him, a black silhouette against the sun, trotting across the top of the valley on one of Mr Morris's horses.

Suddenly, Miles turned around. And, as if he had known that Leah was watching him, he fixed his dark eyes directly upon her. Leah felt his gaze penetrating her. She stood perfectly still, unable to move for a moment, then shuddered and walked quickly away from the window.

Her mum had arrived with the hoover. 'Come on, Leah,

jump to it. You've not cleaned more than a quarter of those panes.'

Reluctantly, Leah moved back to the window.

The figure on the hillock had vanished.

'I wanted to ask you, Doreen, whether Leah would like to earn a bit of pocket money?'

Leah was sitting in the kitchen with her mother, having a cup of tea before the walk back to the village.

Mrs Delancey was standing in the kitchen doorway in a smock covered with a variety of bright, oily colours. She was smiling at Leah.

'Well now, I'm sure that sounds like a fine idea, doesn't it, Leah?' said Mrs Thompson.

'Yes, Mrs Delancey. What would you want me to do?'

'You know I have my nephew, Brett, coming to stay tomorrow. The problem is that I'm deep in the middle of painting for my exhibition. I'm going to have little enough time as it is without having to cook every day. I was wondering if you would like to come and help your mother keep the house tidy and make some breakfast and an evening meal for myself and the children. My own are perfectly capable of fending for themselves, but my nephew . . . well, let's just say he's used to a far grander lifestyle. Obviously, I'll pay you more for the extra hours, Doreen, and give Leah something too.'

Mrs Thompson looked at Leah. 'As long as one of us is around to cook supper for Dad, I'd say it was a fine idea, isn't it, Leah?'

Leah knew her mother was thinking how the extra pennies would come in handy. She nodded. 'Yes, Mrs Delancey, I'd like it very much.'

'Good, that's settled, then. I've got an old bicycle in the barn you can use to get up here. Brett arrives tomorrow afternoon and I'd like you to prepare something special for dinner. We'll eat in the dining room. Get the Wedgwood service out and make a list of the groceries you'll need for the week. I'll ring the farm shop and ask them to deliver. Now, I really must get back to my studio. I'll see you tomorrow.'

'Right, Mrs Delancey,' said Mrs Thompson.

Rose began to walk out of the kitchen, then, in afterthought, turned back.

'If my nephew seems a little . . . different, take no notice. His mother died not long ago and, as I mentioned, he's been used to the best.' Rose seemed to wince. 'Well, as I said, see you tomorrow.' She left the kitchen and shut the door.

'Poor mite, his mother dying when he's so young.' Mrs Thompson rinsed the teacups in the sink.

The door opened and in waltzed Miranda, dressed in a tight red miniskirt and a low-cut cheesecloth top.

'I thought you were coming to see my new outfit, Leah.'

'Well, I . . .'

'Never mind. I've come to model it for you. What do you think? Isn't it great?' Miranda smiled and twirled.

'I think it's—'

'I think it's high time we were leaving to get your dad's tea,' cut in her mother.

Miranda ignored her. 'I got it from that new boutique in Keighley. I'm going to wear it to dinner tomorrow night for the arrival of my cousin.' Miranda gave a large grin. 'You know his father is one of the richest men in the world, don't you?'

'Now don't you go making up stories, young lady,' reproached Mrs Thompson.

'It's true!' Miranda sat down in a chair and swung her legs onto the table, revealing a large expanse of white thigh. 'Dear Mama kept that one quiet, didn't she? Her brother is David Cooper. *The* David Cooper.' She stared, waiting for a reaction, and frowned when none came. 'Don't tell me you haven't heard of him. He's world famous. He owns Cooper Industries? One of the largest companies in the world? God only knows why we have to live in this heap, when dear old Rosie has him for a brother.'

'Don't call your mum Rosie, madam.'

'Sorry, Mrs T,' Miranda replied. 'And here was me thinking that nothing exciting ever happened around this dump when, out of the blue, I discover I have an uncle who's loaded, and his son is arriving here tomorrow. And the best news of all – he's sixteen. I wonder if he's got a girlfriend?' she mused.

'Now, you treat him nicely, Miranda. Poor thing, he lost his mother not long ago.'

Miranda grinned. 'Rest assured I will, Mrs T . . . Anyway, I'm going to try out my new face pack. See you later.' She stood up and skipped out of the kitchen.

Mrs Thompson shook her head. 'Come on, Leah, we'd best be going. It'll be a busy day tomorrow.' She wiped her hands on a tea towel and inclined her head towards the door. 'And I smell trouble.'

3

The long black limousine made its way smoothly through the picturesque Yorkshire villages. People gazed at it curiously and tried to make out the shadowy figure behind the tinted glass.

Brett Cooper stared miserably back at them, making grotesque faces that he knew they couldn't see. The sky had just clouded over and it had begun to rain. The moorland around him looked as desolate as he felt.

Brett stretched forward and pulled a can of Coke from the minibar. The interior of the car reminded him of a luxury tomb, with its plush leather wall-coverings and blinds to all sides so his father could shut out the world.

Brett pressed a button. 'How far now, Bill?'

'Only another half an hour, sir,' the metallic voice replied.

Brett released the button, stretched out his long jean-clad legs and sipped his Coke.

His father had promised to collect him from school and drive with Brett up to Yorkshire to introduce him personally to this aunt of his. But when he had eagerly climbed into the back of the car, he'd found it empty.

Bill, his father's chauffeur, had told him that Mr Cooper sent his apologies, but he'd had to fly off to America sooner than expected.

On the five-hour drive from Windsor, Brett had experienced anger towards his father for repeating, once more, the pattern of his childhood, fear at having to face this unknown aunt alone, and overwhelming sorrow that his mother was not here to stop him feeling as though his father didn't give a damn about him.

Tears filled Brett's eyes as he thought of this time last year. He had flown directly to Nice airport, where his mother had met him. They had driven to the villa she had rented in Cap Ferrat and spent a glorious summer together, just the two of them. His father had visited a couple of times but had spent the days locked in his office or on the yacht, entertaining important business associates who had flown over to see him.

And then, three months later, his mother was dead. He remembered being shown into his housemaster's study to be told the news.

Brett had gone to his empty dormitory, sat on the edge of his bed and stared into space. All that money and luxury, and yet it had not stopped his mother dying. He hated her for not telling him there was something wrong. Didn't she know how he would feel about not being there with her at the end?

And his father – he had known, too, but said nothing.

Brett guessed that his father had made a conscious decision to pour all his efforts into his business. It seemed to be the only thing in the world he cared about – in fact, Brett wondered why he had ever bothered getting married. And yet, his mother had been so loyal. She never complained about the fact she rarely saw her husband, or that she and his son seemed to be at the bottom of his list of priorities. He had only heard them arguing once, when he was a child of four.

'For God's sake, Vivien, please think about it. New York is a marvellous place to live. When Brett goes to prep school, he can still fly over for the holidays. The apartment is wonderful. At least come and see it.'

His mother had replied in her quiet even tones, 'No, David, I'm sorry. I want to stay in England so that I'm here if Brett needs me.'

Brett had started to realise, as he had grown up, that his mother had made a choice that day. And that choice had been him. His father had come home less and less after that, basing himself in New York and rarely pressing his wife to join him there again.

When Brett had first started at Eton, boys had asked him what his famous father was like. He would answer 'great', or 'a really good guy', but the truth was he really didn't know.

When he was thirteen, David had taken to pulling Brett aside and showing him plans for a new apartment block he had under construction. Brett would try to look interested in what his father had to say.

'As soon as you've left Cambridge, you'll be coming into the business to learn how it runs. One day, it'll be yours, Brett.'

He would nod and smile but inwardly grimace. He didn't have the least interest in understanding his father's empire. Brett had no head for figures and found statistics impossible. He had only scraped through the Eton entrance exam by gaining such high marks in his English paper.

During the past two years, Brett had started to wake up in cold sweats as the future that had been mapped out by his father began to dawn on him. Last year, in Cap Ferrat, he had opened his heart to his mother about how he felt. He had also shown her some of his paintings. She had stared at them in surprise.

'Goodness me, darling! I had no idea you could paint like this. They're exquisite. You have real talent. I must show them to your father.'

23

David had glanced cursorily at them and shrugged. 'Not bad. It's good for a businessman to have a hobby that relaxes him.'

Brett had put his watercolours and easel away. His mother had tried to comfort him and encouraged her son to continue capturing the splendid views from their villa.

'It's pointless, Mother. He'll never let me go to art college, never. He's got it all planned. He's so certain about me getting into Cambridge that he never thinks for a minute I might flunk my exams.'

Vivien had sighed. They both knew that if the worst did happen, a place could easily be arranged through a generous donation to the right college.

'Look, Brett, I promise I'll talk to him for you. You're only fifteen. I'm sure that we can make him understand when the time comes. You must continue painting, darling. You show real promise!'

Brett had shaken his head. A month later he had gone back to school and painted his mother sitting on the swing in the garden of their Gloucestershire home. He had copied it from his favourite photograph of her, which showed her delicate beauty at its best. Brett had planned to give it to her for Christmas. But by then she was dead and the painting was still gift-wrapped under his bed at school. He had refused to step into the art room since.

After eight months, Brett still felt as though she had died yesterday. His mother had been the centre of his world, his rock and his security. He felt so vulnerable now that there was no mediator between him and his father.

He had presumed that he would go home to the house in Gloucestershire for these summer holidays, or maybe Antigua. So when he had received the letter, typed by Pat, David's personal assistant, telling him that his father was packing him off to Yorkshire to stay with some aunt he'd never heard of, it had only added to his despair. He'd tried in vain to contact his father in New York and protest, but Pat had intercepted his calls.

'Your father is adamant you should go, Brett, dear, as he has such a busy schedule for the next couple of months. I'm sure you'll be fine. I'm cabling five hundred pounds over to you as spending money. Let me know if you want more, won't you?'

Brett knew there was little point in arguing. What David Cooper wanted, he got.

The intercom buzzed. 'Another five minutes, sir, and we'll be there. You can see the house from here. If you look to your left, it's the one perched on top of the hill.'

Brett looked, and through the drizzle, he saw it. A large grey stone building, set alone in the surrounding moorland. It looked desolate and terribly unwelcoming, like something out of a Dickens novel.

'Bleak house,' he muttered to himself. His heart started beating faster as the limousine climbed the hill. For the thousandth time, he wished his mother was sitting next to him, telling him that everything was all right.

The car came to a smooth halt in front of the house. Brett took a deep breath. His mother wasn't here, and he had to face this alone.

Rose heard the car draw up. She peered out of the corner of her studio window and saw the grand limousine, which boasted tinted glass. She watched as the chauffeur got out of the front seat and walked round to open the passenger door. Rose sucked in her breath as a tall young man got out. The chauffeur shut the door behind him, and she realised that Brett had come alone.

'Thank God,' Rose breathed out. Then, from her unseen vantage point, she studied her brother's son.

Rose recognised the titian hair as her own colour. The boy turned round and she saw David's deep, blue eyes and strong jawline. Brett was an extremely handsome young man. She watched him nervously fiddling with something in the pocket of his jacket as the chauffeur unloaded the suitcases from the boot and walked towards the front door. Something about the boy struck Rose as forlorn. *He's probably far more nervous than I am*, she thought. The bell rang, and Rose quickly checked her appearance in the mirror. She heard Mrs Thompson open the front door, just as Rose had asked. She had packed Miles and Miranda off horse-riding for the afternoon, wanting to have some time with Brett alone.

Rose heard a voice uncannily like David's talking to Mrs Thompson as she led him through to the sitting room. She tentatively opened the door and walked slowly down the hallway. The chauffeur was bringing in the last suitcase.

'Ms Cooper, I presume.'

'No, it's Delancey, actually.'

'Sorry, Ms Delancey. Mr Cooper sends his thanks. He also asked me to give you this to cover Brett's keep.' The chauffeur handed Rose an envelope.

'Thank you. Would you like a cup of tea and something to eat? It's a long drive back.'

'No, Ms Delancey. Thanks for the offer, but I've got to push straight off. I'm picking some people up from Leeds Bradford Airport at five.'

'Sounds as though David works you too hard.'

'He keeps me busy, but I enjoy it. I've been with him for nearly thirteen years and I've known Brett most of his life. He's a good kid and he won't cause you any trouble. If he seems a bit quiet, well, he's not had an easy time of it. He adored his mother. It was such a tragedy.'

'Don't you worry, I'll take care of him. I'm sure we'll get along fine. Drive carefully.'

'I will.' Bill tipped his hat. 'Goodbye, Ms Delancey.'

Rose closed the front door and heard the limousine drive off. She tore the envelope open and found a 'Cooper Industries' compliment slip and a thousand pounds in cash.

'My goodness,' she whispered, 'I'll have to feed him caviar and champagne every night to get through this much.' Rose tucked the envelope into a pocket of her voluminous skirt, wondering how soon she could get the builder in to quote for the roof, and opened the door to the sitting room.

Whatever Brett had expected his unknown aunt to look like, it was certainly not the woman who walked through the door.

His mother had always wondered from whom Brett had inherited his unusual red-gold hair colour, and now he knew.

His Aunt Rose was a full-figured lady, dressed in a brightly coloured blouse and a peasant skirt. Brett could see that she had once been a very beautiful woman. As he looked through his artist's eyes, he saw the fine bone structure, marked by prominent high cheekbones. Her huge green eyes dominated her face and she shared her wide, voluptuous lips with his father. Rose smiled at him, showing an even set of white teeth. Her face looked familiar, and Brett was sure he'd seen her somewhere before, but he couldn't place her.

'Hello, Brett, I'm Rose.' She spoke in a rich, deep voice.

Brett stood up. 'I'm very pleased to meet you, Aunt Rose.' He held out his hand, but, instead of taking it, she clasped him in a tight embrace. He smelled strong perfume and something else . . . yes, he was sure that it was the distinctive smell of oil paint. Rose let him go, sat down on the sofa and patted the seat next to her. He sat down and Rose took his hand in hers.

'It's lovely to have you with us, Brett. You must feel a little strange at the moment, having to come here and stay with relatives you've never met before. I'm sure you'll soon settle down. You must be hungry after that long drive. Would you like something to eat?'

'No, thank you. Bill filled a hamper for me to eat on the way up here.'

'Perhaps a cup of tea, then?'

'Yes, that would be lovely.'

'I'll tell Doreen to bring some through.'

While Rose went to the kitchen, Brett looked around the room. It was untidily crammed with old furniture and bric-a-brac, but what caught his attention were the distinctive paintings on the wall . . .

'How long did the journey take?' Rose sat next to him once more.

'Oh, about five hours. The traffic was good.'

'You must be tired, though.'

'I am, a bit.'

'I'll show you up to your room after we've had some tea. The house is very quiet as my children are out riding. Maybe you'd like to have a lie-down before dinner.'

'Maybe,' said Brett.

There was a pause as Rose tried to think of something to say.

'Ah, here's Doreen with tea. Do you take sugar?'

'No thank you, Aunt Rose.'

'Oh, for heaven's sake, drop the "aunt" part, will you?' Rose smiled. 'You're almost grown up now and it makes me feel ancient. My children call me Rose too. I so hate "Mother" or "Mum".'

Rose bit her lip as she watched the anguish on Brett's face. The confident, arrogant boy whose arrival she'd expected could not be more in contrast to the shy, tense young man who was so obviously still grieving for his mother.

'You'll meet Miles and Miranda at dinner tonight. She's fifteen, only a few months younger than you, so you should be able to keep each other company.'

'How old is your son?'

'Miles is twenty and just home from his second year at Leeds University. He doesn't say much, so don't worry if it takes time to get to know him. I'm sure you'll get along fine.' Rose could hardly believe she was having this conversation. 'Well, if you've finished your tea, I'll take you upstairs to your room.'

Brett followed Rose up two flights of creaking stairs and along a lino-clad passageway.

'Here we are. I'm afraid it's basic, but the view from this window is the best in the house. Well, I'll leave you to unpack. If you need anything, Doreen is usually in the kitchen. I'll see you at eight for dinner.' Rose smiled at him and closed the door.

Brett looked at the room that would be his for the next two months. There was a double bed, with an old patchwork quilt thrown over it. The linoleum covering the floorboards was worn and there were large cracks in the plaster on the ceiling. Brett walked to the window and looked out. The drizzle had turned to rain and grey clouds were covering the tops of the hills in the distance. He shivered. The room was cold and smelled of damp. He heard a faint dripping sound and noticed a small puddle of water near the door. Concerningly, the ceiling above the puddle was sagging heavily.

A lump arrived in Brett's throat. He felt deserted, miserable and completely alone. How could his father have sent him here, to this terrible, desolate place? He threw himself face-down on the bed and started to cry for the first time since his mother had died.

His tears fell for a long time, then, realising that he was physically shivering, Brett climbed under the quilt, fully clothed, and fell into an exhausted sleep.

That was how Rose found him, three hours later. After shaking him gently and getting no response, she tip-toed out of the room and closed the door.

4

Brett opened his eyes and blinked as rays of golden sun streamed in through the window. For a moment, he couldn't remember where he was. As he came to, he sat up and looked out of the window at the beautiful greenery beyond. He could hardly believe that the sun could turn a desolate landscape into a scene of such tranquillity.

Brett turned over and stretched. Then he saw her.

She was standing by the door, holding a tray in both hands. She was tall and almost waif-like in her thinness, and had a head of glorious dark brown hair, reaching nearly to her waist. Her eyes were also deep brown, with long black lashes framing them. Her face was heart-shaped, with lips of a natural red, and a small retroussé nose.

With the sun shining directly onto her, sending dancing lights through her locks, she looked so perfect that Brett wondered if he was seeing a vision of the Madonna. Then he realised that madonnas didn't usually carry breakfast trays or wear sweatshirts and jeans, so she had to be real. Quite simply, this was the most beautiful girl he had ever seen.

'Hello,' she said shyly. 'Mum thought you might be hungry.'

The girl spoke in a soft, Yorkshire accent. So *this* was Miranda, thought Brett. Wow, two whole months with her for company. Maybe this holiday wasn't going to be quite as bad as he'd anticipated.

'That's very kind of her. Actually, I'm starving. I think I missed out on dinner last night.'

'You did.' She smiled, showing her flawless, pearl-white teeth. 'I'll put the tray on the end of the bed. There's bacon and eggs under the dish, and some toast and tea.'

Brett watched as she moved gracefully towards him and set the tray down.

'Thanks, Miranda. I'm Brett, by the way.'

Her lovely face creased as she frowned and shook her head. 'Oh no, I'm not—'

'Was somebody mentioning my name?' A girl with bright blonde hair, a pair of tight riding jodhpurs and a T-shirt that showed a large amount of cleavage burst through the door. The girl would have been very pretty if her face had not been plastered with unsubtle make-up. She bounced over to him and sat on the edge of the bed, sending the tray skidding onto the floor with a clatter of breaking china.

'Sod it! Who put that tray there? Clean it up, will you, Leah?' She smiled at Brett as the other girl knelt on the floor. 'Miranda Delancey, your cousin, or should I say step-cousin, as dear old Rosie adopted me when I was little.'

Brett's heart sank. He watched the girl called Leah struggling to pick up the shards of crockery from the mess of bacon and eggs on the floor.

'Good to meet you,' he said to Miranda, then jumped out of bed. 'Let me help you with that.' He knelt beside Leah.

'Let her do it, it's what she's paid for,' said Miranda, swinging her legs onto the bed.

Brett watched a glimmer of anger cross the brown eyes as he handed Leah the last piece of china from the floor.

'It's done now,' said Brett, standing upright.

'I'll go and get a broom and a cloth from downstairs to clean up the mess. Will you be wanting your breakfast up here still?'

Brett looked into Leah's clear eyes, thinking that breakfast was the last thing on his mind. 'No, I'll come down for it.'

Leah nodded, picked up the tray and left the room.

'Who is she?' Brett asked Miranda.

'Leah Thompson, the housekeeper's kid. She helps around the house during the holidays,' said Miranda dismissively. 'Now, on to more important things, like what you and I are going to do today. Rosie has put me in charge of the Brett Cooper entertainments committee, and I intend to see to it that you are not left alone for a minute.'

Brett was taken aback by the determined gaze in her eyes. He was unused to girls of his own age, being at an all-boys school and spending most of his holidays in the company of adults. Miranda was looking him up and down and Brett felt himself blushing.

'Well? What do you want to do today?'

'I . . . well . . . I—'

'Do you ride?'

Brett gave a swallow. 'Yes.'

'That's settled then. When you're ready, we'll go over to old Morris's place and take a couple of horses out on the moors for a nice long trot. Get to know each other better.' Miranda swept her hand through her hair and stared at him.

'Fine. Er, could you tell me where the bathroom is? I think I ought to wash and change out of these clothes.'

'Down the passage, second door on the left. What happened to you last night? I got all dressed up for dinner especially.'

'I . . . well . . . I was tired from the journey, I think.'

'I hope you don't usually make a habit of sleeping in your clothes.' Miranda jumped off the bed. 'I'll wait for you

LUCINDA RILEY

downstairs. Don't be too long, will you now?' She disappeared from the room.

Brett gathered himself and padded along the corridor. He soon found the bathroom and turned on the taps to run a bath. The water coughed and spluttered and when it finally made an appearance, it was a strange yellow colour.

He took off his crumpled clothes and climbed in, trying his best not to notice the brown, gritty sediment lying along the bottom of the ancient iron tub. When he closed his eyes, he was met by a vision of Leah standing in the doorway of his room. He felt overwhelming disappointment that she was not the girl he would be spending the holiday with.

Twenty minutes later, he was sitting in the comfortable kitchen eating a large plate of bacon and eggs. Miranda was chattering ten to the dozen about her plans for the next two months, and Leah was helping her mother with the drying-up.

'Right, time to be off,' said Miranda. 'It's only a half-mile walk to the farm. We could cycle if you want.'

'No, a walk would do me good.'

Miranda led him out of the kitchen door and Brett stopped and turned round. 'Bye, Leah. See you later.'

'Bye, Brett.'

'Do you not think I should say good morning to Aunt . . . I mean Rose before we go?' Brett asked Miranda, who was striding down the hill at a brisk pace.

'God, no. She's locked away in her studio and it's on pain of death that you disturb her. She only comes out to eat.'

'What kind of studio?'

'Oh, didn't you know? Rosie used to be a famous painter back in the dark ages. She hasn't done anything for yonks, then a couple of years ago she cleared out one of the downstairs rooms and turned it into a studio. She's having an exhibition in London next year. Her big comeback or something. Personally,

34

I think she's wasting her time. I mean, who's going to remember her from twenty years ago?' Miranda sniffed.

Things were falling rapidly into place as Brett walked down the hill. That smell of oil paint when she had hugged him, the paintings on the wall in her sitting room, and Rose's face . . . of course!

'Is Rose's second name Delancey?'

Miranda nodded. 'Yes, why?'

'Miranda, I can tell you now that your mother was the toast of the art world twenty years ago. Arguably, she was the most famous female artist in Europe, then she suddenly disappeared off the scene altogether.'

Miranda wrinkled her nose. 'Personally, I can't stand her paintings. They're so strange. Anyway, you seem to know a lot about her. Interested in art, are you?'

'Well, yes, I am actually.' Brett felt terribly excited, but was puzzled. Why on earth had his father never mentioned that Rose Delancey was his sister? It was something to be tremendously proud of, surely?

'I'm sure Rosie will be able to spare a couple of seconds to discuss her favourite subject with you. Now, how good a horseman are you? The gelding's a brilliant ride, but unpredictable, and the mare . . . well, if you want an easy trot, I'd go for her.'

They had reached the stables and Miranda was leading him along the loose-boxes.

'I'll take the mare, thanks, Miranda.'

The horses were saddled up and the picnic that Mrs Thompson had made them stowed away in the gelding's saddlebag. The two of them trotted at a relaxed pace in the direction of the moors.

'I just can't believe that this is the same place I arrived at last night. I don't think I've ever felt quite so depressed. It was all so black and gloomy.'

35

'It's like that up here. The weather can change in an instant. It's amazing how different the moors look when the sun's shining,' agreed Miranda.

'Who owns all this land?' enquired Brett.

'Farmers mostly. They graze their sheep on it.'

'It looks like it stretches for miles.' Brett gazed across the valley as they trotted onto the open grassland and began ascending the hill.

'It does. That's Blackmoor over the other side of the reservoir. It goes right to the edge of Haworth, three miles away. It gets pretty desolate in the winter up here, you know. We've been snowed in hundreds of times.'

Brett suddenly experienced a sense of well-being. He felt glad he had come. And he couldn't wait to get back and talk to his aunt.

'Phew,' said Miranda, wiping her forehead. 'It's a hot one today. When we get to the brow I think we should sit and have a drink.'

'Fine.'

Fifteen minutes later, the horses were tethered and Brett and Miranda were lying high up the hill in the rough grass, drinking Coke.

'Oh look!' Miranda shot up. 'There's Miles, down there, on the horse.'

Brett sat up and looked down the valley in the direction Miranda was pointing. He saw a small figure in the distance trotting across the moors on a large black horse.

'He spends most of his time riding on the moors when he comes back from university,' Miranda said softly, with a touch of wistfulness in her voice.

'What's he studying?'

'History. I quite miss him when he's not around.' Miranda tugged at a lump of grass. 'We used to spend a lot of time together when he was at home. Miles is different from other people . . . so quiet . . .' Her voice trailed off, then she turned to Brett and the seriousness left her face as she smiled. 'Me, I like lively people, lots of noise and action, you know. I'm moving to London as soon as I leave school. It's so dull here – nothing ever happens!'

'I think it's quite beautiful,' murmured Brett.

'Yes, but you don't have to live here, do you? I mean, I'm sure you go to fancy parties and famous restaurants all the time.'

Brett thought about the number of times he had been paraded around at a function of David Cooper's like a prize poodle, desperate to get home and out of the stiff, formal suit his father liked him to wear.

'Really, Miranda, those kinds of things aren't all they're cracked up to be.'

'Well, I want to try them for myself. I want to be super-rich one day, then I can buy anything I want. I'd have a whole room full of designer clothes, and shoes to match. I'd have a huge house, and a Rolls-Royce, and . . .'

Brett lay back in the grass and wondered why the entire world thought that money bought happiness. He knew it didn't.

Later, they took the horses back across the moors to the stable and walked home.

Mrs Thompson was in the kitchen, preparing supper.

'Have a good ride, both of you?' She smiled.

'Great thanks,' answered Brett.

'Mrs Delancey wants to have dinner in the dining room again tonight, as you missed out on it yesterday. It'll be ready for eight. Now, how about a nice cup of tea?'

At eight o'clock that evening, Brett wandered downstairs and into the dining room. It was deserted, so he went and sat down in an old leather chair, placed by the big, mullioned windows.

Leah came in, carrying a tray of soup bowls, which she proceeded to place on the scratched oak dining table.

'Here, let me help you, Leah.' Brett stood up.

'No, I can manage fine. Mrs Delancey'll be in in a minute.' She seemed nervous.

'Do you live here, Leah?'

'Oh no, I live in the village with my mum and dad.'

'I see. Miranda was saying today that Haworth isn't too far away. I'd love to go and see the Parsonage where the Brontës lived.'

Leah's eyes lit up. 'Oh yes, you must visit it. I've been lots of times. I've read all their books, I think they're wonderful.'

'So do I. Which novel is your favourite?'

'*Wuthering Heights*,' said Leah without a pause. 'It's so romantic.'

Brett watched her blush prettily and move towards the door.

He put a hand on her arm to stop her. 'Well, as you seem to be the expert, maybe you could take me up there one day and show me round.'

She looked at him, paused, then smiled. 'Well, yes, if you'd like to, Brett.'

'I would, very much.'

Rose appeared at the dining-room door and Leah scurried out. She sat down at the top of the table.

'So, Brett, feeling better after your long sleep?' Her eyes twinkled.

'Much. I am truly sorry about last night. I don't know what hit me.'

'The Yorkshire air, probably. Miranda tells me you've been out riding today. It seems to have done you good. You looked so pale when you arrived. Are you settling in all right?'

'Yes, fine.'

'I must apologise for the leak in your room. The builder is coming to take a look at it tomorrow. I'm afraid the whole roof needs replacing.'

'No problem,' said Brett politely. 'Rose, Miranda was telling me today that you have started painting again. I know your work from the fifties and I was wondering if I could come and have a look at your new work sometime.'

Rose's face lit up. 'Of course. You're interested in art, then?'

'Extremely. I presumed your surname was Cooper, like Dad's – not Delancey.'

'I have been in retirement rather a long time. I'm flattered that you know my work. If you'd like to come to the studio after dinner, I'll show you what I've done so far for my exhibition.'

'Great, I'd love to. But I have to admit that I don't understand why Dad has never mentioned you before, especially with me being so interested in art.'

Rose opened her mouth to answer, but at that moment, Miranda bounced through the door. 'Hi, you two.' She was wearing the tight red miniskirt and cheesecloth top. She sat down along one side of the table and patted the chair next to her. 'Come and sit next to me, Brett.'

Brett reluctantly did so as Rose clucked. 'Really, Miranda . . .'

She was interrupted by a deep voice from the doorway. 'Sorry I'm late, everyone. I hope that the meal hasn't been held up on my behalf.'

Brett stared at the man who had spoken, and was immediately reminded of his earlier conversation with Leah. His tall stature, black hair and dark eyes reminded Brett instantly of Emily Brontë's Heathcliff. Brett watched as he kissed his mother and then sat down at the table next to her, before his gaze fell on Miranda. The pair exchanged a look.

Brett recognised, as men could in another male, that Miles was very handsome. As he focussed his eyes on him, Brett momentarily sensed something wild in the young man. The two males held each other's gaze, before Miles broke into a wide, friendly smile and he extended his arm across the table.

'Miles Delancey, pleased to meet you, Brett.' For an instant, Brett felt the power of the well-muscled frame as Miles gripped his hand, then released it.

'And you.'

Leah entered the room with the soup tureen and began serving Rose. Brett watched her, and as he did so, he noticed that someone else was watching her too. Miles was staring intently at Leah as she moved around the table. He didn't take his eyes off her once, and Brett saw the slight nervousness as Leah moved next to Miles to serve him. He continued staring at her as she poured the soup into his bowl.

'How are you, Leah? You seem to have done some growing up since last time I saw you.' As Miles's eyes bored into her, Brett watched her give an almost invisible shudder.

'I'm fine, thanks, Miles.' Leah quickly moved away towards the door with the empty tureen and Miles averted his eyes.

'Do begin, everyone,' said Rose, picking up her spoon.

'Now, I hope you all realise that a big event is going to take place on the twenty-third of July,' said Miranda. 'I'll be sixteen years of age, and we all know what an important birthday that is, don't we? Rose, darling Rose, could I have the teeniest of parties to celebrate?'

Rose looked doubtful. 'Miranda, I have so much work on, the last thing I need is a house full of teenagers.'

'You asked Miles if he wanted a party when he was sixteen.' Miranda's eyes glistened with anger.

Rose knew she was cornered.

'All right, Miranda, you can have a few friends round on the Saturday night.'

'Thank you, thank you, Rose. You wouldn't fancy going out to the pictures or something that evening, would you?'

The look in Rose's eyes made it clear that she would not, and Miranda knew not to push it any further.

She switched tack. 'Mrs Thompson and Leah can make some food and serve it, can't they?'

'Don't you think that Leah should be a guest? After all, she is in your year at school,' Miles said quietly.

Miranda looked at Miles as he smiled at her. She nodded immediately. 'Of course. Now, I shall have to buy a new dress and I think I'll have my hair cut like Farrah Fawcett Major's . . .'

Miranda chatted happily away through the rest of the meal. Miles didn't say another word, and once dessert was finished, he stood up from the table.

'Do excuse me, everyone, but I have some work to do. Goodnight.' He left the room.

'Is Miles going to study?' Brett asked politely.

'No, Brett,' Rose answered. 'His big passion is photography. He spends most of his time out on the moors taking photos, and he's turned one of the smaller rooms upstairs into a darkroom. I expect that's where he's gone now. Some of his photographs are quite beautiful.'

'I should like to see them.'

'Then you must ask Miles to show them to you. Now, how about you coming with me to my studio?'

'Oh, yes please!'

Miranda immediately cut in. 'Oh Brett, I was going to take you upstairs and play you the ABBA album I bought on Saturday.'

'I'm sure Brett can listen another time.' Rose stood up from the table and walked towards the door. Brett followed her, flashing an annoyed Miranda a false smile.

41

He walked with Rose along the corridor to her studio. The room was in darkness, and Rose switched on the light. Brett breathed in the familiar, comforting smell of paint and white spirit. The studio was not particularly large and was cluttered with canvases stacked against the walls. There were the usual artists' brushes, palettes and tubes of paint strewn on a work-bench along one wall.

Brett walked towards the large easel and studied the canvas resting upon it. There was only a basic outline, painted in thick, black strokes. Brett could not make out any particular shapes.

'Don't waste your time looking at that. I only started it this afternoon. Come and have a look at one of the finished prod-ucts.' Rose was removing one of the canvases from against the wall.

Brett knew that it would be recognisable anywhere as a Rose Delancey. The realist style was still strong, but the colours were softer, more muted than in the harsh, sometimes fright-ening, paintings that Rose had become famous for.

'What do you think?' she asked anxiously.

Brett thought how strange it was to have the great Rose Delancey asking him for an opinion on her work. Realism was not his own style – his work reflected the English Impressionists – but he had always admired Rose's work for its strength and individuality, and he could see that her new painting had all that, and more.

'I think that it's wonderful, Rose, really. It is different from your old work, but it has a subtlety to it that makes you want to look closer.'

Rose breathed a sigh of relief. 'Thank you, Brett, dear. I've shown these to nobody else, you know. It may sound silly, but I was frightened that I might have lost my gift for painting.'

'No, certainly not. I can't say how valid my opinion is. I mean, I'm only a novice, but I think you should have every confidence about showing this to someone whose opinion does matter. Can I see the others?'

For the following hour, Rose and Brett pored over the eight other completed paintings. She explained each one in detail and the pair analysed colour, shape and form. Rose explained how she felt she was moving out of the realism for which she had become so famous.

'It's most odd,' she mused. 'When I was very young, I painted in a truly representational style. I was almost too romantic about my subject matter. Then, as I matured to adulthood, I could only see the cold, hard seams and faults of everything I painted and I wanted to highlight this in my work. Critics used to comment that my work was almost masculine. I was also surrounded at the Royal College by the Kitchen Sinkers. And I was heavily influenced by Auerbach and Kossoff, and Graham Sutherland's work. But since I've returned to painting, that feeling has left me. I want people to see beauty, too.'

Brett noticed Rose's eyes had become misty.

'They will, Rose. I promise.'

She turned to Brett and smiled. 'I must be boring you. I'm sorry. Come on. Let's go and get some coffee from the kitchen, shall we?'

Brett helped Rose stack the finished paintings back against the wall.

'Why did you stop painting, Rose?' They were sitting at the kitchen table, sipping their coffee.

Rose's face clouded over. 'It's a long story, Brett. Let's just say I was drained, that I felt as though I had nothing further to put on canvas. I had success so young. It's very unusual for a painter to do that, you know.' She sighed. 'I just woke up one morning and didn't want to do it any more.'

'And it took almost twenty years for the urge to come back?'

'Yes. But I can't tell you how much more pleasure I'm getting from painting now. In those days I felt like a machine, churning out the work, working to deadlines for galleries and collectors. Now, there are no expectations from others, only my own need to paint.'

'I bet you had no trouble securing an exhibition at a gallery.' Brett smiled.

'Actually, it was all rather a coincidence. I'd started painting again last year, and had just finished my first work, when I got a call from an old friend who was at art school with me. He's opening a gallery in London in the new year. I told him I was painting again and he immediately suggested that I have an exhibition. First of all I said no, then after I'd finished the second painting I thought, why not?' Rose looked down at the floor. 'It also comes down to lack of funds, Brett, dear. This house needs thousands spending on it and my coffers are empty. I have to earn some money, and painting is the only thing I do well.'

'I'm sure the interest will be enormous.'

'Thank you for your confidence, Brett, but remember that the public has a short memory. Anyway, enough of me. Have you always been interested in art?'

'Oh yes. It's . . . it used to be my hobby.' Brett checked himself.

'Well, I really do think that you're too young to retire just yet.' Rose laughed.

Brett tried to think of a simple way to explain why he had tried to forget about his ambition, about the painting of his mother, and how he couldn't face putting brush to canvas because it was all so hopeless.

'The thing is, Rose, my father isn't at all keen on the idea of me becoming an artist. He's got my future all planned. Cambridge, then going into his company to learn the business so I can take over when he retires. My mother knew that I wanted to go to art college and she was going to talk to my father about it when the time came. But now . . .' Brett shrugged and looked so forlorn that Rose stretched her hand across the table and took his.

'Brett, whatever your problems – and believe me, no successful artist is without *those* at the beginning of their career – you must keep painting. You might even find it gives you comfort. It certainly did me.'

'Yes, but there seems no point. My father, he . . .'

'He is a very complex man. I understand, more than anyone else, how he can be.' Rose paused and stared deep into her coffee cup. 'However, hold on to your dream, Brett.' She slapped her hands on her thighs. 'Now, I think it's time we both went to bed. Tomorrow, come to my studio and I'll dig you out an easel, some paint and paper. Why don't you spend some time up on the moors? There are lots of splendid views to draw. I want to see if I'm to have competition in the future!' Rose stood up. 'Goodnight, Brett, dear. Sleep well.'

Brett sat for a long time alone in the kitchen, before he slowly made his way upstairs to bed.

There were so many things he had wanted to ask Rose. He wanted to know why his aunt had been kept a secret from him, but the look of sadness in Rose's eyes as she talked about her brother had prevented him from voicing those questions.

Brett switched out the bedside light.

Rose was right. He must continue painting. Although Rose had not actually told him that she too had faced problems when she was younger, he knew instinctively that she had. He suddenly wondered whether the fact that his father seemed so intent on ignoring his artistic leanings had something to do with Rose.

There was a mystery that he wanted to unravel, but in the meantime, he must paint.

And he knew exactly who he wanted to start with.

5

'You'll have to amuse yourself today, Brett, darling. I'm off to York to buy something incredible to wear to my sixteenth birthday party and have my hair done. Anyway, I'm fed up with sitting on a pile of sheep-doings while you sketch some mouldy old view.'

Brett breathed a sigh of relief. Having Miranda with him while he was trying to paint was proving to be an irritating distraction. But apart from that, during the past ten days he had felt happier than he had since his mother died. He had completed four paintings. Doing what he loved most, combined with the fresh northern air, had provided a healing tonic.

Miranda got up from the table in the kitchen. 'I'll be back for tea. See you later.'

When Miranda had gone, Brett surreptitiously turned around and watched Leah, who was quietly drying the dishes with her mother.

With the presence of Miranda, who was proving an able bodyguard, he had had little opportunity to speak to Leah. He knew he must seize his chance.

'I was thinking I might go up to Haworth to see the Parsonage today. Trouble is, I don't know how to get there.'

'Oh, it's easy. You just get on the Worth Valley railway from the station in the village. It's only ten minutes to Haworth and the ride is lovely. If you hurry, you might get the ten o'clock,' said Mrs Thompson.

'Great. I was wondering if I could borrow Leah to show me round. She seems to be the expert on the Brontës and I don't want to miss anything.'

Mrs Thompson frowned. 'Well, Mr Brett, I don't know about that. We've got all the upstairs sheets to change and—'

'Oh, please, Mum. You know how I love Haworth.' Leah's eyes pleaded with her mother.

Mrs Thompson thought about how hard her daughter had worked for the past two weeks. She was a good girl and deserved a treat.

'All right, lass. As long as you're back by four to make your dad's tea. Have you got the train fare?'

'Don't worry about that, Mrs Thompson. I'll pay, as I've asked Leah to come with me.'

'I've got enough, Mum. Thank you.' Leah's eyes were sparkling.

'You'd better make it sharpish if you're to get the ten o'clock, mind.'

A few minutes later, they were hurrying down the hill towards the village. Now that Brett was actually alone with Leah, he felt completely tongue-tied.

They had just had enough time to purchase their tickets from the quaint station office when the train pulled in. Brett opened the door to a carriage full of visiting German tourists, but managed to locate two seats.

He could not help but stare at the beautiful girl sitting next to him. Leah was looking out of the window and he admired her faultless profile. The rest of the journey was conducted in total silence, and Brett realised that Leah was as shy as he was.

On arrival in Haworth, they followed the crowds of people off the train and walked along the road towards the centre of the village.

'This way,' said Leah, and Brett followed her as she moved gracefully up the steep, cobbled contours of the High Street. It was packed with people bustling in and out of the many gift and souvenir shops.

'We'll probably have to queue. They only allow so many people in at a time,' Leah remarked.

Brett nodded, knowing that he was making a complete ass of himself, unable to think of anything to say. Leah led him up some steps at the top of the High Street and along a narrow path, flanked by a graveyard on the left-hand side.

'There it is. Isn't it beautiful?'

The Parsonage stood tall and proud, washed by rich golden sunshine. Brett found it hard to believe that so much tragedy had taken place inside.

The queue was not as bad as Leah had anticipated, and within ten minutes they were in the sitting room, staring at the chaise-longue where Emily Brontë had taken her last breath.

Leah immediately came to life, leading him from room to room and chattering incessantly. Brett relaxed too, asking Leah questions and receiving knowledgeable and interesting answers.

'I find it so difficult to believe that Charlotte Brontë was so tiny. That dress looks as if it would only fit a doll! I feel like a giraffe compared to her.'

The two of them were standing in front of a glass cabinet containing items reported to belong to the famous Charlotte.

'I can assure you that you don't look like a giraffe, Leah.' Brett smiled and Leah blushed heavily.

An hour later, they were in the gift shop, where Brett insisted he buy a stack of postcards to send to his chums from school.

'Now, I would like to treat my tour guide and fount of knowledge to lunch. Can you recommend anywhere?'

Leah was nonplussed. Whenever she came up here, she brought sandwiches and had never been out to eat in a restaurant in her life.

'Er, well, not really.'

'Not to worry. Let's walk down the High Street and see what we can find.'

What they found was the Stirrup Café, which provided lunches of traditional Yorkshire fare. They found a table at the back of the crowded room and placed their orders. Leah felt awfully grand.

'So, what does your father do?' asked Brett.

'Nothing. He has very bad arthritis and can't walk.'

'I'm sorry, Leah.'

Leah waved away his embarrassment. 'That's okay. He's the most positive man I know.'

Two Cokes arrived with the waitress and they both took a sip.

'Do you always spend your holidays working for Rose?'

'No. It's because of the exhibition and you being here.'

'Gosh, I'm sorry I ruined your holidays, Leah.' Brett smiled.

'Oh, no, I didn't mean it like that. I meant, we need the money and . . .' Leah stopped herself. She'd heard Miranda talk about how rich Brett's father was. He wouldn't understand. 'Are you enjoying staying up here?' she asked.

'Very much. Especially today. Thank you for coming with me. I've been trying to get a chance to talk to you, but Miranda . . .' Brett's voice trailed off.

'She's very pretty, isn't she?'

Brett looked at the completely natural beauty sitting opposite him and smiled. 'Yes, if you like that sort of thing.' He steeled himself. 'I think you're much prettier.'

Leah looked down and blushed once more. The arrival of two shepherd's pies spared her from having to think of a reply.

'God, this is good.' Brett tucked in hungrily. 'They really know how to cook up here. When my father told me to come here for the summer, I didn't want to, but I'm so glad I'm here. It's a beautiful part of the world.'

'Yes.' Leah felt young and unworldly next to this boy who spoke so eloquently in his clipped English. It was hard to believe that he was only a few months older than she was.

'When we've finished this, is there anywhere else we could go? I fancy a walk.'

'We could go up onto the moors at the back of the Parsonage. Or there's the ruins of Top Withens, which is the farmhouse they think Emily based *Wuthering Heights* on, but we won't get there. It's too far.'

'Well, we could just see how far we get.' Brett shrugged, desperate for the day not to be over yet and for them to have further time alone together.

The two of them retraced their footsteps to the Parsonage and set out across Haworth Moor, once more lapsing into silence as they walked side by side.

After a while, Brett threw himself into the grass.

'I must be getting old,' he quipped. 'I'm exhausted.'

Leah sat down, a fair distance away from him. Brett shielded his eyes against the glaring sun and stared at the imposing house they had left behind in the distance.

'The Parsonage looks quite beautiful today, but I can imagine how bleak it must be up here in the winter. You can almost hear Heathcliff knocking on the window.'

Leah nodded. Brett looked at her, staring out across the moors, hands gracefully wrapped around her knees.

'You remind me of Cathy, sitting there. Apart from the T-shirt and jeans.' He laughed. She smiled at him and all he wanted to do was to pull her into his arms and kiss her. But he couldn't pluck up the courage.

Leah was thinking how romantic it would be if he were to take her hand. She'd never had the least interest in boys before, but Brett . . . No, she was just a poor Yorkshire girl from a small village. Surely the sophisticated Miranda was much more his type.

They sat like that for a while, Brett willing himself at least to move closer to her. Eventually, he did so, and sat there, tearing at the grass with his hands.

'I . . . I've really enjoyed today, Leah. I hope that we'll be able to spend some more time together. Actually, I've got something to ask you.'

'What is it?'

'You can say no if you want, but I'd really like to sketch you.'

'Sketch me?' The astonishment in Leah's voice was plain.

'Yes. I think you're . . . very beautiful.'

No one had ever suggested to Leah before that this might be the case. Apart from Megan the witch, all those years ago . . . Leah did her best not to shudder.

'Would you let me, please?'

'Well, if you really want to. I don't have much time, mind. Can't you paint Miranda instead?'

Brett was firm in his response. 'No.' It was now or never. Brett reached towards her and put his hand on top of Leah's. 'It's you.'

Leah thought she might die of pleasure as she let Brett take her hand in his.

Spurred on by this, Brett moved closer and put his free arm around Leah's shoulder.

'I'd prefer it if Miranda didn't know, or she'll want to come too. I'd like it to be just you and me while I paint. Why don't we arrange a place on the moors near the house? We could meet there every day for an hour or so. When is best for you?'

Leah hardly knew what she was saying as she felt the warmth of his body next to hers. 'The afternoon. About three o'clock.'

'That's settled, then. We'll find a good place on the way back.'

Leah looked at her watch. It was gone half past two. Although she wanted to stay here for ever, she knew they must be getting home.

'We have to go.'

'Okay. But first . . .' He kissed her chastely on her closed lips. He wanted to be more passionate, but understood he must go slowly. So he drew his mouth away, put both arms around her and held her in a tight embrace.

Leah wondered if she was in the middle of a lovely dream as she sat with her head on his shoulder, eyes tightly closed. Her first kiss, in a place she loved, with a boy so different from any of the brash, uncouth lads in her class. It felt so wonderful that she wanted to cry.

Eventually, Brett released her and they walked hand in hand down the hill. Silence, so uncomfortable at the beginning of the day, was now completely natural for the two of them experiencing their first taste of love.

6

'Oh Mum, I haven't got anything to wear to Miranda's party next week,' wailed Leah.

'You've got the dress you wore to Jackie's party last year. That'll do fine.'

'But, Mum, I've grown since then and that dress is so . . . babyish.'

Doreen tutted. 'Listen, madam, you're only fifteen and—'

'Sixteen at the end of August,' retorted Leah.

'You're only fifteen and that dress will be fine if I let it down,' said her mother firmly.

'Can I go into Bradford and just have a look? I've got some money saved from working up at the house. Please, Mum.'

'You've never been interested in clothes before, my girl.'

'I know, but I'm growing up now, and all Miranda's friends will have beautiful clothes.'

'They've got the money. We haven't.' Mrs Thompson looked at her daughter's crestfallen face and her heart softened. 'Tell you what: we'll go into Keighley tomorrow and see if we can find some material that I can turn into something quickly. Will that do?'

'Oh Mum, thanks.' Leah gave her a hug.

'Right. I'm off to the big house. You get your dad's tea sorted and I'll see you later.'

Mrs Thompson went out of the kitchen door and Leah got on with peeling the potatoes for tea. Once she had put them on to boil, she sat down at the table. A smile lit her face as she dreamily remembered the afternoon she had just spent with Brett.

Every day, at half past two, Leah would leave the big house as if she was going straight home, then scamper across the heather as fast as she could. They had found a lovely, concealed spot on the moors and Brett would be waiting for her, sketchpad and charcoal in hand. Leah would sit very still for half an hour as he sketched her. After that, Brett would put his arms around her and they would lie back in the rough grass and talk. Leah still pinched herself in disbelief that this was really happening. She could no longer think of him as Mrs Delancey's nephew, or the son of a very wealthy man. He was just Brett, who talked to her about how much he wanted to be an artist, how heartbroken he was about his mother dying, and how he was dreading returning to Eton, leaving her and Yorkshire behind.

Leah sighed and got up from the table to turn the potatoes down. She wondered what Miranda would say if she knew what was going on. It was obvious that she liked Brett a lot, and Leah still couldn't believe that Brett preferred *her*.

Leah took the toad-in-the-hole out of the oven, mashed the potatoes, adding lots of creamy butter, and doled them out onto two plates. Then she called her dad to say that tea was up.

Harry Thompson wheeled himself skilfully along the narrow corridor and positioned himself at the kitchen table.

'Mmm, this smells good, lass. You're getting to be as good a cook as your mum.'

'Thanks, Dad.' Leah sat down opposite him. 'Tuck in before it gets cold.'

'Aye, lass. So. How's it going up at the big house?'

'Fine. It's nice to have the extra pennies.'

'And what's this rich young nephew of Mrs Delancey's like, then?'

'Oh, he's very . . . nice.'

Harry did not miss the look in his daughter's eyes. He'd had his suspicions over the past three weeks, seeing the spring in her step, the flush in her cheeks and the dreamy expression on her face when she thought no one was looking.

'I see. Anything you want to tell me?' He smiled at Leah.

Leah blushed a deep red. She'd never been able to keep anything from her father.

'Oh Dad, promise you won't tell Mum. She mightn't let me work up there if she knew and . . .' The whole story came tumbling out. It was such a relief to tell someone. 'I don't know how I'm going to live when Brett goes away,' Leah finished, tears coming to her eyes.

'You've got me, pet. You can cry on my shoulder,' Mr Thompson replied. He hesitated before speaking again. 'Now, I know that Mum says he's a little gentleman, but he's from a different world. Don't let yourself get hurt by him, will you, pet?'

'Brett would never hurt me,' Leah said defensively.

'I'm sure he wouldn't, lass.' Harry gave his daughter a warm smile. 'You enjoy yourself. Being in love for the first time is magic. If you ever want to talk, I'll always be there to listen.'

Leah nodded, stood up and moved round the table to give her father a hug.

'Thanks, Dad. I love you very much, you know. Now, you go and watch *Coronation Street*, I'll do the washing-up and bring us in a cup of tea.'

Harry nodded and pushed himself out of the kitchen, troubled by the obvious strength of feeling his innocent daughter had for a boy who would walk out of her life in less than six weeks' time.

* * *

'Wow, this summer's turning out to be one of the hottest ever,' said Brett, staring up at the perfect deep blue sky.

Leah nodded, shifting her position in his arms to become more comfortable.

'You swear you're going to write to me at least every day when I go back to Eton?'

'Only if you do the same,' answered Leah.

'And I was thinking, I could come and spend the half-term up here, and maybe Christmas.'

'Yes.' Leah just couldn't bear to think about Brett leaving. She changed the subject. 'When are you going to let me see the sketch?'

'When I've finished it. You are impatient, aren't you?' Brett leaned above her and began tickling her mercilessly.

'Stop it! Stop it!' laughed Leah, loving every moment of it. She wriggled away from him across the grass and looked at her watch with a sigh. 'I ought to get going. Dad'll be needing his tea.'

'Okay, but first . . .' Brett grabbed her and pulled her into his arms. He kissed her passionately and placed his hand on her neck, before moving it down to the soft swelling underneath her blouse. He sighed with relief that Leah did not stop him. Tentatively, he undid the top button of her shirt, and his hand moved slowly underneath.

'No!' Leah pulled away from him angrily.

Brett jumped. 'God, I'm sorry, Leah. I thought you . . . we . . .'

'Yes. But I've told you, I don't want to go any further.'

Brett was visibly crestfallen. 'Don't you like me enough?'

'Of course I do. But Mum's warned me what trouble a girl can get into.'

'Do you think what we're doing can get you into trouble? I mean, Miranda must have been up here on the moors with half the boys in Oxenhope from the way she carries on, and—'

'Then why don't you go and find her?' Leah's eyes filled with tears. She stood up and began to make her way down the hill.

'Leah, I . . .' Brett sighed and sank down onto his haunches as he watched her jog gracefully over the moors away from him. He felt rotten. The last thing he had meant to do was to upset her, but she was driving him crazy. Of course he understood. She was so innocent, so naive, and seemed so much younger than he was. But the contours of the body that he felt beneath her clothes portrayed a different story altogether. She was in his thoughts night and day.

He was in love with her. And he would tell her at Miranda's party next week.

Leah kept running until she was far enough away from Brett, then she threw herself down on the moors to have a good cry. It was so unfair. Brett knew she didn't like him to touch her there, and yet she ended up feeling so guilty when she stopped him.

'And what's wrong with you?'

A shadow came across the bright sunlight and Leah looked up. Miles was on his imposing black horse, staring down at her. The involuntary shiver she always felt ran up her spine as he dismounted. She wiped away the tears from her face and stood up, desperate to get away.

'Nothing. I'm fine. I've got to go home now.' She turned to go, but he put his hand on her shoulder to stop her.

'Had a row with your new boyfriend, then?'

'I . . . what do you mean?' Leah stood stock-still, his hand burning into her shoulder. She did not want to turn round and look into those dark eyes.

'I saw the two of you on the moors together in the afternoon. You have grown up, haven't you?'

She was rooted to the spot, paralysed with fear. He let go of her shoulder and walked round to face her.

'Don't worry, I won't tell anybody. It can remain our little secret, can't it?' He smiled at her. Then Miles reached out his hand, and ran his fingers down her neck to her waist. This movement galvanised Leah into action and she ran, as fast as her legs would carry her, across the moors and down towards the familiarity and safety of home.

That night, Leah had a terrible nightmare.

A man was chasing her over the moors. He was gaining on her, and she knew exactly what he would do if he caught up. Her legs were getting slower and slower, and the valley below echoed with the voice of Megan the witch. 'Evil things . . . doomed . . . you can't alter destiny . . . you must beware him . . .'

7

'Well now, Dad, doesn't our Leah look a picture?' Her mum was smiling with pride.

'She does indeed. That dress is quite beautiful. It looks like it's out of one of those fashion magazines. You're right talented with a needle, aren't you, love?' Mr Thompson gazed fondly at his wife.

Leah stood in her mother and father's bedroom, staring at the mirror in disbelief. The dress was very simple – made of cheap, white cotton – but her mother had managed to fit it perfectly to Leah's tall, graceful body. It was sleeveless, with a boat-neck and a nipped-in waist with a pleated skirt. It would have looked like a child's party frock on anyone else, but Leah's height and slimness added just the necessary degree of sophistication and in turn made her look years older.

'Now, young lady. You just make sure you behave yourself. I'll be serving the food and drinks so I won't have time to watch you. Mrs Delancey's invited half of South Yorkshire,' Mrs Thompson clucked. 'Anyway, no slinking into the toilet to put some of that warpaint on your face, young miss. That pale lipstick is enough for a girl of your age.'

'Yes, Mum,' Leah said obediently. She glanced at the clock by the bed. 'We'd better go.'

Doreen nodded. 'Go and get your coat, Leah. It'll be cold on the walk back.'

Leah did so, and went back into the bedroom to kiss her father goodnight. It broke her heart sometimes to leave him alone.

''Night, Dad.' She kissed him.

''Night, love. You look quite the little grown-up in that. Have a good time and behave yourself.' He smiled and winked at her.

'I will.'

Mother and daughter left the house and started the walk up the hill in the sultry July air.

Miranda finished outlining her lips with 'strawberry red', put a tissue between them and pressed hard. She looked at the lips' outline on the tissue and wondered for the thousandth time why Brett was not bursting with desire to kiss them.

She had tried everything from outrageous flirtation to demure stand-offishness, but nothing seemed to work.

Miranda stood up and surveyed herself in the mirror. Perfect. The tight black dress showed off her voluptuous body. Surely even Brett would not be able to resist her tonight. She already knew how to use her face and curves to make the boys at school prepared to do anything for one look at the suspenders she wore under her school uniform. Miranda was not top of her class academically, but she knew how the world worked.

Miranda wanted out of this dump of a house, out of the small, repressive village full of nobodies leading boring, little lives. But above all else, she wanted wealth. Money equalled power and control, and there was only one way Miranda could get it.

Love was for the foolish. It made you helpless and stopped you from getting what you wanted. Miranda didn't ever intend to fall into that trap.

But Brett's reaction had disconcerted her. He wasn't behaving in the way she had come to recognise. He seemed immune to the spell that had so far enchanted her male classmates. It was beginning to aggravate her. He was her passport out of here. Put simply, she had to have him.

Miranda smiled at her reflection as she stood up. Brett didn't stand a chance.

'Thank you, Rose, it looks quite lovely.' Miranda surveyed the barn that had been cleared by men from the village and festooned with streamers. The mobile disco was being set up at the front, and Mrs Thompson was busy in the kitchen preparing the food.

Rose looked at her daughter, wishing she had the courage to tell her that the skin-tight short black dress, overdone make-up and high stilettos were doing her no favours. However, Rose had put a lot of effort into this party, hoping that it might make Miranda easier to deal with, and the last thing she wanted was to create an argument.

'That's all right. Now listen, Miranda, a few ground-rules for you and your friends. They're allowed into the house to go to the bathroom, but the rest of it is off limits. I don't want anyone sneaking off into the other barns. And apart from the fruit punch, which does have a little wine in, I don't want anyone drinking alcohol. I'll be in the sitting room with the adults and, as long as there isn't any trouble, I'll stay there. But—'

'It's okay, I understand,' Miranda interrupted impatiently. 'You just enjoy your party and I'll enjoy mine. Do you like my outfit, by the way?' She gave a twirl.

Rose gritted her teeth. 'Yes, it's . . . very . . . striking.'

'I thought so too. I'll see you later. I just want to go and check my make-up before everyone starts arriving.'

Miranda made her way upstairs as best she could in the tight dress and high heels. She walked along the corridor to the bathroom, passing Brett's bedroom. She could hear him whistling. She crept to the door, which was slightly ajar, and peeped through the crack. Brett was sitting on his bed with his back to her, wrapping a flat, rectangular object in an old blanket. She knocked and walked into the room.

Brett was obviously startled, for he jumped and quickly slid the object under the bed before turning round.

'Jesus, Miranda, you shouldn't creep up on people like that.'

'Sorry, darling.' She sat on the bed and crossed her legs, revealing the top of one of her black stockings. 'Was that my birthday present?'

'Er, no. But this is.' Brett passed a neatly wrapped package to her, hoping that it would deflect Miranda's interest in what was under the bed.

'Can I open it now?'

'If you'd like. Happy birthday.'

Miranda tore at the wrapping paper, finding a blue velvet box inside. She opened it and looked at the dainty gold locket. Not her scene at all, but obviously worth a packet. She took it out of the box and laid it across her fingers.

'Thank you, Brett. It's lovely.' Miranda fiddled with the clasp of the locket and managed to open it. 'See, I can put a picture of someone in here and wear it next to my heart. Do you have a picture of yourself I could put in?'

'No, not one small enough, anyway. I'm glad you like it, Miranda. I didn't know what to get you, so I asked Mrs Thompson to help me.' Leah had chosen it, actually, but Brett didn't think Miranda would be too pleased about that.

'Could you put it round my neck? I'll wear it tonight.'

'Of course.' Brett knelt on the bed behind Miranda and fastened the clasp. Before he could move, she had swung round and put her arms around him. Her face was inches away from his, and he could smell the heavy scent she was wearing.

'I think I should give you a kiss for that, don't you?' Miranda locked her lips against his.

'No, Miranda, I . . .'

Before he could pull away, her other hand swiftly took his up towards her breast.

After all those fruitless afternoons on the moors and tantalising dreams of Leah night after night, Brett struggled not to respond. He relaxed his lips, and let his hand roam over one breast, then the other. He knew that this was wrong, dangerous, but his body, not his mind, was in control. Miranda did not stop him when he slipped his hand inside her dress.

In return, Brett felt Miranda slowly undoing the zip of his trousers.

'Oh God,' he stuttered. Feeling a woman's touch for the first time was unparalleled and carried an intensely aroused Brett beyond the point of no return.

Pent-up passion spent through Miranda's hand, Brett was aghast. He could only think of getting away from her as quickly as possible. He wrenched his mouth from her vice-like kiss and moved off the bed towards the door.

'Miranda . . . I . . .'

There was the light of victory shining in her eyes.

'I'm sorry.' It was all he could think of to say as he bolted for the bathroom and locked himself in.

He sat on the edge of the bath with his head in his hands. How could he have done that, after all he'd said to Leah? It was as if he'd been possessed for those few minutes – not himself, unable to think about anything except his own physical gratification. Were all men like this? Did they all become powerless when faced with their own selfish desire for sex?

Was this why he was constantly reading of ruined careers after involvement with unsavoury women?

He couldn't tell Leah. She would never, ever forgive him, and he wouldn't blame her.

Brett had been so excited about tonight. He was going to tell Leah that he loved her, and present her with the finished charcoal sketch. He had even found a hidden spot in one of the barns, and when Miranda had burst in on him he was wrapping the sketch in a blanket, ready to sneak it downstairs for later.

Brett stood up and undressed. He washed his body, face and hands as if to cleanse himself of Miranda's touch. Then he took a deep breath and decided that to keep Leah, he would just have to live with his shameful secret and make it up to her in other ways.

She immediately became a shining icon in his eyes; pure, untouched, innocent, so unlike Miranda who had tempted him and succeeded.

'Shit! The sketch!'

Brett unlocked the door and ran back down the corridor to his bedroom, which was empty. He checked under the bed and, to his relief, the sketch was still there. He hoped that Miranda had forgotten about it, for he was aware that while she could not harm him, she could harm Leah.

It was the first thing Miranda had done when Brett had left the room. Happy in her triumph, in the knowledge that however much money, wealth or power men had, they were all the same underneath, she reached under the bed and drew the object out.

The shock was terrible. Miranda turned ashen and anger burned inside her. Leah's beauty and innocence, captured so perfectly by Brett, shone out from the sketch.

But Miranda couldn't see it. All she could see was the mousey kid who washed Rose's dishes to earn some pin money.

'Bitch!' she said under her breath. That was probably why Brett had been so stand-offish with her – he was getting it from that common little brat.

Miranda's first instinct was to smash the frame and tear the sketch to shreds. No, Brett would know it was her. There had to be a better way for her to get revenge.

'I'll fix you,' she said to the sketch as she rewrapped it and placed it under the bed. Then she stood up, tidied her hair in the mirror and went downstairs to greet her guests.

'Mamma Mia' burst through the speakers in the barn as the DJ welcomed everyone to the party. A few people edged onto the makeshift dance floor and started to move to the beat.

Miranda was surrounded by friends handing her presents when Brett entered, fresh from secreting Leah's sketch in the spot he had found in the end barn right on the edge of the moors.

He was unaware that someone had watched him from start to finish.

Brett spotted Leah. 'There you are. My, don't you look beautiful.' He kissed her and wrapped an arm round her shoulder.

'Brett, don't. Miranda's just over there and she might see.'

'I don't care any more. She can't stop us.'

'No, but—'

'Sshh. Come on. Let's go and dance.'

The barn was filling up. Some boys from the village had brought cider and beer and Miranda was drinking from their proffered bottles. She looked around, and the sight of Leah and Brett together heightened her anger.

'Come and dance with me.' Miranda grabbed the nearest male, pulled him onto the dance floor and jived seductively to the music, swigging from the bottle of cider in one hand.

Brett had his arms round Leah and they were swaying slowly to the music.

'Are you happy, Leah?'

She looked up at him. 'Yes.'

'Good. I've got something for you. It's in the last barn, on the edge of the moors. We'll have to go there separately so no one sees us, but will you come? I promise to behave myself,' he pleaded.

'All right.' Leah smiled.

Mrs Thompson was bringing in the food from the kitchen and putting it on the trestle table at the back of the barn. She immediately espied Leah dancing with Brett.

'That'll lead to trouble,' she muttered under her breath. Once the song had finished, she clapped her hands together and shouted, 'Food up!'

People drifted over to the laden table, and Mrs Thompson was kept busy serving sausages, baked potatoes and salad.

'I'm keeping my eye on you,' Mrs Thompson whispered to Leah, as she filled her plate.

Leah looked at the floor in embarrassment. 'Honest, Mum, we were only having a dance, that's all.'

'See that it stays that way. No disappearing.' Mrs Thompson passed on to the next hungry customer.

Miles watched Leah and Brett from his vantage point in the corner of the barn. Leah was turning into such a beautiful girl, just as he had known she would. But that boy she was with . . . he wasn't good enough to lick her boots, even if his father did own half the world.

Miles had photographs of her, taken secretly, from the time when she was a tiny, delicate five-year-old, pottering around the farmhouse behind her mother. The camera loved her, her ethereal beauty enhanced by the sharpness of the lens.

And now there was a pretender to his throne. He was looking forward to tearing that portrait to shreds like the garbage it was.

Brett had to understand. Leah was not ready yet. She was pure and perfect. Miles had known this when he had touched her the other day. He'd had to mark her for his own.

Miles sauntered out of the barn, heading towards the edge of the moors; a dark solitary figure in the moonlight.

Leah entered the end barn, having slipped out the minute her mother had taken a pile of dirty dishes back to the house. There was only the ghostly moonlight to see by, and she hoped that Brett had arrived first.

'Brett?' she whispered. She felt relief as she heard a noise from the far end. Then the sound of something smashing. 'Brett, Brett, are you all right?' She stumbled in the direction of the noise and saw a circle of torchlight shining on the floor. It was immediately switched off and everything was silent once more.

'Brett, where are you?' Leah had reached the spot where the torch had been, and could hear someone breathing. She reached out and put a hand on something warm.

'Thank goodness, Brett. What was that noise?'

The arms reached out for her and she snuggled into them. But something didn't feel quite right. She looked up, her eyes now adjusted to the dim light, and screamed.

A hand covered her mouth, and she struggled, but he held her tight.

'I'm not going to hurt you, Leah. Stop struggling, for goodness' sake.'

Feelings of revulsion and fear rose in Leah.

'No!' She wrenched herself away with all her might. The motion toppled her backwards against the wall. She heard the tear of material as her dress caught on something and she slid down to the ground.

'Leah, Leah, are you okay? Damn, I can't see a thing!'

Leah picked herself up and ran towards the shadowy figure

of Brett standing near the entrance to the barn. She threw herself into his arms, sobbing loudly.

'What on earth's the matter?'

'Over there . . . he was in here and I thought he was you and . . . he wasn't.'

'Okay, okay, calm down. I'm here now,' soothed Brett. He looked towards the back of the barn and could see nothing.

'You stay here, and I'll have a look.'

'No! Let's just go.'

'But there's something I wanted to show you.'

'I want to go back to the house. Now. My dress is all torn and—'

'Okay, I can show you another time.'

Brett turned her round to walk out of the barn and saw Miranda standing there, arms folded.

'Well, well, well. We've had a busy night, haven't we, Brett?' She looked at the tear in the dress across Leah's shoulder.

'Hello, Miranda,' Brett sighed. 'I wanted to tell you about—'

'About the fact that you've been screwing her as well as me?' Miranda's words were slurred.

Brett's jaw clenched. 'Shut up, Miranda.'

'Oh no, I think little innocent Leah has a right to know where lover boy was earlier this evening, don't you?' She laughed viciously.

Leah was standing there silently, staring straight ahead, not wanting to hear.

'Go on then, Leah, ask him. See if he denies it,' Miranda taunted.

Leah looked up at Brett, her eyes begging him to do just that. But she didn't have to ask. The guilt was written right across his face.

She gave one huge sob and ran out of the barn, straight into the arms of her mother.

8

'Come on now, Leah, tell Mum what happened.' Mrs Thompson wrapped a cardigan round her daughter's shoulders. The girl was shivering violently and she couldn't get a word out of her. Mrs Thompson had sent Brett back to the disco. She'd had a quick word with Miranda, who had obviously been drinking. Miranda had said she'd heard screaming and found Brett and Leah in the barn alone together.

Mrs Thompson looked at her daughter's torn dress and feared the worst.

'Did he, did Mr Brett . . . ?' Mrs Thompson could not speak the words. Thank goodness she'd gone looking for Leah once she'd noticed that her daughter and Brett were missing. Leah did not reply. If that boy had touched her daughter, well . . . there'd be hell to pay, however rich his father was.

'Leah, did Mr Brett . . . ?'

'No, Mum.'

'Then what happened? How did your dress get torn?'

Leah sat, tight-lipped and pale as a ghost. Mrs Thompson realised that she would get no more out of her tonight.

'All right, love. We'll talk about it tomorrow. I think we need to get you home and tucked up in bed.'

Mrs Thompson didn't want Harry knowing about any of this, not with his health the way it was. She went into the

69

sitting room where Rose was entertaining her guests and asked Mr Broughton, a local farmer, whether he'd mind giving Leah a lift down the hill as she wasn't feeling too well. He agreed, and Mrs Thompson bundled Leah into the back of the car, telling her to go straight upstairs to bed when she got home.

Doreen went back to the kitchen and started making headway into the large pile of dishes in the sink. The kitchen door opened and Brett came in, looking shame-faced and ashen.

'Is she all right, Mrs Thompson?' he asked quietly.

'She is. I've sent her home to bed.'

'I didn't touch her, you know, really. I wouldn't. I like her too much to do anything to upset her.'

'That's not what Miranda said when I asked her. She said she heard screaming and went to the barn to find you and Leah alone together.'

Brett ran a hand through his hair. 'Oh God, did she?'

'Yes, she did. Anyway, I'll be speaking to Leah tomorrow and she'll not be back working up at the house for the rest of the summer. I think you've caused enough trouble for one night, young man. I'd take myself off to bed if I were you.'

'Yes, you're right. Please, Mrs Thompson, send Leah my love and my apologies.'

Mrs Thompson said nothing, just continued with the dishes.

Brett slunk miserably up the stairs. Everything was ruined. And he was to blame. If only he'd been stronger, if he'd resisted Miranda, then none of this would have happened. As for what had gone on in the barn, it was his word against Miranda's. She was paying him back for deceiving her, and he knew Leah would never want to see him again.

Brett undressed and lay miserably under the covers. He closed his eyes and dreamed of his lost love.

9

David Cooper swivelled his chair away from his desk to gaze out of the full-length window overlooking Central Park. The trees were like tiny, green dots far below and the cars looked like children's toys.

He thought how his physically elevated position reflected his standing in life. He rarely came into contact with any of those everyday people far below him, rushing about their business along Fifth Avenue. Everyone he met these days was very rich, very powerful, and a mirror-image of himself.

The pleasure of making money had ended for him on the day his wife died. He'd loved her, of course. But the extent of the loss he was now suffering had shocked him. Vivien's death had brought back the realisation of his own mortality.

He hadn't touched another woman for the past nine months.

David knew his son thought he didn't give a damn about his wife dying. He'd only seen Brett twice since she'd passed: once at the funeral, and then at Christmas. They'd not grieved together.

He wondered how Brett was getting on in Yorkshire with his sister. Rose . . . having not seen her for over twenty years, he still maintained the image of the exquisitely beautiful girl she had been in her twenties.

David was thinking of the past a lot these days. Having survived only by blocking it out, he had spent his life planning the future. But now he was starting to look backwards, to let old memories resurface.

Some of them were painful – too painful to be unlocked. But reflecting on his financial success made him see just how far he had come in the last twenty-eight years.

David sat there, in his forty-foot office, remembering the time when he had run his business from the sitting room of his tiny flat in Bayswater.

He had started with a rundown tenement building in Islington in the late forties, buying the land it stood on for a song and refurbishing the building into four smart studio flats. Young people didn't buy property in those days, so he had rented them out and used the money he received to buy another, similar building. By the mid-fifties, he had twenty such buildings, providing him with enough steady monthly income to ask the bank for larger and larger loans.

There were still sites in the centre of London untouched since the war. He built office blocks on them and sold them for a fortune to the growing number of companies opening at the time.

By the mid-sixties, he had the largest construction company in Britain. He began to look abroad, at the newly growing holiday market, and bought sites along the beaches in Spain, the Balearics and Italy. He built hotels on the land, holding on to portions to sell back to the governments five years later for triple the price.

Now, ten years on, he owned land in almost all major developed countries and was starting to cast further afield for business opportunities.

He had been named as one of the top ten richest men in Britain and made the top fifty in America.

One hell of an achievement.

The thrill of a successful business deal had made up for the part of him that couldn't function. He knew his colleagues, his wife and son saw him as a cold man. Emotionless.

Now that she was dead, David wished that he'd had the courage to confide in Vivien, to tell her why he'd been incapable of affection . . . but it was too late.

He knew that this sudden memory surge was the reason he'd decided Brett should go to meet Rose.

David was not going to pick up his son from Yorkshire. He had given himself the pleasure of knowing it was an option, but seeing her again after all this time . . . He wasn't up to it at the moment. But he might pop into that little gallery he'd just bought in London when she held her exhibition there, just to see. In spite of everything, he still cared about her, deeply.

David turned and studied the painting on the wall behind his desk. He sighed. He sometimes felt sad at the easy way that everything could be bought and sold, especially people. He stood up and picked up his slim Cartier briefcase. He had to be at Sardi's in thirty minutes for lunch with a newly elected senator.

As he left his office and waited for the lift, he wondered briefly what this man's price was.

10

'Well, Brett, it's been lovely to have you with us. I do hope you'll come back and visit soon.' Rose kissed him. 'And keep up the painting. The ones I've seen show great potential.'

'Thanks, Rose. I've really enjoyed being here. I'll try and get to your exhibition.'

Bill and the limousine were waiting outside for him.

'Bye, Brett, it's been nice knowing you.' Miranda came running down the stairs and gave him a peck on the cheek. Brett couldn't bring himself to do the same, so he smiled and waved and got into the back of the big car.

'Have a nice holiday, sir?' Bill asked on the intercom. 'You look well on it, I must say.'

Brett thought about the past two months. The first five weeks had been wonderful, with his rediscovered painting and Leah. But the past month had been dreadful, as he was unable to get her out of his mind.

As promised by Mrs Thompson, Leah had not been up to the house again, and he had not seen her since the night of the party. Brett had spent most of his time on the moors at the spot where Leah and he had met every day, hoping and praying she would come. He had asked Mrs Thompson time and again how she was, but she would just purse her lips and say, 'Fine,' and that would be the end of the conversation.

He'd been so desperate in the last week that he had gone down to the village just to see if he could catch sight of her, but he didn't.

'Yes, Bill, it was . . . different.'

'Good, sir. Your father sends his regards. He'll be down to visit you at half-term. He's in South America for the next six weeks.'

Brett felt lower than he had when he'd arrived in Yorkshire. As the miles increased between him and the girl he loved, he thought his heart might break.

'Bye, Leah, I'll never forget you,' he whispered as they crossed the Yorkshire border and sped down the motorway towards Windsor.

11

Rose shivered violently, despite the three sweaters and scarf that she was wearing. She blew on her hands, which were numb from the cold and becoming too inflexible to paint.

The snow was piled in great drifts outside her studio window. The thaw had begun yesterday, but it always took longer for the drifts on high ground to melt.

Rose stoked the small, ineffectual fire and warmed her hands. The freezing January weather made her feel miserable and depressed. She turned to look at the painting on the easel. Self-doubt hit her once more.

'Oh,' she groaned. 'Is it worth it? Am I going to be torn to shreds by the critics?'

Come on, said a voice inside her, as she switched on the old kettle. *Just think of the central heating you could install if the exhibition is a success.*

Rose sat in front of the fire, warming her hands on the coffee cup and drinking from it slowly. She sighed, picked up her brush and palette and walked back to the easel.

'Think positive, Rosie, old girl. Two more to go and you're there. And this painting must be worth at least four and a half radiators.' She smiled and put her brush to the canvas.

* * *

An hour or so later, there was a knock on her studio door.

'Come in.'

'Rose, can I see you for a moment, please?' Miranda was standing at the door, looking unusually pale.

Rose had noticed how quiet she'd been for the past few months. It had, in fact, been a blessed relief. In the four and a half months since Brett had gone home, and with Miles back at university, Rose had virtually managed to complete her work for the exhibition.

Now she wondered whether she had missed something. Miranda looked quite dreadful. She put down her brush.

'Of course, darling. Come and sit down. What is it?'

Miranda promptly burst into tears. Rose could not recall ever seeing a teenage Miranda sob in front of her before. She knelt next to her and put a comforting arm round her shoulders.

'Whatever it is, I'm sure it can't be as bad as all that.'

'It is, it is,' Miranda sobbed.

'Come on, then, tell Rose what the problem is.'

'I think I'm pregnant.' The words burst out in a rush.

Oh God, thought Rose. *I should have seen this coming. One of the village boys, perhaps, when I was locked away in my studio.*

'Have you missed your last period, darling?'

Miranda nodded. 'And the one before that, and the one before and . . . I don't know how many.' She looked up and Rose could feel nothing but sympathy. After all, she herself had been through this.

'Try to think clearly, darling. There's probably still plenty of time to—'

'About five, or maybe six . . . I don't know.'

'Well, what I'm going to do now is telephone a very good clinic I know in Leeds. I'll make an appointment for tomorrow and if the snow will let us, we'll go and see them. You may not be pregnant at all. It could be some kind of woman's problem and—'

'Feel this.' Miranda's hand took Rose's and led it under the layers of sweaters to her stomach. Rose felt the definite bulge.

'Why didn't you come to me before, Miranda? Surely you must have realised a long time ago?'

This induced a fresh stream of tears. 'I know, but I kept hoping that I was wrong and thinking that next month it might be all right.'

'Okay, okay,' soothed Rose, remembering so vividly the self-same nightmare. 'Don't worry, we'll sort it out. Now, how about a nice cup of tea?'

She led Miranda into the kitchen and prepared two mugs. Miranda's usual high-handed attitude had disappeared completely. There was now a frightened little girl sitting at the table.

Miranda sipped the tea while Rose made an appointment at the clinic for the following day.

'Right, all fixed up. We're going to see a lovely woman doctor called Kate.'

'Thank you, Rose,' Miranda said quietly.

'What for?'

'For being so nice. I know I'm a pain sometimes and I'm sorry.'

'That's okay.' Rose was desperate to ask who the father was while Miranda was being so pliable, but she thought it better to wait until they had seen the doctor tomorrow.

'I'm scared.'

Devoid of the usual make-up, Miranda looked young, her eyes big, blue and fearful. Rose went to her and gave her a hug.

'Don't worry, darling, we'll sort it out.' She spoke with as much confidence as she could muster.

* * *

'I'm afraid you're over six and a half months pregnant, Miss Delancey. Only two weeks short of the allowed limit for termination by the National Health Service and, in my opinion, too near to risk it. The baby is due on the twentieth of April.'

Rose sighed deeply. It was no less than she had expected.

Miranda sat stock-still, staring at the doctor.

'So you're saying I can't do anything about it?' Her face was deathly pale.

'I'm saying that in my opinion it would be a risk to your health that I wouldn't like to take.'

'Absolutely,' said Rose. 'I'm not putting you in jeopardy. I'm sorry, but you're going to have the baby, Miranda, dear.' She squeezed her daughter's hand tightly.

'Does the father know about this?' asked Kate softly.

Miranda stared at her hands and shook her head.

'Do you know who the father is, darling?'

Miranda looked at her mother and for an instant Rose saw the flicker of fear run through her daughter's eyes. It vanished in an instant and Miranda stared silently ahead.

'No.'

'But darling, I think that—'

'No! It's nothing to do with him.'

Rose saw Kate send a warning glance in her direction.

'All right, Miranda. If you don't feel like talking about it at the moment, that's fine. Now, so far as the procedure for ante-natal care is concerned, I want you to come back tomorrow and I'm going to give you a full check-up. You have only three months until the birth of the baby and we need to look after you both. Do you smoke, Miss Delancey?'

Rose drove her ancient Land Rover back to Oxenhope with a silent Miranda next to her. She racked her brain to try to think of one particular boy that Miranda had mentioned

during the past few months. If she was over six months pregnant now, it would mean that conception had been in the
middle of July . . . Of course – Miranda's birthday party. Rose
knew that she had been much the worse for wear by the end
of the evening . . . it might have been any one of the twenty
or so young boys who had turned up. Perhaps Miranda couldn't
even remember, and that was why she was being so cagey.

'You're going to have to leave school, darling, at least for
the time being. I shall postpone my exhibition until the baby's
born and you're settled.' Rose was desperate to tell her how
stupid she'd been not to confide in her before so they could
have at least made plans, but her guilt over her self-centredness
of the past few months prevented her from doing so. Rose
felt it was her fault and, therefore, her responsibility.

Miranda only nodded and continued to stare out of the
window.

When they arrived back at the farmhouse, Miranda went
straight up to her room, threw herself on the bed and lay
staring up at the ceiling.

The father? Should she tell him? Surely he'd understand,
help her?

She sat up, jumped off the bed and searched for a notepad
in her chest of drawers. Armed with a biro and paper, she lay
back on the bed again, propping herself up with pillows.

'Dear . . .'

Miranda threw the notepad onto the floor with a cry as
tears streamed down her face.

12

Leah sat in her tiny bedroom staring into space. The news had been all round the school today. Miranda Delancey was pregnant and was leaving until after the birth of her baby. There were all sorts of ideas about who the father was; Miranda was never short of admirers, but no one was absolutely positive.

Leah knew for definite.

The tightness in her chest increased, and the lump in her throat produced one small tear that fell slowly down her cheek.

'Nothing more than I expected,' clucked Mrs Thompson when she'd returned home from the farmhouse with the news. 'That one's always been trouble. A right little madam. That poor wee mite inside her, not knowing who its dad is. Mrs Delancey told me Miranda is refusing to say.'

Leah understood why Miranda wouldn't say anything to Mrs Delancey.

Brett. The father of Miranda's baby. The boy Leah thought had loved *her*.

Leah had spent the past six and a half months believing that she was the unhappiest girl alive. Her young heart had been so consummately, completely given to Brett that she doubted whether she would ever recover.

Knowing that Brett was still living so nearby had been the hardest part. Imagining Miranda in his arms had been terrible too. At least when her mother had said that Brett had left to go back to school, the distance had eased the pain slightly.

Leah had swung from the terrible anger of being deceived to the devastation of knowing she would never see Brett again.

There had been times when she had imagined that Miranda had been lying, just to get her own back, but now Leah knew that she had been telling the truth.

Leah wished that she could hate Brett – really, *truly* hate him so that the longing in her heart would go away. But, even now, she could not. She often thought of that terrible night in the barn, when that creep had grabbed her. Leah was sure it had been Miles, but daren't say anything that might risk her mother's job. Brett had saved her.

She still loved him.

Leah, always quiet before, had retreated further and further into her own world. Now she was studying for her mock exams and used revision to try and take her mind off her broken heart. Her mother had assumed that the long silences at supper were to do with 'growing pains', as she put it, but her father knew the truth. He would wink at her and tell her funny stories to try to make her smile.

But no one could truly understand. If she spoke about Brett, her dad would just tell her to forget him, and that was something she couldn't do.

Ever.

13

'Keep pushing, that's a good girl, nearly there now. Come on, just one more push and . . .'

Miranda, red-faced, exhausted and with not an ounce of energy left, gave one final push. As she screamed, her cry mingled with that of the first sounds of her newly born child. She saw the strange blueish thing being held by the midwife and sank back, uninterested in anything else except closing her eyes.

'Come on now, dear, hold baby.' The midwife placed the bawling infant into her arms. 'It's a beautiful little girl.' She smiled as Miranda looked down at the tiny creature with the ugly, screwed-up face.

She had wondered how she'd feel when she held her child in her arms for the first time. Fear, maybe? Affection? But Miranda felt neither. She felt nothing at all.

She handed the screaming bundle back to the midwife. 'Too tired now,' she said, and closed her eyes once more.

The midwife tutted in disapproval, but carried the baby off to the nursery.

Rose came rushing through the door five minutes later. She stroked her daughter's sweat-matted blonde hair away from her face.

'Well done, darling. I've just seen her and she's absolutely beautiful. I'm so proud of you,' she smiled.

Miranda nodded, keeping her eyes firmly closed and wondering why people kept saying that the baby was beautiful. She didn't think it was.

'Anyway, I'm going to let you get some sleep now, darling. I'll be back to see you later.' Rose kissed her daughter gently on the cheek and crept out of the room. After checking with the doctor that mother and baby were going to be fine for the next couple of hours, Rose left the hospital, retrieved her car from the car park and set off towards Oxenhope. She hadn't been home for twenty-four hours, since she had found Miranda standing in a pool of water in the kitchen and in a terrible state of panic. Rose had managed to keep her calm on the journey to the hospital, inwardly feeling as frightened as Miranda, remembering the pain of childbirth and wishing she could endure it for her.

Thankfully, however, although long, the birth had been straightforward and Rose found tears filling her eyes as she neared home. It was a glorious April day and the fresh smell of spring permeated the air.

'Rebirth,' Rose whispered emotionally. 'I'll do the best I can, I swear,' she murmured, knowing the problems were only just beginning.

Mrs Thompson had offered to take over the day-to-day care of the baby when and if Miranda returned to school. Rose somehow doubted that her daughter would do so, never having been academically inclined. And the attitude from the other students in her year, especially the boys, was enough to deter even the most confident girl.

But there was no doubt that Doreen Thompson would prove useful. She had been very good with Miles when he was small. Rose had managed to delay the exhibition until the beginning of August, and Mrs Thompson's help was going to be invaluable while she was in London.

She drove up the hill and parked the car in front of the farmhouse. The builders were still at work on the roof, and the barns adjacent. Rose had hired the barns out to a local farmer for a little extra monthly income, so they were being cleaned out and swept ready for a herd of cows to take up residence.

'Mrs Delancey, how did it go?' one of the builders shouted from the roof as she stepped out of the car.

'Just fine. It's a little girl and both mother and baby are doing well.'

'That's cracking news.' He smiled. 'I've left something on the kitchen table for you. One of the lads found it while he was clearing out the barns. He thinks it might be one of your drawings.'

Rose frowned and nodded. 'Thanks, Tim.' She opened the door to the kitchen, thinking it may have been junk stored there by the previous owner.

It was lying on the table, frame smashed, but sketch untouched. Rose gasped. It was the most exquisite charcoal drawing of Leah Thompson. She picked it up, carried it into her studio and placed it on an easel. Then she sat down and studied the signature in the right-hand corner. 'B.C.' Of course. It was Brett's work.

Rose was completely dazzled by the sketch. Her nephew had shown her his landscape work and she had been impressed by his obvious talent, but this . . . It had a maturity and depth to it that belied the artist's age and experience. The face staring out at her was one of great beauty. The eyes, my, they were hypnotic. You could hardly drag yourself away. In them, Brett had caught Leah's innocence perfectly.

And she knew that it had been drawn through the eyes of love.

Rose sighed and wondered why Brett had never shown this to her. Why, if she had seen this and recognised the talent that he had in common with his aunt, she thought proudly, then she would have given him more encouragement.

Her eyes filled with tears as she stared at the sketch.

David must not be allowed to discourage his son. She went to a drawer, pulled out a pad of writing paper, found a paint-splattered biro and sat down in her chair.

After staring at a blank page and chewing the end of her pen for five minutes, she put the pad down.

No, she had a much better idea of how to help Brett.

14

'Rose, darling, how absolutely marvellous to see you again, after all these years.' Roddy clasped her in a tight bear hug, then pulled back and looked her over from top to toe. 'Mmm, still the same beautiful Rosie.'

'It's very kind of you to say so, but I think I've put on quite a few pounds since you saw me over twenty years ago.' She smiled wryly.

'Darling, it suits you. You always were far too skinny. Oh!' Roddy clapped his hands together, 'I can hardly believe you're here.' He put his arm through Rose's. 'Follow me. I've a bottle of your favourite Veuve Clicquot chilling in my office. We'll take a look round the gallery later. Your paintings arrived safely yesterday, by the way, and I have to admit I was tempted to look at them immediately.'

Rose walked through the spacious, newly fitted gallery with Roddy, its deserted walls a reminder of why she was here. Butterflies fluttered in her stomach.

'To you, my darling. I just know that the exhibition will be a huge success,' said Roddy, handing her a champagne flute.

Rose lifted her glass and drank, wondering how Miranda and little Chloe were doing. She'd felt so guilty leaving them, but with Mrs Thompson clucking round them like a mother hen, Rose knew that they'd be fine. She could only hope that

Mrs Thompson didn't do all the work, as Miranda often used her as an excuse to have as little to do with the child as possible.

'Of course, you're going to come and stay with me in Chelsea for the next week.'

'Well, actually, Roddy, I've booked myself into a hotel and—'

'Bugger the hotel, I insist you stay with me. I have a super flat that I bought a year ago. It's divine and I'm looking forward to cosy nights in with gin and tonics while you tell me everything that's happened over the past twenty years.'

Rose had to smile at her friend. He was completely unchanged by the years except for the fact that he was sporting a toupee. His wiry frame was, as always, dressed immaculately in a designer suit.

She had met Roddy in 1948. He had been in her year at the Royal College of Art. Then, it was as if he had sensed the secrets in her past, and never once had pried into those things that were too painful for her to remember.

In return, she had moved into his comfortable flat in Earl's Court when she'd finished college, and provided a listening ear to the complications of Roddy's sex life – she could hardly keep up with the constant rotation of men that her friend always seemed to be juggling. Roddy came from dubious nobility in Devon and was becoming a well-known figure at the Colony Room and French's, where promising young artists gathered in the fifties.

Having decided that he harboured little passion for painting himself, but adoring the atmosphere and the people, Roddy had concentrated on putting his more libidinous talents to good use. It used to be a joke in their tightly knit crowd that the only well-known young artist in London Roddy had not seduced was Rose herself. When she had eventually left for Yorkshire, he was off in the South of France living with a very wealthy art dealer.

'Who owns this gallery, Roddy?' she asked. 'Cork Street is a prime location.'

Roddy filled her glass to the brim once more. 'Well,' he said, 'I got a call from a company in New York offering me a job as manager here. I was at a bit of a loose end, so I came to see the place. You should have seen it, ooh.' Roddy shook his head. 'A shell, that's what it was. Anyway, I called them in New York and told them to contact me when they'd refurbished the place. Then they told me I could have *carte blanche* to design it myself, with money being no concern. I couldn't resist!' Roddy swigged his champagne. 'Then a very nice suit from New York flew over to take a look at the finished product. He loved it, I'm glad to say. In fact, it was his idea to have an exhibition of fifties artists.' Rose looked quizzical. 'It's all above board and everything,' Roddy assured her. 'We pay our VAT and tax on time, so you're all right, dearie. It's not being funded by Mafia money or anything. To be honest, it's a wonderful arrangement. They just let me get on with it.'

'Are you doing well?'

'We've only been open since the New Year, and you're our sixth showing. But with my connections, we're going to do just fine.' He gave her a wink. 'I intend to bring the fun back into the art world. It's become so staid and snobby since our merry little band grew up and went their separate ways. I've invited everyone to the private viewing. Sontag, Lucie-Smith and a few others are going to pop along to say hello to their old stablemate. Just to see if you really are still alive.' He chuckled.

'Oh dear, Roddy, you make me feel like an ancient monument. I'm only forty-six, you know.'

'Sorry, sweetie, but people do love a mystery. No one knows why you ran off into the deep blue yonder at the peak of your career.'

And God help me, I hope they never do, thought Rose.

'I've arranged lots of interviews for you. There's *The Guardian* tomorrow, *The Telegraph*, and John Russell on Thursday. The . . .'

Rose listened as Roddy reeled off a lengthy list of newspapers and wondered what had possessed her to do this. Could she handle it? Could she keep her cool and lie smoothly to journalists trained in the art of interrogation?

She had to. Twenty years of self-denial was too long a punishment for her crime. She owed it to herself to grasp at this chance. So she nodded and smiled and went with her old friend to examine her paintings.

Roddy spent a long time studying the work, as Rose sat nervously sipping champagne. Finally, he turned to her, his beady eyes surveying her face. 'I think I detect a touch of romanticism in this one. Have you fallen in love, darling?'

Rose laughed and shook her head. 'No, Roddy. I know my new work is softer, the colours less stringent and the lines muted.' Panic surged inside her. 'Oh dear, you do like them, don't you? Or have I lost my touch?' Rose bit her lip, hating the old feelings of insecurity as someone surveyed her innermost thoughts on canvas.

'Well, they are different from your previous work, but still carry the great Rose Delancey touch. You've matured. Maybe the break you've taken was the right thing to do, because these –' Roddy swept his hand along the length of the paintings – 'are wonderful.' His eyes greedily devoured the twenty paintings. Rose could almost hear the cash register ringing inside his head. 'Now, I'm going to take you out to lunch at San Lorenzo, then we'll come back here and set to work on placing the pictures round the gallery. How does that sound?'

'Just fine, Roddy, just fine.' Rose's relief was evident as she smiled at him.

They took a cab to Beauchamp Place, and Lucio, the maître d', settled them at a discreet table under the large sycamore tree that grew inside the restaurant. Over a sumptuous meal of grilled red mullet with fennel seeds and veal San Lorenzo, accompanied by a bottle of Frascati Fontana Candida, Roddy went through the list of paintings, and they discussed a rough price guide.

'Do you not think we're being a little over-ambitious, Roddy? After all, I have been off the scene for twenty years and my style must be dated compared with what the youngsters are doing these days.'

'Absolutely not, darling. For starters, the more figurative work you're doing is immensely popular at present, and look at Lucien's work! He sells for a fortune. We have to make you exclusive, to make the dealers and collectors feel as though they will be buying a piece of British art history. People want to pay for the pleasure of owning something rare, not some rubbish from the bargain basement.'

'I suppose you're right.' Rose sighed, realising that she was out of touch with the marketplace. The figures Roddy was quoting her seemed absurdly high and would replenish her bank account to an extremely comfortable level.

'I still think it's a gamble to put myself in the price bracket of some of the top artists around today.'

'Trust me, Rose. You're my number one project and establishing the gallery depends on your success. By the time I'm finished with you, every art collector from here to the poles will know you're back in business. I intend to make you bigger than you were in the fifties.'

'Well, let's just see how the exhibition goes, shall we?' Rose was determined not to get carried away.

'Okay, darling, I understand your apprehension. Now, I'll order coffee and then you can tell me about the land of whippets and Wensleydale and damp.'

'Well, I don't have a whippet. But I do live with my two children, and . . . well, I've just become a grandmother.'

'Rose!' Roddy almost choked on the dregs of his Frascati. 'I didn't even know you were married.'

'I'm not. Actually, one of my children – Miranda – is adopted.'

'I see. And the father of the other one?'

'Someone. Just someone.'

'The lady of mystery once more.' Roddy smiled. 'Ah well, I shan't interrogate you. But surely, Rose, you could tell me why you disappeared the way you did? I promise not to say a word to anyone. I've been theorising along with the rest of the art world for the past twenty years. Rumour had it that you'd run off to some harem in the Sahara with that sheikh who kept buying your paintings. Someone else suggested you'd been kidnapped by the German count, and there was an idea that—'

Rose chuckled and shook her head. 'Nothing so exciting, Roddy. I went to Yorkshire, that's all.'

'I have to tell you that when I arrived back from France and found your note saying you were running out on me and the flat without so much as a goodbye or a forwarding address, I could have happily killed you. It was over a year before you wrote to me from Yorkshire, and that was only so I could send your post on. But no matter, I forgive you, I suppose.' Roddy sniffed.

'I am sorry, Roddy. I felt terrible about it but it was what I had to do, I'm afraid.'

'But why, Rose? Everything was going so wonderfully. Your career, all those simply gorgeous, wealthy men desperate to marry you. Not that you ever seemed interested in any of them. I'm still convinced you had some sort of secret aristo-cratic boyfriend who you wouldn't tell me about. I remember that you used to disappear on "trips" every now and then. Surely you can tell me now, Rose.' Roddy gave her a wink.

Rose took a sip of her coffee. 'Enough of the past. All I can tell you is that I'd run out of steam. I needed time to sort myself out and I didn't want to paint any more, okay, Roddy?'

Roddy looked at the frown across Rose's brow and knew that he'd dug deep enough. 'Of course. Let's finish our coffee, then go back to the gallery and set to work.'

Rose found the rest of the afternoon exhilarating, as she and Roddy spent hours hanging paintings in one order, then deciding they looked wrong, taking them down and starting all over again.

'God, I'm exhausted. Time for a break.' Roddy went off towards the small kitchenette at the back but reappeared two minutes later holding a small frame.

'I think we've missed one out. I found it in the storeroom where the others were. Let's have a look at it.' Roddy removed the sheet and placed the sketch against a wall.

'Surely this can't be yours, Rose, darling?'

'Er, no. But what do you think of it?'

Roddy studied it thoughtfully. 'I think it's quite lovely. And the girl is stunning. Who's it by?'

'A friend of mine. He doesn't know I've brought it here, but I thought the same as you and wanted a second opinion. The artist is still very young.'

'Do I smell a protégé here?' smiled Roddy.

'Not exactly, no. He's my nephew, actually.'

'Aha! David's son, is it?' Roddy stared at her for a reaction, but got none. 'Looking at it again, I have to say that there is a similarity between you, not in your style, of course, but in its mesmeric quality. I'll hang it if you like, round the corner. It can start my small section of new artists.'

'Oh, well, all right then. But it's not mine to sell.'

'Of course not. But we'll hang it nonetheless, and see if there's any interest in it.'

'Fine. Now, how about a cup of tea?'

A week later, Rose stood in front of the wall-to-wall mirror in Roddy's guest suite and studied her reflection. For the first time in twenty years, she rued the fact that she'd let her lithe figure slip away. In Yorkshire, there had seemed little point in caring about her appearance. No one had been around to notice. But tonight the vultures would be out in force and it wouldn't just be her work that was on show.

She straightened the belt of the loose-fitting black gown and decided that she looked like a madam in a bordello. The Dior dress, which had been far too expensive, was covered with tiny, sparkling sequins. When she had tried it on in the salon, she had thought that it made her look sophisticated and perhaps slimmer, but as she looked at it now, she knew it had been a mistake.

'Shit!' Rose tore the dress off, left it in a heap on the marble floor of Roddy's bathroom, and hunted through the wardrobe for one of her favourite caftans. It was years old, picked up at an ethnic shop in Leeds for next to nothing, but she felt comfortable in it. She stood once again in front of the mirror and immediately felt better. The dark green of the caftan set off her emerald eyes and titian hair. She added some heavy gold chains and a couple of thick gold bangles.

Rose took deep breaths to try to calm herself. She was as nervous as a kitten.

'Come on, girl, you've been through much worse. This is your night tonight. Think of the money and try to enjoy it.'

Rose walked down the corridor to find Roddy, decked out in a dinner jacket, waiting for her in the sitting room.

'Do I look okay, Roddy? Tell me honestly.'

Roddy held out his hands to her. 'Stunning, absolutely stunning. That caftan is wonderful. Balmain, or Galanos, perhaps?'

Rose smiled and took Roddy's hands. 'Neither, I'm afraid. These days, even Marks and Sparks is above my price range.'

'You just wait until after tonight. You'll be able to buy the entire range of any major fashion house once the art world has greeted the return of their very own prodigal daughter.' He checked his watch. 'Right, the taxi's outside. I suggest we go. And don't worry, my darling. You'll be coming back to this flat a queen.' Roddy touched Rose's cheek gently and proffered his arm. She smiled and took it.

By nine o'clock, the gallery was jam-packed. Champagne was flowing freely and Rose was surrounded by faces she hadn't seen in twenty years. With one eye cocked on the art critics, slowly perusing each of her paintings, she chatted away calmly to the many people who had come to support her. It was like being in a time warp: the same crowd, in the same atmosphere . . . and yet so much had changed. The silver hairs and crow's feet that had appeared on the people with whom she'd partied until dawn years ago were testament to that. It was strange to see many of the young, devil-may-care artists she had known transformed into sober-suited males with responsible jobs and wives to match.

Everyone asked her the same questions, time and again. After a week of practice with the media, she was adept at answering, the rehearsed words falling smoothly and naturally off her tongue.

She glanced around and saw Roddy talking earnestly to an art collector whom she knew from the fifties. He had been wealthy then, and had bought three of her paintings. She only needed someone as influential as he to take the plunge and the rest would follow suit.

Rose checked her watch slyly, wondering where on earth Miles had got to. He had promised to be here by eight thirty and there was no sign of him.

'Rose, darling,' Roddy interrupted her thoughts. 'Didn't I tell you? I just knew that you would be a great success. Now, I want you to come and say hello to Peter. You must remember him. He bought three of your paintings years ago and is oh so interested in buying two of this collection. So be nice to him and . . .'

Peter Vincent was the collector Rose had seen Roddy with before. She put on her most charming smile and went to shake his hand.

Miles entered the gallery. The waitress offered him a glass of champagne, but he refused and took orange juice instead. He glanced around the packed room and spotted his mother deep in conversation.

He hated crowds like this. They made him feel claustrophobic and unimportant. Just another sliver of humanity carved off the main joint. But his mother had begged him to come and he could hardly refuse. So he had come to London and spent the past two days hawking his portfolio of photographs around magazines and newspapers.

And this afternoon, he had found himself a job. Only a temporary contract, but it was with an important fashion magazine. He was flying off to Milan next month to cover the haute couture fashion shows for next year's spring and summer range. He wouldn't be taking the pictures, but working as an assistant to one of the magazine's hottest photographers, Steve Levitt. In between changing rolls of film and carrying equipment around, he might just get a chance to shoot some of his own stuff.

Miles wandered around, looking at the paintings hanging on the wall. He found his mother's work strange and could not associate it with Rose. He could see her talent, but he preferred the uncomplicated reproduction of reality that his photographs showed.

He turned a corner, glad that this part of the gallery seemed to be less crowded than the rest, and found himself looking at the sketch of Leah. Her beautiful face shone out at him, but he knew that this was nowhere near as good a representation as the many photographs he had taken of her over the years.

'Bastard,' he muttered under his breath.

'Pardon?' A fair-haired man was standing behind him, studying the drawing.

'Sorry, I didn't say anything,' said Miles.

'Oh.' The man raised an eyebrow. 'You don't by any chance happen to know who this girl is, do you?'

'I think you'd better ask the gallery owner. Sorry I can't help you further.' Miles moved away, and skulked out of the gallery.

Steve Levitt nodded and stared at the sketch again. The girl was radiant. Youth, innocence and beauty, just what Madelaine looked for on every street corner every day of her life. And the kind of face that Steve dreamed of photographing. He pushed his way through the crowd and found Roddy standing with Rose Delancey.

'Steve, lovie.' Roddy kissed him on both cheeks. 'Have you met Rose Delancey?'

'Yes.' Steve grinned. 'Years ago, but I'm sure she won't remember me. I was nothing but a starving photographer desperate to make a crust in those days.'

'Oh, but I do remember you. You once took a photograph of me walking in Regent's Park with a man I was trying to keep under wraps and sold it to half of Fleet Street.' Rose chuckled.

'Oh God, you do remember me!' Steve put his hands up in mock horror. 'Guilty as charged, I'm afraid.'

'I'm sure Rose will forgive you. You know Steve is now *the*, I mean *the,* top photographer in London. Even the society hags are turning to him instead of Bailey,' pronounced Roddy.

'I manage.' He smiled. 'Actually, I was wondering if you could help me, Roddy. There's a charcoal sketch round the corner of the most stunning girl. Do you know who she is? I'm sure Madelaine would love to get her hands on her.'

Roddy shrugged. 'I'm afraid I don't. How about you, Rose?'

'As a matter of fact I do. But who's Madelaine?' she asked suspiciously.

'The *châtelaine suprême* of the biggest modelling agency in London,' said Roddy.

Rose was intrigued. 'Oh. Well, the girl in the sketch will only turn seventeen at the end of the month and—'

'Perfect. We like 'em young these days.'

'Her name's Leah Thompson. As a matter of fact, she's my housekeeper's daughter.'

'A real-life Cinderella.' Roddy smirked.

'If you wouldn't mind, Roddy, I'd like to bring Madelaine in to show her the sketch tomorrow. Then we could get the girl to come to the office and—'

'Just hold on one moment,' interrupted Rose. 'The poor girl lives in Yorkshire and is just about to start her A levels. I hardly think her parents would like her to go skipping off down to London.'

'In that case, Madelaine will have to come to Yorkshire. She's very good at dealing with difficult parents, I can assure you.'

Rose stayed firm. 'Let's just slow down here. You know nothing about Leah, you've never seen her in the flesh and—'

Steve broke in. 'If she's half as lovely as she looks in that sketch, she'll be as big as Jerry and Marie in a couple of years. You've seen her, Rose. How tall is she?'

Rose sighed, knowing that Leah's height, which she estimated to be over five foot nine, would make Steve's eyes light up further. She imparted the news reluctantly.

'This girl gets better and better.' Steve beamed. 'Well, good to see you after all these years. I hope you've forgiven me for the shot in Regent's Park. That photo was actually what gave me my big break.' He turned to Roddy. 'I'll bring Madelaine along tomorrow to see the sketch, if that's okay with you?'

'Perfectly,' Roddy replied. 'Then I can announce that not only did I rediscover one of the greatest living artists, but I helped launch a young model on the path to a glittering career.'

Steve waved as he left the gallery. Roddy hugged Rose tight. He was tingling with excitement. 'Well, there's an almost definite sale from Peter on two, I've got an American who's coming back tomorrow to study *Light of my Life*, and a collector from Paris who is a dead cert for *Tempest*. You may have made a fortune tonight, darling. Let's mingle and see if we can spot any more would-be purchasers. The night is still young, Rose.'

As Roddy led her across the still-crowded gallery, Rose allowed herself a small smile. It was good to be back.

15

'What can I say, my dear? I think a triumph would sum it up. You're back, Rose.'

As she listened to his voice on the telephone, Rose could tell that Roddy was grinning from ear to ear.

The day after the opening of the exhibition, Rose had insisted on getting a morning train home to Leeds, concerned about Miranda and the baby. Her friend had protested strongly, saying that there were still buyers he wanted her to meet, but Rose would not be swayed.

She was sitting in her studio, surrounded by the Sunday papers, most including good to glowing reviews of her exhibition.

'Thank you, Roddy, for all your help.'

'Don't thank me, darling. You're the artist. I think you could probably afford to go out and buy yourself some new canvas and brushes. We've sold six of your paintings, for a grand total of fifteen thousand pounds.'

'My God, that's incredible!' said Rose.

'Nothing compared to what you're going to earn in the future, but it's a start. Now, the other thing is that Steve Levitt brought Madelaine into the gallery yesterday to see the sketch of Leah. My dear, Madelaine nearly hailed a taxi for Yorkshire there and then.'

'Blimey,' Rose breathed.

'Quite. Steve's off to Paris on a shoot next week, but he wants to bring Madelaine up to meet this little girlie of yours in the flesh when he gets back at the beginning of September. I thought I might tag along to see where my number one artist lives and works. We'll drive up in the Jag and be there for lunch. How does that sound?'

'Fine, Roddy, but I'm really not sure what Leah's parents' reaction will be to all this.'

'I suggest that you ask Leah and her mother to come round after lunch. Then Madelaine can set to work.'

'I don't know whether I want to be a part of all this. She's due to start a new term at school soon and—'

'Look, give the girl a chance to make up her own mind. She can always say no to Madelaine if she wants.'

Rose gave in. 'All right, Roddy.'

'That's my girl. Tell Leah it's a huge honour that Steve Levitt is prepared to drive up to the wilds of Yorkshire *avec* Madelaine Winter.'

'I'll see her mother tomorrow and ask her.'

'Great. And I may have some more good news for you about your paintings. I've someone coming to the gallery tomorrow who's interested in three of them. I'll be in touch. *Ciao*, my darling.'

The telephone clicked off. Rose wandered into the kitchen, where Miranda was sterilising bottles for the baby. Little Chloe was gurgling happily in her carrycot on the kitchen table.

'Hello, darling.' Rose cooed at the baby, who grasped her finger in one of her tiny hands. 'She's a strong little mite. That grip is incredible. I'm sure she's grown while I was away, haven't you, beautiful?' Rose picked Chloe up and hugged her.

'If you say so,' said Miranda morosely.

Rose looked at her daughter and sighed. Since the birth of Chloe, Miranda had become a different girl. All her spark

101

seemed to have left her, and from being almost obsessive about her appearance, now Miranda never bothered to put on make-up. Her lovely blonde hair was scraped back in a tight ponytail. She'd been wearing the same pair of jeans for weeks.

'That was Roddy on the telephone. I've had a piece of good news. He's sold six of my paintings for a large sum of money. I think that calls for a celebration. Tomorrow, I'm taking you into York on a spending spree.'

'And what about the baby?' Miranda picked Chloe roughly out of Rose's arms and sat down at the table. The little girl spluttered as Miranda rammed the bottle into her mouth.

'I'm sure Mrs Thompson won't mind babysitting. You know she adores Chloe. Anyway, I've got to speak to her about Leah.'

Miranda looked up. 'What about Leah?'

Rose knew she had to play this very carefully. Her daughter was demoralised as it was. 'It seems a photographer might be interested in taking her picture. It's a friend of Roddy's and he's coming up here in September for lunch.'

'How come this man knows what she looks like?' Miranda's eyes were hard, questioning.

'There was a sketch of her at the exhibition,' said Rose quickly. Embarrassed, she stood up. 'I'll see you later, darling.'

Miranda closed her eyes as Rose left the kitchen. She listened to her daughter suck contentedly on her bottle.

She hated the permanent smell of dirty nappies, talcum powder and milky sick that pervaded all her clothes. She hated getting up at all times of the night to feed the bawling Chloe, and having her life *ruined* by someone who depended on her for her every need. She was only seventeen and she felt her life was over before it had begun.

The whole episode had taught her a lesson. She hated men. Hated them with a vengeance. Why wasn't the father's life being ruined like hers was? A year ago, she'd had her future mapped out. She was going to control them, use them to get what she wanted. Now, she was the victim.

She took the empty bottle away from Chloe's mouth and heaved the baby onto her shoulder to wind her.

Chloe's arrival had started her thinking about her own mother. For the first time in her life, she was wondering who she was, why she'd abandoned Miranda when she was so small. Sometimes, Miranda wished she could do the same with her own daughter.

She understood now. Everyone was selfish, out for what they could get. There was nobody who really gave a damn about her.

All her dreams of a better life had been ruined by Chloe's arrival.

Tears of self-pity plopped slowly down her cheeks.

16

Rose saw the green Jaguar pull up at the front of the farm-house, and she eyed the woman who emerged from the front passenger seat.

Madelaine Winter, ex-model and owner of the most successful agency in Europe, was still a very beautiful woman. Rose knew that Madelaine was older than she was, but had to admit she looked younger. Her thick, black hair, worn in a tight chignon, betrayed not a hint of grey, and the figure that had graced all the major catwalks into the early sixties was still perfect. The red suit she was wearing was Chanel, and her make-up was impeccable. Rose felt, once again, frumpy and old, and determined to go on an immediate diet.

'Darling! We made it! Good grief, it's like the end of the world up here! However do you stand it?'

Rose smiled at Roddy, kissed him, then shook hands with Steve and Madelaine and led them into the sitting room.

'What a fabulous view,' said Madelaine, looking out of the window.

'It is, indeed.' Steve joined her.

'I must say, I hope this girl is worth it. We got held up in a jam on the motorway and it'll take hours to get back,' Roddy moaned.

Rose thought how strange it was to have these three smartly dressed Londoners standing in her sitting room. They looked totally incongruous with their surroundings. Leah was going to be overwhelmed and Rose wondered whether she had done the right thing in encouraging Mrs Thompson to let her daughter meet them.

'I've prepared a light lunch, but I suggest we have a drink in here first.'

'Sounds perfect. I brought a tiny bottle of champagne with me to celebrate the fact that I sold your tenth painting yesterday.' Roddy produced a magnum from the plastic bag he was carrying.

'Congratulations, Rose. London is still talking about your exhibition.' Madelaine smiled, showing a perfect set of neat, white teeth.

Rose found some glasses and Roddy proposed a toast to her.

'And to Leah,' interrupted Steve.

'Now, talking of Leah, her mother is in the kitchen preparing our lunch. Leah's joining us later. Doreen's not too happy about all this so I'd tread very carefully if I were you. She's a straight-up-and-down Yorkshire woman and a damn good housekeeper. I wouldn't like either Doreen or Leah to be coerced by you.'

'Don't worry, Rose. I'll tread carefully, I promise,' Madelaine reassured her.

At that moment, the door opened and Miranda entered the room. Rose drew in her breath. Her daughter was wearing one of her tight miniskirts and a low top. Her face was once more plastered with make-up. Rose couldn't help but feel a little embarrassed.

'Miranda. This is Madelaine Winter, Steve Levitt and Roddy Dawes. Everyone, this is my daughter, Miranda.'

Miranda smiled and posed in the doorway for a second, before coming into the room. 'I thought I might join you for lunch, if that's okay by you, Rose.' Miranda was speaking in a slow, husky drawl.

'Of course, darling. Miranda has just presented me with a beautiful granddaughter.'

Miranda shot Rose a look of venom across the room.

'Let's go and have something to eat, shall we?' said Rose quickly.

They settled themselves down in the dining room, Miranda pointedly waiting until Steve had taken his seat before placing herself next to him.

'Ahh, here's Doreen with the soup. Doreen, I'd like you to meet Steve Levitt. He's the gentleman I was telling you about.'

'Good to meet you, Mrs Thompson. I'm looking forward to seeing Leah immensely.'

Mrs Thompson nodded.

'And me. My name's Madelaine Winter. I run Femmes, a modelling agency.'

'Nice to meet you, Mrs Winter,' Doreen croaked, overwhelmed.

Rose felt immense sympathy for the woman. She knew that if Madelaine wanted Leah, there wasn't a damn thing Mrs Thompson could do to stop her. She would be outmanoeuvred and brushed aside as a small irritation.

Mrs Thompson finished serving the soup and left the room.

'I actually have a surprise for you, Steve,' said Rose.

'And what might that be?'

'I hear *Vogue* has hired an assistant to help you in Milan.'

He sighed. 'Yes. Jimmy, my loyal and faithful servant for two years, has left me in the lurch to start up on his own. Diane at the magazine said she'd get me someone. It's only for a week. If he's awful, I can always find someone else when I get back.'

'I hope you don't think he's awful, because he happens to be my son, Miles.' Rose smiled.

'Your son?' Steve was amazed.

'I know. It's a total coincidence. I didn't realise until Sunday night when he told me on the telephone he was working for you in Milan.'

'Is he here?'

'No. He's in London. I'm sure you won't be disappointed with him. He's a very talented photographer and he's been told to be on his best behaviour.'

'Small world,' mused Steve.

Rose watched Miranda all through lunch, dismayed at how she was flirting outrageously with Steve, tossing her hair and leaning forward so that the entire table received an excellent view of her cleavage.

'Does your daughter know she's on a loser?' whispered Roddy. 'Take it from me, he's as gay as I am.'

Rose nodded as they went through to the sitting room to have coffee, and squirmed as Miranda sat impossibly close to Steve on the sofa.

Mrs Thompson followed them in five minutes later with a tray of coffee and a terrified Leah trailing behind her.

Miranda looked at Leah Thompson. She couldn't understand why Steve was interested in her. Leah was just a thin, lanky kid with no sex appeal. Not a patch on her!

'I think it's time you fed Chloe, darling,' said Rose.

Miranda scowled. 'She'll be fine. She's fast asleep upstairs.'

'Well, go and check on her, will you?'

Miranda stood up reluctantly.

'I'll see you later, Steve.' She shot him a winning smile and left the room.

Steve was staring at the girl in the doorway. She was wearing a pair of old jeans and a T-shirt which hung off her with effortless grace. Her hair was wonderful. Long, lush and a natural burnished mahogany. He thought her face was perfect for the camera, with its high cheekbones and big brown eyes. And to top it all, the girl was at least five foot nine and waif thin. He watched Madelaine staring at Leah, and when she shot him an almost imperceptible nod, he knew that he'd found something special.

'Leah, let me introduce you to Steve Levitt and Madelaine Winter.' Rose stood up and steered Leah over first to Steve, then to Madelaine. She shook their hands shyly. 'Now, come and sit down by me, and you too, Doreen. Madelaine would like to talk to you both.'

Madelaine smiled at Leah kindly. 'Leah, do you know anything about the world of modelling?'

Leah shook her head. 'Not really, no.'

'Well, you must have seen models on the covers of glossy magazines?'

'Yes.'

'Well, Steve here, who takes those pictures, and I, think that you could be on the covers of magazines too.'

'Me?' Leah said, astonished.

Steve nodded. 'Yes, you, Leah. That's why I brought Madelaine up to see you for herself. She runs one of the biggest agencies in London.'

'What's an agency?' enquired Leah.

'Well, I have a number of girls that I look after. I find them modelling work, I agree the money they will be paid and make sure that they get it,' said Madelaine. 'And I would very much like to look after your career, Leah.'

Mrs Thompson was sitting silently next to her daughter. Leah looked at her for help, but there was none forthcoming. Mrs Thompson was as overwhelmed as she was.

'I'm just about to start my A levels,' Leah managed, and her mum nodded in agreement.

'Well, there's no reason why you couldn't continue your

studies in London. You'll have plenty of time to study when you're travelling,' reassured Madelaine.

Fear filled Leah's eyes. 'I'd have to leave here and move down to London, then?'

Madelaine nodded. 'Yes, but you'd be able to visit your parents as often as you wanted, and I'm sure you'd have a lot of fun with the other girls,' she soothed.

'But, I . . .' Leah searched desperately for another excuse. 'I only turned seventeen last week.'

'The perfect age, my dear. I much prefer to take girls from scratch and build them up. That means they don't have any bad habits from other agencies.'

'Oh,' said Leah. She turned to Doreen. 'What do you think, Mum?'

Mrs Thompson exhaled. 'I'm not sure, Leah. I don't know anything about this modelling business. And I'm not keen on you going down to London and living by yourself.'

'You could go with her to start off with, Doreen,' said Madelaine.

'No I couldn't. My husband, Harry, is in a wheelchair. He has arthritis and needs care.'

'Oh, I'm sorry.'

Rose noticed the flicker of interest that passed across Madelaine's elegant brow.

'Well, I can certainly sort out somewhere for Leah to live, probably in a flat with another of my models. Of course, another point that must be taken into consideration is the fact that Leah would be earning quite a lot of money if she does well. I expect you'd like to be able to help your mother with your father's care, wouldn't you, Leah?'

Madelaine smiled sincerely at Leah. Rose was aghast at the merciless emotional blackmail that the woman was employing. She watched as Leah wavered.

'Of course, but—'

'I think the best thing to do would be to have Leah and Doreen come down to London for a couple of days, and see how Leah likes it,' cut in Rose firmly. 'I'm sure Madelaine would pay for someone to look after Harry whilst you're gone.'

'Good idea,' said Steve. 'I can take some shots of Leah to see how they turn out. Then Doreen and Leah could visit your offices, Madelaine, and have a chat.'

'That sounds fine. I can go into more detail with you both about the way the industry works.' Madelaine was beaming. She knew that once she got them to London, she was well on her way to securing a contract with Leah Thompson.

'Great!' Roddy slapped his knees and stood. 'Now, I really think we should be thinking of getting back to London. We're going to hit the rush hour head on and I have a dinner engagement at eight.' Steve and Madelaine got to their feet.

'I'm off to Milan for the fashion shows next week, but Madelaine will call you and we'll arrange a date for the week after. Goodbye, Leah. I look forward to seeing you again very soon.' Steve shook Leah's hand.

'Goodbye, my dear. We'll be seeing you shortly.' Madelaine smiled at Leah, then followed Rose, Roddy and Steve out of the door. Leah and Mrs Thompson were left alone in the sitting room.

'What do you think, Mum?' Leah's eyes were wide.

'I think we could both do with a nice cup of tea. Come on, love.' Mrs Thompson put an arm round her daughter's shoulders and they went into the kitchen.

'Rose, promise me you'll work on that mother in the next week. Leah is sensational. I must have her,' pleaded Madelaine.

'I'll do what I can, but I rather think it's Leah you'll have to work on. She didn't seem too keen on the idea of leaving home.'

'Honestly, it's the dream of so many girls to become stars. We've picked the only one who doesn't have a clue what she has to offer,' said Steve.

'Ah, but that's part of her beauty,' Madelaine reminded him. 'We don't want to lose that. Anyway, thanks for lunch, Rose. *Au revoir*.' Madelaine got into the car and Roddy kissed Rose goodbye.

'I'll be in touch soon if there's any further developments on the sales of your paintings. Now you get back into that studio of yours and start work. I'll be needing plenty more Rose Delanceys to sell in the next year.' Roddy smiled.

Rose waved at the car as it disappeared down the hill, then she went back into the house. Leah and Mrs Thompson were sitting in the kitchen, drinking tea.

'I don't know, Mrs Delancey. What do you think about this modelling carry-on?'

Rose shrugged. 'Well, Doreen, Leah ought to feel very honoured that the best photographer and agent in the business came all the way up here specially to see her.'

Leah blushed. 'I can't believe they think I'm pretty enough to be a model, Mrs Delancey.'

'Let them worry about that. These people are professionals. They wouldn't waste their time if they didn't think you'd be successful.'

'I don't know.' Mrs Thompson was shaking her head doubtfully.

'Look, Doreen, I think you should go down to London with Leah and then decide. What I will say is that Madelaine is the best in the business and she really looks after her girls. And if Leah does make it as a successful model, she could earn a lot of money.'

'I wouldn't like to be in London by myself, but on the other hand, if I made some money, then Dad and you . . .' Leah's voice trailed off.

'Now, don't you go making your decision on the money. Apart from the fact that it would be yours anyway, me and Dad've managed just fine up until now, and I daresay we'll continue to do so,' said Mrs Thompson firmly.

Miranda entered the kitchen with Chloe on one shoulder.

'Hello, my pet,' cooed Mrs Thompson, taking the baby from Miranda.

'How's the new Twiggy?' drawled Miranda.

'She's hungry, same as your baby,' said Mrs Thompson sharply. 'Why don't you nip off home, love?' she said to Leah. 'You could tell your dad all about Mrs Winter and get started with the tea. I've got to clear up here.'

'All right, Mum. Bye, Mrs Delancey. Bye, Miranda.' Leah opened the kitchen door and set off on the walk home.

Outside, she breathed in the fresh autumn air. She loved the beginning of September, when the moors were starting to turn a soft gold and she awoke in the morning to see the mist hanging gently over the hills.

How could she leave all this? And what about her mother and father? They would be left all alone if she went off to London. On the other hand, if what Mrs Winter said was true and she could earn a lot of money, it would be a dream to help them. They'd struggled for such a long time.

But the realisation that she might lose every bit of what she had taken for granted for the past seventeen years made her suddenly intensely grateful for the life she had at present.

Leah passed the spot where Brett and she had spent such wonderful times together. She stopped and sat down. Twelve months had passed, and still she woke every morning after a night of vivid dreams of him. She was haunted by a boy she truly wanted to hate, but could only love. Maybe going away would help her forget.

When Leah arrived home, she went straight to her father's room. He had fallen asleep while reading a book, and his glasses were perched right on the tip of his nose. Leah felt a surge of love as she studied him.

Mr Thompson stirred and opened his eyes. He smiled when he saw his daughter standing in the doorway.

'Hello, love. How did it go up at the big house with the folks from London?'

Leah went and sat on the pouffe by his side. 'They want me to go to the city and be a model.'

Harry inhaled deeply. 'Do they now? And what do you think about that, then?'

Leah shook her head. 'I don't know, Dad. Mrs Delancey says it's a big opportunity, but I'd have to go and live in London. I'd miss you and Mum and Yorkshire something rotten.'

Mr Thompson looked at his beautiful daughter and smiled at her concerned face. He'd been so worried about her for the past year. The lass had taken her first affair of the heart very hard. But he knew she'd get over it in time, and this modelling business seemed like just what was needed to bring back her confidence. It would break his heart to see her leave, but he knew that Leah had something special. She deserved to go out into the world and find her future.

'Well now. I know you'll miss Mum and me, pet, but employment's bad up here and someone's offering you a job. And a glamorous one at that!'

Leah took her father's hand. 'I'd have to leave school, and I worked so hard to get good results in my O levels. I want to take my As and think about university.'

'Well, it's a decision only you can make, Leah. But opportunities like this don't come along very often. I'll support you whatever you want to do. You're a good girl and although I don't want you to go, I think you're worth more than ending up in an office as a secretary with a brood of kids. You're a lovely looking lass, Leah. You take after your dad, of course.' Mr Thompson smiled. 'Come and give me a hug.'

Leah put her arms around his neck and thought how wonderful it would be to have the money to shower him with presents in return for the kindness he had shown her. She held him tight. 'I love you, Dad.'

Mr Thompson felt a lump in his throat. 'Go on now, go and put the tea on. Your dad's hungry and you're not a super-star yet, you know.'

He watched Leah leave the room and reached in his cardigan pocket for a tissue to wipe his eyes. Leah was what he lived for. And he knew he was going to lose her.

17

'They're absolutely fabulous,' Madelaine said excitedly, as she spread the photos across her desk for Leah to see.

'Are they really me, Mrs Winter?' Leah said in amazement as she looked at the beautiful girl in the pictures.

'Please, call me Madelaine, and yes, they are you, Leah. It's amazing what a good make-up artist and photographer can do, isn't it?'

'I look so much older.'

'Well, I would say you look more sophisticated, yes. And the clothes you're wearing help too.'

Mrs Thompson was touching the photos reverently. 'I must admit that Mr Levitt's done a good job. I can hardly believe this is our Leah.' She smiled proudly.

Madelaine breathed a sigh of relief. Having spent a large amount of money putting the pair up at the Inn on the Park for the past three nights, hours reassuring Mrs Thompson that she'd personally take care of her daughter when she was in London, and even paying for a nurse to stay with the disabled husband, she was delighted to see that familiar look of motherly pride. Now it was only Leah she had to convince.

'Did you enjoy the photo session, Leah? Steve said you both had a good time.'

115

'Yes, I did, Mrs – Madelaine. He's a very nice man.'

'So, do you think you're prepared to do this kind of thing full time?'

Leah looked at Madelaine. Guilt for all the money that had been spent putting her and Mum up in that plush hotel – and the thought of how she could help her parents with what Madelaine had said she might earn – made it difficult for Leah to say no.

This was exactly what Madelaine had intended.

'What about my A levels?' She looked at her mother.

'Well, as Mrs Winter has said, you could try modelling for a year, and if you really didn't like it, you could always do the exams the year after next. It's a wonderful chance, Leah,' Mrs Thompson encouraged.

'Well, I suppose I could try it for a while to see how I got on,' she said slowly.

'That's fine, Leah, although I'll have to sign you up to the agency for a year. Standard procedure, I'm afraid.' Madelaine picked up the contract and handed it to her. 'Now, why don't you sign that and then we'll all go out to lunch and celebrate.'

Leah looked at the five pages of small type in front of her.

'Go on, dear, I'm sure Mrs Winter would understand if you really didn't like it and wanted to come home.'

'Absolutely, Doreen.' Madelaine nodded.

Leah took the heavy gold pen that Madelaine handed her, uncertain.

'Do I need to read it through first?' she asked.

Madelaine shrugged nonchalantly. 'It's all legal gobbledegook. It basically says that Femmes will be your sole representatives and will take a percentage each time we get you a job.'

Leah looked at her mother, who nodded. Then she took a deep breath and scribbled her signature in the appropriate place.

'Wonderful!' said Madelaine. 'Now, before we get down to the hard work, let's go and enjoy ourselves.'

Madelaine took them to a plush restaurant just around the corner from her office in Berkeley Square. She ordered champagne and, over a dozen minuscule courses, talked to Leah about the future.

'This afternoon, I'm going to take both of you round to meet Jenny at her flat. She's one of my up-and-coming young models and has a spare room. She's a couple of years older than you and a nice, sensible girl. She can look after you and show you round London. I'm sure you'll both like her,' Madelaine said, beaming. 'Tomorrow, I want you to come into the office at nine o'clock. I'll book a hair appointment with Vidal and send you off to Barbara in the afternoon. She'll teach you how to do your make-up. And I might send you to Janet, a friend of mine who teaches elocution, just to tone down that Yorkshire accent.'

Leah listened as Madelaine planned her life, and she watched her mother agreeing with everything she said.

'Doesn't it all sound exciting, Leah? Say thank you to Madelaine for all she's done for you.'

'Thank you,' Leah repeated.

'I'm going to try and book you for the ready-to-wear collection in Milan next month. It's where most of the girls start. The fashion editor of *Vogue* won't even look at you until you've made it in Europe.'

Madelaine continued to chat away in the taxi on the way to visit Leah's new home. It was in a place called Chelsea and the taxi stopped outside a grand white house.

'It's a very safe area, Doreen, so there'll be no worries on that score.' Madelaine pressed a bell and a girl in an old tracksuit answered the door.

'Madelaine, darling.' The girl kissed her on both cheeks. 'Come in. And this must be Leah. Hi, I'm Jenny. Come on up.'

As the three women followed Jenny up the two flights of steep stairs, Leah thought that her new flatmate was the prettiest girl she had ever seen. She was about the same height as Leah, with long blonde hair and a pair of huge blue eyes. *Far lovelier than I am*, Leah thought.

Jenny showed them round the flat, which was small but elegantly furnished. Leah's intended bedroom was no bigger than a broom-cupboard, but it was prettily decorated with candy-stripe wallpaper and matching curtains.

Mrs Thompson's 'oohs' and 'ahhs' as she looked round the miniature kitchen, crowded with every modern appliance on the market, made Leah long for her basic but cosy kitchen at home.

Jenny suggested coffee as Madelaine and Doreen went into the sitting room and sat down.

'Stay and help me make it, Leah. You look scared stiff.' Jenny smiled kindly.

Leah relaxed a little. 'I am, a bit.'

'Don't worry. I was just the same when Madelaine found me walking along a street in Bristol. I'd never even been to London before.'

'Nor have I,' said Leah.

'Madelaine'll look after you, and I'll be here to show you the ropes. Just keep your head down and do what Her Majesty asks you to.'

'Her Majesty?'

'Yes, all the girls on her books call Madelaine the Queen behind her back,' said Jenny conspiratorially.

Leah gave a giggle and carried the tray of coffee into the sitting room feeling a little better.

However, as she stood on the platform of King's Cross station that evening, she sobbed her heart out.

'Come on now, Leah. Anybody would think you weren't ever going to see me or your dad again. Madelaine says you can come up next weekend if you want to visit us.'

'Oh Mum,' Leah wailed, hanging on to Mrs Thompson's coat.

'Honestly, you're acting like a ten-year-old. Pull yourself together and think how many other girls would give their eye-teeth for the chance you're getting,' Mrs Thompson chastised.

Leah blew her nose hard and walked down the platform to see her mother onto the train.

'Don't bother waiting for it to pull away. You go and get in that taxi. It must be costing Madelaine a fortune.' Mrs Thompson kissed her daughter and opened the door to a carriage.

'Bye, love. Be a good girl and do everything Madelaine tells you to. I'll write as soon as I can.'

'Send my love to Dad, won't you?'

''Course I will. Make us both proud of you, pet.'

Despite her best efforts, tears were forming in Mrs Thompson's eyes. She waved hastily and disappeared to find a seat.

Leah walked miserably back up the platform towards the waiting taxi. She opened the door of the big black car and jumped in.

'Where to, miss?'

She read out Jenny's address and the driver set off, taking Leah to begin her new life.

119

18

'It's good of you to see me at such short notice; I wanted to catch you while you were in Washington, Mr Cooper.'

David studied the heavy-set man with the distinct accent. 'What exactly is it that you want to discuss?'

David felt slightly irritated. He'd an important business meeting and he was not interested in some charity organisation, probably here to beg for money. Pat usually dealt with this kind of thing and he wondered how this one had slipped through the net.

'First, Mr Cooper, I have to apologise. I am here under false pretences. I do not work for the organisation you think I do.'

Jesus, this was all he needed. David sighed. 'Okay, so who do you work for?'

'Would you sit down, Mr Cooper? Then I shall explain.'

A frustrated David shook his head, but complied. 'Let's not waste any more time. What can I do for you?'

The man began to talk to him softly, and soon, all David's irritation had vanished.

When the man had finished, David sat in silence, staring into space. The colour had drained from his face.

'How did you find me?' David asked, eventually.

'One of our organisation recognised your face from a news cutting. He knew you many years ago.'

David nodded slowly. 'Bravo. And now you *have* found me, what is it that you want?'

'We know that you are about to start doing business with this man.' He passed David a file with the name of the man on the cover.

'It is the man you are dealing with, is it not?'

David nodded slowly. 'Yes. What's the problem?'

'Have you met him yet?'

David thought carefully. 'No. I've corresponded with him quite heavily and we've spoken briefly on the telephone. We're supposed to meet for lunch in a couple of weeks' time.'

'Then I'd like you to read that file. It is, of course, highly confidential, and should any word of this leak out, thirty years of intelligence work will be for nothing. I will leave it with you.' The man stood up. 'I want you to read it from cover to cover. I think you might find what it contains a little disturbing. There is a . . . connection between the two of you of which you will be unaware.'

David swallowed hard.

'When you have finished, I would like you to ring me on this number.' He held out his hand, and David shook it.

'Goodbye, Mr Cooper.'

The man left the room and David went across to the drinks cabinet. He poured himself a large whisky with ice and settled down in the comfortable hotel chair to read the file.

An hour later, tears were pouring down his cheeks and he was on his fifth drink.

'Jesus,' he moaned. He went into the bathroom and splashed his face with cold water.

So many years ago, so much pain. All these years of blocking out the past, and now . . .

He wandered back into the sitting room of the hotel suite and poured himself yet another whisky.

David knew he had to make the biggest decision of his life.

Then he remembered the vow he had made when he had been so much younger.

His hands were still shaking from shock. His mind forced him back into the past, opening doors into the dark recesses of his memory that he had not entered in such a long time . . .

19

'Mama, may I go and see Joshua? He has a new trainset and has asked me to help him build it.'

Adele smiled fondly at the boy in front of her. No one could resist him, herself included. He was so clever and had the kind of cherubic, innocent face that made it impossible for a bad or evil thought to pass across it.

'Of course you may, as long as you have finished the reading that Professor Rosenberg set you.'

'Oh yes, Mama, I finished it hours ago. English is such a strange language. It has words which mean more than one thing. It confuses me sometimes.'

He spoke so seriously, so fluently for a boy of ten. His teachers were predicting a great future for him.

'All right, then. You may ask Samuel to take you round in the car. I will want to hear you play your violin when you return.'

'Of course, Mama.'

'Give your mother a kiss, David.' She beckoned.

He came forwards and pecked her on the forehead.

'Goodbye, Mama.' He smiled and walked out of the drawing room.

Adele exhaled contentedly and thought once more how lucky she was. And how glad that she had taken such a dreadful risk over ten years ago and eloped from Paris with the young Polish artist with whom she had fallen so deeply in love.

In the summer of 1927, Adele had been on a tour of Europe with her maiden aunt, Beatrice. It was a final hurrah before her return home to England, where she was to be married off to a man deemed suitable by her father, and packed off to India. While visiting Paris, Beatrice had gone down with a bad case of food poisoning, leaving Adele free to explore the city by herself. During a warm Wednesday afternoon stroll, she had chanced upon the bohemian district of Montmartre. Enticed by the noisy chatter of artists sitting outside a bustling cafe, Adele took a seat at a neighbouring table and ordered a *citron pressé*. It was only a few minutes before one of the men had asked her to help settle an argument: did she think that Picasso or Cézanne was the greatest creator of their time? Adele had joined their table, and there she was introduced to Jacob Delanski.

She had been spellbound by the young, tall Polish man, admiring his blond hair, penetrating blue eyes and infectious laugh.

The wine flowed freely that afternoon, and after a few hours, Jacob worked up the confidence to ask Adele if he could paint her. She had no difficulty answering in the affirmative, and for the following week, Adele would leave the comfort of her suite at the Ritz Hotel to go to Jacob's cramped attic on the Rue de Seine.

Jacob, with his charismatic personality and sheer exuberance gained from being young, talented and in the most exciting city in the world, had overwhelmed Adele. She'd been used to her regimented, Victorian-style upbringing, and the formal, stiff young army officers in England thought suitable by her father to escort her to balls.

Now here she was in a Montmartre studio, drinking wine at three o'clock in the afternoon, listening to Jacob telling her that he loved her and wanted to marry her.

Adele had protested that it was impossible, but Jacob had silenced her, telling her that she was wrong, that destiny had taken a hand. He'd made love to her then, and she'd known Jacob was right, that they must never be separated again. She knew that her father would come searching for her in Paris, so the two of them had agreed to travel to Jacob's native Warsaw. Adele had left the Ritz in the early hours with one small valise, the overwhelming passion she felt for her beautiful, talented lover blinding her to the momentous decision she was taking.

When Jacob and Adele had arrived in Warsaw, they had taken shelter with one of Jacob's oldest friends in Wola, an artisan district of the city.

Their first priority was to get married, but this presented a problem. Jacob was Jewish, and Adele was a British Christian. There was not a rabbi or a priest in the city that would conduct the service. Quite simply, one of them had to change religion, and Adele agreed that it should be her.

She took herself to preparation classes, and Jacob struggled to find work to put food on their table. Finding commissions lacking, he went to see his father, who offered help on the condition that Jacob denounce his ambition to paint, and accepted his rightful position at the family bank. Jacob refused and found himself a job at a library, which gave him and Adele enough money to find a room of their own, and to throw a small celebration after their wedding, which his parents did not attend.

Things had been dreadfully hard at first, but they'd survived on love, with Jacob never failing to bring a smile to her face when she felt low. His lust for life was infectious, and Adele learned that there wasn't a problem that couldn't be solved by persistence and optimism. A year after their marriage, she gave birth to a baby boy, whom they named David. Their single room was soon filled with soaking nappies and the smell of paint, as Jacob was more determined than ever to make himself a success, and to show his parents he didn't need their help.

Soon after David's birth, Jacob had been asked to paint a portrait of a wealthy relative of one of his friends, which provided enough money for an upgraded two-roomed apartment. Three months after that, Jacob was asked to paint another member of the same family, and word soon started to spread. His ambition was realised, and Jacob was able to give up his job at the library.

By the time Adele gave birth to Rosa in 1931, the family had moved from the overcrowded city to Saska Kepa, a housing district joined to the centre of Warsaw by the new Poniatowski Bridge. Jacob was establishing an excellent reputation as a portrait painter, with his good looks and charm earning him large commissions from middle-aged matrons anxious to be flattered both on and off canvas.

As Jacob's fame and prosperity grew, his parents, although uncomfortable about his choice of career and gentile wife, softened in their feelings towards their son. They too moved away from the city, joining Jacob and Adele in Saska Kepa, and communication was re-established. They saw the care Adele took to bring up her children in the Jewish tradition, and after hearing that she had been of noble birth in England, they accepted the marriage and doted on their grandchildren.

Adele had understood perfectly well why Jacob could not give up his religion for her; it would have been like asking him to change his very core. But she was determined that her children would grow up knowing something of her own heritage. So, since they'd been babies, she had spoken English to them – although French had been the common language between the family, as she struggled to get to grips with Polish. And now, at ten and seven respectively, David and Rosa could converse with ease in three tongues.

When the children lay tucked up in their small beds at night, Adele would sit and tell them stories of her life in London. She shared tales of the enormous house overlooking Hyde Park that she had lived in as a child, of Big Ben, the Houses of Parliament and of Old Father Thames, who ran through the capital of the world. She promised, as their eyes hung heavy with sleep, that one day she would take them there.

Adele would often think about her parents, wondering how they had reacted to her disappearance. She had felt dreadful leaving poor Aunt Beatrice to break the news, but there had been no choice. By now, they probably thought she was dead.

Adele was brought out of her reverie by a knock on the drawing-room door.

'Come in!'

Christabel, the round-faced nanny, led Rosa towards her by the hand.

'Hello, darling.'

The little girl, a minute replica of her mother, with her thick, titian hair, held her small arms up. Adele lifted her and hugged her tight.

'Tell Mama what you have to show her,' said Christabel fondly.

Rosa's large emerald eyes grew wide as she handed her mother a piece of paper from a pocket.

'Here.' She presented it proudly.

It was a small painting of a bowl of flowers. Adele drew in her breath as she realised that this was her seven-year-old daughter's work. She could hardly believe it. The use of colour, shape and intricate detail showed the hand of a far more mature artist. Adele put Rosa down on the floor and took a moment to study what was in front of her closely. It was quite remarkable. She questioned whether she was looking through an unbiased eye . . . but sensed strongly that she was.

Rosa was standing patiently in front of her, arms folded neatly over her spotless white pinafore.

'Why, darling, this is wonderful! Are you sure you are telling me the truth? Did you really paint it yourself?'

Rosa nodded. 'Oh yes, Mama, I really did.'

'I can vouch for that, ma'am. I watched her with my own eyes. She has a drawing book full of them upstairs.'

'My goodness! Well, Rosa, I think we should take this to show Papa, don't you?'

'Yes. And David?' Rosa's eyes lit up.

'Of course.' Adele was always touched by the closeness of her two children, she herself having been an only child.

When Jacob saw his daughter's painting, he felt awed. He knew that within her lay a talent that made his own pale into insignificance, and he wasted no time in harnessing it. From that moment on, Rosa joined her father in his purpose-built studio at the back of the house for two hours every morning. He taught her everything he could, and watched with pride and amazement as her effortless grasp of the knowledge he imparted far outstripped her tender years. Although Jacob and Adele didn't speak of it to Rosa, whose sheer delight in her ability to bring things to life on a sheet of paper was part of her gift, they acknowledged that she carried a prodigious talent.

Outside of the studio, young David was showing a flair for the violin. On his tenth birthday, Jacob and Adele had bought him the Ludwig, a rare and valuable Stradivarius. The family would sit, night after night, listening to him drawing melodious sounds out of the beautiful instrument.

'I told you, didn't I, that our best chance of happiness was in being together?' Jacob would whisper to his wife when they climbed into bed.

'Yes, my love.' She would kiss him. 'Life is perfect.'

They would fall asleep in each other's arms, innocently unaware of the horrors to come.

On 1 September 1939, Germany invaded Poland. Over a million men, equipped with superior air power, easily overcame Poland's inadequate army. Two weeks later, Russia sent its troops into the east of the country. Soon after, Polish forces crumbled completely and the nation was divided between Russia and Germany.

The battle for Warsaw raged on. Night after night, Jacob, Adele, David and Rosa sat huddled in their cellar. Jacob was filled with a growing fear. He'd heard of the atrocities committed against the Jewish people in Berlin and had watched as a new wave of anti-Semitism washed over his home country. A policy of 'evacuating' Jews from many small Polish towns and villages had sent them flooding into Warsaw to escape brutal pogroms. Thousands had died already, yet as Jacob listened to the explosions that rocked Warsaw day after day, he knew that this was only the beginning.

On 27 September, Warsaw surrendered. For the first time in a week, Jacob ventured outside and was horrified by the devastation brought on the once-magnificent city. The Royal Castle had been burned to the ground, and the newly refurbished Central Railway Station was unrecognisable.

The streets were deserted as he hurried to his parents' house.

His heart lurched as he saw the next-door building still smouldering, its innards hanging out.

'Dear God, Jacob. What is to become of us now the Nazis are here? You should have got Adele and the children out while you had the chance.'

Jacob gazed at his mother's pale face. 'I know, Mama, but Adele refused.'

'Well, she's missed her opportunity. Now she'll have to stay here and die with the rest of us.'

'Mama, do not talk like that! There are three million Jews in Poland. We shall stand up and fight back.'

Surcie Delanski considered her son's defiant stance, his youth and strength. But she knew, deep in her heart, that the battle was already lost.

After Warsaw surrendered, the Polish government went into exile in Paris. The new General Government of Poland was formed, with Hans Frank appointed governor general. He issued orders for the Jewish community in Warsaw to set up their own council, under German instruction.

Jacob's father was a member. He relayed to his son the latest set of German instructions to be followed by the Jewish population.

'As from tomorrow, all Jews will have to wear identifying armbands. Parts of the city will be closed to us.'

Jacob put his head in his hands. 'Papa, I can hardly believe this! Is the council not fighting back?'

'How can we, when we are already subjected to a reign of terror? Random shootings, Jews being bundled into lorries and taken to labour camps . . . Thousands have died already.' He looked grave. 'And there will be worse to come.'

'You say we are not allowed access to certain parts of the city? That is ghettoisation.'

Samuel Delanski nodded sadly. 'Yes. And we believe that is exactly what they want. My son, I implore you to sell what you have now. Raise as much money as possible before it is too late. Thank God I had the sense to withdraw the funds from my account at the bank. I knew the Nazis would close it. Some of my friends have lost everything. The net is closing in. You must insist that Adele leaves the city with the children. She still has her British passport, does she not?'

'Yes, Papa.'

'You must get your family out, Jacob.' He cast his eyes to the floor. 'I am sorry to say, but they stand a much better chance of survival without you. An Englishwoman and her two Christian children.'

Jacob was not unaware of the truth. 'Adele will not go without me. But I shall try to persuade her one last time.'

'Good. I have a friend who is helping people to make their way to Gdynia. There are a few boats still sailing to Denmark from there. If they get that far, they can go into hiding until a boat sails for England.'

That night, Jacob related to Adele what Samuel had told him. As he knew she would, Adele adamantly refused to leave without her husband.

'But do you not see, Adele, that without me, you have every chance of reaching safety? With your passport, you and the children are English. No one need ever know that you converted when you married me.'

Adele's eyes were full of tears. She shook her head. 'I will not leave if you do not come with me. I cannot abandon you here to face an uncertain future.'

Jacob looked at his wife. The love he felt for her burned stronger than ever. She had the chance to escape this madness, and yet she was prepared to stay and suffer with him.

He gave it one last try. 'Adele, *kochana*, you understand that

I cannot possibly come with you. If we were caught, we would face immediate death. But think of the children. Think of how they will suffer if they stay. *Please*, my love, I beg you.'

She sighed, stared upwards, then took his hands in hers.

'Jacob, that day when we ran from Paris to be together, you begged me to follow my heart. I did so, and at that moment, I knew that I had sealed my fate. There is no going back. I took my decision to be your wife and convert to your faith. I will not deny our love. Ever. So please, my darling, accept that we will be together, as a family, until the day we die.'

She put her arms around him and he grasped her tightly to him.

He nodded slowly. 'Until the day we die.'

As Samuel Delanski had predicted, orders were given by Hans Frank for Jews in Warsaw to be sealed inside the northern part of the midtown by the end of November 1940. Having had prior warning of this, Samuel had managed to organise a small apartment within the ghetto area in the brushmakers' district on Lezno Street. It had only three rooms: one for Jacob and Adele, another for Samuel and Surcie, and the sitting room provided enough space for a mattress for David and Rosa. Compared to the conditions others were living in, the apartment was a palace.

Jacob had sold everything he owned to raise cash. Pooled with Samuel's money, they surmised they had enough to keep them in food for two years or more.

Four hundred thousand Jews were sealed into the area. It stretched only three-quarters of a mile square, and consisted of only twelve blocks, from Jerozolimska Street to the cemetery. The overcrowding in the ghetto was unimaginable, the sanitation appalling, and already there were food shortages.

Adele spent most of her mornings queueing outside one of the few licensed bakeries to bring home bread.

Samuel and the community council tried hard to bring some kind of normality to the ghetto citizens. Schools were set up and ran without fail every day; debates were organised, theatre groups formed and a fine symphony orchestra gave weekly concerts.

But by the end of 1940, the number of Jews forced out of the villages in the provinces had swelled the population to over half a million. Rations to the ghetto had been decreased and were barely enough to feed half the population. As a result, many were dying of starvation and the black market was rife. Those who made the dangerous runs out of the ghetto to bring back supplies were charging outrageous prices. The Delanskis had no choice but to pay or starve.

It was a strange life, fraught with terror as friends disappeared and the streets rang with the sound of bullets, but Adele and Jacob desperately tried to keep some kind of routine for the children's sake.

The children attended school in the morning, then Jacob sat with Rosa in the afternoon and painted, using the backs of old canvases to extend the life of their small supply of fresh paper. It whiled away the hours as Adele tried to cook a palatable dinner from her supplies of potatoes and other decaying vegetables. Nine-year-old Rosa seemed blissfully unaware of her surroundings, although she sometimes crept closer to David at night when the sound of gunfire frightened her. Her sweet nature endeared her to the neighbours, who would often find her a spare apple in exchange for a sketch.

At night, the family would huddle together around the small fire, and David would play his precious Stradivarius, which Jacob had not been able to bring himself to sell.

The following April, Surcie Delanski went down with an attack of typhoid that was sweeping the ghetto. She died a week later. Samuel Delanski followed her in July.

Unable to speak from grief, Jacob hauled his father's body onto one of the carts provided for the purpose. It was already overflowing.

After the death of his parents, Jacob became quiet and withdrawn. He stopped painting and would sit for hours staring out of the window at the dreadful poverty and suffering in the street below their apartment.

Adele despaired as she watched her beloved, exuberant husband retreat further into himself with each passing day. When she tried to comfort him, he would stare at her as if he did not know her. Try as she might, she could not shake her husband out of his increasing misery.

Adele was left to care for the children, which meant organising a supply of food. Already weak from lack of nutrition and caring for two fatally ill people, she passed out in a dead faint on the floor of the tiny kitchen.

Horrified, David picked her up. She was light as a feather and he could feel the bones beneath her worn dress. He spoon-fed her a little broth that was simmering on the stove. In that moment, David knew that his precious mama had been neglecting her own rations to feed her family.

Tears came into Adele's eyes as she watched her son.

'Eat this. All of it,' he demanded.

'No, David.' She pushed the bowl away.

'Mama, everything is all right. From now on, I'm taking charge. By tonight, I promise there will be fresh food on the table.'

A determined David left the apartment half an hour later. At six, he returned with a sack of fresh food.

From thenceforth David would go out once a week and return with a sackful of supplies as dusk fell. He always smelled fetid, and Adele guessed that he was making the journey through the sewers to reach the city outside the ghetto.

Rosa never questioned how he got the food. She knew David was subjecting himself to terrible danger and she couldn't bear to think about that.

The winter of 1941 wiped out thousands more in the ghetto. Coal was virtually impossible to get hold of and even David, with his now excellent knowledge of the black market, was struggling. The money was starting to run short and he guessed he only had enough to feed the family for another few months. He was just thankful that spring was on its way.

David's trips to the other side also provided him with a useful amount of intelligence. He heard from one of his sources that the ghetto of Łódź had been emptied, with Jews deported to Chelmo, and that the same was happening in Lublin. There were dreadful rumours that Chelmo was a death camp, where Jews where being annihilated by the thousand.

David longed to confide this news to his father, to hear him say that his information *must* be wrong, but Jacob was now confined to his own world. These days he rarely got out of bed. So David shouldered his terrible fear alone.

In July 1942, on the day of Tish B'av, a Jewish holiday to commemorate the destruction of the Temple in Jerusalem, David was making his way back to the apartment with a precious haul of five potatoes.

A Nazi patrol, an everyday sight on the streets of the ghetto, whisked past him and stopped in front of the building housing the Jewish council. David did not think much of it, guessing that the Germans were continuing their round-up of Jews for their forced labour battalions – so he did not pause to listen to what the commandant had to say. The golden rule was to keep as far away as possible.

Later, as the four Delanskis were sitting eating their paltry meal, there was a knock on their door.

David went to open it and found a pale-faced friend of his who lived with his family in the apartment below theirs.

'Come in, Johann. What is wrong?'

'My father sent me to warn you. Today he saw the Germans rounding up old people and tearing children out of their mothers' arms. Those they captured in the Umschlagplatz were marched to Stawki Street near the railway sidings, where there was a line of freight cars. The old and young were bundled into the cars and the train left. Nobody knows for sure where it was heading.' Tears were in Johann's eyes. 'There is panic on the streets. People are spreading rumours of death camps. David, keep Rosa inside. She should not attend school. I must go. There are others who need to be warned.'

'Thank you, Johann.'

David shut the door, his heart thumping. The liquidation of the ghetto, as at Łódź and Lublin, had begun here.

Adele knew the minute she saw her son's face that something was wrong. Later, when Rosa was sleeping, and Jacob was in the bedroom, Adele beckoned her son into the kitchen.

'What did Johann want, David?'

He explained his friend's warning. Adele's green eyes darkened with fear.

'David, I have seen in your face that you know more about what is to become of us than you say. But you must tell me now all you know. We shall share it between us. Rosa is too young to understand and your father . . .' She closed her eyes for a moment, and gathered herself. 'So, David, is this rumour about the death camps true?'

He looked at his mama and nodded slowly. 'Yes. People believe so.'

David sat on the floor, and Adele wrapped her arms around him. He told her everything he had heard, and wept at the relief of confiding his terrible knowledge.

Adele sat silently, listening to him, before offering some comfort. 'I admire your strength and your courage, for shouldering this alone. I want you to know that it was my decision to stay in Poland with your papa. He blames himself for what has happened to his family, but my love for him . . . Well, maybe one day you will understand why I could never leave. He has only ever seen the beauty and joy of this world, finding a way to block out the dark realities. But now there is no joy for him to see. He has had to withdraw into himself to survive. He lives in the past, to stop the guilt. Do you understand?'

Suddenly, for the first time, David did.

'Now, I want to give you something. Here.' Adele took the gold locket from around her neck and handed it to her son. 'Open it.'

David did so. Inside was a photograph of his mother, taken when she was much younger.

'Remove the picture and turn it over.'

David observed the tiny writing. 'What is this?'

'It is the address of your grandparents in London. If by any chance we are . . . separated, you must try and reach them. God willing, they are still alive. Explain who you are. The locket will prove it. Now, memorise the address and put it round your neck. You must swear to me that you will never take it off again.'

David followed Adele's instructions and tucked the locket under his shirt.

'I swear, Mama.'

Adele stood up and fumbled in the back of one of the kitchen cupboards. She withdrew a slim, blue book. 'Here. I want you to keep this as well. It's my British passport. You can use it as proof of who you are, just in case.' Adele held out her arms. 'Come and hug me. If anything happens to me or your father, look after Rosa for us. She has a great gift and it will be up to you to help her develop it.'

Adele held her son for a long time. David knew that they shared an unspoken knowledge of the future.

Throughout the summer, the German patrols combed the streets of the ghetto, rounding up victims and sending them off on trains to their inevitable deaths. The Delanski family stayed in their apartment twenty-four hours a day, with only David venturing out to find food. Adele begged him not to take the risk, arguing that it was better for them to go hungry than for David to be caught and sent away, but they both knew the family had to eat.

After one fruitless expedition that had only yielded half a loaf of mouldy bread and two old carrots, David rounded the corner onto Lezno Street just in time to see four German patrols marching a group of people off down the road. Once they were out of sight, he flew along the road to the apartment.

Sobs consumed him as he entered his devastated, empty home. David sank to the floor, grinding his knuckles into his eyes.

'Mama, Papa, Rosa. No!'

Not knowing how much time had passed since they had been taken, David picked himself up and walked into his parents' bedroom. Their drawers had been opened and the contents flung all over the floor. His mama's jewellery box lay empty on the bed.

David felt inside his shirt for the locket, its presence comforting him slightly. Then, with a racing heart, he dived under the bed, hoping and praying they had not found it . . . No, the Stradivarius, with the passport hidden in the lining of the case, was untouched.

He brought the violin out and put it under his chin, still weeping. He lifted the bow, but as the first sweet sound filled the room, the familiar melody brought back powerful memories of his beloved family, and was too much for him to bear.

Then he heard something else, a noise so faint in the room that he thought he had imagined it. David sat motionless, straining his hearing. There it was again. Was it . . . someone crying? Could it be?

'Rosa! Rosa, *kochana*, where are you?'

He stumbled round the room, following the sobs to the heavy mahogany wardrobe. With every muscle in his body straining, he managed to heave it along the wall. Behind, there was a small door, only two feet high.

He opened it and Rosa, shaking with fear and half hysterical, fell into his arms.

'David, David! The soldiers came and took Mama and Papa away. Mama hid me in here. I was so frightened. It was so dark and I couldn't breathe and . . .'

'Hush! David's here now. Hush.' He stroked her hair gently, remembering the promise he had made to his mother.

He vowed then that he would protect Rosa until the day he died.

After two weeks of living in the sheer terror of being discovered, and surviving on the scraps of food that David had found in the other empty apartments in the block, he knew that he would have to venture out or face starvation.

Rosa refused to be left alone and would start screaming the minute David left her by herself. Only when she at last fell asleep on the mattresses, positioned by David next to the tiny cupboard just in case, could he leave her alone and ferret for food. However, he had scavenged everything he could from the rest of the building, and needed to go further afield. He couldn't risk her waking while he was out.

'Sweetheart, why don't you draw me a picture? I have to go out and find something to eat. I won't be long, I—'

'No!' Rosa clung to him. 'Don't leave me alone, David, please!'

It was no good. He would have to take her, otherwise her hysterical screams would draw unwanted attention.

He drew a deep breath. 'All right, you can come with me. But you must promise to do everything I say.'

David went to a floorboard in the kitchen, under which was the box where the money was kept. He groaned when he saw how little was left.

Then he had an idea. It was only a chance, but someone might be interested in it.

David picked up the violin case that contained his precious Stradivarius.

'I'm taking my paper and pencil in my bag, in case I see anything to draw on the way,' Rosa said pedantically.

David didn't argue. 'Right. Come on then. And remember, you must do exactly as I say.'

Rosa followed David into the deserted streets. It was a hot, sunny day, and the stench of rotting bodies was almost unbearable. David darted across roads, pulling Rosa into the shelter of doorways if they heard footsteps. He only prayed that one of his contacts in the black market had also escaped unscathed. He felt eyes were watching him as he pulled a tired and sulking Rosa behind him.

When they arrived at the apartment of one of David's suppliers, they found it deserted. The cupboards were bare and Rosa was complaining of thirst.

David put his head in his hands. This was impossible. Rosa was slowing him down and making their presence obvious. He would have to leave her.

David noticed a big teddy bear sitting on a chair in the bedroom. Rosa's eyes lit up as he gave it to her.

'This bear is called David too. He's going to stay here and look after you while I find us some supper. Now, no complaints. I'll be back before you know it, otherwise there's no water and nothing to eat for David Bear. You must not move from here.' He gave his sister a smile. 'David Bear has promised to tell me if you so much as squeak.'

To his relief, Rosa nodded, completely entranced with her new toy. 'All right. I'll draw David Bear as a present for you,' she announced.

David slipped out of the apartment and ran swiftly down the road.

He was back an hour later, still clutching the violin. It was hopeless. Everyone else was starving too. No one was interested in a musical instrument, no matter how precious it might be.

David opened the door to the sitting room and his heart stopped. Rosa was sitting on the floor, hungrily eating an apple, while a German officer studied a piece of paper. She looked up and grinned.

'Hello, David. This man gave me an apple. He liked my picture of David Bear and asked me to draw one of him while we waited for you to come back.'

The officer stood up, the squeak of his boots sending shivers up David's spine. He smiled, almost pleasantly.

'You are David Delanski, and this is your sister, Rosa.'

David nodded. He couldn't speak.

'Good. Your sister is a talented young lady. Her sketch of me is most accurate. I have heard of your father. He was talented too. Come, it is time for us to leave.'

The soldier clicked his heels and pulled Rosa to her feet.

'Can I take my bear with me?'

For a moment, David saw a fleeting glimpse of sympathy cross the Nazi's face as he stared down at Rosa's innocent face.

'Why not?' He shrugged. A few more hours of pleasure seemed little to ask.

They were bundled into the back of the officer's car, and driven to Stawki Street, where the sight of the freight trucks sent pangs of terror through David.

The platform was crammed with frightened faces, and the trucks were being filled to bursting point with humanity.

David got out of the car, and Rosa followed. She reached up to the officer and planted a kiss on his cheek.

'Thank you for the apple,' she said.

The officer watched as David and Rosa were bundled into an already packed truck.

He saw the little girl's face register fear as the sliding door of the vehicle was closed.

He wandered back to his car, then stopped and said something to one of the guards, pointing to the truck housing David and his sister.

It was Rosa's kiss that saved her life.

In the present, David stared unseeingly out of his hotel window. He arose from his chair, his face betraying the dreadful suffering he had just relived, and poured himself another large whisky. He swallowed it in one.

He picked up the receiver and dialled, accepting his life was about to change.

'For you, Rosa,' he muttered, as his call was answered.

20

London, October 1977

'Last call for Alitalia flight AZ459 to Milan. Please board at Gate 17.' The robotic voice repeated the message as Leah and Jenny dashed through passport control and ran towards the gate.

'Shit! I knew we should have left more time. I can't believe the traffic was so dreadful,' gasped a red-faced Jenny.

'Madelaine will never speak to us again if we miss this flight!' cried Leah.

Ten minutes later, after pleading with the gate attendant, the two girls were on board the plane as it was taxied down. Leah's beautifully polished nails were dug into the sides of her seat.

'Here we go,' said Jenny gaily. 'I love this feeling, don't you?'

Leah closed her eyes as the engines roared and the plane soared into the sky.

'There, we're up. You can open your eyes now.' Jenny laughed. 'Gosh, I'm glad to be sitting down after all that running.'

'Would either of you like a drink, ladies?' asked the air hostess after the seatbelt signs had been switched off.

Jenny nodded. 'Yes, I'll have a vodka and Coke. What do you want, Leah?'

'Just a Coke, please.' Leah was still trying to recover her stomach.

'Honestly, you'll have to be more adventurous than that when we hit Milan. Absolutely everyone drinks and they'll think you're an awful square if you don't.'

Leah wrinkled her nose. 'I honestly don't like the taste, Jenny.'

'Nor did I at first, but you get used to it after a while.'

'Anyway,' answered Leah, 'I'm underage.'

'So are most of the girls when they start, but that doesn't stop them. Cheers. Here's to your first assignment.' Jenny took a healthy slug, then turned around and surveyed the cabin. 'Oh look, there's Juanita. She's on Madelaine's books too. And Joe, he works for *Harper's*. The usual crowd always end up on the same plane. You'll get to know everyone soon enough. I must just go and have a word with Juanita. Won't be a minute.'

Jenny slipped out of her seat and Leah closed her eyes, trying to will this terrifying new flying experience to be over as quickly as possible.

She found it difficult to believe that she'd been in London for over a month. The time had flown by, every day filled with photo sessions for her portfolio, make-up lessons, elocution and deportment. Leah hadn't even had time to form an opinion on whether she loved it or hated it. Now Madelaine was sending her on her first assignment.

Jenny had been marvellous, taking a sisterly interest in her and teaching her all sorts of things that she hadn't known.

'What on earth are you doing, Leah?' Jenny had stood there one night, horror-struck by the sight of her new friend tucking into fish and chips. 'Give me those.' Jenny had grabbed the remainder of the meal and chucked it in the bin.

'What's wrong? I'm starving.'

'Never, ever eat chips.' Jenny waggled her finger at Leah. 'They make your skin oily. Here, have an apple instead.'

Leah found it difficult to adjust to the different kind of diet, and would often nip to the chip shop around the corner to eat a crafty feast when Jenny had gone out for the evening. She honestly didn't know how Jenny survived, seeming to live on fruit and muesli. When Leah had attempted it, she just became ravenously hungry.

'I give up,' said Jenny, when she came home one day to find Leah enjoying a huge chocolate eclair. 'What I hate about you more than anything else is that you can eat as much of whatever you fancy, and *never* get spots or put on weight.' She had stomped off to have a bath.

Jenny had tried to persuade her to go out in the evenings, but Leah was too tired and shy to enjoy the round of parties and nightclubs that the other models went to. She usually sat at home and watched television, then spoke to her mum on the telephone.

She missed her parents something rotten and felt terribly homesick on occasions. Madelaine had kept Leah too busy for there to be time for her to go back to Yorkshire.

'The girls and I reckon you're the Queen's new protégée. She's taking a lot more care of you. I was thrown on a plane to Paris the day after she signed me,' Jenny had commented without a hint of jealousy.

Jenny did not need to be jealous. Her career had really started to fly during the past six months, and when she returned to London from Milan, she was doing a six-page spread for British *Vogue*.

'Hi there. Can I come and keep you company for a while? You look a little lonesome.' Leah opened her eyes and saw Steve Levitt hovering over her.

LUCINDA RILEY

'Sure,' she replied. He sat in Jenny's empty seat. Of all the new people she had met, Leah liked Steve best and had enjoyed his photo sessions immensely.

'Is it always like this?' Leah indicated the group that had gathered behind them, perched on the end of seats and armrests, smoking cigarettes and drinking.

'I'm afraid so. The fashion world is a very small place. Everybody knows each other. You'll join the club soon enough. They're a nice bunch but . . .' Steve raised an eyebrow. 'Don't confide a secret to anyone. It'll be all over town the next day.'

'I'll remember that, Steve.'

'Good. Would you like a drink?' He was holding a bottle of wine and pouring himself a glass.

Leah sighed. 'All right then.'

Steve noticed her reticence. 'It's not in your contract, Leah! Don't have one if you don't want one.'

'I know. But I don't enjoy drinking, I don't smoke or take drugs. Jenny says they'll all think I'm square.'

Steve took a swig of wine and shook his head. 'You just carry on in your own way, Leah, and let them all accept you for what you are.'

'That's easy to say, but I want them all to like me.'

'Of course you do. It's tough being the new girl, but everyone has to go through it. They're bound to be a little wary of you at first.' Steve leaned in to whisper. 'The word's out that Madelaine thinks you're destined for big things.'

'I just hope I can remember everything Madelaine's told me, and don't trip up on the catwalk.'

'You're a natural, sweetheart, you'll be fine.' He gave Leah a fatherly smile. 'One small word of warning, though. This crowd are mostly okay, but some of the girls will stop at nothing to get ahead. Just be careful, and be on your guard against anything offered to you at parties. And I mean *anything*.

Milan is notorious for its eventful social life after the shows, but there's a side to it that isn't so pleasant. Stick with Jenny. She's fairly straight.' Steve chuckled at the worry lines creasing Leah's beautiful face. 'You'll be fine. Right, I'd better go back.'

'Is Miles with you?' She knew that Rose's son had assisted Steve on a previous trip to Milan, but she hadn't come across him at a shoot.

Steve frowned. 'No. That relationship didn't really work out. I've got a new assistant called Tony, whom you'll love. See you later, cherub.'

Leah relaxed a little, glad that she wouldn't have to cross paths with the man who made her stomach turn. Steve pecked Leah's cheek and walked back to his seat.

The taxi drove Leah and Jenny the six miles from Linate Airport into Milan, the richest city in Italy.

Leah, having never been out of England, stared with excitement as the taxi negotiated the maze of narrow streets and squares. Cars were bumper to bumper, with drivers tooting their horns and shouting out of windows. The atmosphere was cosmopolitan and electric, with a mixture of skyscrapers and gothic pinnacles – particularly the magnificent Duomo – dominating the skyline.

'Rush hour in Milan! This is all you'll see of the city, so enjoy it while you can.' Jenny laughed.

The taxi dropped the pair off outside a large white building in the Piazza della Repubblica.

'This is it, sweetheart. The Principe di Savoia. It's the best hotel in Milan.'

The women checked in and were shown to their separate rooms, planning to meet in the bar at half past seven.

Leah was overwhelmed by the luxury of her suite. She took ten minutes to explore it fully, pressing every single knob, and jumping out of her skin when the television or radio came blaring out unexpectedly.

She lovingly hung up the clothes that she had brought with her. Madelaine had taken her out shopping when she first arrived in London, and spent hundreds of pounds on a new wardrobe for her. She had suits by Bill Gibb, cocktail dresses by Zandra Rhodes and a shimmering evening dress by Jean Muir.

'It's important to have a British model wearing British designers wherever possible. If Jean saw you in that dress, she'd have you on the catwalk tomorrow.' Madelaine had smiled.

Leah showered, put on the soft terry-towelling robe provided by the hotel, then sat down to apply a light make-up, the way Barbara Daley had taught her.

'When you're out in public, whether in a professional capacity or a social one, you must always look your best. The myth of a model is ruined instantly if the public see her looking like a hag in the supermarket on Monday morning. Wear what you want at home, but outside your front door, you're a professional.'

Leah had nodded at Madelaine and said she understood completely. She brushed her long hair vigorously, turned her head upside down as Vidal had shown her, then threw it back. The light perm the stylist had put into her hair had given it more body, and three inches had been cut off so that it hung in a thick, glowing sheen around her shoulders.

Jenny had said that tonight was a casual, informal drink in the hotel bar to which some of the designers turned up. Leah looked in her wardrobe and took out a black crêpe jumpsuit, chosen by Madelaine from Biba. She matched it with a thick, black belt and a pair of high-heeled pumps.

Leah studied her image in the mirror and felt reasonably

confident about her appearance. However, she was less sure that she could ever master the art of small talk.

But she didn't want to let Madelaine down. So she took a deep breath and prepared to do her best.

Carlo Porselli looked across the crowded bar which was filled with models, photographers and fashion editors, chatting away loudly. His eyes fell on the doors of the lift, which opened to reveal a woman he had not seen before.

He'd always shrugged his shoulders when other designers had claimed that they had found their 'muse', believing that clothes should be made to make any woman feel good in them. But as the vision approached him, he swiftly changed his mind.

'Who is that? *Molto, molto bella.*'

'It's Madelaine's new model.' Jenny was sitting next to him in the bar, draining her fifth vodka and Coke. 'She lives with me. Her name's Leah. She's in your set, along with me, Juanita and Jerry.' She waved her hand. 'Hey, Leah, come and sit by me and meet Carlo. We're modelling his ready-to-wear on Friday. He's the hottest young designer in town.' She pulled up a chair for her companion. Carlo stood up, took Leah's hand and kissed it.

'*Buonasera, signorina*. It is a pleasure to meet you.'

'And a pleasure to meet you,' said Leah in a stilted voice. They sat down. Carlo clicked his fingers and a waiter came running. 'We shall all have champagne to celebrate Leah's first fashion show.'

'I'd prefer a Coke, if that's all right with you,' said Leah quietly.

'Ahh, the young girl, she looks after her so beautiful figure and face. *Per favore*, a Coca-Cola and a bottle of Berlucchi.' The waiter scurried away and Carlo turned his attention to Leah. 'So, it is your first time in Milan, *sì*?'

'Yes.'

'It is the most beautiful city in the world, especially in late autumn, when the noisy tourists have gone home and the leaves are falling from the trees. You must allow me to show it to you.'

Jenny chuckled. 'I don't think Leah's going to have any time for sightseeing, Carlo. As from tomorrow, we work night and day.'

'Time can be made,' said Carlo dismissively.

The drinks arrived and the waiter poured the champagne into three glasses. Leah picked up her Coke and sipped it.

'Here. You will insult me if you will not take one tiny sip.' Carlo held out a glass to Leah and she took it reluctantly.

'Okay.' She put it to her lips and sampled the drink. The bubbles raced down her throat and she spluttered helplessly.

Carlo threw back his head and laughed. 'Ah, well, it is not the reaction I had hoped for, but I can see we have to protect your innocence against the predators who would take advantage.' He looked at Jenny, who nodded knowingly.

'Carlo's talking about the playboys. This week is hunting season. There's a line of Ferraris parked outside the hotel as we speak.' Jenny pointed to the other side of the room. 'You see those men talking to Juanita? And the three with the models at the bar?'

Leah nodded.

'They're very rich international businessmen. They'll take their pick tonight and then plague you with flowers and trinkets until you give in and go out to dinner with them. After that, they'll try anything to . . . well, you know.'

'Yes,' said Leah, blushing.

Carlo sighed. 'I'm afraid it is so. I apologise for the bad behaviour of my countrymen. But it is the Italian blood. We cannot resist a beautiful woman.' He stared hard at Leah once more. 'So, are you looking forward to this week?'

'I'm a little nervous.'

'But of course. That is only natural. I am sure that you will shine like a bright star in the sky.' Carlo drained his champagne flute. 'Now I must take my leave and go back to work. There is much to be done before Friday. *Buonanotte*, Jenny. You make sure that this little one is taken under your arm.' He kissed her on each cheek.

'Wing, Carlo, not arm.' Jenny giggled.

'Goodnight to you, *piccolina*. I see you soon.' Carlo kissed Leah's hand and walked out of the bar towards the hotel entrance.

'Are you sure you don't want any champers?' Jenny took the half-full bottle and refilled her glass.

Leah shook her head and watched Juanita being escorted from the bar by one of the young playboys.

'Of course,' muttered Jenny, noticing too. 'She's unbelievable, that one. She's engaged to that pop star, but goes for anything in tight pants with an overflowing wallet.'

'Carlo seemed nice,' Leah prompted.

'Oh, he is these days. But apparently he used to be just as bad as the rest of the young men in this town. Then he started designing four years ago and seems to have reformed. His father's stinking rich.' Jenny looked around her to make sure there were no eager ears, and leaned in close. 'Someone was telling me last year that he's in with the big "M".'

'Big "M"?' Leah whispered back.

'The Mafia,' Jenny hissed. 'Mind you, most of them here are. A lot of the modelling agencies are run by crime syndicates. Last year, one agency which refused a takeover deal was bombed!'

Leah's eyes were opening wider and wider. Madelaine hadn't told her about any of this.

'*Scusate, signorine*. Can we buy you both a drink?'

Two good-looking Italian men were standing behind them.
'No thanks, we're fine,' said Jenny firmly.

'Then could we at least sit down and have the pleasure of your company?'

'Actually,' said Jenny, 'we were just leaving, weren't we, Leah?' She stood up and Leah followed suit. '*Ciao*, gentlemen.' Jenny smiled politely and set off towards the lifts with Leah in tow.

'I think an early night is in order for both of us. Call room service if you're hungry,' said Jenny as the lift opened onto their floor. ''Night, Leah. You've just completed lesson one and passed with flying colours. You're going to be fine.' Jenny kissed her and disappeared into her room.

21

'Good luck, darling, you'll do just great.' Jenny squeezed Leah's hand as the pulsing beat of their entrance music started. Leah was glad that the designer had placed her at the back, and she was modelling only two cocktail dresses.

'Go!' said the choreographer, and Leah walked out into the blaze of lights behind the other girls. A round of cheers and applause came up from the audience. She followed the weaving pattern that the choreo had taught her, and managed to smile when it was her turn to walk onto the circular platform at the front to show the dress she was wearing. Flashbulbs popped in her face as she turned, walked back up the catwalk and offstage towards her designated dresser and hairstylist.

There was no rush for her, but she watched with interest as some of the older, more experienced models swore blatantly as they deftly changed into their next outfit, then rushed up the stairs to walk serenely down the catwalk.

The whole show was over in less than forty minutes and there was a lot of kissing and congratulations back-stage with the designer. This was followed by drinks in the salon, and the models had been asked to stay in their dresses. Leah was wearing a red satin halter top and a heavy black satin harem skirt.

'Congratulations. I told you it was a cinch, didn't I?' Jenny cooed. She had been one of the two main models tonight, and Leah thought she looked stunning in a pinstripe velvet dinner suit, with a silk wing-collar blouse and long bow-tie at her neck. 'Now, stay as close as you can. This is when things can go wild.'

Leah nodded and followed her friend into the salon, where Jenny was immediately surrounded by a posse of photographers, then kissed and congratulated by the fashion editor at *Vogue*.

Leah took a glass of orange juice from a passing waitress and sipped it slowly, feeling uncomfortable. As she had been told, everyone seemed to know each other.

'*Cara*, you were perfect!' Carlo swung Leah round and kissed her on each cheek. 'Of course, tonight's designer makes clothes that do not flatter a woman as I do, but still, I had eyes only for you.'

'Oh, thank you, Carlo.'

'I will be using you to show off your true potential on Friday.' Carlo indicated the world-famous designer standing behind him. 'I hope you are not modelling too many dresses tomorrow night at *his* show?'

'I'm not sure yet,' replied Leah, honestly.

Carlo took her hands. 'Well, I want you for me. All for me. You are the woman to take my designs into immortality.' He was staring at her again with those powerful brown eyes, and Leah was at a loss for words.

'Carlo, *caro*!' A stunning woman with jet-black hair and flashing green irises kissed Carlo directly on the lips. A conversation in fast Italian followed, with Carlo pointing in Leah's direction a couple of times.

'Excuse me for being so rude, but I have not seen Maria for many months. She has been away in America earning lots of dollars for a cosmetics company.'

Maria spoke English in a particularly thick accent. 'I am pleezed to meet you, darleeng.' The look on the woman's face belied her words.

'Maria has flown over specially to do my collection. You will be working together on Friday.'

'I see you then, no?' Maria turned and kissed Carlo once more. As she walked away, she turned and looked at Leah, muttered something in Italian, and disappeared into the crowd.

'Sorry about that. I got caught up by the photographers.' Jenny joined them. 'Was that Maria I saw walking away from you?'

Carlo nodded. '*Sì*, Jenny.'

Jenny raised her eyebrows. 'How . . . wonderful that she could be here. Now, you two, we're off to the Astoria Club. Gianni's hired it for the night. Sally and I are going with him in his car.'

'Ahh, then I will drive Leah there. Do not worry, Jenny, I have her under my arm.'

'Wing, Carlo,' Jenny drawled. 'Okay, I'll see you there. Behave yourself, Leah.' She winked.

Carlo clapped his hands. 'Right. We go.'

'I must change first,' said Leah, and Carlo nodded.

Leah went into the dressing rooms and slipped into her Jean Muir evening gown.

'Ahh, that is much more you. I like Muir's line. It is similar to mine,' Carlo commented as if the great British designer had copied *him*. He grabbed Leah's hand, pulled her through the crowd of people, and out into the cool air of the Via della Spiga.

'Before the Astoria, I want to take you somewhere. It is not far. We can walk.' Carlo set off down the street, his hand gripping Leah's. He observed her worried look and smiled.

'It is okay, *cara*. Jenny trusts me, no?' He let go of her hand and gestured around him. 'See, we are in the Quadrilatero. In

these few streets you will find every great Italian designer.'
Carlo turned right, and Leah followed him down a quieter
street. Instead of the grand neo-classical white *palazzi* and big
luxury shops of the Via della Spiga, the Via Sant'Andrea was
a tranquil, eighteenth-century world. Leah stopped to peer in
the windows of an old boutique.

Carlo put a firm hand on her back. 'Come, come. We have
little time.' Leah apologised and followed him once more.
'See, that is Giorgio's salon. You are there on Thursday, are
you not?'

Leah nodded. Carlo stopped two hundred yards further
along the road. 'We are here.' He pulled Leah up some old
stone steps. On the gold plate by the bell, it said 'Carlo'.

He was unlocking the door. 'My assistant, Giulio, will still
be here and I want him to meet you. Wait a moment.'

Carlo indicated an ornate chair and disappeared into the
depths of the salon. Leah looked round the room. It was
incredibly plush, with huge chandeliers suspended from the
hand-painted ceiling, and long moiré silk curtains hanging from
the tall windows.

Carlo reappeared with a short middle-aged man behind him.

'Leah, please, stand.' She did so. Carlo looked back at the
older man.

'Am I not right?' he asked.

'*Sì*, you are.' The other man nodded slowly.

Carlo walked towards Leah. 'This is Giulio Ponti. He has
been employed by many of the major houses in Milan, and I
kidnapped him to come and work for me, just as I have
kidnapped you tonight.' He paused, then turned to Giulio. 'I
want her to wear the wedding dress on Friday.'

Giulio stared at Carlo as if he was mad. 'But . . . we have
fitted it exactly to Maria.'

Carlo looked annoyed. 'That is why I have brought Leah

here tonight. I want her to put on the dress and you must refit it to her. I am sure there will not be that much difference.'

'Well . . .' Giulio stepped forward reluctantly and surveyed Leah. 'Same height and hips, I think, but Maria . . .' Giulio gestured without a hint of awkwardness. 'She has more here.' He indicated Leah's chest.

'Attch, that can be fixed in a *momento*. Leah, go into the dressing room on the right upstairs. You will find the wedding dress. Please put it on. We will come up shortly.'

Leah nodded and started to walk up the stairs at the front of the salon. Giulio was talking in fast Italian, and Leah could make out only the name 'Maria'. She soon found the dressing room, and opened the door.

The shimmering white dress was hanging in a corner. As instructed, Leah removed her own dress and slipped the gown over her head. Giulio had been right. It fitted perfectly everywhere but the bust, where it was only slightly too big. There was a knock on the door.

'I'm ready,' she called out.

Carlo and Giulio entered, and stood staring at her. Carlo nodded, a smile appearing on his lips. 'I was correct. Leah must wear this dress on Friday.'

Giulio nodded reluctantly. 'She brings to it the natural innocence and joy of a bride on her wedding day.'

'Just as I thought,' replied Carlo with deep satisfaction. 'Please proceed with the fitting.'

It took Giulio only ten minutes to make the slight alterations. When he had finished, they left Leah alone to change, and she joined them in the salon.

'Now we go to the nightclub.' Carlo grinned at Leah, and she thought he looked like a little boy who had just succeeded in getting his own way.

'You will explain to . . .'

Carlo waved a dismissing arm in the direction of Giulio as he took Leah's arm and led her towards the front door.

'I will handle it. There is no problem. *Arrivederci*, Giulio.'

When Carlo and Leah arrived at the Astoria nightclub in his red Lamborghini, the paparazzi gathered round them. Carlo smiled and put an arm round Leah's shoulders. Flashbulbs went off again. He answered their questions in Italian, waved and ushered Leah inside. Then he guided her into the leather seat of an unoccupied booth.

'Wait there. I go for some champagne and, er, Coke.' He winked and set off towards the crowded bar.

Leah, still dazed and feeling exhausted from the night's events, saw Jenny walking towards her, glass in hand.

'Wherever have you been? I let you out of my sight for a moment and you disappear. I was worried sick!' said Jenny crossly.

Carlo reappeared behind her. 'She has been with me, Jenny. And she is perfectly safe, is she not?' He shot her a winning smile and placed the drinks down on the table.

'I suppose so, but next time let me know where you're going. I promised Madelaine I'd look after you. I want to go back to the hotel in a minute. And Leah looks exhausted.'

'Come, sit down for *un momento*, and let me show you what I have for you,' said Carlo. 'I know you like it and it is the best in Milan.' He produced a small phial from his top pocket and handed it to Jenny.

Jenny looked hesitant. 'I shouldn't. I've had enough already.'

Carlo shrugged. 'Then you keep it as a present, *cara*.'

'Okay. Thanks, Carlo.' Jenny slipped the phial into her evening bag, watching Leah's inquisitive eyes on her. She shot Carlo a look. 'I'll come back in half an hour,' she said firmly, and left the table.

'So. We dance?' Carlo stood up and offered his hands to Leah.

'Oh, umm . . . sure.' Leah was wishing that she was tucked up in her comfortable bed at the hotel. Her feet were killing her, but she knew that this was the kind of thing she had to do with grace, if she was to be successful.

As they stepped onto the dance floor, the music changed to a slower beat and Carlo pulled Leah into his arms. She smelled the strong aroma of his aftershave, then sniffed at the fug hanging in the air. It was a strange smell, something she didn't know.

'Oh *cara, mia cara*,' Carlo was murmuring. He tipped her face up to his and studied it. 'I will make you so famous. Our names will be joined together for ever. You are my muse! Say you'll stay with me tonight.' He leaned forward and kissed her on the lips.

'Hey, no! Carlo, stop it!' She wrenched herself out of his arms and ran towards the exit. Once outside, Leah swiftly located a waiting taxi and gave the driver the name of her hotel. When she was safely in the confines of her hotel room, she flung herself on the bed and burst into tears.

It was all too much. A little more than a month ago she'd been living with her parents in a small northern town, just seventeen years old and oblivious to this world. Now here she was, rocketed into a glittering arena of unknown territory, trying to ward off strange men.

She felt completely out of her depth and wanted to go home to the safe world she knew.

There was a knock on her door and Leah held her breath. The knock came again.

'Leah, it's only Jenny. Can I come in?'

Leah stood up and unlocked the door. Jenny's eyes were full of sympathy when she saw her friend's blotched face.

'Sweetheart, I'm so sorry. It was my fault. I shouldn't have left you with him. Come on, you go to the bathroom and wash your face while I make you a cup of tea.'

Leah nodded silently. After she had wiped away her mascara, she felt a little better. She opened the bathroom door and Jenny handed her a steaming cup of Earl Grey.

'What did he do to you?'

'He tried to kiss me,' Leah said quietly.

Jenny gave a sigh of relief. 'Thank God that was all. I've known them try much more at a nightclub before. I'll murder him tomorrow. He promised me he wouldn't touch you.'

'It's not your fault, Jenny. I just don't think I'm cut out for this kind of thing, that's all.' Leah could feel a lump rising in her throat again.

'Don't you think we all feel that way when we start? Trust me, Leah, I was greener than you are when I first began and I really learned the hard way.' Her blue eyes saddened as she recalled the past.

'What happened to you?'

Jenny took a deep breath. 'Remember I told you that Madelaine sent me off to Paris the day after she signed me?'

'Yes.'

'Well, I had no one to look after me. No one told me that the model groupies will do anything to get you into the sack. So, when this dishy French bloke started wining and dining me and sending flowers to my room, I believed everything he said. I was overwhelmed by the attention.' Jenny sank down onto the bed. 'One night he fed me coke in a cigarette, took me back to his house and . . .' Jenny began to cry. 'I tried to tell him "no". But he was forceful. He shouted at me. So I gave in. I never saw him again after that night.' Jenny sniffed. 'By the way, "coke" is a drug, not something brown and fizzy that you drink.'

Leah nodded. 'Was that coke in the tube Carlo gave you?'

Jenny's mouth tightened. 'Yes. But don't you dare tell Madelaine, Leah Thompson. If she found out, I'd be off her books in a flash. I don't use it very often, but everyone does it in the fashion world. You can't avoid it.'

Leah sat next to Jenny on the bed and put an arm around her. 'If that man raped you after giving you that stuff, why would you—?'

Jenny cut her off. 'You get a taste for it, that's all. Anyway, I want you to tell me where on earth you and Carlo disappeared to earlier.'

Leah pulled a face. 'To his salon to try on a wedding dress. He wants me to wear it on Friday.'

'Jesus!' Jenny looked horrified.

'What's the matter?'

'Maria always wears the wedding dress for Carlo. She's been his number one model since he opened. They had an affair for three years until she went off to America six months ago. Does she know about this?'

Leah pulled a face. 'Carlo mentioned that he was going to tell her.'

'Jesus, Leah. He's really dumped you in it. Carlo's so spoiled. He just brushes people aside to get what he wants and leaves others to pick up the pieces.' She took a deep breath. 'Seriously, you're going to have to be on your guard against Maria. She's a bitch at the best of times and this . . .' Jenny could not finish the sentence.

'I just want to go home,' Leah said in a small voice.

Jenny gave her a hug. 'I'm sorry, darling. I didn't mean to frighten you. Of course you don't want to go home. To be chosen from nowhere by the great Carlo Porselli to model his wedding dress is the biggest honour you could have! It means that you're going to be incredibly successful. I only mean to say that this game is a rat race. You have to grow up very fast, but if I can do it, you can, darling.' Jenny squeezed her.

'But what if Carlo tries to touch me again?'

Jenny shrugged. 'Do you not like him? He's obviously fallen for you in a big way.'

Leah grimaced.

22

Leah awoke to her alarm call at ten to seven on Friday morning, pulled her exhausted body out of bed and went to take a shower. As she came out, she heard a knock on the door.

'Who is it?'

'Reception with a delivery, Mees Leah.'

Leah opened the door to find the bell boy struggling with a huge bouquet of white roses.

'*Grazie.*' Leah tipped the young man and he handed her the bouquet, which she carried to the bed. She opened the card.

Tonight will be a night you will never forget, my bride. Carlo.

Leah had not seen him since Monday evening. He hadn't turned up at any of the other designers' shows, and Leah had been glad of it. She had spent the week on a steep learning curve and was starting to realise that although modelling might be glamorous, it was mainly a lot of hard work. Every day, she had been up at seven and in a designer's salon in the Quadrilatero by nine, where the models had then been put through their paces for the evening's show. They practised with the choreographer, had trial runs with the hair and make-up stylist, and finished with a full dress rehearsal. They would usually have no more than half an hour's break to grab something to eat before getting ready for the main event.

Then there had been the socialising afterwards. Most of the models stayed out until the early hours, going to parties and nightclubs. Leah didn't know how they managed to look so fresh the following morning. There would be a lot of groans and aspirin passed around first thing, but the previous night's hectic activities seemed to be something the girls took in their stride.

For Leah's part, she had got into the habit of having one drink at the party in the designer's salon after the show, then quietly slipping back to the hotel, content to have a long bath and enjoy the splendour of her suite. She wasn't part of the crowd, and although some of the girls called her a 'party pooper', they mostly left her alone.

Jenny would usually regale her with the latest gossip over coffee in her room the following morning. Leah had asked her why the famed playboys seemed to be leaving her well enough alone, and Jenny had smiled wisely.

'Carlo's put the word out that you're off limits. None of them would dare touch you. They're too scared of him. I told you that he and his father hold a lot of sway in this town.'

Leah had been grateful to Carlo for that. Wild parties, drink and drugs just didn't appeal, and she knew her mother would kill her if she got involved in anything like that.

She also knew that tonight would be a different kettle of fish.

Leah wondered what the other girls would think when Carlo announced later on that she would be wearing the wedding dress this evening. If the backbiting she had witnessed in the dressing room when a model got the best clothes was anything to go by, she was in for a rough ride.

'Keep your head, Leah, and be sensible,' she muttered as she went down the corridor and knocked on Jenny's door.

Jenny opened it, looking ravaged and still dressed in her nightie.

'Come in, sweetie. I'm running late. God, do I have a hangover! Put on the kettle for some coffee and I'll jump in the shower.'

Leah did so, then picked up Jenny's beautiful Chanel evening gown, which was lying in a heap on the floor, and hung it.

'Mmm, that's better,' said Jenny as she sat naked on her bed and sipped her coffee. 'I met someone last night.' She eyed Leah over the rim of her coffee cup.

'But, Jenny, I thought you said that you wouldn't touch any of those playboys with a bargepole.'

Jenny giggled. 'He's not a playboy. He's a prince.'

'Oh.'

'Oh?! Oh?! Your best friend meets one of the world's most eligible bachelors, spends the evening with him, and all you can say is "oh"?'

Leah gave her friend a smile. 'I'm sorry, Jenny. Tell me about him.'

'Well, his name's Ranu, and he's the Crown Prince of some-where in the Middle East. His father is reputedly the richest man in the world. You must have heard of him, Leah. The gossip columns are always full of Ranu holding huge parties on his yacht or private island in the Caribbean. They're always trying to marry him off to one beautiful woman or another.'

Leah shook her head. 'I honestly haven't heard of him. What was he like?'

Jenny's face became dreamy. 'Oh Leah, it was the most romantic night of my life. When Giorgio, the designer, said that Ranu was desperate to be introduced to me, I wasn't particularly thrilled. I mean, the man hasn't exactly got the best reputation. But then Ranu came over and . . . he's so sweet, Leah. Such a gentleman. We went to this party at a grand *palazzo* on the shores of Lake Como and he stayed by my side all evening. Then he brought me home and he didn't even try to kiss me. Can you believe it?! Before I got out of the car he turned to me and said in that terribly sexy voice of his, "I want to see you again, Jennee." I love the way he pronounces my name, with the accent on the "y".'

Leah thought she might be sick. She had believed that sweet, sensible Jenny was above being fooled by the things these men said.

'I know what you're thinking, but I just can't explain . . .' Jenny was now up and pulling her faithful rehearsal tracksuit on. 'He's different, I know he is. He's coming to the party tonight and I want you to meet him and tell me what you think. Now, enough of me. Are you ready for your big day?'

Leah nodded. 'I think so.'

'Good. Remember, ignore anything that the girls say. They'll only be jealous because you've got a big break and you're new on the circuit. Just watch out for Maria. I'll be interested to see how Carlo handles her. Come on, we don't want to be late.'

When Leah and Jenny arrived at Carlo's salon, most of the other girls were already there, drinking coffee and smoking.

'Okay, ladies, gather round. I wish to go through the schedule, and Carlo wants a word with you all.' Giulio was looking tired and red-eyed. Leah and Jenny took two seats at the back, and Carlo climbed up onto the front of the catwalk that had been erected for the show.

'*Buongiorno*, ladies. I hope that none of you were later to your beds than midnight . . .'

A titter came up from the seats. Carlo raised his eyebrows and continued, 'We have a very busy day today. This year the format will be slightly different, with one notable change. The beautiful Maria, who has so kindly joined us from America, has been asked by her company there to keep a low profile so as not to interfere with the marketing and promotion in the United States. She will, of course, still be in the show, but under the circumstances we have decided that someone else must wear the wedding dress.'

'Good try, Carlo,' muttered Jenny, knowing that not a person in the room believed him.

'Having looked at all your measurements, the girl who is the closest to Maria is Leah. Therefore, she will wear the wedding dress tonight.'

An audible gasp went round the room. People began nudging each other and turned around to stare at Leah, who blushed and studied her hands. Then they turned to gauge Maria's reaction. She was in the front row, shrugging her elegant shoulders and smiling graciously.

'*Va bene*, I leave you in the capable hands of Giulio, who will go through the running order, and Luigi, who is staging the show. *Grazie*, ladies.'

As Carlo left the stage, the girls began whispering. A few of the older models gathered round Maria, and others turned to Leah and whispered insincere congratulations. After a moment, Maria stood up and walked over to her successor. Every single head in the room turned to watch.

To Leah's surprise, Maria smiled and kissed her on both cheeks. 'Thank you, darleeng, for 'elping me out. These Americans are oh so possessive with me. Good luck. If you need any 'elp, you ask, okay?'

Leah let out the breath she'd been holding as Maria went back to her seat and Giulio climbed up on the catwalk to start going through the running order.

For the rest of the morning, Leah concentrated on mastering her moves. She was partnered mostly by Maria, and the older model could not do enough to help her. In fact, Maria fussed over her like a mother hen, brought her coffee when she was too busy to get it herself, and generally treated her like a long-lost daughter.

At lunchtime, Leah and Jenny nipped out for a breath of fresh air.

'I can't get over the way Maria's looking after you. All the other girls have commented on it. She seems a little too sweet, though, so don't be totally taken in, will you?'

Leah shook her head, but had to admit that Maria's concern seemed genuine enough.

The thing that terrified Leah most about the evening was the quick changes. She had watched the other girls go through them night after night, and wondered how they handled it. Leah was wearing half a dozen outfits tonight, and she and the other girls knew that they were the finest garments.

The dress rehearsal was a disaster. Leah missed two of her cues and Giulio shouted at her.

An hour before the show, Leah was sitting having her hair styled, in a state of frenzy. Maria came up behind her.

'Ah, leetle one, you are nervous, no?'

Leah nodded as she stood up from the chair and the next girl sat down.

''Ere, I give you these to calm you down.' Maria handed her three small white pills.

Leah shook her head. 'No, thank you, Maria.'

'They are only aspirin. See, I take them too.' Maria popped another two white tablets into her mouth and reached for a glass of water to swallow them.

'Well, I . . .' Leah relented. She had a stinking headache from the bright lights and having her hair pulled this way and that. And Maria had taken them too, so they couldn't do any harm.

'Thank you,' she said as she took the glass of water and swallowed the pills.

Half an hour later, Leah was in her first outfit, a scoop-necked ribbed sweater and skirt, in the soft wool that had been so popular with all the designers that week. She was trying to keep calm. Ten minutes before the show began, Carlo appeared in the dressing room, resplendent in a white dinner suit.

'Good luck, girls. I am sure you will do me proud.' He made his way over to Leah and took her hands. 'You look incredible, *cara*.' He kissed her on each cheek. 'In an hour's time, you will be the new star of the fashion world, trust me.'

'Okay, girls, everyone in order, please.'

Leah took her place. As she did so, her stomach gave a giant somersault and her palms became clammy.

'It's nerves, Leah, really.' Jenny looked at Leah's pale face and the tiny line of sweat on her forehead. She touched her hand reassuringly. 'You'll be fine once you get out there, I promise.'

Leah nodded. Jenny was probably right, but her stomach really did feel very strange.

She moved towards the catwalk entrance and listened to the hum of the audience. Tonight, she was the model leading the rest of the girls down for the first number. There was a hush as the compere spoke, then the familiar beat of the music. The pain in her stomach was getting worse.

'Okay, go!' instructed the choreographer.

Leah walked out into the lights and received a round of applause. When the first number was over, she ran off towards her dresser, feeling a little calmer, but decidedly ill.

The next twenty minutes were a nightmare. She completed six changes, feeling sure she was going to pass out at any moment. She desperately needed to go to the bathroom, but knew there wasn't a minute to spare. Somehow, she gritted her teeth and managed to smile as she went through her paces on the catwalk.

'It's nearly over, you're nearly there, just the wedding dress now,' she told herself as she rushed off the catwalk towards her dresser. She was halfway through taking off the evening dress when she knew that she could hold on no longer.

'I'm sorry, I have to go to the ladies'.' Leah fled in the direction of the toilets, leaving her dresser holding the wedding dress in astonishment.

'*Mamma mia!* What to do! What to do!'

Giulio came rushing down the stairs from the side of the catwalk.

'Quick! There is no time to lose! Maria, come here and put the dress on.'

Maria gave a triumphant smile and sauntered over.

'But my company will not like it,' she drawled as the dress was put over her head. 'Attchh, it is tight around the top.'

'Then take off your bra, quickly!' screamed Giulio.

Maria gave another grin. 'If you insist.'

A minute later, Maria walked onto the stage and an audible gasp went up from the audience, followed by thunderous clapping. The rest of the girls joined her, and a bemused Carlo jumped up onto the catwalk to receive an ovation.

Jenny found the pathetic figure in the ladies, crumpled in a heap in one of the cubicles.

'Oh darling, whatever is it? We must get you to a hospital immediately.'

Leah shook her head. 'I don't need the hospital.'

'You look ghastly, Leah. Where's the pain? In your stomach?'

Leah nodded. 'I just can't stop . . . going. Excuse me.' Leah pushed Jenny out of the cubicle. She emerged five minutes later, doubled over, and sank to the floor again.

'It looks like you've got food poisoning. But you hardly ate anything today. I watched you. Can you think what it might be?'

'Did Maria wear the wedding dress?' asked Leah.

Jenny nodded. 'Yes. She caused a sensation. She couldn't wear a bra under the dress, so you could see *everything* through the chiffon. I don't think it was quite what Carlo had intended, but it'll certainly make all the papers tomorrow morning.'

'She gave me some tablets. She said they were aspirin and took two herself. The pain started about an hour after I'd taken them,' Leah said quietly.

Jenny was dumbstruck. 'Oh my God. I bet the bitch has given you laxatives! I've heard about models doing that before, but I can't believe Maria would stoop so low. Do you really think it was the tablets?'

'Yes. I've eaten nothing today, and I haven't been sick or anything. I just keep wanting to go.'

'Jesus Christ!' cried Jenny as Leah once again had to close the door and avail herself. 'Right. I'm getting your jeans and you can change while I call a taxi to take you back to the hotel. Then I'm going to see Carlo. Maria's not going to get away with this.'

'Leave it, Jenny. I can't prove anything,' said Leah from inside the cubicle, but Jenny had gone.

Leah lay in bed feeling exhausted, sick, and very sorry for herself. She'd only just made it back to the hotel in time to rush to the ladies, and had spent the past hour in her bathroom. She could hardly believe that anyone could do such a wicked, dreadful thing.

But tonight had confirmed her theory. She just wasn't cut out for this. Anyway, she'd been made a laughing stock in front of the entire fashion world and no one would ever want to employ her again. She decided that tomorrow she would buy a ticket home with her wages and go straight back to Yorkshire, where she belonged.

A solitary tear rolled down her face, but she stopped herself crying by thinking that this time tomorrow she'd be tucked up tight in her own little bed, with her mother looking after her.

Leah drifted off to sleep, grateful that the worst seemed to be over.

A persistent knocking woke Leah from her dreams.

'Who is it?' she called weakly.

'Carlo. Please, let me in.'

'I'm not well, Carlo. Please go away.'

'*Cara*, I implore you. Open the door. I will not leave until you do.'

Reluctantly, Leah staggered to her feet, unlocked the door, and only just made it back to the bed before her legs gave way beneath her.

Carlo came and sat on the end of the bed, his eyes full of anxiety. He took her hand. 'How are you feeling?'

'I think I feel a bit better than I did. I'm so sorry, Carlo.'

Carlo frowned. 'Don't you dare apologise. Jenny told me what Maria did, and a word in the right ear confirmed that it was indeed true. This is all my fault. I was so stupid to think she would accept it with good grace. I am so, so sorry, *piccolina*.'

Leah shrugged. 'It's made me realise that the modelling world isn't for me. I'm going home tomorrow,' she said sadly.

Carlo's brown eyes flashed. 'You will do no such thing! Here, take a look. He put a copy of *Il Giorno* into her hands. There, on the newspaper's front page, was a big picture of Leah in her penultimate evening dress, with big words in block capitals running along the top of the photo.

'What does it say, Carlo?' She handed back the paper and he translated.

'It says, *Who Is She?* I will read you the rest.' Carlo cleared his throat. 'This is the face of the mystery model who caused a sensation at Carlo's ready-to-wear collection last night. She did not appear at the party afterwards and no one has seen her out on the town on any night this week, apart from on the arm of Carlo himself at a nightclub on Monday evening. Even then, she stayed only five minutes before leaving alone. There is talk that she may be Russian aristocracy, descended from the tsar himself . . .'

Leah could not resist a giggle at this point.

'No one in the fashion world can understand why the flamboyant Carlo allowed Maria Malgasa, his ex-lover, to wear the wedding dress. Some suspect it was a peace offering to pacify the fiery Maria, as there is certainly no doubt of his new star. The mystery model's natural beauty and radiance on the catwalk only served to make the rather vulgar display of Maria's flesh – one could see parts of this lady that usually appear only in *Penthouse* – seem more contrived.'

Carlo grinned at Leah over the top of the paper. 'Do you wish me to continue?'

'No.'

'So, do you see that Maria's plan has backfired on her? The fact that you did not wear the wedding dress and were absent from the party has only made the media's interest in you greater.' Carlo put his hands out towards Leah. 'It is good that you do not enjoy the social life as the others do. It has made you a mystery, and there is nothing the press likes more.'

Leah turned her head away. 'I'm still going home, Carlo.'

He sighed. 'It is your decision. I understand that you are upset by the terrible thing this woman has done. But do you not see the best way to pay her back? You can become the true star which she is so scared of you being. Stay, and outshine her! If you creep home, she will clap her hands, thinking she has won. Do you understand?'

Leah nodded slowly, saying nothing.

Carlo narrowed his eyes. 'How old are you, Leah?'

'Seventeen. Just.'

He inhaled deeply. 'Ahh, my *piccolina*, now I understand. You are too young to have to deal with all this. From now on, you will have Carlo by your side, protecting you.' He brushed her hair away from her face. 'I am sorry for trying to kiss you. I thought that you look so *bellissima* and sophisticated. If you will stay, I promise I will never touch you again. You have my word on that.'

Leah turned her face to look at him. He appeared solemn and sincere.

'You must stay, Leah. It is your destiny.'

'Okay,' she said.

The next morning, Leah emerged from the lift to find a posse of photographers waiting for her.

Her new life had begun.

Part Two

August 1981 to January 1982

1

'This is it, chaps. Raise your glasses to our last week as care-free young men. Soon we'll all be getting up at dawn, instead of skulking out of bed at eleven after missing the first lecture. We'll be working through until eight at night, rather than sleeping off last night's hangover in the afternoon. Who knows, some of us might even go on to become pillars of this green and pleasant land. But for now, let's indulge in the thing undergraduates do best: drink!'

Each one of the five young men sitting round the table in the dingy west London pub groaned and raised his glass.

'And to think I complained about the amount of work my sadistic tutor piled on me,' moaned Rory.

'At least you get long lunches in the City, which is more than you can say for the medical students,' muttered a jealous Toby.

'I think Brett's got the best deal of the lot of us. Working for Daddy on a starting salary that most of us will end our careers being pleased to earn. You've got a cushy number if ever I heard of one,' teased Sebastian, without a hint of malice.

Brett shrugged. 'I know, guys, it's tough at the top,' he joked, wishing he could swap places with any one of them. His four good friends from Cambridge had all *chosen* their future careers, and he would have gladly given up his fat salary to do the same.

Brett had enjoyed his three years at university and was enormously sorry that it was all coming to an end. He had not worked particularly hard, finding the Law course unfulfilling, but he had found his niche and best friends in the more bohemian quarters of the university.

He had become involved with the Footlights dramatic club, painting scenery and even performing in a couple of the revues. And to his surprise, he had still managed to come out of Cambridge with a decent second-class degree.

Brett looked round the table sadly. None of them had decided to take their particular artistic talents any further. They had made their career choices, accepting that the fun they'd had for the past few years would come to an end the minute they received their degrees. Being an undergraduate at Cambridge and behaving in an outrageous manner was part of the fun, before they all settled down to lead nice, civilised lives in respectable professions.

Brett seemed to be the only one who could not accept this. Next week, he would begin working for his father. He was dreading it. In the cloistered world of Cambridge, Brett had been just another student set on having a good time, but even now, only two months after leaving, he could feel the difference between himself and his friends.

'I'll get this, chaps.' Brett opened his wallet, removed a gold American Express card and placed it inside the tatty plastic folder.

'Cheers, Brett,' Sebastian said casually. 'Now, I don't know how the rest of you feel, but I'm not ready to go home yet. And it just so happens that I have some invitations to the hottest party in town tonight. Bella, my sister, got them for me. It's at

Tramp, for the birthday of some model or other. Sounds like there'll be some beautiful women there . . .' He raised his eyebrows.

Brett's heart skipped a beat.

He knew that Leah Thompson was hugely successful, and reputedly one of the highest-earning models in the world. The chances of their paths crossing again were small.

He really had done his best to forget her, but Leah's face suddenly staring at him from the cover of every top magazine during the past few years had made the process somewhat difficult.

He had tried relationships with a number of undergraduates, each one considered a catch for any young man at Cambridge, but that feeling he still harboured for his first love was never replaced. No matter whose soft, feminine flesh was beneath him, he still closed his eyes and imagined Leah.

Rationally, Brett wondered if the experience of his first emotional involvement with a girl had been blown out of all proportion, but his heart still stopped every time he saw a picture of Leah and he found himself dreaming about meeting her again one day.

'Come on, let's get a taxi. We don't want all the best girls to be snapped up before we arrive.' Sebastian stood up from the table as the waiter discreetly returned Brett's gold card.

The doorman hailed them a black cab and they set off in the direction of Tramp.

'*Cara*, tonight you look more radiant than I have ever seen you.' Carlo stood on the doorstep of Leah's mews house in Holland Park and kissed her on both cheeks.

'Thank you, Carlo,' Leah smiled. 'Now come in and meet my mother.'

She ushered him into the hallway, the white dress he had

designed especially for her tonight rustling slightly as she moved. Carlo followed her into the big, comfortable living room, where a woman in her forties was sitting, looking uncomfortable in a formal Yves Saint Laurent black dress.

'Mum, this is Carlo.'

Doreen Thompson stood up. 'It's a pleasure to meet you, Mr Porselli. Our Leah's told me so much about you.'

Leah put a hand on her shoulder. 'Don't you think Mum looks lovely? We went shopping yesterday and chose her dress specially for tonight.' Leah glanced at her proudly.

'Mrs Thompson, you look *bellissima*. I can see where Leah gets her beauty from.'

Doreen fidgeted embarrassedly. 'Well, it's very nice of you to say so, Mr Porselli, but I'm much happier in a skirt and a pinny.'

Carlo looked confused. 'Pinny?'

'Mum means apron,' translated Leah. 'Well, I think that you look a picture. Here, champagne for both of you.' She handed them each a glass.

'Ah, *sì*. It is a night of celebration, but also of sadness. For I am losing my muse to the Americans next week.'

'Honestly, Carlo. Don't be so dramatic! I'm moving to New York because of the cosmetics contract, but also because I seem to spend most of my time over there anyway. You know that's where the action is at the moment.'

Carlo nodded. '*Sì*, Leah. But New York is far away from Milan and that is why I am sad.'

'I'll be over for your show in just over six weeks' time. Now, before we go, I've got something for you, Mum. I know it's my birthday, and you're meant to buy *me* presents. So, before I give it to you, I want you to promise me you'll accept it.' Leah's face was serious as she went to the antique mahogany writing desk and took out an envelope. 'Here.' Leah handed it to her mother. 'Go on, open it.'

Mrs Thompson fingered the vellum envelope and looked at her daughter's excited face. She opened it slowly and drew out a sheaf of papers. She was confronted by incomprehensible legal language, but noted her and Harry Thompson's names printed three or four times on the first page.

'What is it, Leah? It looks like a will,' frowned Doreen.

Carlo and Leah both laughed. 'It's not a will, Mum. It's the deeds to a new bungalow in Oxenhope. I bought it for you and Dad.'

Mrs Thompson sat down silently, shuffling the papers. Leah moved and knelt in front of her. Doreen looked up and saw the tears shining in her daughter's eyes.

'Leah, love, I can't accept this.' Tears were coming to her eyes too. 'You've given me and your dad so much already.'

Leah took her mother's hand. 'You must accept it, Mum. It's one of the reasons I model, to be able to give you and Dad presents. This bungalow has been specially adapted for Dad's wheelchair. It's brand new, with a nice sitting room, a big bedroom for you both and a spare room for when I visit.'

'Oh Leah.' Mrs Thompson promptly burst into tears and the two of them hugged each other tight. 'Thank you. I just hope you haven't used up all your money. You must keep it for yourself. You've earned it, after all.'

'Don't worry. I've got enough to keep me going for years, and Carlo's shown me how to invest it.' Leah smiled. 'I'm going to come to Yorkshire this weekend and show you and Dad around the place,' she said proudly.

Carlo stood watching the tender scene in front of him, then coughed. 'Come, ladies, it is time to go.'

He had waited a long time for this night and he couldn't wait for it to begin.

* * *

LUCINDA RILEY

Miranda Delancey followed the rest of the guests into the famous nightclub. There was a crowd of photographers waiting outside, and she felt like a star. Inside, the place was jam-packed, and she glanced at the banner hanging from the ceiling.

Happy twenty-first, Leah, from all your friends, it read.

Jealousy surged once more inside her. Miranda could hardly believe what had happened to Leah Thompson while she had been stuck at home with dirty nappies and baby sick . . . although she had to admit that it had been nice of Leah to send 'Rose and family' an invitation to the party.

Chloe, Rose and Miranda had travelled down from Yorkshire yesterday. Rose had business to attend to with Roddy, promising to babysit Chloe at his flat so that Miranda could go to the party.

Well, tonight was her chance. And she meant to take it.

As Leah's limousine pulled up in front of the club, the paparazzi gathered round. The proprietor of Tramp greeted her on the steps. Carlo brought up the rear with Mrs Thompson, who was a bright shade of red.

'Carlo, give Leah a birthday kiss, will you?' one of the photographers shouted.

Carlo nodded, swept a surprised Leah off her feet into his arms and kissed her hard on the lips.

'Wonderful!' The flashbulbs popped, just as the taxi bringing Brett and his friends pulled up behind the limousine.

Brett stood transfixed on the pavement as he watched the tall Italian place Leah's feet on the ground once more, put an arm round her exquisite, bare shoulders and disappear inside. Brett felt sick. He had a sudden urge to run away from the club as fast as he could.

'Listen, chaps, I think I've changed my mind. I'm going to head off home. You four go, and I'll . . .'

A barrage of fraternal abuse followed, and he was propelled up towards the doorway by his friends.

By the time they had entered the club, Leah was surrounded by admirers. Brett slunk into a corner where he could remain unnoticed, and prepared to sulk the evening away.

Carlo watched Leah from a distance.

He felt a surge of pride as he remembered the pathetic figure lying in bed in the Milan hotel room, determined to give up on her career and return to anonymity. The poised, elegant female, with the crowd of admirers hanging on her every word, had been his creation. She was at her peak.

Like a piece of raw silk, he had fashioned and shaped her into something extraordinary that belied its humble origins. He had done it with time, skill and patience, taking care to pay attention to detail, as all great designers should. For four years, he had longingly watched those long, sensuous limbs covered in his own garments, but had never once touched her.

Carlo knew that the time he had taken to perfect Leah would be worth it later tonight.

She was twenty-one years old today and Carlo had waited long enough.

'Hello, beautiful. Want to dance?' A tall, older man was bearing down on Miranda. He had a strange foreign accent.

Miranda downed her vodka and Diet Coke. 'Why not?' she said. The man guided her onto the floor and began moving to the beat. She recognised the awkward rhythm as that of an older gentleman who had tried to adapt his skills learned as a teenager in the ballroom to the aggressive music of the modern disco.

Miranda surveyed him. He was a big man, probably in his mid-sixties. Even in the dim light, she could see his face was covered in small blue veins, and that he was severely lacking in the hair department.

Well, love's young dream he was not, but Miranda had noted the gold Rolex peeping from the sleeve of his well-cut, expensive suit. She jumped into action, using all the tricks that she'd seldom employed in the last four years. She moved sensuously, like an animal, brushing against the man just close enough for him to glance down the low cut of her tight gold lamé dress.

The song finished and the man steered her over to the bar.

'Champagne?' he asked.

Miranda nodded.

'So, what's a nice girl like you doing in a place like this?' he quipped boringly as Miranda smiled seductively at him.

'I'm an old friend of the birthday girl.'

'Ahh, Leah Thompson. She is very beautiful, as are you.' The man's finger traced the contours of her chest.

'What about you?' Miranda enquired.

The man gave a shrug. 'I make it my business to know when there is an unmissable party in the city.' He winked. 'Let's go and find a quiet corner and you can tell me all about yourself.' He picked up the bottle of champagne and walked away from the bar, with Miranda following a step behind.

Leah came face to face with Brett Cooper, who had decided to take his leave minutes before, as she emerged from the powder room.

Her heart started to bang mercilessly as she willed herself to remember how he had betrayed her, but all she could see was the boy who had for so long been a part of her dreams.

Brett had grown taller. His youthful features had defined themselves and he resembled Rose more than ever.

As they stood there, memories of those perfect days on

the moors came flooding back, negating the terrible way they had parted.

'Hello,' they said together, and then laughed.

'Happy birthday, Leah.' The sound of his voice saying her name after all this time sent a tingle up Brett's spine.

'Thank you.'

Brett racked his brain for something to say to keep her here.

'You look quite beautiful.' It was corny, but he meant every word of it.

Hearing those words from the lips of Brett meant more to her than any of the hundreds of others who had told her the self-same thing that evening.

'Thank you. You look well. Were you leaving?'

Brett squirmed. 'Er, well . . .'

'There's just about to be a toast for my birthday. At least stay and have some champagne,' Leah said too quickly.

Brett sighed in relief. 'Thank you, I'd be delighted.'

He followed her back inside, just as the music stopped and the club owner moved to the centre of the dance floor. He clapped his hands.

'Ladies and gentlemen, if there are any present.' He laughed. 'I . . .'

'Leah, where have you been? Come with me.' Carlo was frowning as he led Leah off towards the club owner, leaving Brett alone.

She turned back and mouthed, 'See you later,' as Carlo pulled her onto the dance floor.

'I now hand you over to Mr Carlo Porselli –' a cheer went up from the crowd – 'who, as I'm sure you all know, gave our birthday girl her first big break and who is also our host for the evening.' Another resounding cheer went up as the assembled company took a sip of their champagne, courtesy of Carlo.

Brett could see the possessive way the Italian looked at Leah. During his speech, he talked of Leah almost as if she was something he owned. She stood sweetly next to him, head down in embarrassment as Carlo extolled her many virtues.

'Please, will you raise your glasses in a toast? To Leah!'

'To Leah,' chorused the crowd.

'To Leah,' whispered Brett, almost to himself.

'And now, I would like the pleasure of being the first man to dance with you on your special day.' Carlo held out his hand to Leah and led her to the centre of the floor. The crowd cleared around them as the slow, rhythmic beat of 'Woman', Lennon's huge number one hit, echoed out of the powerful speakers.

Brett cringed as Carlo put his arms round Leah and held her close. From the way they were dancing, it was obvious that the two of them were involved romantically. He couldn't bear to watch and turned away.

'Oh Leah, how long I have waited for this night,' Carlo murmured into her hair.

Something about the tone of his voice was different. She thought it similar to that first night in Milan when he had tried to kiss her. Leah immediately felt uncomfortable.

The eyes of the crowd were fixed on the two of them with interest. Leah could almost feel a sense of anticipation.

'Kiss me, Leah,' Carlo whispered, as he tipped her face up to his.

'Carlo, I—'

But his lips were upon hers before she could protest. She pulled away and buried her head in his shoulder as the crowd burst into a spontaneous round of applause.

'Please, Carlo, I'm embarrassed.'

'Still so shy, little one. No matter. There will be plenty of time to be alone later. I want you to come back to my hotel. I have your birthday present in my room.'

The song finished and the DJ began playing a Shakin' Stevens record. The floor filled with eager dancers.

'Excuse me, Carlo, but there is someone I have to see.' Leah extricated herself from his arms and looked around for Brett. She espied him heading for the exit, and moved quickly across to him.

'Trying to sneak out again?'

Brett looked embarrassed. 'Well, yes, actually.'

For all her sophistication, Leah had no knowledge of how to give the impression casually that she didn't want a man to leave.

Brett summoned up some courage. 'What about one quick dance before I go?' he asked bravely.

'Aye aye. Don't tell me you've managed to scoop the belle of the ball tonight?!' Brett's friend Toby joined them, with a dishevelled debutante leaning on one of his shoulders.

'Leah and I are . . . old friends. Come on.' Toby's appearance gave Brett the excuse he needed to take Leah's delicate white hand and lead her onto the dance floor.

Brett wished with all his heart for fate to conspire, and the DJ to place a slow song on his turntable so that he could hold Leah in his arms. Instead, the up-tempo disco beat throbbed unmercifully.

The song came to an end, and the haunting voice of Diana Ross, singing a duet with Lionel Richie, spilled out across the dance floor. Brett took his opportunity and pulled Leah close to him.

'It really is great to see you again after all this time,' he ventured.

'It's good to see you too,' Leah replied.

Feeling her perfect body against his own sent an electric thrill up and down Brett's spine. He pulled her closer.

'I'd love to see you again, Leah. I'd like a chance to explain, about, well, what happened. The problem is, I'm flying to

New York on Sunday. My father has his main office over there and I start work for him next week. Perhaps I could write to you?'

Leah giggled. 'Don't bother buying any airmail envelopes, Brett. I'm off to New York, too. I fly out on Tuesday to start a campaign for Chaval Cosmetics.'

Brett's jaw dropped. 'Wow! What a coincidence! Where are you staying?'

'For the first couple of weeks I'll be at the Plaza Hotel, then I'm going to find an apartment with Jenny, my best friend. She's over there at the moment, working for another cosmetics company.'

'Are you going alone or is Carlo coming with you?' Brett asked cautiously.

'Alone. Carlo has the shows for his collections coming up. He has to fly back to Milan tomorrow.'

Brett tried his best to hide his satisfaction. 'Could I call you at your hotel?'

Leah nodded. 'Yes.'

'Leah.' A hand roughly swung her around. 'I think it is time we left.' Carlo was swaying slightly and Leah could see he was drunk.

'Carlo, I'm afraid I'll have to go straight home. My mother is staying with me, remember? You can give me the present another time.'

The Italian looked as though he was about to explode. '*Permesso*,' he said to Brett, and dragged Leah off towards the front door.

'Stop it, Carlo! You're hurting me!' She tried to free her wrist from his grasp.

'I am sorry, but you must come with me. I have it all arranged.' He was pulling her down the steps and Leah was only glad that most of the paparazzi had gone home.

'Carlo! I said stop it!' She tried to wrench her arm free. This was not the Carlo she knew and she felt a tingle of fear.

At the bottom of the steps, Carlo hailed a cab and Leah struggled helplessly to remove her arm from his vice-like grip.

'I'm not coming with you, Carlo. You're drunk.' He was trying to pull her inside the taxi, and she was doing her best to resist.

'Leah! Get in here! It is all planned!'

'No!' she shouted in desperation.

Two strong arms clasped her shoulders and pulled her backwards and out of Carlo's grasp.

'I don't think the lady wants to come with you, Mr Porselli.'

Leah recognised the voice and turned round to see Miles, with three cameras slung around his neck, standing behind her. He pushed Carlo roughly inside the back of the cab and shut the door.

'Take this man to his hotel.'

The driver saluted Miles and the taxi moved off along the road.

'Thank you, Miles,' Leah managed. Her sentiment could hardly extend to gratefulness after that night in the barn. 'I don't know what's come over him tonight. I've never seen him like that before.'

Miles said nothing. He just stared at her in that strange way of his.

'Leah. Are you okay?' Brett was running towards her, concern written over his face.

'Yes, I'm fine, thanks to Miles.'

'Oh. Hello, Miles.' Brett stuck out his hand, and Miles reluctantly took it. 'What are you doing here?' Brett asked curiously.

'Plying my trade,' said Miles coldly.

'Miles is a freelance photographer. His work is always

appearing in the national newspapers.' Leah failed to mention that Miles spent his time hanging round the entrances of nightclubs and restaurants to catch the rich and famous committing *faux pas*, and selling them to the gutter press in Fleet Street.

'I'll find you a taxi,' said Miles.

'I have to go and fetch my mum. She's still inside.'

'I'll go and find her. You get in the car.' Miles flagged down a passing cab, opened the door for her, then disappeared inside the club.

'Goodbye, Leah. I'll see you in New York.' Brett smiled.

'Yes, I'm looking forward to catching up.'

There was a pause as the pair stood alone on the pavement, staring intently at one another. Brett was just about ready to pull her into his arms when Miles emerged with Mrs Thompson. He kissed Leah chastely on the cheek, waved goodbye to a surprised-looking Doreen, and set off down the street.

Brett strolled home to his father's small Knightsbridge flat, needing the cool night air to clear his thoughts.

Both of them in New York. It had to be fate. What about that Carlo chap? Maybe Brett was too late already, but he had to try. He'd been offered a second chance. This time, he'd get it right.

Not too far behind, Miles also walked home to his tiny rented flat in Chelsea, thinking of Leah. When he got back he grabbed a half-full bottle of whisky from a kitchen cabinet, and poured himself a large glass to calm his rage.

He'd had to use the utmost restraint not to wring that bastard Carlo's neck. Did he not realise that Leah was special? She was a creature to be feted and adored, not treated as if she were some cheap whore. Downing his drink, Miles located the key to his secret room, unlocked the door and entered.

Photographs he had taken of Leah, spanning the majority of her life, adorned every inch of the walls. This was his temple. Miles stood in the centre of the room, inhaled deeply, and slowly turned three hundred and sixty degrees. He breathed Leah in; basked in her ethereal glory. The images had a soothing effect, as they always did.

After a lingering moment, Miles left the room, locked the door behind him and picked up the telephone. He dialled the number and a female voice answered. Following a minute's conversation, he replaced the receiver, glad that she lived only a few streets away.

He opened his cameras, removed the films and stored them in the fridge, just as he always did.

Then he waited.

Ten minutes later, the doorbell rang and Miles let the girl in. Without any preamble, he took her into the bedroom and systematically removed his clothes as she removed hers. Then he switched off the main lights, leaving only the dim glow of the nightlight next to his bed. It was a familiar routine.

The girl was ready for him, her long limbs stretched in anticipation across the bed. This one had lasted longer than most of the whores he bedded. She accepted his rough games, was amenable to his unusual demands and had the added advantage of long mahogany hair. In the half-light, with her hair partly covering her face, he could almost believe that it was Leah.

Miles knelt astride her, enjoying the sensation of dominating the woman beneath. He never kissed them. This wasn't love. There was only one woman who could offer him that.

During the act, Miles enjoyed the screams of pain as the girl writhed beneath him. 'Turn over,' he ordered.

The girl looked frightened. Tonight, there was something different in the client's eyes. Something manic.

'Miles, I . . .' She started to crawl across the bed, but he dragged her back and slapped her hard back and forth across her face until her lip began to bleed.

'Turn over, whore!'

Too frightened to do otherwise, the girl followed his instruction and watched the blood from her lip drop onto the pillow beneath her.

'Miles, please, stop . . .'

Miles couldn't hear her. With a roar, he completed the act. As the girl lay whimpering, her face buried in the pillow, Miles stood up, walked to the en suite bathroom and shut the door behind him. When he came out, the girl was fully dressed and standing by the door, her face swollen, her eyes full of tears.

'Men like you should be locked up. Don't ever call me again. If you do, I'll report you.' She let the door off the latch, before turning to face Miles once more. 'You're going to kill someone one day.' The girl scurried down the corridor, and Miles heard her hurried footsteps descending the two flights of stairs. He smiled, then shrugged.

He would have to find a new one tomorrow.

Miles climbed into his crumpled sheets and pulled off the bloodstained pillowcase with distaste. He felt good now, and calmly closed his eyes.

2

Miranda awoke and felt a thunderous banging in her head. Disoriented, she sat up and looked around. The room did not look familiar and she struggled to remember where she was. In any case, she was naked, with her dress thrown over a chair across the room, along with her underwear and shoes. On the bedside table was a thick pile of cash atop a note. She read it.

Dear Miranda,

Thank you for last night. It was most enjoyable. I am entertaining this weekend on my boat in St Tropez and would like you to join me. Please return here at six p.m. so that we can travel together to the airport.

My assistant is arranging a passport for you, as you mentioned last night that you do not possess one. He will call you this morning.

The boutique downstairs will send up a selection of clothes for you to choose from. Here is some spending money for you to buy yourself a present this afternoon.

The note was signed with an illegible squiggle, punctuated by a kiss. Miranda racked her brain to try and remember the man's name and the complete events of last night. She recalled drinking a lot of champagne and the man leading her unsteadily out of the nightclub. But after that, it was all a blur.

193

'Shit!'

Rose would be in a frenzy. She lifted the telephone by the bed, struggling to remember Roddy's number.

'Reception,' a crisp voice answered. Miranda realised that she was in a hotel.

'Er, yes. I wonder if you would call directory enquiries and get me a number.' Miranda gave the woman Roddy's surname and address.

'Certainly, madam. And can I order breakfast for you?'

The thought of breakfast made Miranda's stomach churn.

'No thanks. But some coffee would be nice.'

'Right away, madam. I'll call you back as soon as I have that number for you. And can I tell the boutique to send up the clothes you ordered?'

Miranda was lost for words. 'Sure,' was her eventual response.

While Miranda waited for the telephone to ring, she thought about what she was going to say to Rose. Surely she couldn't turn down this opportunity? She had to follow her catch to France. This was what she'd dreamed of all her life: an invitation to join the jet set.

Rose would understand.

'Don't be too jealous, Leah!' She giggled as reception rang to provide Roddy's number.

Miranda thought for a while, then dialled. Roddy answered.

'Hi, Roddy, it's Miranda.'

'Oh, thank God! Where are you? Your mother's been half out of her mind with worry. I had to stop her from calling the police.'

Miranda cringed. 'I'm fine. Tell Rose I'm twenty-one and not a child any more.'

Roddy managed a small chuckle. 'Well, you might have told us where you were going, sweetie. Your mother has been on the phone to everyone this morning. No one knew where you'd got to.' Roddy's criticism elicited no response from Miranda. 'Anyway, your mother wants to get back to Yorkshire with Chloe. What time are you coming here?'

Miranda sniffed. 'Actually, I'm not coming back with her. A friend of Leah's has invited me to a party for the weekend. Tell Rose I'm fine, that I'll see her on Monday, and ask her to kiss Chloe for me. Bye, Roddy.' Miranda put the telephone down before he could reply.

A twinge of guilt pricked at Miranda as she thought of her daughter. But, she comforted herself, she had given all her attention to Chloe for four years. Didn't she deserve some fun too?

The telephone rang again. Reception announced the caller as 'Ian Devonshire'. Miranda had no idea who he was, but instructed them to connect the call.

'Hello?'

'Hello, Miranda. My name's Ian Devonshire. I work for Mr Santos. He's asked me to sort you out a passport *tout de suite*.'

'Okay.' A smile crept onto Miranda's lips at the service that was being provided. And she now knew her lover's name.

'I need to take your second name and a few details so that I can get hold of a copy of your birth certificate from Somerset House.'

'My surname is Delancey. My date of birth is the twenty-third of July 1960.'

'Thanks. I'll come by the hotel at midday with the forms. You can sign them and I'll take them to the passport office. I've a friend there who'll process your application this afternoon. Can you get two photographs of yourself done by lunchtime? There's a booth at Charing Cross station, just down the road from the Savoy.'

The Savoy! Was that really where she was? A frisson of excitement ran through Miranda. She confirmed that she'd get the photos done and meet Ian in the American Bar downstairs at midday.

As she put down the phone, there was a knock on the door. She jumped out of bed too fast and felt dizzy and nauseous.

'Just coming,' she called as she looked around the room in desperation for something to cover her nakedness. She ended up pulling the sheet from the bed and draping it round her, toga style.

After she opened the door, a young man wheeled in a trolley containing her coffee, plus a red rose and a bottle of champagne on ice.

'I didn't order the champagne,' she said hurriedly.

The boy smiled. 'Compliments of Mr Santos.'

There was another knock on the door.

'May I open it for you, madam?' The boy asked.

Miranda nodded. Another porter in the same smart uniform wheeled in a large pile of boxes and bags.

'A selection of garments from the boutique, madam. Mr Santos has asked you to choose whatever you want. If there is nothing here that you like, please come downstairs, where I'm sure the manager can find something to suit you.'

Both men stood staring at her expectantly, and it suddenly dawned on Miranda that they wanted a tip. She remembered the pile of notes by the bed, and went to pick them up. She gasped as she realised that the pile of thirty-odd bills were all fifties. She had no choice, so handed the boys one note.

'Share it between you,' she said grandly, vaguely noting the look of disappointment on their faces. No doubt Mr Santos would have given them one each. Once the hotel staff had left, Miranda walked over to the heavy mahogany door on the opposite side of the large bedroom. She opened it, expecting to find a bathroom, but instead found herself in a sumptuous sitting room, with large picture windows flanked by gold damask curtains. She wandered over to them, threading her way through the heavy, expensive furniture.

Miranda drew in her breath as she looked out over the Embankment and the silver water of the Thames running beneath her. This *had* to be a penthouse suite. She returned to the bedroom and grabbed as many of the clothes boxes as she could. Once she had transferred everything to the sitting room, she poured herself a coffee.

She knelt on the floor, surrounded by the boxes. Where to start? Why, the largest, of course. She excitedly removed the lid. On the top, resting on the tissue paper, was a small gold-edged card reading: *The Savoy Hotel, with compliments.*

Miranda jumped up and did a little jig around the room, hardly believing this was happening. She bent down and pulled back the layers of soft tissue paper. Inside was the most exquis-ite evening dress she had ever seen. It was fashioned out of black silk and carried the name of a world-famous designer on the label.

Hurriedly, Miranda divested herself of her sheet, put the dress on, and went back into the bedroom to look at herself in the full-length mirror. It fitted her perfectly. She twirled, with one hand holding her hair up in a knot on her head.

'Watch out, Leah, I'm coming to get you,' she gloated as she ran back to the sitting room to open the other boxes, like a child on Christmas morning.

An hour later, the room was scattered with tissue paper, labels, and thousands of pounds' worth of expensive clothing draped over the furniture. Miranda was sitting in black silk undies with a Hermès scarf tied round her neck, admiring the soft leather shoes on her feet.

Disappointedly, she noticed that there was only one small package left to open. She grabbed it and tore the lid off. Inside were two leather-bound boxes, one smaller than the other, which she investigated first. She found a pair of twinkling diamond earrings shaped like teardrops. In the larger box was a fabulous necklace to match.

'Wow,' breathed Miranda.

Having recovered from her hangover, she went over to the trolley and poured herself a glass of champagne.

'Here's to you,' Miranda toasted herself. She took a sip and made room among the clothes to sit on the sofa. All this for a quick shag that she couldn't even remember.

'I must have been good.' She smirked as she took another sip.

Eventually, Miranda showered and chose a pink silk blouse matched with a beautifully cut Chanel suit. She left the room, made her way downstairs and asked the concierge directions to Charing Cross station.

After a brisk walk down the road, she changed one of the fifty-pound notes at the ticket office.

Miranda checked her watch as she waited for the photos to drop out of the slot. Ten to twelve. Just enough time to get back to the hotel and meet Ian Devonshire in the bar.

Not really considering the possibility that there was anything strange about the morning's happenings – for Miranda had been quite sure for her entire life that someday this *would* happen to her – she sauntered back to the Savoy, went into the bar and sat down.

'Miranda?'

'Yes.'

A plain young man sporting a smart suit and a thick pair of glasses sat down opposite her.

'Ian Devonshire.' He presented his hand, which Miranda shook. 'Good to meet you. Can I offer you a drink?'

'Yes please, a white wine for me.'

Ian ordered, then pulled a sheaf of papers from his briefcase. He looked a little awkward.

'Now, I presume you know that you're . . . you weren't . . .' Ian looked hopeful that Miranda might be able to finish his sentence for him, but she had no idea what he was driving at. 'Are you aware that you're adopted?'

'Yes,' she confirmed, and Ian looked relieved. 'Have you got my original birth certificate there, then?' Miranda asked.

'Yes.'

'Can I take a look?'

Ian handed her the piece of paper, and Miranda gazed at it with interest. 'So, my birth name was Rosstoff.' She glanced up at Ian, an idea running through her mind. 'You know, I prefer my original name. Can I have "Rosstoff" on my passport?' Miranda calculated that Rose would find it more difficult to trace her if she decided to stay away for . . . a little longer.

'I don't see why not. I'll ask my friend.'

Miranda smiled. 'Good.'

'Now, I just need you to sign here.' Ian indicated the spot on the passport form. 'And check that the details I've filled in are correct.' Miranda complied. 'Super. I'll get this off to the passport office straight away and have the documents back to you by four this afternoon.'

'Mr Santos must be a powerful man to be able to arrange all this for me,' Miranda fished.

Ian nodded his head. 'Absolutely. Although he doesn't visit London very often, he has plenty of connections.'

'Where does he live?' Miranda enquired.

'South America,' Ian replied, not making eye contact.

'Do you do this kind of thing for him often? I mean, arrange passports?'

Ian shrugged. 'As I said, he's not here too often. Anyway, I'm afraid I must leave you and get on with the job in hand. It's nice to meet you, Miss Delancey . . .' He put a finger in the air and corrected himself. '. . . Miss Rosstoff. Have a good trip to France.'

Ian left the bar and Miranda sat sipping her drink thoughtfully.

Who was this Mr Santos? She tried to remember if she'd ever heard his name mentioned on television or in the papers.

No. For a second, a flicker of doubt passed through her mind. Should she be going off with some strange man all alone? He could be involved in the Mafia, for all she knew. Or human trafficking.

On the other hand . . . here she was at the Savoy, dressed in thousands of pounds of designer clothes. All the hotel staff seemed to know Santos, and Ian had seemed very straight down the line.

Suddenly exhausted, Miranda stood up and walked towards the lift, too engrossed in her own thoughts to notice a man who had been sitting quietly in a corner of the bar stand up too.

He watched her call the lift, and left the hotel.

Miranda opened the door to her suite. The chambermaid had obviously been in, for all the clothes had been replaced in their boxes, and the bed made.

She sank down onto the comfortable bed gratefully, deciding to take a nap and then spend the rest of the afternoon preparing herself for Santos's return. Miranda closed her eyes, her mind whirling from the events of the past few hours. Feeling more content now than ever before, she drifted off to sleep.

3

'Hello, David.' The tall, bearded man shook his hand warmly. 'How are you?'

'Well, thanks. I was beginning to think I wouldn't be hearing from you again. It's been over eight months since we last had contact.'

The man narrowed his eyes. 'There are reasons for that, I assure you. As you are learning, this game of chess is incredibly long. Each move has to be thought out with absolute precision. This particular operation has taken years – no doubt with more to come.'

David sat down behind his desk and invited his guest to take a seat.

'Did you proceed with the security checks we suggested?' asked the man.

David nodded. 'I did. The team has been over this office with a fine-tooth comb. I can assure you that it is perfectly safe to talk.'

The man sighed. 'Talking is something that is never perfectly safe. However, I wished to see you at your office to avoid arousing suspicion. Underground car parks at midnight and arranged meetings on deserted beaches at dawn are for the movies. This is reality.' There was an uncomfortable pause between the men. 'Things are beginning to progress, both on our side, and from your point of view. Am I right?'

David swallowed hard. 'Yes. I have done as you asked. You can understand how difficult all this has been for me. But the project began six months ago and I am winning his trust.'

The man looked pleased. 'You are performing well. But I warn you, he is a clever individual.'

'You've been watching him for all these years?'

'Yes.'

'Then why wait until now to make a move? It seems that you're moving at a snail's pace.'

The man shrugged. 'In dealing with cases like this, and I can assure you that there are many others, watertight evidence must be gathered. We have found that as time passes, our enemies grow more confident, less careful, and eventually they make a mistake. If it takes a lifetime, that is of little importance.'

David stared silently at the man. 'I'm finding it all very difficult,' he muttered.

The man leaned back in the deep leather chair. 'Yes, I imagine you are. But you are perfect for this, Mr Cooper. Not forgetting your *personal* motivations to help us, you harbour certain similarities to the target. You both have a past that you have chosen, understandably, to forget. You are both powerful, well-known and beyond reproach in your business dealings.' The man sucked his teeth. 'Generally, like for like produces a good bait.'

David was unsure of what to say. The response had hardly been full of sympathy. He had learned over the last four years that these people weren't in the habit of doling out such a thing.

The man spoke again. 'We ask you to continue your joint business venture and take time to get to know him. Become his friend. To trap him, there are certain circumstances that must be arranged. You will be informed of those nearer the time.'

David tapped his index finger slowly on his marble-topped desk. 'I have to tell you that . . . on many occasions I've considered refusing this task.'

The man let out a low chuckle. 'No you haven't, Mr Cooper. You were carefully selected to perform this role for us. I do not wish to remind you of who you are, but . . . it is time for the circle to close. And it is your right to close it.' He reached his hand out across the desk. 'Goodbye, David.'

The man walked across the spacious office, opened the door and closed it behind him.

David let out a breath and rubbed his forehead. He felt drained and exhausted. He hadn't slept last night, his mind dizzy with thoughts of today's meeting.

It had been four years since the past had crept back into his life, but the nightmares still woke him. The memories were undimmed by the passage of time.

David ran a hand through his hair. They were expecting too much, surely? He was putting not only himself, but his entire business at risk.

But then, as he always did, David remembered the promise he had made when he was fourteen years old . . .

4

Poland, 1942

David felt that even death could be no worse, as he sat, holding a weeping Rosa to him in a tiny corner of the train truck, listening to the hum of the train as it rattled across Poland. Others had come prepared, with food supplies and drink, but all they had was the violin, some paper and pencils and Rosa's precious teddy bear. Only when Rosa screamed in desperation for a drink and something to eat did an older woman take pity on her and hand her a small phial of water and half a cold sausage.

The heat in the closed truck was unbearable, and the stink of excrement mixed with disinfectant on old straw would live in his memory for ever. David talked little to the others, simply listening to their conversations as they pondered what fate awaited them at the end of their journey. He already knew. He hoped it would be fast, however they did it, for Rosa's sake, if not his own.

The women were pulling their jewellery from their necks, arms and fingers and hiding it in their underwear. David followed suit, secreting the precious locket with the passport in the lining of his violin case.

As the journey progressed, a man next to him keeled over from a heart attack and died in David's lap. *A blessed escape,* he thought quietly, as the man's wife cried piteously for the rest of the night. She held her dead husband to her bosom, the man's legs still straddled across David.

At first light, the train screeched to a halt. David peered through the tiny barbed-wire grille and saw a sign on the platform: *Treblinka*. He could make out several railway workers alongside some SS officers. The train moved again, stopped, then lurched backwards, throwing the occupants of the carriage violently against each other.

David could see that their carriage, alongside a few others, was being pushed into a siding. The light faded as dense forest surrounded them, before some huts came into view, and behind them, what appeared to be a huge pile of shoes. The train entered a clearing, and David glimpsed barbed-wire fencing enclosing some sort of camp. Before that was a strip of land broadened into a makeshift platform. There were SS men everywhere, some carrying whips. Sentries stood in black uniforms by the fence, holding rifles.

As the train halted again, other occupants of the carriage piled behind David, desperately trying to see out of the grille. Few had the chance. Immediately, the doors were opened, and the sentries clambered in to start hurling the occupants out.

'David! David!' Rosa's screams filled his head as she was dragged away by a guard and disappeared into the mass of crying, screaming people on the platform.

Still clutching his precious violin, David moved along the platform as they were herded towards an open gate in the middle of the fence. He called Rosa's name over and over, but it was impossible to make himself heard above the dreadful noise of desperation.

'Oh Mama, oh Mama,' he repeated as he was pushed towards a yard, with cries of '*Schnell! Raus!*' resounding from the sentries.

As they entered the yard, women were being ordered to one side, and men to the other. David searched desperately for a sight of Rosa among the women, but it was impossible. Unaware of the tears that were streaming down his face, he sat down with the others and started to take off his shoes, as directed by a group of Jewish men wearing armbands. They were handing out pieces of thread so the prisoners could tie their shoes together.

As one of the men with armbands approached, he looked down at the violin sitting next to David.

'Is that yours?' he asked in Polish.

David nodded.

'Do you play?'

'Of course.'

The man looked relieved for David. 'I'll tell the guard.' He continued handing out the bits of thread, then disappeared.

David could see that the women were being ordered into a hut on the other side of the yard. It was not large enough to accommodate them, so some were made to stand outside and remove their clothes.

A sentry instructed the men to do the same. As David was about to remove his trousers, he was hauled to his feet.

'Play!'

David turned around to see an SS officer behind him, pointing to his violin.

Disoriented, David swayed silently. A whip cracked across his bare chest.

'Play!'

David opened his case with trembling hands. He put the violin under his chin and picked up his bow. Try as he might, no tune would come into his brain.

The rest of the men stared up at him silently. They were all naked.

'Liar!'

As David watched the whip come towards him for a second time, his brain jumped into action. He lifted his bow and began to play the soft, soulful melody of Brahms' Violin Concerto. The sweet sound filled the yard. Some of the naked men wept.

'Enough. Wait over there!'

David managed to snatch up the violin case before he was dragged by the arm and pushed into a hut. He peered through a hole and watched as the naked men were pushed through an opening in the fence. The women had gone too.

Packages and clothes were strewn across the wasteland.

David sank to his knees, head in hands. Weak from fear, lack of food and sleep, his mind wandered back to the times his family had gathered together in the drawing room and he had played the violin which had just saved his life.

His imagination dared not conjure up what was happening to his little sister, his precious Rosa. His only hope was that it was all over for her now and she was at peace.

He heard a noise in the yard, which prompted him to look through the hole once more. About fifteen of the Jewish men with armbands appeared. Under the supervision of the sentries, they started to clear the bundles of clothing.

David looked around the hut. There were piles of rags strewn over the floor, alongside cups, plates and pyjama tops. This was obviously some kind of dormitory. Still naked from the waist up, David grabbed a shirt lying on the floor next to him and pulled it over his head. He noticed that the material was good; the shirt almost brand new.

The door to the hut opened and a stream of bleeding Jewish prisoners entered, followed by a sentry.

'Follow me!' he barked at David.

David hugged his violin case as he crossed the yard. The sentry led him towards another hut. Inside were groups of men dressed in all manner of strange attire. They were sitting at long wooden benches and eating hungrily from their bowls. The soldier pointed to an older gentleman with a somehow familiar face. 'Get your soup, then see Albert Goldstein. He is in charge.'

David took a bowl of the delicious-smelling soup from a woman standing behind a trestle table. As he sat next to the man designated as his superior, recognition struck him. This was one of Warsaw's most eminent musical directors.

'Mr Goldstein . . . I cannot tell you how honoured I am to meet—'

Albert Goldstein waved him quiet. 'Eat, then we'll talk.'

David did so, amazed at how palatable the meal was – better than anything he'd eaten during his time in the ghetto. The food nourished him and his dizziness slowly abated.

When Albert had scraped out every last mouthful from his bowl, he turned to David. 'So, what do you play, boy?'

'The violin, sir.'

Albert wiped his mouth with his hand. 'I might have guessed. Our last violinist met with . . . an accident.' He raised an eyebrow. 'Are you good?'

'I am nothing compared to the men I have seen you conduct, sir. But, for my age, I was considered a talent in Warsaw.' Albert gave him a nod. 'Could you tell me, please, where we are and what will have happened to my sister?'

The older man stared at him, sorrow in his eyes.

'How old are you, boy?'

'Fourteen, sir.'

'Your sister?'

'Eleven, sir.'

Albert sighed deeply. 'Come, we will go to our quarters.'

David followed Mr Goldstein back across the yard and into yet another hut. This one was cleaner than the last, and had several thin mattresses on the floor. The maestro pointed to one in the corner, which was without a blanket.

'There. That was Josef's, and now it will be yours.'

'Josef?'

'Yes. The last violinist.'

'Please, sir, can you explain this place to me? Where did the other people from my train go?' David knew the answer in his heart, but he needed to have it confirmed.

Albert looked him in the eye. 'To their deaths. I am sorry to tell you that you are in Treblinka. It is not a labour camp. It is a place where the Germans bring Jews to exterminate us. Your neck was saved by that.' He pointed to David's violin.

David's eyes filled with tears. 'And my sister?' he asked bravely.

Albert shook his head sadly. 'Women are of little use, especially children. Do not hope. It is best to understand now the mentality of our captors.'

A small cry escaped David's lips.

'Every single person still alive in this hell-hole has lost their families. We all live with the guilt daily: that we are alive and they are not. But as you will see, your little sister may have had a blessed escape. What you will witness every day . . . it will turn your heart to stone.' Albert was staring at the floor.

'What do you mean, sir?'

'The musical trio of which you are now a member is forced to play as the officers send families to their deaths.' Now Albert's eyes reddened. 'It helps drown out the screams of those inside the gas chamber and keeps those who are waiting their turn calm. Boy, you will watch as people in their thousands walk to their deaths, believing they are going to the shower.'

David could stand no more, and sank to the floor.

'I am sorry, boy, but it is for the best that you are aware of the situation. It is also our duty to entertain the German guards and their Ukrainian whores after dinner.'

'Ukrainian?' David enquired.

'Yes. Not just women, either. You'll find most of the soldiers here are Ukrainian, operating under German instruction. They're effectively prisoners, too. This entire area was controlled by the Soviets after the annexation in 1939 – Poles, Ukrainians, Belarussians . . . but then came "Operation Barbarossa". Now the Germans run this entire district.' David's face was ashen. 'Maybe now you see that you were not the lucky one. The massacre continues throughout night and day. And we must watch it happen.'

David tried to gather himself. 'My parents, they too were taken from Warsaw.'

'What is your name?'

'David Delanski, sir.'

Hope jumped into Albert's eyes. 'Delanski? As in Jacob Delanski?'

David nodded.

'You are his son?'

'Yes, sir.'

Albert smiled. 'Then I have good news for you. Your father is alive. He is the camp painter. He lives in this very dormitory and produces portraits for our captors.'

David's eyes shone. 'Sir! I can hardly believe it!'

'Quite. It is only moments such as these that make me believe there is still hope in the universe. But there is no room for sentimentality here. I must warn you now that every second you live, your life is in peril. The officers take pleasure in shooting for the sake of it. In their eyes, there is always another Jew to replace you with. And please, be very careful around the deputy commandant . . .' Albert shuddered.

'What's his name?' David asked.

'Kurt Franzen. Never, ever do anything to attract attention to yourself while in his company. He is the most evil, sadistic man I have ever had the horror to encounter. No doubt you will meet him shortly. Now, let me tell you the rules of the camp.'

David listened as Albert explained that his father, Jacob, was part of a small group of '*Hofjuden*', the privileged Jews, who performed services for the Germans. Among them were carpenters, mechanics, shoemakers and jewellers. There was no shortage of food or clothing, due to the large amount of supplies coming in daily to the camp with those who had no further use for such things.

'Physically, we are comfortable, more comfortable than perhaps you were in the ghetto, if you can avoid the beatings. Stay out of trouble and try to hang on to your sanity. Now, let me hear you play. We will be called out soon for roll call and we must perform perfectly to avoid flying bullets.'

The other member of the trio joined them and for the next two hours they practised well-known pre-war tunes that brought tears to David's eyes.

Roll call arrived and David followed Albert out onto a small wooden platform positioned in the middle of the assembly yard. David looked down at the sea of people lined up in front of them. Three names were called out by a German officer. The men stepped forward, their faces creased in fear. They were positioned in a line in front of the wooden platform and, one by one, thrown across a small stool and whipped.

David wobbled as faintness hit him. He thought he would fall off, but a vice-like grip on his arm stopped him.

'I told you not to draw attention to yourself,' hissed Albert under his breath.

After the lashing was complete, the SS guard turned towards the ragged figures on the wooden stand and nodded.

The trio began to play.

Twenty minutes later, they queued up in the mess hall for their food. David searched the room for a sight of his father, and spotted him sitting at a table on the other side of the room.

'Papa!' He left the queue and ran over. David's joyous greeting seemed to carry no meaning for the gaunt man sitting in front of him. Jacob simply took no notice of his son and continued eating.

'Papa? It is me, David! Your son! *Jak się masz?* How are you?'

Jacob stopped eating and sat stock-still. The man sitting next to him moved out of his chair to allow David to sit down.

'He doesn't hear us, but try again,' the man said softly.

David sat and put his hand on the thin wrist of his father.

'Papa, please. It's David.'

Jacob's hollow face turned towards his, and David watched as the empty eyes filled with recognition.

'Is it really you, David? Am I dead and in Heaven?'

'No, Papa. You are alive. They let me live because I play the violin. Is Mama . . . ?' David's voice trailed off.

Jacob looked past his son. 'She was taken.' He stared silently into the distance. Then his eyes landed back on David's face, as if he was remembering.

'Rosa?'

David shook his head.

'So young, so much talent. Tell me, why do *we* live?' Jacob searched his son's face for the answer, but found none. He stood up.

'Goodbye, my son.' Jacob left the table. David was about to stand, but a hand pulled him down.

'Listen. You must understand that your father has lost the will to live,' the man whispered. 'He has stopped painting for the past two days. He just sits and stares at his easel. The Germans are growing angry. He has little time left.'

'Then I must help him.'

'There is nothing you can do. Rumour has it that a new artist was brought in on the last train.'

'I am his son! I will go to him!' David pushed the man roughly away and walked towards the door of the mess hall. Back in the dormitory, Albert and Filip, the cellist, were getting ready for their evening session. There was no sign of Jacob.

'Have you seen my father?' David asked Albert.

'Yes. He was wanted in the room where he paints. It's next door to the furrier's shop, just to the left at the end of this row of huts. You'll see an easel by the window.'

'Thank you.' David made to leave.

'Don't be late. We start in ten minutes!' shouted Albert.

Outside, David noticed that the fast darkening sky was lit by a terrific red glow. A dark, murky smoke was billowing out across the camp, and the air was thick with the dreadful stench of burning flesh. He ran along the huts, saw the easel and entered the small room behind it.

Jacob was sitting on a chair, motionless in the dim room.

'Father!' David ran and knelt in front of him. As he did so, the door opened and an SS officer entered, carrying a painting in his arms.

'Father, please,' he whispered.

'*Schnell!* Attention!' shouted the officer. He put the painting on the easel, and moved it next to another painting, which David recognised as his father's work. The officer left the hut, and was replaced by another, who held an oil lamp in one hand. David could just make out another, smaller figure holding his other hand, hidden behind him.

He turned back to Jacob. 'Father, please, I—'

'What did you say?' cried the officer. 'Rise, both of you!'

David stood up and looked into a pair of such malevolently evil eyes that his body shuddered involuntarily.

'I asked you a question. What did you say a moment ago?' The SS officer's face was just inches away from David's.

'I said "Father," sir.'

The officer's eyes darted in the direction of Jacob, who was standing, still staring straight ahead. He put the oil lamp on a table and its glow lit the room.

'Well, this is quite the coincidence. Truly, a Delanski family gathering.' The man's harsh German accent blunted the mellow language of David's homeland. The officer pushed the small figure behind him into the middle of the room. 'Three of you in one room. Say hello to your brother and father, Rosa.'

David gasped as Rosa's terrified expression gave way to joy. She ran to him. He closed his arms protectively around her, hardly daring to believe that it was her. Then Rosa saw Jacob. His eyes were still fixed on a point above them.

'Papa!' she squealed. She threw her arms around his neck and covered him with kisses.

The officer seemed to be watching the scene with a degree of pleasure.

'Well, it seems as though you have solved my problem. I was going to call one of the *Hofjuden* to help me, but I believe that your opinion will be far more discerning. See here.' The officer pointed his stick at the two paintings, standing side by side. 'One is painted by your father, the other by your sister. One of the guards told me that she could paint, so I had her draw this for me this afternoon. It is a sketch of my dog, Wolf.' The officer turned to face David. 'Of course, it is bad economy to have two artists in the camp. So, I would ask you to choose which painting you think best.'

It took David a few moments to comprehend what he was being asked to do. The horror of it struck him as he turned to see his sister, now clasped in the tight embrace of her father. Jacob was looking down at his daughter, caressing her hair disbelievingly.

'Well, Herr Delanski? Which is it to be? Rosa's, or your father's?'

David looked desperately around for help, for some heavenly guidance. There was none. Surely this wasn't happening. How could anyone make such a decision and expect to retain their sanity?

'I want an answer, boy!' The officer was drawing out his pistol. David knew what he must do. He got down on his hands and knees in front of the officer.

'Take me, sir. Please, I beg of you. Then there will be one less mouth to feed, as you requested.'

The officer shook his head very slowly, a look of mock concern on his face. 'But we can't do that, boy. You are needed for our little orchestra. *Choose!*'

David was dragged to his feet by his collar and stood in front of the paintings.

Help me, Mama!

It was an inner scream as he stared desperately and unseeingly at the two paintings.

'Well, boy. If you find it impossible to choose, clearly you think neither of the artists is worthy. I will have to look around for another from the next intake.'

'*No!*' David turned, his entire body shaking, tears streaming down his cheeks. Rosa and Jacob were staring at him.

His father gave him an imperceptible nod and, with a slight movement of his head, indicated Rosa.

David heard the pistol being drawn behind him.

His breathing was so fast he could hardly speak.

God, Mama, Papa, forgive me.

'Rosa.' It was no more than a whisper.

'I am sorry, boy. Did you speak?'

'Rosa.'

'Louder!'

'Rosa!' David screamed and ran towards the door. The SS officer who had brought in the paintings was blocking the exit. He pushed David roughly back into the room.

'Good. I agree with you. My dog's portrait is indeed excellent. Rosa! Come and stand by your brother. He has chosen you to continue your father's work.'

Jacob kissed the top of his daughter's head as she clung to him. Then he gently pushed her away. David held out his arms and she ran to them.

The officer pointed his pistol at Jacob. He fired three times.

The air was filled with Rosa's hysterical screams. The officer took hold of her arm and pulled her away from David.

'Please, sir, can she not at least stay with me for a short time?' David begged, as Rosa screamed his name over and over again.

'I will take care of our little protégée.' He pushed Rosa roughly out of the door and into the arms of the other SS officer. Then he turned back into the room.

'My name is Franzen. Do not forget it. I will be meeting with you again soon, I am sure.' He smiled once more, then left David alone with the bullet-riddled body of his father.

David had little idea of how much time had passed. One day of terror, humiliation and pain melted into another. He knew it must be approaching winter when the camp awoke to frosts. The snow started to fall and David watched the naked men and women turn blue as they waited in line to go to their deaths.

Now he understood why his father had disappeared inside himself. The horror of what he had witnessed daily was a surreal nightmare from which he never awoke.

216

Every day David lived, he prayed to die.

He would lie awake at night and ask God why innocent people were being punished in this way. There was never an answer, so eventually, David had stopped praying. His faith disappeared along with his perception of reality. He had accepted that no one was coming to save him and his sister. He was going to have to do that himself.

Rosa was alive and well. She was living in the Ukrainian women's quarters. Franzen, from whom he had witnessed unspeakable atrocities, seemed to have taken a shine to her. He had instructed one of the women he treated as his personal whores to take Rosa under her wing.

Her name was Anya, and she worked in the kitchens at the camp. She was sixteen, very pretty and sweet-natured, and doted on Rosa. David could see that she was more frightened of Franzen than his sister was.

David sighed and turned over, knowing he must sleep. Ideas of escape buzzed about his mind. During the past few months, he had managed to hide a pile of paper money, gold coins and jewellery under the floorboards in his dormitory. He knew all the other prisoners did the same. Such things were found secreted in the possessions of those who had already died, and Ukrainian guards were prepared to swap fresh fruit and meat for money when rations to the camp were diminished. David thought of his treasure as his passport, which he could use once he had managed to get Rosa and himself away from the camp.

Tears stung his eyes as he realised how useless it all was. The dense forest and easily bribed Ukrainians who lived outside the camp in the surrounding villages made escape almost impossible. Since he had been in Treblinka, every prisoner who had tried to escape had been captured, returned and shot by Franzen in front of the rest of the camp. Then he had taken every tenth man from roll call and murdered them too.

There *had* to be a way. If they stayed much longer, they would die anyway. David closed his eyes and tried once more to sleep.

'So, Rosa, *Liebchen*. Let me see the picture you have painted today.'

Rosa stood nervously in front of Officer Franzen's desk and passed her canvas across the table. He took it and smiled widely.

'How pretty. I think you are getting better, yes? Come and give Uncle Kurt a kiss, Rosa.' He held out his arms.

Rosa walked round the table. She was pleased that he always seemed to like her art, and enjoyed her daily reward of sweets. Uncle Kurt had been very kind to her since she and David had arrived at Treblinka. He always made sure that she had warm clothes, tasty food, and gave her lots of presents. It made her feel very special.

But when she had to kiss him, his thick moustache would spike her lips, and his breath always smelled of cigarettes.

Franzen picked her up and sat her on his knee, then tapped his mouth. Rosa was familiar with the routine. She gave him a kiss. When she went to pull away, Franzen grabbed the back of her head, and tried to open her teeth with his tongue.

Franzen smiled at Rosa. 'Good, good. You are getting better. Tomorrow I will teach you another game you will enjoy.'

'Yes, Herr Franzen.' She climbed off Franzen's knee and headed towards the door. Once it was closed behind her, she ran as fast as her legs could carry her to her dormitory, where Anya was lying on her mattress, her eyes closed.

'Are you feeling all right, Anya? You look unhappy.'

Anya opened her eyes and looked at Rosa. 'Yes, of course. I am fine. It is time you slept. I must get ready for this evening.'

While Rosa undressed and donned an oversized nightie, Anya put on a dress that she had found among the piles of clothing brought in yesterday to the sorting hut. It said it was made by Chanel. She hoped Franzen would like it and it would hide the growing bulge in her stomach. If he saw that . . . she knew her life was over. She'd heard dreadful stories from others who had witnessed women being shot by the SS officers when they grew tired of them.

She put on some lipstick and piled her soft golden hair on top of her head.

Although just five years older than Rosa, Anya was already a grown woman. She had come into the camp a year ago, when her parents, half-starved and desperate for money, had heard of a vacancy in the kitchen through a neighbour in their village. Her father had encouraged it, but her mother had begged him not to make Anya work for the Nazis. Despite her mother's protests, the fact was that the family needed to eat.

So Anya had begun to work at Treblinka.

A week after she had arrived, Franzen had invited her to his quarters. He had offered her wine and food, the quality of which she had never experienced before. She was grateful, and did not initially reject Franzen's advances when they came after the meal. But he would not stop when she had requested, then demanded, then begged. That night, he had raped her, and ordered her to live at the camp. If she were to refuse him, he said he would have her parents shot.

For the past year, Anya had been subjected to such acts of humiliation and indecency that she felt no more human than the camp's prisoners. Sometimes, if she refused, Franzen would produce his pistol and make her perform with it pointed at her head. He had shared her around, too, with countless others. It was often to reward another officer for doing good work.

In public, he showered Anya with presents, and treated her as though she was a goddess. As a result, the prisoners spat at her when they passed, but she knew that if she didn't give Franzen what he wanted, then others would be chosen instead.

The only person that she had ever seen him show kindness towards was Rosa. Franzen had taken a shine to the girl from the moment she had arrived at the camp. She believed his affection was genuine, and thanked God, for Rosa's sake.

Of course, Anya had thought countless times of escape. Each night, as she lay on her mattress, mortified and ashamed of what Franzen had made her do, she vowed that it would be the last time. And now there was no choice. She was pregnant and guessed that she was over five months gone. Anya could not hide it from him much longer. He liked her because of her slim, supple body, which was fast disappearing. The child wouldn't save her. Anya wouldn't be deemed worthy enough to birth a member of the 'master race'. She had no idea if Franzen was the father, either. It could be any one of the dozen other SS officers she'd been used by.

Recently, she had heard him talking with the commandant of the camp. They were discussing the fact that soon Treblinka would be only a peaceful farmyard with no trace of what had gone on there.

Anya applied some lipstick in her precious broken piece of mirror and saw the fear in her eyes. If she tried to run, her parents, and no doubt Anya herself, would be shot.

Although sometimes she wondered if she would not be better off dead.

'Hello, Rosa!' Franzen smiled. 'What have you painted for Uncle Kurt today?'

'A picture of a lake,' she replied.

'A lake, you say? Wonderful. Bring it here and let me have

a look.' Rosa padded round to join Franzen on the other side of his desk, and laid out her work.

He inspected it, nodding in approval. 'It is very beautiful, Rosa. Just like you. Here –' He reached into a drawer and produced a paper bag full of red liquorice. Rosa went to take a piece, but Franzen grabbed her hand.

'You must be hungry today!' Rosa nodded. 'Here. Let Uncle Kurt feed you.' He took a piece of the liquorice. 'Open wide.'

Rosa followed the instruction, and Franzen popped the red sweet onto her tongue.

'Is it good?' he asked.

'Yes, Uncle Kurt. Thank you.'

'It is my pleasure. You are a very special young lady, with a very special talent. And you deserve your rewards.' He gave her a large smile, and Rosa responded in kind.

'Do you like that Uncle Kurt looks after you, Rosa?' She nodded enthusiastically. 'Because I cannot look after everyone, you know. You always have a full belly, don't you?'

'Yes.'

'And a very thick blanket to keep you warm at night?'

'Mmm-hmm.'

'Nobody else has those things, Rosa. Only you.' He looked at her intently. 'Don't you think you are lucky to have Uncle Kurt to protect you?' Rosa nodded once more. 'Good.' Franzen stood up from behind his desk, and crossed to the sole window in his office. He looked out and inspected the area, before drawing the curtains. 'Don't you think that *I* deserve a reward for looking after you so well, Rosa?'

'Of course, Uncle Kurt. I will paint you extra pictures!'

Franzen chuckled. 'Thank you, Rosa. I love them. But the reward I am referring to is a little different. You can give it to me right now.' Rosa looked confused. 'Would you like

221

another piece of liquorice?' He grabbed a red sweet from the bag, and this time forced it into Rosa's mouth.

Rosa tried not to gag. Looking up into his face, she saw something in Franzen's eyes that made her afraid. His friendly demeanour was gone, replaced by something darker.

'You are important to me, Rosa. Very important indeed. I am going to keep protecting you. But you have to learn to do something for me in return.'

'What?' asked Rosa, her voice trembling a little.

'Something that only two people who have a *very* special bond would ever do.' He advanced on her. 'Do not be afraid. I will show you.'

Franzen strode towards the door of his office, locking it.

Anya knew something was wrong the minute Rosa walked into the dormitory. Her face was deathly white and her small hands were shaking.

'What is it, Rosa? Tell Anya.'

Rosa shook her head, not trusting herself to speak. Anya's stomach turned as she feared the worst.

'Franzen. What did he . . . ?'

Rosa did not have to answer. Anya swept her into her arms and the little girl began to shake.

'Oh my poor darling, my darling.' Anya stroked Rosa's hair.

Enough. Neither of them could take any more.

David took his usual place in the tailor's shop after dinner. The few prisoners in positions of authority gathered there to meet, as it was the largest and most pleasant hall in the camp.

Albert nodded in his direction and the trio began to play. David was thankful for this time, as it was the one moment in the day when life veered somewhere towards normality.

People would smile and dance. Here, David could lose himself in the music and forget about his aching bones and how hungry he was.

Recently, the trains had stopped coming, and so had the supply of food. Most in the camp were starving and the Ukrainians were charging phenomenal amounts for smuggled supplies.

As was usual, a few Germans started to drift in and took to the floor. Franzen entered the hall with Anya and joined the dancers. David watched as they waltzed gracefully to the music, as if they were in one of Warsaw's dance halls, not the middle of hell on earth. After ten minutes, David saw Anya excuse herself, and make her way over to him.

'Play *Blue Danube*, can you?' she asked, then leaned closer. 'I must talk to you. The furrier's hut tonight after the dancing. I'll wait for you there.' She took a step back. 'Thank you,' she said performatively. She walked back across the floor to join Franzen.

The furrier's hut was in complete darkness.

'Anya?' David whispered hoarsely.

'Over here.'

He moved towards the sound of her voice and at last saw her, sitting against one of the mountains of fur coats.

'Why did you wish to see me, Anya?'

'Because Rosa and I must escape and we need your help.'

'Is Rosa all right?'

'No, David. Franzen's interest in your sister is not innocent. He has been making her do indecent things.'

A deep moan came from inside David.

'That bastard! I'll go now and kill him with my own bare han—'

'Hush, David! I have a plan for escape. I too am at risk.

223

When he discovers I am carrying a child, he will shoot me. Now, listen carefully, while I explain . . .'

Roll call finished the following morning and the prisoners went off about their gruesome business. David's heart ticked steadily against his chest as he went back to his dormitory.

Everything was in place. He just had to time it right, and in two hours, he should be leaving this hell. He accepted that other prisoners would suffer if he went, but he had to escape, if only to tell the world of the madness that had existed here, and the chance to get Franzen.

As Anya had promised, David had found the gasoline in the tool hut – only a small canister, but enough to do what was required. The plan was to set light to the fence that hid the gas chambers – for it was camouflaged by a mountain of dry twigs. In the ensuing confusion, he planned to make his way to the train, which Anya had said was due to leave today, to take discarded clothing to the Fatherland. David would have to pass right below the watchtower, but hoped that all the attention would be on the fire, on the other side of the sorting area.

It was time to go. He walked nonchalantly across the path to the gas chambers and into the assembly yard, his violin case in his hand, before diving into the hut that served as an undressing area for the women. He rooted under the wooden bench for the gasoline, which he had stored there last night, alongside three matches given to him by Anya. This was the most dangerous part of his plan. He had to get to the other side of the yard which provided no cover from the watchtower.

David peered out of the hut. Seeing that the coast was clear, he bolted across the yard and sheltered underneath the five-metre-high fence. Acting as quickly as he could, David poured the gasoline on the dry branches nearest to him, then struck the match along the hard gravel floor. It lit, then went out.

He tried again, but the second attempt yielded the same result. David had one match left.

Please, Mama. Help me.

He struck it, sheltering the flame with his hands, and put it to a twig. It caught with such ferocity that he jumped backwards in fright.

David heard a shout, turned, and saw the men from the watchtower looking at him. A second later, bullets rattled around his head.

The fire had taken a firm grip of the fence, and the guards began to scurry down the tower. David seized the moment and raced back into the women's changing room. He scampered down to the other end of the hut and peered through a hole. There was the train. He watched as the surprised Ukrainians, who were loading the piles of clothes, dropped what they were doing and heeded the calls of the Germans to help them with the fire.

When the platform had emptied, David opened the door. Ten yards between him and the carriage. He saw Anya clambering inside.

'David! Come on! Quick! Cover yourself! Rosa is already buried.' David leaped across the platform, threw his violin case into the carriage and jumped up inside. He plunged into the massive pile of clothes, trying to ease his breathing. A small hand was touching his shoulder. He wriggled round, grasped it with his own and squeezed.

After what David would always remember as eternity, the train began to move. Tears of relief came to his eyes. He held Rosa's hand tightly. She moved through the clothes and snuggled up to him.

'I love you, David.'

'I love you, too, Rosa. And one day I'll make that man pay for what he did to Papa, and to you, Rosa. I swear.'

She fell asleep as the train gently rocked her. David looked down at her sweet, innocent face and knew that he meant it with all his heart.

The intercom buzzed, bringing David sharply out of his reverie and back to his smart New York office. He wiped his sweating brow and dried his eyes.

'Yes?'

'Mr Brett Cooper is in reception for you, sir.'

'Thank you, Pat. Give him a coffee and tell him I'll be with him in five minutes.'

'Right you are, sir.'

'Damn!' For the first time, David wondered whether he'd taken the right decision to keep his past from his son. He'd done it with the best intentions, wanting to protect him, but now, as it crept into his own future, threatening to change him, he wasn't so sure his decision was the right one.

Of one thing there was no doubt. David was being handed an opportunity to take revenge. Whatever it cost him, David was prepared to pay the price.

He collected himself as best he could and pressed the intercom.

'Okay, Pat. Tell Brett to come in.'

Maybe one day, when it was all over, he'd tell Brett. But this was his war, not his son's.

The door opened and his red-eyed, exhausted son walked across to his desk.

'Hello, Dad. Good to see you.' Brett stood with his hands in his pockets and admired the room. 'Wow, this place is amazing. It's much nicer than the London office.'

'Yes. You'll get used to everything being ten times larger than it is in England. How was the flight?'

'Okay, thanks. I didn't sleep much, so I feel a bit rough.'

David smiled. 'Well, I'm not going to recommend that you

do a serious day's work here, but what I do suggest is that we spend an hour going through the plan I've drawn up for you, which will take us to midday. Then I'll take you to lunch at the 21 Club, after which I'm packing you off to my apartment to get some sleep. How does that sound?'

Brett gave his father a weary smile. 'Marvellous. I'm glad to be here, Dad.'

'And I'm pleased to have you, Brett.' David was relieved that his son finally seemed to have accepted the idea of working for Cooper Industries and had forgotten all those silly thoughts of being an artist. At present, that was something that he could *not* deal with.

What David didn't know was that Brett's happiness was almost entirely due to the fact that Leah Thompson would be arriving in New York in less than forty-eight hours.

Father and son spent an agreeable hour going through Brett's work plan. David wanted him to spend four months in the New York office, learning how the hub of the business was run. Then he would be sent off for a year around the world to visit Cooper Industries sites in their various stages of development.

'I don't believe in any of this "starting in the post room" sort of business, Brett. Everyone in the company knows that you'll take over from me sometime. However, you won't officially hold a position for the next eighteen months, during which I expect you to turn your hand to anything. The most important thing is to earn the respect of the people you will one day control. Humility and a willingness to learn are what I want to see. You're here to learn from every single person on the payroll. Right, speech over! Let's go to lunch.'

After a pleasant meal, David and Brett hailed a cab and went back to David's brand-new duplex apartment, situated on Fifth Avenue, six blocks from the offices of Cooper Industries.

'I thought this could be your suite. It's got a nice view of the park.'

Brett looked around the grand sitting room, then wandered into the spacious bedroom, with marble bathroom en suite.

'It'll do fine. Thanks, Dad.'

'I did think about getting you a separate apartment, but I'm hardly here and you'll be off in four months' time.'

'Sure, I understand.'

David knew that he didn't have to impress his son, but he was keen to make the effort. 'Oh, there's also Georgia, the resident cook, who's always on hand to knock you something up.'

'It's great, Dad, really.'

'Right. I'll leave you to get some sleep. I'm out tonight at a business dinner, but I'll be around tomorrow morning. If you need anything, just press the housekeeper's bell by your bed.' David turned to walk out of the room. He stopped and looked back at his son. 'I really am glad you're here, Brett,' he said simply, and left.

Brett sank onto the bed and closed his eyes. Although his body was begging for rest, his mind was too alert for sleep to envelop him. He gave up twenty minutes later and decided to explore his new home.

The duplex was on a grand scale, with the formal sitting room and dining room on the top floor, opening onto a terrace that overlooked Central Park. David's suite of rooms led directly off his comfortable office. The lower floor, where Brett's suite was, also housed the huge kitchen, three further suites, and rooms for the staff. Brett was used to luxury, but even he had to admit that this was something else.

He wondered what Leah would think of it, then stopped

himself. He was automatically assuming that she would want to see him again.

Brett wandered back into his room, and lay down on his bed once more. Less than two days until she was here.

With his mind full of pictures of her, he finally fell asleep.

5

New York, August 1981

'Leah, darling! I can't believe you're here.' Jenny hugged her friend tight. 'I've missed you. Sit down and I'll order some champagne.'

'Mineral water for me, Jenny.'

'Oh, you bore! You simply can't sit in the Oak Room on your first night in New York and toast it with mineral water!' she laughed.

Leah had to agree. 'Okay. I'll have one glass.'

Jenny ordered a bottle from a passing waiter. 'It's good to see you haven't changed. I just wish I had your discipline!' She smiled ruefully. 'Let me look at you.' Jenny surveyed her and gave a melancholic sigh. 'Still as beautiful as ever. Not an inch of fat on you, nor a touch of a crow's foot under your eyes. Lucky old you.' She rolled her eyes. 'Whereas I'm starting to show my age.'

Leah studied her friend. Although she didn't want to admit it, Jenny looked tired and haggard. Her eyes were red and there was a noticeable roundness about the delicate contours of her face.

'Don't be silly, Jenny. You look just the same as ever,' she lied smoothly.

230

Jenny shook her head. 'I look like shit, Leah. Don't worry, I can take it. I had a call from Madelaine this morning to say that if I don't lose half a stone and clean up my act, my cosmetics company aren't going to renew my contract next month. She wants me to go off to this detox spa in Palm Springs for a week. Trouble is, you can't drink, or smoke, and you live on rabbit food most of the time.'

'Sounds like a great idea to me.'

The two girls clinked glasses and drank a toast to the future.

'I hope I've made the right decision, moving to New York,' Leah mused. 'I've only got a month's work to do for Chaval, then I'm back on assignments again.'

'Oh, come on, Leah. You're being paid half a million dollars for twenty-odd days' work, and I bet they'll renew your contract. Your face is going to be all over America. Magazines and photographers will be screaming for you here.' Jenny looked a little sad. 'They did for me when I first arrived.' She drained her glass. 'Now, I want to hear all about your birthday party. I'm so sorry I couldn't make it. The stinky old company wouldn't rearrange a shoot,' she moaned, pouring herself more champagne.

'Well, it was eventful,' said Leah, thoughtfully. 'I met Brett, my first crush, who I hadn't seen for years. Plus, Carlo disgraced himself and had to be packed off in a drunken stupor to his hotel.'

Jenny giggled. 'Sounds like a good night. But I've always told you to watch Carlo, Leah. The guy's madly in love with you. He honestly believes that he made you who you are.' Jenny narrowed her eyes. 'I reckon he's trying to call in his chips.'

Leah frowned. 'What do you mean?'

'He's behaved as if he owns you for the past four years, and he's moving in to take what he believes is his due.' Jenny raised an eyebrow. 'The entire modelling world, plus the press, have assumed that you two have been at it for years anyway.'

Leah was mortified. 'Jenny! Please! I'm grateful for what Carlo's done and I regard him as a very good friend, but I don't and never have felt . . . that way about him. I'm sure Carlo knows that.'

Jenny sighed. 'Oh dear, Leah. You may have grown up in some ways, but in others, you're terribly naive. Anyway, let's drop the subject. Tell me about this old flame from the party.'

Leah shrugged. 'I met him when I was fifteen. He did the dirty on me, actually.'

'Well, I hope you didn't give him the time of day.'

Leah examined her nails. 'I'm afraid I did. We danced together and I said he could contact me here in New York. By coincidence, he flew out to work here a couple of days ago.'

'Don't tell me that the virginal twenty-one-year-old actually has a stirring in her loins?'

Leah rolled her eyes. 'Honestly, Jenny. You make me sound like a relic. I haven't had time over the past few years and—'

'You haven't been out of Carlo's sight for long enough to even think about other men, let alone do anything about it,' finished Jenny. 'You like this boy, don't you?'

Leah paused, then looked at her friend. 'I shouldn't; he did something absolutely rotten to me years ago, but yes, I do. Very much.'

Jenny took another healthy slug of champagne. 'Good. It's about time you joined the human race. It is perfectly natural to fancy a guy, you know!'

'Yes. Anyway, while we're on the subject, how's your prince?'

Jenny poured herself a third glass of Veuve Clicquot. 'He's not rung me for a couple of weeks. He's been with his father on some urgent family business. I'm sure he'll call when he hits New York.'

Leah was glad that Jenny had not seen copies of any recent British papers. Prince Ranu had been in most of the gossip columns, photographed entwined with the daughter of a wealthy Russian aristocrat. One columnist had even mentioned that there was talk of a possible engagement.

'You don't love him, though, do you, Jenny?'

Her friend was silent as she traced the line of her glass. 'As a matter of fact, I do. I adore him. Four years on and I still feel the same as the first night we met. If he asked me, I'd marry him tomorrow and get out of this stinking rat race.' Jenny glanced at Leah sadly. 'I know. You don't have to tell me. He's having an affair with that Princess De-La-Unpronounceable-Surname. It's not the first time, I can assure you. But he always comes running back to me in the end, begging for forgiveness.'

'Why on earth do you forgive him, Jenny?'

'Why are you prepared to forgive this boy you re-met at your birthday party?'

Leah blushed. '*Touché.*'

'I'm sorry. That was below the belt, but it illustrates the point. I love him, Leah. And he's rich. Very, very rich. He can have any girl he wants, when he wants. He doesn't need to be faithful, because there'll always be another, younger, prettier female in the queue behind me. So I figure that the only chance I have of eventually getting him is to hold on fast to my place in the queue.'

'Oh dear.' Leah did not know what else to say.

'Don't worry. You see this boy again, then you'll understand.'

'But I won't fall in love, Jenny.'

'Oh no?' Jenny's eyes twinkled. 'Famous last words, Leah Thompson.' She ordered another bottle of champagne.

6

'Leah, it's Brett.'

'Hello, Brett.'

'You sound sleepy. Did I wake you?'

'Er, no. Sorry.' Leah sat upright on the big kingsize bed, her head still woolly, her heart pounding at the sound of his voice.

She had returned to the Plaza an hour ago after a heavy lunch with the PR people from the cosmetics company, and an afternoon of press interviews. Jet-lagged and exhausted after a sleepless night, she had fallen onto the bed and closed her eyes.

'I was wondering if you fancied meeting for a drink tonight.'

Leah could see her pale face and dishevelled appearance in the mirror on the wall opposite. Getting ready and going out was the last thing she had on the agenda. On the other hand . . . She hated herself for wanting to see him so badly.

'Okay then.'

'Great. I'll meet you in the hotel lobby in forty minutes!'

Leah sighed. Forty minutes to transform herself. She'd better get moving.

After showering and drying her hair, Leah tried on her entire wardrobe of clothes, discarding one expensive outfit after another.

'Shit!' she screamed aloud in frustration. She spent her life as a professional clothes horse and tonight she was acting as though she was a teenager on a first date.

Leah finally decided on a dress designed especially for her by Carlo. Then she sat in front of the mirror and pulled her hair into a myriad of different styles, all of which, she was convinced, looked dreadful. Realising that she was already ten minutes late, she pulled her hair out of the top-knot and let it hang loose around her shoulders.

'You'll just have to do,' she muttered, grabbing her handbag and heading for the lift.

Brett was standing nervously in the lobby, checking his watch as the lift doors opened and Leah emerged. As she came out, he noticed every male head turn and watch her. Brett felt a surge of pride as one of the most beautiful women in the world spotted him and walked across the room.

Brett thought Leah looked even lovelier tonight than on her birthday. She had a radiance about her, and with her long hair flowing naturally around her shoulders, he was reminded of the very first moment he had seen her, silhouetted by the early morning sun in his Yorkshire bedroom. Of course, her beauty had matured, with the addition of her designer clothes, and with the polish of gracing catwalks for the past few years. Brett felt like a schoolboy as she casually kissed him on both cheeks.

'Hello.'

'Hello.' Brett could almost feel himself blushing. 'Shall we go to the bar here?'

As they walked into the Oak Room, both of them desperately tried to think of something to say. With nothing forthcoming, they sat down in silence.

Brett broke the tension. 'What would you like to drink?'

'Mineral water, please.'

'You don't drink?'

'Rarely.'

'Gosh. How impressive!'

Brett ordered water and a beer, thinking how composed and cool she was. It was understandable, after what he had done to her all those years ago.

'How was your flight?' they asked simultaneously. The subsequent laughter helped to relax them both. 'Mine was fine,' answered Leah.

'And mine. I'm still feeling jet-lagged, though.'

'God, me too,' said Leah. 'I was awake all last night. I spent most of it staring out of my hotel window. This city just never goes to bed.'

'Tell me about it. I keep feeling as though I want to take a shower. The grime and dust seem much worse here than in London.' Brett picked up his beer. 'Anyway, cheers. It's wonderful to see you again.'

'Thank you.'

'It's hard to believe that we're both in New York at the same time.'

'I know.' Leah stopped herself from thinking it was fate. 'So, tell me what you've been doing with yourself over the past few years.'

Brett sketched an outline for her. He spoke of Cambridge and his friends with an obvious fondness. Clearly, he'd not spent his time there pining for her, Leah thought irrationally.

'So here I am in NYC to learn how my father runs his company,' Brett finished. 'Now, what about you? My life is cripplingly dull in comparison. I could hardly believe it when I saw your face staring at me from the cover of *Vogue*! I want to hear all about it, Leah.' Of course, her career rise had been better documented by the press than the prime minister's. What Brett really meant was: *Tell me about Carlo.*

'I'll start at the beginning, Brett. If I can shock you a moment, *you* are responsible for my being spotted.'

He looked amazed. 'How on earth do you mean?'

'Rose took the sketch you did of me on the moors and hung it in the gallery at her first exhibition. Steve Levitt, the photographer, saw it, and here I am.' She smiled.

Brett was flabbergasted. 'Good grief! Where did Rose find it? Has she still got it?'

Leah shook her head. 'No. That's the mystery. It disappeared a few days after the exhibition. It hasn't been seen since. Do you still paint, Brett?'

'No, is the simple answer. I've grown up a little. The world isn't about silly childhood dreams.' He smiled sadly.

'Your dreams were hardly silly. You had real talent, Brett. I think you should use it, if only as a hobby. You've obviously inherited Rose's gift.'

'Maybe, except our styles couldn't be further apart. She's done well over the past few years. I wrote to congratulate her on the latest exhibition, actually. I thought it was magnificent.'

'You should see the farmhouse these days. You'd hardly recognise it. It's furnished with all mod cons and Laura Ashley sofas.' Leah took a deep breath. She had to know. 'And Chloe has shot up since I last saw her.'

'Chloe?' Brett asked, a blank look on his face.

'Miranda's daughter.'

He felt a knot in his stomach at the mention of her name. 'Good God. Is she married already?'

'No. And she won't say who the father is. Chloe's four now. Miranda told Rose she was pregnant just after you left Yorkshire.' Leah took a sip of her drink to give her something to concentrate on.

A cold chill ran through Brett's bones. It was time.

'Look, Leah, about Miranda. Will you let me explain?'

'If you want to. But it's pretty obvious. Chloe is your daughter, isn't she?'

Leah watched as Brett turned white.

'Don't worry, I'm the only one who knows.'

'No! Jesus, no. No. That's absolutely impossible. No way, no how.' Brett couldn't have been more emphatic.

'But Miranda said that night that you two – oh Brett, please don't lie to me. Guilt was written all over your face.'

He put his hands up. 'Leah, I swear to you that Chloe couldn't possibly be my child. Miranda and I . . . oh dear . . . well, we kissed and cuddled and stuff, but not . . . you know.'

'Then why did Miranda tell me that you did? And why won't she say who the father is?'

'The answer to the first question is simple. Miranda wanted revenge. The second, I honestly don't know.'

'Well,' sighed Leah. 'I'm afraid it confirmed your guilt in my mind when Miranda was so secretive about Chloe's father. I thought that it was because it was you and she was too scared to tell Rose.'

Brett ran a hand through his hair. 'Look, Leah. I can't prove it, but I swear to you, I am not guilty of that crime. I was stupid and selfish, yes, but I paid for that when I lost you. I understand how you must feel at the moment, and that's totally fair enough.' He looked at her pleadingly. 'But would you please give me a chance to prove that I really am a decent sort of guy these days?'

Leah suddenly felt extraordinarily tired.

'I'm sorry, Brett, but I'm exhausted. I've got a very heavy day tomorrow and I really must get some sleep.'

Brett exhaled. 'Of course.' She hadn't forgiven him. 'But would it be okay if I called you again?'

Leah thought for a moment. 'Yes. But I'm going to be pretty

busy for the next week, and Jenny and I are going out apartment hunting at the weekend.'

'Will you let me know your new address and telephone number?' Brett pulled a card out of his wallet and handed it to her. 'Leave a message with Pat, my father's PA, if I'm unavailable.'

'Will do.' Leah stood up. 'Thanks for the drink.'

He walked with her to the lift. 'You won't forget to call with your number, will you?'

'No.' The lift doors opened. 'Goodnight, Brett.' She kissed him on both cheeks and stepped inside.

'Goodnight, Leah.' The doors closed and she was gone.

Brett sauntered outside and hailed a passing yellow cab. He checked his watch. Half past nine. So much for his dreams of whisking her up to her hotel room and making passionate love until the dawn broke. He sighed. There was no one to blame but himself. Leah held all the cards, and he would just have to wait in the agony of anticipation to see if she called.

7

Miranda stretched luxuriously, opened her eyes and stared at the mirrored ceiling above her. She liked what she saw. Her naked body was partly hidden beneath the white satin sheets, and her blonde hair was splayed across the pillow.

She sat up and looked round the comfortable bedroom. Her new home. All this luxury, a bank account with as much as she could ever wish to spend, and a wardrobe full of beautiful designer clothes. Miranda smiled and hugged her knees. Everything she had ever wanted had become hers in a matter of days. And it had all been so easy.

Quick, painless sex was the exchange for all this.

She and Santos had flown to Nice and travelled on to the port of St Tropez on Saturday morning to begin their weekend cruise round the Mediterranean. He had been so sweet to her while they were on his boat, introducing her to his many associates, most of whom worked for him.

Miranda had never seen such luxury before in her life. She had imagined a yacht to be a small vessel with a couple of cramped cabins below deck, but this thing . . . Why, it was like being on the *QE2*. It had three floors of sumptuous suites for the fifteen guests, a magnificent glass-enclosed lounge, a formal dining room and five enormous sun terraces.

For the two days she had been on board, Santos had

showered her with gifts and affection, making it plain to the male guests that she was his. As such, they had treated her with respect and deference, as if she herself was the hostess.

Miranda had done her best to try to extract information on Santos from his friends, but had only come up with the fact that he lived somewhere in South America, was over sixty and was incredibly wealthy . . . All of which she had gathered anyway.

When he had visited her in her cabin late at night, Miranda shut her eyes and pictured her diamond necklace, her beautiful clothes and the luxurious private jet, occasionally emitting what she hoped were realistic groans of feminine pleasure. Then Santos would kiss her, put on his silk robe and depart for his own cabin.

On Sunday evening the boat had pulled gently back into St Tropez and the guests began disembarking and climbing into their waiting limousines. Miranda watched them wistfully from one of the upper sun decks, accepting that her return to Yorkshire and normality beckoned. Until Santos sidled up behind her and handed her a key.

'Your limousine is waiting to take you to the airport, Miranda.'

'Are you not coming with me?'

'I cannot. I must go home. That key will open the door to an apartment in London. The driver who collects you from Heathrow will take you there. I will call you later.' He kissed her. 'Goodbye, my sweet woman.'

After Miranda had touched down in London, she was whisked through customs and out to a waiting Rolls-Royce. The car drove her through the darkening streets of the city and stopped in front of a palatial white stucco building, which overlooked a park.

'Please follow me, madam,' the chauffeur said formally, and led Miranda through a large lobby and up to the third floor in a small lift. After a short stroll along a luxuriously carpeted corridor, he opened the door on a tastefully furnished one-bedroom apartment.

The chauffeur had taken her suitcases inside, then tipped his hat.

'The number to call if you need me is on the list by the telephone. Goodnight, madam.'

Miranda had the distinct feeling that the chauffeur had been through all this before. As such, she spent the following hour combing the apartment for any signs of previous female occupants, or of Santos himself. She had found nothing in any of the scented drawers, nor down the back of the plush washed-silk sofa. But she did come across an envelope by the telephone, with her name on it. Inside was two thousand pounds cash, plus assurance that she would be receiving two credit cards in her name, both charged to the account of Mr F. Santos. That, plus a bank account opened for her, containing the sum of ten thousand pounds, an amount topped up on the last day of every month by another five thousand.

Miranda had sat in shock. This was better than she had even dreamed about. She was rich.

At nine o'clock that evening, the ornamental telephone had jangled loudly in the silent apartment. She'd picked it up.

'Hello?'

'Hello, Miranda,' Santos cooed. 'Have you found everything to your liking?'

'Yes, my darling. Everything's wonderful,' she replied.

'Good, good.' There was a pause as the bad line betrayed the distance between them. 'I hope that you understand that all these things come with certain conditions. I do not wish you to go out of the apartment at any time without calling for Roger, the chauffeur, to escort you in the Rolls-Royce. And no guests. Men are forbidden in your apartment, apart from Ian, whom you met at the Savoy. He will visit you from time to time and if you have any problems, you must contact him. I will ring you at nine every evening to make sure you are well and happy. Camila, the housekeeper, lives in the apartment below you. She will cook all your meals and take care of household duties.'

Miranda was unsure of how to respond. 'Of course, my love,' was what she offered.

'Good. One last thing. Always have a suitcase packed, for I may ring you at any time and ask you to join me abroad.' The tone of his voice changed. 'Under no circumstances will you ever attempt to contact me.' An uncomfortable pause followed. 'Well, I hope that those little rules will not stop you enjoying your new home. There is champagne in the fridge. Drink a toast to us both. Goodbye, Miranda.'

The telephone had clicked and Miranda replaced the receiver. She sank down onto the sofa and tried to take in what Santos had said.

All this luxury came with a much higher price than she had at first thought. After a moment, the cold truth dawned on her. Santos had just bought and paid for her. She was his possession and, therefore, he had the right to dictate how she lived her life.

She was a mistress.

'Mistress.' Miranda uttered the word to see how it sounded on her tongue as she stared up at the mirrors on the ceiling.

After four days of being alone, Miranda was finding the silence in the apartment deafening. She was used to the morning sounds of Mrs Thompson bustling in the kitchen, Rose's loud singing as she painted, and the sweet, high-pitched voice of her daughter, Chloe.

She suddenly felt dreadfully homesick. Miranda reached for the telephone by her bed and dialled.

* * *

The telephone rang and Rose hurried to pick it up.

'Hello?' her voice was hoarse from a lack of sleep and too many cigarettes.

'Rose, it's me.'

Rose choked back a sob.

'Miranda! Thank God. Are you okay?'

'Never been better,' the voice sang down the receiver.

Rose wanted to strangle her daughter. She had spent the past four days out of her mind with worry.

'Where are you, Miranda? I've been worried sick. You might have called. We were expecting you home days ago and—'

'For God's sake, Rose, I'm twenty-one and I can take care of myself. I'm in London and I'm absolutely fine.'

'You may be twenty-one, young lady, but you are still my daughter and—'

'Okay, okay. I'm sorry, Rose.'

Rose took a deep breath. 'All right. Now what train are you catching? I'll pick you up from Leeds.'

'Actually, I'm not coming back to Yorkshire just yet.'

'Why ever not, Miranda?'

'Because I've met some people down here and I want to stay a bit longer. Will you take care of Chloe for a while?'

Rose bit her lip. 'Of course, but . . . where are you staying? Who are these people? Have you got enough money . . . ?' Rose's attention was caught by a small plump hand pushing open the sitting-room door.

'Mummy? Where's Mummy?' The angelic face, a replica of Miranda's at the same age, creased into a frown.

'Come to Granny, darling.' Rose held out her arms and Chloe walked over to her. 'There's someone who wants to speak to you, Miranda. Chloe, say hello to Mummy.'

'Hello, Mummy. Can you come home?'

'Hello, Chloe, darling. Don't worry, Mummy will be home soon.'

Rose settled her granddaughter on her knee. 'She misses you badly, Miranda. She asks every day where you are.'

'Yes, well. I have to go now. I'll ring again soon. Give Chloe a kiss for me. And don't worry, Rose. I'll be fine, really. Goodbye.'

The line went dead. Rose slowly replaced the handset and studied the beautiful little girl sucking her thumb contentedly in her lap.

'When is Mummy home, Granny?' The little face looked up at her with such trust and innocence in her big, blue eyes that Rose's own filled with tears and she hugged Chloe tightly to her.

'I don't know, sweetheart. I really don't know.'

8

Jenny threw herself lengthways onto the comfortable cream sofa and smoothed her hair away from her sweating brow.

'Never again.' She shook her head.

'You're absolutely right.' Leah collapsed in an armchair on the other side of the room. 'I am never again helping you move your stuff from one apartment to the other. Really, Jenny, you've only been here for nine months. I can't get over how much junk you've collected!'

She smiled. 'Sorry. But it's going to be worth it, isn't it?' She looked proudly around the new apartment.

The two of them had spent the previous weekend trailing around rental accommodation, until at last they had found their new home. It was not nearly as large as some of the vast lofts they had seen in Soho, but both girls found too much space intimidating, being used to their smaller, English living spaces.

The apartment was on the twelfth floor of a luxury high-rise building on East 70th Street. Both of them had known the minute that they had walked through the door that this was the one. It boasted a large sitting room, with doors opening onto a balcony overlooking the bustling street below. Along the corridor was a small but serviceable kitchen and dining area, two double bedrooms with en suite bathrooms, a guest room and a toilet. It was tastefully decorated in soft beiges and creams, and the stripped floors strewn with pastel rugs. Consequently, the rent was as impressive as the apartment, but Leah's cosmetics company was paying, so that was no problem.

'I adore it. It has such a cosy feel,' Leah remarked. 'Coffee, Jenny?'

'Something stronger for me. I think I deserve it. I must have lost five pounds lugging all those boxes around today.'

'Okay. You can have a small vodka with lots of ice.' The two girls walked along the corridor to the kitchen. Leah began digging through boxes for a jar of coffee.

'It's a great place for a party. I think we should have a housewarming next weekend. I can introduce you to a few people in this town,' said Jenny, leaning against the cramped breakfast bar.

'Great. Could we throw it on Saturday night? That'll give me twenty-four hours to recover from Mexico.' Leah was due to fly down to a shoot on Monday morning, and would not be back until the following Friday night.

'Leave it to me. I've nothing on at all next week. Consider me Head of the Party Planning Committee!'

Leah sighed as she fished the coffee out of the bottom of a box. Jenny had told her that she had 'nothing on' since Leah had arrived in New York. This, for a top model, was unheard of.

Madelaine had called Leah in the middle of the week and imparted some worrying words.

'I'm glad you're going to be living with Jenny, Leah. She needs somebody to keep her under control. You've noticed the drink problem, I presume?'

'Well, Madelaine. I've noticed Jenny enjoys a drink but—'

'She's turned up on two shoots in the past month stoned

247

out of her mind and pissed. She's put on weight and her skin looks like concrete. Word is getting round. I've told her that the cosmetics company are seriously considering cancelling her contract if she doesn't get her act together. And I'm struggling to find her anything to do while she waits for the new campaign to start. She's got a couple of months to sort herself out. Help her, Leah. I know how close you two are.'

'I'll do my best, Madelaine. I'm sure she'll be fine. She's still one of the best around.'

'Maybe, but there are a thousand beautiful girls out there just ready and waiting to jump into her shoes. This is her last chance. Tell her that from me.'

Leah had found little chance to tell Jenny anything in the past week. She'd been through a gruelling schedule of shoots, interviews and a big campaign launch for Chaval last night. Now she had twenty-four hours before she flew to Mexico. Leah was hardly the right person to play minder. But tonight, she'd have to have a talk with her.

'There.' Leah put the vodka on the kitchen table and sat down opposite Jenny.

'Cheers. Here's to our new home.'

Leah winced as Jenny downed the entire glass in one slug.

'Mmm. That feels better. Do you fancy sending out for some Chinese? I'm starving.'

'Okay.'

'I'll go to the store on the corner and get a couple of bottles of wine. We'll have a cosy night in.'

An hour later, they were sitting out on the balcony, eating and watching the sun set over New York. Jenny had ordered a feast of Chinese food and they were washing it down with white wine. In the time that Leah had managed to consume half her glass, Jenny was on her third.

248

'You realise that is the last Chinese you're going to have for a while, don't you, Jenny?'

Jenny was licking her fingers. 'What do you mean?'

'I spoke to Madelaine last week. She really is worried about you.'

'You mean she's a bossy, interfering old hag who enjoys poking her nose into other people's business.'

'Come on. You know that's not true. You used to adore her. She genuinely cares about us, that's all.'

'Yeah, as far as her bank balance is concerned,' countered Jenny.

'She's a businesswoman. And her business is selling us. When one of her "products" isn't performing, she—'

'Products!' exploded Jenny. 'You just hit the nail on the head. Well done, Leah. We're not human. We're just walking, talking Barbie dolls without a grey cell in our heads!'

'I'm sorry, Jenny. I didn't mean it like that.' Leah looked at her friend's angry face, wishing she knew how to approach this more tactfully. 'The thing is, Madelaine thinks you may lose the cosmetics contract.'

Jenny looked down at her feet. 'I know. I told you that.'

'Surely you don't want that to happen?'

'Of course I don't!'

'Then surely it's worth going without a few drinks and a few joints, and doing some exercise classes?'

Jenny stared out into the dusk, then shrugged. 'It's okay for you, Leah. You don't like alcohol, never touch drugs and could eat chips all day without putting on an ounce. I'm not made like that. I was born to be excessive.' Jenny downed the remainder of her glass of wine. 'Oh, what's the point? It's a vicious circle. I get depressed because I know I'm overweight and drinking too much, so what do I do to feel better? I eat more and get pissed or stoned. It's all useless!' She burst into tears, stood up from the table and ran into the sitting room, knocking Leah's barely touched wine over and spilling it on the patio.

Leah followed her inside and sat beside Jenny on the sofa. She gently put an arm round her shoulders.

'Don't cry, sweetheart. I'm sorry I've upset you.'

'Don't be. I know you're only trying to help. And that bastard Ranu! He's not called me for weeks.' There was a fresh flood of tears. 'Oh Leah, I just feel so low. Everything was wonderful two years ago,' she sobbed. 'Now I'm in such a mess, and I don't know how to start putting it right.'

Leah grabbed her friend's shoulders. 'Jen, listen to me. You're twenty-three years of age. Most other girls are only beginning their lives, and you're talking like yours is over. Don't you realise how lucky you are?' Leah gave her a sympathetic smile. 'The pressure's just got to you, that's all. You're strong, Jenny. You can do it, I know you can.'

'I don't know if I can.' Jenny sniffed quietly.

'Well, I do. Remember how you looked after me when I first started? If it hadn't been for you, God knows where I'd have ended up. Now it's my turn to do the same for you. Madelaine's willing to pay for you to go to this detox centre in Palm Springs for a week. If I were you, I'd take up her offer.'

Jenny was silent for a while. 'You're right. I owe it to myself,' she eventually said, boldly. 'I'm going to end up dead if I carry on like this.' She turned and looked at Leah. 'God, you've grown up. However did you get to be so sensible?'

'It must be my Yorkshire blood.' She hugged her. 'Now, why don't you ring Madelaine and tell her you'll go to Palm Springs?'

'Okay.' Jenny stood up, retrieved the bottle of wine from the balcony, and poured the contents into a plant pot beside the sofa.

'To the new me.'

'To the new you.' Leah smiled.

9

Exactly a week later, the apartment was vibrating to the throb of music and people were jammed wall to wall.

Jenny was nursing a glass of Coke and smiling through love-filled eyes at her Arab prince. Leah had breathed a sigh of relief when Jenny had called her in Mexico last Thursday to tell her that Ranu was in town. It was just the boost her friend needed. He had even offered his private jet to fly her to Palm Springs on Monday morning.

Leah was standing in a crowd of people she did not know, mostly models and photographers, artists and designers; the cream of the New York 'in crowd'.

Everyone knew who Leah was, though. They asked her the same set of questions: how was Carlo? Was she really paid half a million for the cosmetics contract with Chaval? How long was she in New York for?

Leah puffed out a breath. Maybe it was because she was tired, but she wasn't in the mood for small talk. She wandered out of the sitting room and headed for her en suite bathroom, wanting some space and a little quiet. Leah closed the door behind her and stared at her reflection in the mirror.

'The most valuable face in the world.'

That had been one of the headlines last week when the

press had got hold of the figure she had been paid for the Chaval contract.

Often, she could not reconcile her face with the person she was inside. The former was world famous, the latter, well, nobody ever bothered to look. They weren't interested.

Leah propped her face up with her elbows. She thought how lovely it would be to have a day of anonymity, to meet someone who had no idea who she was and treated her accordingly.

She brushed her hair and wondered if Brett would come tonight. After swinging backwards and forwards all week, she had decided to give him the benefit of the doubt. Leah had left a message with Pat at Cooper Industries, as instructed, giving details of the party and address.

She realised that she was shirking her duties as hostess. Leah reluctantly came out of the bathroom, opened her bedroom door onto the corridor, and immediately bumped into a tall, dark-haired older man.

'Sorry,' she muttered.

'Oh, don't worry. In fact, I was looking for you.'

'Were you?' she answered wearily, not in the mood.

'Yes. My name is Anthony Van Schiele.'

If it was meant to mean something to Leah, it didn't.

'Hello.'

'I believe that you are working for me.'

'Am I?' Leah didn't understand.

He was smiling down at her with a twinkle in his eyes. 'Yes. I own Chaval Cosmetics . . . among other things.'

'Oh dear. I'm so sorry. I had no idea.' Embarrassment was plain on Leah's face.

'Don't worry. Most people who work for me have no idea either. I only acquired the company a few months back, and there's nothing worse than a dictatorial new owner who upsets the apple cart.'

Leah was warming to his relaxed attitude, a seemingly rare commodity in New York.

'Well, it's good to meet you, Mr Van Schiele.'

'Likewise. I was wondering if you would allow me to take you to dinner, to celebrate our partnership?'

Leah was in no position to refuse. 'Of course.'

'Wonderful. I'll meet you at Delmonico's at eight on Wednesday, if that suits?' Leah gave a nod. 'Perfect. I have to go now, but I look forward to seeing you then. Goodbye, Miss Thompson.' He bowed formally and walked towards the door. As he pulled it open, Brett stepped in and came towards her.

'Hello, Leah.' He kissed her on both cheeks and offered her the bottle of champagne he was holding. 'Happy house-warming.'

'Thanks, Brett. Come through and I'll get you a drink. Beer?'

'Great. This is some party. Do you know all these people?' Brett whispered in astonishment.

'No.' Leah giggled. 'Unfortunately, they all seem to know me.'

'You do happen to be rather famous. Even my father sounded jealous when I told him I was coming to Leah Thompson's party.'

'As you're here and you brought me a bottle of champagne, I shall make an exception and have a glass. We'll toast the British.' Leah yelped as the cork flew off with a loud bang. She suddenly felt as high as a kite and unusually flirtatious.

'To the British!' She raised her glass.

'Yes, to us,' he replied.

They moved through to the sitting room, where 'Satisfaction' was blaring over the hi-fi. Brett caught her arm.

'Come and dance. I love this song!' They joined the stamping, shouting mass on the makeshift dance floor in the centre of the room. As the song ended, Brett picked her up and twirled her round in his arms. 'God, I'm happy,' he said, as he put her down.

'So am I.' Leah beamed.

And she meant it. It was as if she had come alive inside from the moment Brett had walked into the apartment. Her senses were tingling and the world suddenly seemed to be the most extraordinarily lovely place.

A Lionel Richie record followed the Rolling Stones and slowed down the pace. Brett wrapped his arms around Leah and she nestled into them contentedly.

The pair were interrupted by Jenny. 'Darling, Ranu and I are going to his place. Will you be okay by yourself?'

Leah turned around, irritated at being disturbed. 'Of course. Jenny, this is Brett.'

The two shook hands.

'And this is Ranu, Brett.'

'Hello, Brett, how are you?' Ranu turned to Jenny. 'We know each other already. He was six years below me at Eton.'

Brett nodded. 'Yes. I fagged for Ranu for a term. He was a hard man to please.'

Although he was joking, Leah could see the obvious dislike in Brett's eyes.

'We must get together and go out to dinner when I'm back from Palm Springs,' said Jenny. 'Bye, Brett. Bye, Leah. I'll be back some time tomorrow.' She winked at her friend as Ranu led her out of the sitting room.

Brett shook his head. 'Is Jenny seriously involved with Ranu? He's a first-class pillock with too much money. Everyone disliked him at Eton.'

'I'm afraid so,' Leah confirmed. 'Don't worry, Jenny can look after herself,' she added with a conviction she didn't feel.

For the rest of the evening, Leah played hostess, checking people's drinks and being dragged from group to group to be introduced to the elite of the New York fashion world. Brett tagged along beside her, looking bored. It seemed impossible to have two minutes alone with her.

But eventually, the last of the hardened partiers drifted out of the apartment, leaving Leah and Brett standing in the middle of complete devastation.

'Oh God.' Leah groaned, surveying the bottles, glasses and overflowing ashtrays strewn with gay abandon around the sitting room. She collapsed on the sofa. 'I haven't got the energy.'

'Come on. I'll help you. It won't take a minute once we get started.' He pulled her up. 'You'll only have to face it tomorrow morning if you don't do it now.'

For the next hour, the two of them worked hard to put the apartment back together again. The dawn was rising as Leah flopped back down on the sofa.

'Coffee?' Brett offered.

'Mmm. Yes, please.' She closed her eyes.

Brett made two steaming cups and sat down on the floor in front of Leah.

'Come on, sleepy. You're far too big for me to carry into the bedroom. Drink this. I'll put the fire on. It's cold in here.'

Leah forced her eyes open and watched Brett lighting the ornamental gas fire. A tremor ran through her as she realised they were alone for the first time in a very long while.

She sipped the coffee slowly.

'I love the dawn in New York. I've seen it quite a few times in the past week. For some reason, I haven't been able to sleep,' Brett mused as the fire jumped to life. He placed himself on the big sheepskin rug that Leah had bought that morning, and looked out of the balcony windows across the skyline.

They drank their coffee in silence, a sense of anticipation stopping all conversation.

Leah put her empty cup on the floor. As she brought her hand back, Brett caught it and held it tight. He stared hard into her eyes as his face came nearer and he kissed her.

Her lips opened to him willingly, and his arms locked around her.

Every nerve-ending in Leah's body tingled in ecstasy. She gasped as his mouth travelled down to her neck, and he pulled her gently down onto the sheepskin rug. Brett propped himself above her as his hand hovered over the buttons of the black camisole top she was wearing.

'May I?' he asked.

Leah nodded shyly, and Brett reverently undid each of the tiny seed-pearl buttons, until the garment fell away.

'Leah, you are so beautiful, too beautiful.'

Leah lay there, eyes closed, enjoying the new sensations permeating her, but also knowing that she must make a decision. She had guarded her innocence for so long it had become almost sacred.

Leah suddenly understood why. She had been waiting for him.

Brett must have sensed her thoughts, for he stopped kissing her and looked into her eyes.

'I want, very badly, to make love to you.'

He spoke to her gently, and Leah read the honesty in his eyes.

She nodded, tempted for a second to tell him that he would be the first, but too embarrassed to voice the words.

That they should be joined together as one seemed only natural. She knew she had always been waiting for him, that no one else could make her feel complete as this man could.

Leah's physical and emotional feelings locked tightly together into a climax of pure joy.

Afterwards, she lay nestled in his arms on the rug in front

of the fire, staring up through the windows at the purple glow of dawn.

Leah knew that tonight she had found the key to her future. Brett was the other half of her. He was the missing link to her soul.

Brett felt it too. He had tried to deny it, but as he looked down at her, he knew that loving her was his destiny and would rule his existence from now on.

Deep in their own thoughts, they lay cradled together, knowing with utter certainty that they had just sealed their fate.

10

Jenny flew off to Palm Springs on Monday and Brett decamped from his father's duplex to Leah's apartment.

They spent the evening reminding themselves of the pleasure they had experienced early on Sunday morning, finding it only better than they remembered. Leah was eager to learn how to please him, and found she was able to touch him without a shade of embarrassment.

They slept little, and Brett went into the office on Tuesday morning feeling as if he had returned from the moon. His thoughts were distracted, and he was unable to concentrate. As his father talked at him, Brett found his mind straying to Leah and counted the minutes before he was released from the real world to go back to his dream-like existence with her.

When he arrived at the door of the apartment, she was there waiting to greet him, her hair dripping wet from the bath, and her beautiful face devoid of make-up.

'I missed you,' he said as he threw his arms around her and drank in her heavenly smell.

Having made love again, Leah padded naked into the kitchen and threw some spaghetti in a pan. Brett showered and then sat at the kitchen table, content to watch her as she expertly prepared a Bolognese sauce.

They sat down in front of the fire with a bottle of red wine and the pasta.

'Wow, you're a great cook as well. What more can a man ask for?'

Leah giggled. She looked so sweet, sitting there in her robe on the sofa. Brett could hardly believe that this was the same woman whose beauty and sophistication stopped traffic when it was displayed on the many billboards that were being placed across the length and breadth of America.

'How about I take you out to dinner tomorrow night? I went to the 21 Club with Dad last week and it was excellent.'

Leah's face dropped. 'I can't tomorrow night. I've got to have dinner with Anthony Van Schiele. He owns Chaval.'

A flicker of fear surged through Brett. For the past two days nothing had come between their precious evenings together. The thought of Leah spending time with another man made him feel physically sick. But he knew that this was only the beginning of the inevitable insecurities. He was in love with one of the most beautiful women in the world and he would have to deal with the consequences.

'Fine. I understand,' he said with mock indignity.

Leah immediately put down her plate and came to sit on his lap.

'I don't want to go, Brett, but I have to.'

'I know you do, darling. I have plenty to catch up on workwise, so I'll spend the evening at home and try and get some sleep.'

Brett felt bereft as he left her at the entrance to the apartment the following morning.

'See you tomorrow. Just remember I love you.'

'And I love you.' She kissed him and climbed into the limousine waiting to take her to Chaval.

Brett hailed a taxi and rode to work feeling quite ridiculous as tears threatened to fill his eyes at the thought of waiting until the following evening to see her.

'Miss Thompson. As always, you look quite enchanting.'

Anthony Van Schiele greeted her at the entrance of Delmonico's, and the maître d' ushered them to the best table in the splendid dining room.

'Can I get you anything to drink?' he asked.

'Yes. A bottle of my usual white wine and some mineral water with lots of ice for Miss Thompson.'

Leah was impressed that Anthony Van Schiele had taken the trouble to discover what she drank.

'Please, call me Leah.' She smiled.

'And you must call me Anthony.'

Leah looked at the man across the table and thought how attractive he was. She would hazard a guess that he was in his early forties, although he looked younger, with his dark brown hair only tinged by grey at the temples. His physique was slim and toned, but his eyes were what gave him his gravitas. They were a soft grey, underlined by years of smiling and with a kindness that shone out of them. There was something trustworthy and strong about him.

'So, how is the campaign going? I've seen the posters . . . Well, who in New York hasn't?' He twinkled. 'I think they're wonderful and that you are going to earn a great deal of money for our little company.'

Leah tried not to laugh at Anthony's description. Chaval Cosmetics was probably one of the largest and most successful companies of its kind in the world.

'I hope so too. Everything seems to be going well.'

'I trust that marketing vice president of mine is treating you well and not working you too hard?'

'Oh yes. Henry's been most kind.'

'Good. Any complaints, you just give me a call,' he said with sincerity. 'How are you settling down in New York? Have you been out much?'

'No. To be honest I've been too tired. The frenetic pace that this city moves at is starting to exhaust me.'

Anthony nodded. 'Ah, yes. Personally, I can't stand it. I find it intimidating and impersonal. I have a house in Southport, Connecticut, where the pace is slower and the air is clear. Although I must admit that New York seems to be suiting you. You look quite radiant tonight.' Anthony took in Leah's glowing, luminescent skin, which was selling many millions of dollars of Chaval cosmetics.

Despite the fact that Leah had been convinced she would have a miserable time, she found that the evening flew by. Anthony treated her with total respect, complete decorum, and seemed genuinely fascinated by her thoughts and opinions. Because of this, she found herself bringing down the usual barrier and telling him things about herself that she usually kept private.

She was amazed when she glanced at her watch in the powder room and noticed that it was getting on for eleven.

Leah sat down at the table and took a small sip of her cappuccino. 'So, are you going back to your house in Southport tonight?'

'Yes. I do try to go home every night, unless business keeps me here very late. I have an apartment at the top of the Chaval building where I can put my head down for a few hours.'

'I'll bet your wife doesn't see a lot of you,' commented Leah.

'My wife died two years ago, so I'm afraid there is no one at home who misses me,' he answered quietly.

Leah blushed. 'I'm so sorry, Anthony.'

'Thank you. But it was a blessed relief. She had been in

pain a long time.' He looked off into the distance. 'Sometimes, I still arrive home expecting her to be there, in her chair by the fire, waiting to greet me. People tell me time heals the pain, and I wait for that to be true.'

A wave of pity engulfed Leah. Instinctively, she reached across the table and squeezed his hand.

Anthony was touched by her concern. 'I'm sorry, Leah. I didn't bring you here to depress you. It's just a little tricky when others look at rich, successful people like us and only see the outer trappings, which I suppose spell happiness.'

Leah nodded eagerly, finding it refreshing to have found someone who voiced the feelings that she herself had.

'I know. Because of my job, no one ever seems to want to take a look at who I am inside. They're only interested in my face, nothing more.'

'I'm interested, Leah,' he said quietly. 'If you ever feel the need to talk, you know where I am. But now it's time to take you home. I can't be responsible for Chaval's most precious employee arriving for a shoot with bags under her eyes!'

Anthony escorted her from the restaurant. Outside, the chauffeur immediately sprang to attention and opened the rear door of the gleaming black limousine. Leah stepped inside and Anthony joined her. They drove through the busy streets in companionable silence until they reached her apartment block.

Anthony reached for her hand and kissed it.

'Thank you for a delightful evening. I'd like to do it again sometime.'

To her surprise, Leah answered without hesitation. 'Yes, so would I.' She made to get out of the car, but Anthony stopped her.

'You're a real person in a very unreal world. Hold on to that for me, won't you?'

She nodded and stepped out of the car. 'I will. Goodnight, Anthony, and thank you.'

As she waited for the lift, Leah thought about the unusual man she had spent the evening with. A peculiar bond had formed between the two of them and Leah knew that she had just made a friend.

11

The telephone rang shrilly through Leah's dream. She forced her eyes open and leaned over to pick up the receiver.

'Hello.'

'*Mia cara*. It is I, Carlo.'

She looked at the luminous dial on the clock.

'Carlo, it's four o'clock in the morning! What are you doing? You know I have to be up at the crack of dawn.'

'*Scusa, cara*, but I could not wait another second to speak to you. I have missed you so much.'

Leah knew that Carlo was waiting to hear that she had missed him too, but the truth was that she'd hardly thought of him since her arrival in New York.

Leah was silent. Carlo continued, 'Are you missing me as I have missed you?'

'Of course, Carlo,' she answered mechanically. An arm was encircling Leah and pulling her back into the warmth of the duvet. When she didn't respond, another arm snaked around her and grabbed hold of a breast.

'Stop it,' she whispered.

'Pardon? Is someone there with you, Leah?'

'No, of course not.' Brett subsided next to her. 'Anyway, the show's only three weeks away. We'll see each other then.' Leah saw Brett open his eyes and frown up at her. 'Look, I've got

264

to go. I want to try and get some more sleep. I've got a big shoot tomorrow.'

'Okay. I understand.' The petulant tone implied that he didn't at all. 'You do miss me, don't you, Leah?'

'Of course, Carlo.'

'I hope that you are behaving and saving yourself all for me. I have spies everywhere that will tell me if you are being a naughty girl.'

'Yes, Carlo. I'll see you in Milan.'

'Yes. I will wait with bated breath until then. *Buonanotte, cara.*'

Leah slowly replaced the receiver and lay back against the pillows.

'I presume that was Mr Porselli checking up on his protégée,' said Brett.

'Yes.'

Brett propped himself up on one elbow and stared down at her coldly. 'And what was all that about not being able to wait until you see him in three weeks' time?'

Leah sighed. 'Oh Brett. Don't be silly. You've got the wrong end of the stick. Carlo's just . . .'

'I'm jealous, Leah. Is there any truth in the rumours about the two of you?'

'Of course not, Brett.' Leah felt at once irritated and defensive. 'Carlo's been extremely good to me, but there's never been anything physical between us. Never.' *Or any other man*, thought Leah ruefully, wishing she could voice the words. 'I get so angry when the press make up their ridiculous stories. I thought you were above believing all that rubbish they write.'

Brett saw the anger in Leah's eyes. He lay back on the pillow next to her.

'Okay, okay. I'm sorry. I love you so much, I'm just insecure, that's all.'

265

'Brett, darling. Please. You have to trust me.' Leah's hand crept under the duvet and found his. 'I love you too. There'll never be anyone else. Ever. Promise.' She squeezed his hand and he snuggled in to her shoulder.

"Night, sweetheart. Sorry.'

Five minutes later, Brett could hear Leah's regular breathing, but sleep would not come so easily for him. The way Leah had talked to Carlo just then . . . he was sure that there had been something between them. He remembered the night of Leah's twenty-first, when the two of them had danced together. In three weeks' time, Leah would be off to Milan and back into Carlo's clutches. How he'd cope with the thought of them alone together Brett really didn't know.

All thoughts of Carlo were washed away as Brett and Leah spent an idyllic weekend exploring the delights of New York together.

They went shopping at Rockefeller Center on Saturday morning, then in the afternoon took a long stroll in Central Park and watched the children play on the carousel. In the evening, Brett took her to Sardi's and they both stared like stage-struck kids as the stars of Broadway sat not inches away from them. Afterwards, they caught a cab back to Brett's father's duplex and sat out on the terrace in the balmy September air, sipping coffee.

'This place is just beautiful,' said Leah in admiration. 'You must feel like you're slumming it when you come and stay at mine.'

'Your apartment has got heart.' Brett gestured round him. 'This hasn't.'

Brett persuaded Leah to stay with him that night, saying that his father was out of town on business and there would be no embarrassing breakfast meetings for her to endure.

Unfortunately, Brett was wrong, and as the two of them climbed the stairs in their bathrobes to enjoy the superb view over Central Park from the terrace as they ate breakfast, David was already there, reading the papers.

Leah stared at Brett's father. David Cooper looked nothing like his son or his sister, Rose. He had blond hair, flecked with grey, a deep tan, and piercing blue eyes that studied Leah with as much interest as she studied him.

'Well, I see we have a guest for breakfast. Leah Thompson, I presume.' He rose to shake her hand and Leah noted that David was slightly smaller than she was, with a firm, stocky body.

She held out her hand and David grasped it firmly. 'We've never met, but your face looks awfully familiar,' he joked.

Leah laughed with him, although she had heard the line a thousand times before.

They sat down at the table on the terrace and the maid brought them coffee and croissants. As Brett chatted easily to his father, Leah found herself comparing David Cooper to Anthony Van Schiele. The aura of power he exuded was breathtaking, but just as Anthony Van Schiele was unassuming about his vast wealth, David Cooper seemed to wear it like a mantle. Leah felt intimidated by his presence and slightly uncomfortable. She was glad when he stood up from the table, politely said goodbye to Leah and left the two of them alone.

'Sorry about that. Dad had a change of plans at the last moment,' said Brett, munching a croissant. 'So, what do you think?' He glanced casually at a newspaper.

'What do I think of what?'

'Dad, of course.'

'He's not a bit like you,' Leah answered carefully.

'That's what everyone at work says. Most of the staff are petrified of him.'

'I'm not surprised.'

Brett looked at her, his eyes demanding further explanation.

'I mean, he just . . . oozes power. He seemed very pleasant, though,' she added.

'He is, once you get to know him. That's one of the reasons I'm glad I've come to work for him. I hardly knew him as a child. He was away so much. I think that fear was passed on to me. But since I've been here in New York, he's seemed different, softer somehow.' Brett shrugged. 'I really admire what he's done, you know. He built up this huge business from scratch all by himself. So many of the big conglomerates over here are second- or third-hand wealth. What my father's accomplished in thirty-odd years has taken other companies generations.' Brett pulled a face. 'I'm afraid you don't do that by being a sweetie to your employees.'

'Of course not.' Leah was surprised that Brett felt he needed to defend his father.

'Now, what would you like to do today, darling?'

Leah thought for a moment. 'How about taking one of the boats that go round Manhattan? It looks as if it's going to be a lovely day.'

They took a yellow cab down to the 42nd Street pier, where they boarded the Circle Line and found themselves a couple of seats at the front of the boat. Leah and Brett enjoyed the cool breeze as the engines rumbled to life and the boat headed out across the river.

They listened to the crackle of the speakers, as the captain gave a running commentary while they passed the Statue of Liberty.

Brett was propped up on his elbows, staring out to sea. 'The immigrant boats used to come in this way, carrying their passengers to a new life in the promised land. I wonder what went through their heads as they saw America for the first time?' he mused. 'God, I'd love to paint this,' he added quietly.

As the boat completed its tour and chugged back towards the jetty, Brett leaned over to Leah and took her in his arms.

'Do you ever wish you could hold a moment and the way that you're feeling for ever?'

'Yes.'

'Well, this is one of my moments. I love you, Leah. I've never been happier than the past two weeks. I can't imagine life without you.'

Other passengers forgotten, they kissed and held each other until the boat was tied to the jetty and it was time to get off.

'I know where I want to spend the afternoon, if you wouldn't be too bored.' There was a sudden eagerness and a light in Brett's eyes as he thought of it.

'I'm sure I won't. Where?'

'The Museum of Modern Art.'

'I'd love to go.'

Leah felt a frisson of pleasure as the train rattled through the subway stations. This was the real New York: the air of tension and danger, the filthy carriage with its smell of sweat, dope and perfume, and its occupants, who lived in the hope of one day joining her and Brett in their rarefied world of money and comfort.

Leah emerged from the subway feeling as though she'd been on a different planet. As she walked hand in hand with Brett along the street, she was reminded of how much her life had changed in the past few years. And how much she now took for granted. She felt a little ashamed.

She spent the rest of the afternoon following Brett around the huge collection of priceless paintings in the museum, listening in awe as he talked knowledgeably about what they were seeing.

He made her understand Van Gogh's *Starry Night*, Picasso's *Les Demoiselles d'Avignon* and Matisse's *Dance*.

Brett seemed to be in a different world, as if something had come alive inside him. By the end of the afternoon, Leah knew that Brett had a love and a joy for art that she could only envy and admire, for she herself had no such passion.

'Who is your favourite artist?' asked Leah.

Brett's eyes widened. 'I can't answer that. I find a painting that I love, something that is a pure work of art for its atmosphere, statement and use of colour. Then I'll find another that I can't take my eyes off. I have a soft spot for Manet, Seurat . . . and Degas! He captured his dancers' vitality and grace so perfectly. I love them all, Leah.' He laughed. 'In some ways I'm glad that I didn't go to art school. I don't study paintings from a technical viewpoint, because I don't know how. I believe that a painting should be a work of beauty, something that you never cease wanting to look at. With too much knowledge you can find fault with each one and it takes away the sheer joy.'

'But you know so much about all of them.' Leah was holding Brett's hand as they walked out of the museum.

'Oh, I'm no expert,' he admitted.

'You must continue painting, Brett.'

Brett pulled a face. 'Maybe. Come on, we'll discuss it over caviar and blinis at the Russian Tea Room. My father said it's a must, and we can walk from here.'

Fifteen minutes later they were sitting on a comfortable red velvet banquette, sipping strong tea. Leah eyed the small pancakes filled with red and black caviar suspiciously.

'Mmm. Wonderful. Try one, Leah.'

'Okay. But I must warn you, I'm a fish and chips merchant myself.'

Brett laughed as Leah bit gingerly into the blini and found she enjoyed the unusual taste.

'Just because you're working for your father doesn't mean you should stop painting. You really do have talent.' Leah was determined not to let the momentum of Brett's enthusiasm at the museum go to waste.

'How do you know I'm talented?'

'Because I watched you when you used to paint up on the moors. It was a complete natural ability. If I had a talent like yours . . .' Leah shook her head. 'But I don't. I have no talent at all.'

'What on earth are you talking about, silly? You're one of the most successful models in the world. Surely that takes a little bit of talent,' Brett chastised, mouth full of his fourth blini.

Leah sighed. 'No. At least I don't think so. I just happen to have a pretty face and a good body and I wear clothes well. That's not something that comes from inside me. I don't have a natural gift for the arts or a superb mathematical brain that can do some good for mankind.'

Brett looked at Leah and mused at how she was constantly surprising him. When he had known her that first summer in Yorkshire, he too had fallen in love with her outer packaging and her sweet, gentle nature.

But as he grew closer to her, he was starting to realise that there was so much more to discover.

'We live in an immediate world, Leah. And the most immediate thing about you is your beauty. You mustn't resent it, because it's part of you and it's brought you success. And, I'd guess, quite a lot of money.'

Leah nodded. 'I know, Brett.' She paused and exhaled. 'But sometimes, when I'm standing in the same position for an hour or so, I watch the people hurrying around fiddling with the lights, the camera lens, or a piece of hair that's out of place. They all care so deeply about it. I mean, one photo. It's hardly going to change the world, is it? It just seems so false

271

and futile. And there's me, earning all that money for doing nothing, really, when there are people with real talent who are struggling to earn a crust, like the graffiti artist who painted that dragon on the train, or the young actors who work in here as waiters.'

Brett reached for Leah's hand. 'Sweetheart, I understand completely what you're saying. However, there is an answer to the puzzle, a way that you can reconcile yourself to what you do.'

'And what is that, Brett?'

'Well, you're in a very privileged position. People know you and your face. At present you are an ambassador for a cosmetics company. But in the future, you could use your money and your fame to much better purpose. If you want to do some good for the world, you couldn't be in a better position to do it.'

Leah thought about what Brett was saying. A look of relief crossed her face. 'You're right, Brett. In the future I can do some good. I'd never thought about it like that. Thank you.'

'For what?'

'For giving me a reason to get up at six in the morning and wear a professional smile on my face for the rest of the day.'

He squeezed her hand. 'Just remember, darling, there are real people around you. And it's wonderful to see that you haven't been sucked in to the hype and false glamour of the world you live in. That's why I love you so much.'

When they arrived back at Leah's apartment, they were greeted at the door by a radiant Jenny, just returned from her week in Palm Springs.

'Leah, darling, I've missed you!' Jenny flung her arms round her friend. Then she stepped back. 'How do I look?'

'Absolutely wonderful. Doesn't she, Brett?'

'She sure does.' He smiled.

'Come and sit down and I'll tell you all about it. I've just made some herbal tea. Want some?'

Leah sniggered and Jenny gave her a playful punch.

'Okay, okay. I know it sounds weird for your vodka-swigging best mate to be drinking dandelions, but, Leah, I'm converted!' Jenny went to the kitchen, poured some yellow liquid into three mugs and brought them into the sitting room.

'There you go. Try it. It's very good for you.'

Leah raised the cup to her lips and was immediately hit by the familiar, noxious smell. There was a strong memory attached to it; for a moment, Leah felt dizzy and disoriented.

She was back in Megan's kitchen, eleven years of age and terrified.

Leah banged the mug down onto the table beside her, as if to break the spell. The yellow liquid spilled over the edge and formed a small puddle.

'Are you okay, Leah?' Brett was looking at her pale face with concern.

'It's not that bad, Leah, honest.' Jenny giggled. 'Anyway, let me tell you all about the spa. You have *got* to go. It was absolutely amazing and I feel like a new woman. They've worked out a diet for me and shown me the exercises I have to do to keep the weight down, and I haven't had a drink or a fag since I left New York. I feel fantastic!'

Leah felt a glow of pride for Jenny. She certainly looked revitalised. Constant exercise had shed the pounds and toned her body back to its old sleekness. Her golden hair was hanging in shiny waves around her shoulders, her skin looked healthy and, most importantly, her eyes were sparkling with their old zest.

'I'm so pleased, Jenny. Now all you have to do is keep it up.'

'I will, Leah. I have to, don't I?' she said simply.

12

The telephone rang at nine o'clock exactly.

Miranda's heart beat hard against her chest as she picked up the receiver.

'Hello.'

'You are alone?'

He asked that every day.

'Yes.'

'Good. Have you missed me?'

Miranda gritted her teeth.

'Of course.'

'I have also missed you. I am touching myself now while I think about you. Are you doing the same?'

Miranda looked at the hand placed firmly around the stem of her glass of vintage red wine.

'Yes.'

'I do not believe you.'

'I promise I am.' Miranda tried not to let revulsion creep into her voice.

'Ahh, that feels so good. Is it good for you too?'

'Yes. Wonderful,' Miranda answered flatly.

'I'm sending my jet to London to collect you on Friday.' Santos's tone had changed completely from a few seconds before. 'Roger will be outside at four o'clock and you will be met at the other end by a limousine.'

'Where am I going?' she asked.

'To the boat. I shall look forward to seeing you for what will be a most enjoyable weekend. Sleep well, Miranda.'

Miranda replaced the receiver slowly. She had come to dread nine o'clock, and as it approached, she would pour herself a large glass of wine and steel herself for Santos's call.

For the first couple of weeks in the flat, he had been sweetness itself. Then the tone of his voice had begun to change. He had started urging her to say obscene things to him down the phone. She tried to protest, but he had shouted at her. Santos frightened Miranda when he was angry, so she had done as he asked.

Miranda ran a hand through her thick, blonde hair. She couldn't live like this any more. Things hadn't worked out at all like she had hoped. She'd lived like a princess for the past six weeks, eating sumptuous meals and wearing elegant, expensive clothes. She was chauffeured around in a Rolls-Royce and spent afternoons at Harrods increasing her wardrobe or buying gorgeous little dresses that she sent to Chloe in Yorkshire.

But all this she did alone. Miranda saw no one except the hard-faced German housekeeper, Maria, and Roger, the old cockney chauffeur, who insisted on following her in and out of every place she cared to visit. She'd tried to talk to them out of desperation, but Maria could hardly speak any English, and Roger replied to her general chatter in monosyllables.

Recently, she'd started dreaming vividly about Chloe. The nightmare was always the same: terrifying, horrifying.

Chloe was running across the moors, a dark figure chasing her. She was crying and calling out for Miranda. 'Mummy, Mummy! Where are you? Help me!' Miranda would stretch out her arms as her child came nearer, but Chloe would not see her, and would run past. Miranda's screams joined her daughter's as the menacing figure caught up with Chloe, and she stood watching helplessly.

Miranda would be woken by her own sobbing; sweating and shaking uncontrollably.

She'd pace around the flat until the dawn broke, petrified of the darkness, berating herself for the way she had resented Chloe since she'd been born. She'd never shown her child the love and affection she deserved. Chloe had to find that from others, such as Rose or Mrs Thompson.

She wanted to make things right. She wanted to wake up in the morning in her own pretty bedroom in Yorkshire, cuddling Chloe, and hear the curlews crying as they flew across the moors.

Tonight, the homesickness was unbearable.

Miranda was scared, very scared. She wanted desperately to run away, but she knew she was trapped.

She sat there for the rest of the evening, swilling the red wine down her throat and sinking slowly into oblivion.

When the bell rang next morning, Miranda was still on the sofa. Her head clattering, she staggered to the intercom.

'Hello.'

'It's Ian.'

'Okay.' She pressed the button and a couple of minutes later Ian was standing at the door with a look of concern on his face.

'Morning, Miranda. Gosh, are you all right?'

His obvious sympathy made Miranda burst into tears. Ian led her to the sofa, sat her down and waited patiently until she had finished crying. Then he went to the kitchen and made her a cup of strong black coffee.

'Drink this, and try to calm down.'

He sat there silently, watching her. Miranda found his presence comforting somehow. He was not the kind of man she would have glanced at twice two months ago, with his glasses and his kind, plain face. But now, Ian provided the touch of normality and dependability that was so lacking in her strange life.

'Now, I want you to put your best frock on and I'll take you out to lunch.'

She nodded and retired to the bedroom to shower and change.

'There, you look your pretty self again now,' Ian said kindly. He offered her his arm. 'Come on.'

They went downstairs and Miranda was surprised and pleased to see Ian opening the passenger door of a brand-new Range Rover.

'It's okay. You are allowed to come with me. I'm tried and trusted and I thought you'd prefer to go in my car.'

Miranda slipped in, just grateful to be away from that flat and the prying eyes of Roger and Maria.

Ian drove through London in silence, then parked his car down a small cobbled side alley, just off Kensington High Street.

'There's a very good bistro I know along here. I thought we could have a bite to eat and a chat.'

Inside the small restaurant, they sat down at a table in the corner and Ian ordered a bottle of wine.

'Hair of the dog for you, I think. Come on, it'll make you feel better. If you can't beat it, then make it worse. That's what I always say.' He laughed.

Miranda, for the first time in weeks, managed a giggle too.

'Now. I've brought you here because Roger called me to tell me what happened last night and I wanted to talk to you.' Ian's face was serious. 'I don't know how much you know about Mr Santos.'

Miranda shrugged. 'Almost nothing.'

'That's not surprising. Outside of the business world he keeps a low profile. He could go anywhere across the globe and not be recognised. His circle of friends, some of whom you met on board the boat, is small and elite. Most of them have worked for him for a long time and he trusts them. He does not socialise outside this set and it was a rare occurrence that you met him in London at a nightclub. However, his last, er, lady friend had been disposed of and he was on the hunt for a new one. You were it.'

Prey. Hunted, captured, like a helpless fly lured into a spider's web, thought Miranda.

'Does he always treat his . . . lady friends in this way? Like captives?'

Ian looked at her across the table, his eyes soft. He sighed.

'Miranda, I have worked for Santos for over ten years, ever since I came out of school and he gave me a job when I was desperate. He has been a generous employer and I've certainly been a loyal employee. I'm going to break that rule for the next ten minutes because I honestly don't think you realise what you've got yourself into here. Usually, the girls he chooses are professionals: hard, worldly wise and prepared to do anything for a fur coat and a life of luxury. You're not really like that, are you?'

Miranda shook her head. 'I thought I was. I mean, I wanted all those things too. But not like this.'

'Well, I have to tell you that you've got yourself into a hell of a hole. For all Santos's anonymity, he controls one of the most powerful business empires in the world. He has fingers in every pie, although most of the time he'll use a frontman to do the negotiating and the other party will not be aware that Santos owns the company. That way, he's managed to collate vast wealth and power across the globe without anybody realising it.'

'Why does he do that?'

Ian shook his head. 'I've no idea, but it's always been the case. For example, I work for a company in London and only myself and one other director report to Santos. The rest are unaware of the real owner. Strange, I know, but then Santos is a strange man.'

'Ain't that the truth,' breathed Miranda. 'So, am I his only mistress?' She hated using the word, but knew it was the only accurate description.

'Of course I couldn't say for sure, but yes, I believe so. Santos is married. His wife is German. I've only met her once. Don't do anything to incur the man's wrath. He's dangerous when angry,' Ian said quietly.

A shiver of fear went through Miranda. 'What do you mean?'

'I'm not saying any more, but I don't want to see you get hurt, or your child.' It slipped out before Ian could stop it and he regretted it immediately as he looked at Miranda's horror-stricken face.

'How do you know about Chloe?' Miranda asked, trying to control herself.

'Well, the shopping trips for children's clothes, the phone calls that Maria has overheard. That's what she and Roger are paid such a lot of money by Santos to do. They put two and two together very quickly. Luckily they've told me and not him. I cannot stress to you how important it is that Santos remains unaware of your little girl. It's leverage he'll use if he has to. So, no more phone calls or letters. You must cut off all contact immediately to protect the both of you.'

Miranda took a few deep breaths to try and calm herself as the fear rose inside her. 'I don't understand why, Ian. Why does he keep me a prisoner? Why does he pay people to spy on me? Why can't I speak to Chloe?' Tears of helplessness sparked in her eyes. This was like some dreadful nightmare.

Ian looked nervous. 'I would be in terrible trouble if Santos found out about what I've told you. He's bought you, and he possesses you. It's the way he is with all his women. If you are good to him and do everything he says, you'll be fine. If not . . .'

The threat hung in the air.

Miranda steeled herself. 'I'm going to leave. I'll go to King's Cross and get on a train back to Leeds. What's going to happen, really?'

Ian looked grim. 'You'll be stopped.'

'By you?'

He shifted uncomfortably. 'More likely Roger. As you know, he's far less sympathetic. If he goes straight to Mr Santos . . . I would worry for your family.'

Miranda was shaking her head from side to side in disbelief. 'Can't you help me, Ian? Isn't there anything you can do?'

Ian cast his eyes down. 'My parents are elderly and I need the money I earn.'

'What about the police?' Miranda was getting desperate.

'He has half of them in his pocket, not to mention government officials.' Miranda put her head in her hands. 'I'm sorry, I don't mean to frighten you. It's terrible that you've become embroiled in all this. But you have, and I just needed to warn you. I'll do everything I can to assist you in your current situation, I promise.' There was an uncomfortable pause as the hopelessness of the scenario descended on the pair of them. Now, shall we order?'

Ian tried to lighten the atmosphere for the rest of the lunch, making jokes and telling silly stories. Miranda hardly heard them. She picked at the food on her plate without enthusiasm and was glad when Ian asked for the bill.

She looked out of the window in silence during the journey home.

'I won't come in, as I've work to do. Are you going to be okay?'

'Yes,' she answered in a flat voice.

'I believe you're going off on Friday to join Santos for the weekend.'

'Yes.'

'As I said, just be nice to him. You'll probably have a good time. I'll pop in and see you when you're back. Take care, Miranda.'

'Thanks for lunch.'

Ian watched her as she sadly made her way to the door of her apartment and disappeared inside.

'Poor kid,' he breathed, as he started the engine and drove off down the elegant tree-lined street.

'*Buongiorno*, Leah! You are looking radiant, *cara*. It is so good to see you.' Carlo was like an excited little boy as he fussed round Leah, finding her a chair in the crowded salon and ordering one of his assistants to get her a cup of coffee.

Leah looked around the salon and smiled. She couldn't help remembering the morning when Maria Malgasa was the star of the show and Carlo had treated her like a queen. She looked behind and noticed a couple of new, younger faces sitting nervously at the back, as she herself had once done. They were staring at her with awe, and she gave them a friendly smile.

The twice-yearly shows were a chance to catch up with the fashion crowd. After her first year, Leah had always enjoyed them immensely. Of course, now she was the star of the September haute couture collection, not just the October ready-to-wear, and photographers were as eager to catch Leah on film as they were Carlo's creations.

But this year, as she listened to Giulio go through the running order, she did not feel the same buzz of excitement. Perhaps it was jet lag after the long flight, or more likely that she felt bereft at the thought of being without Brett for the week. That, plus having to face Carlo's smothering attentions after she had become used to life without him.

And this year, Jenny wasn't here. None of the designers had wanted to use her when Madelaine had offered her services. They wouldn't take her word that Jenny was back to her old self. Leah had even gritted her teeth, called Carlo and begged him to give Jenny a chance.

'Even for you, darling, the answer is no. She is *finita*. Washed up, as the Americans say.'

Leah had assured him that Jenny was booze and drug free and looking great, but the fact that her cosmetics contract had been cancelled hadn't helped Jenny's cause. Jenny herself had taken the news relatively coolly when Madelaine had called to tell her.

'It's their loss. There'll be other contracts.' She had shrugged.

Leah had felt awful when Jenny had helped her pack for her trip to Milan, but was grateful that the romance with her prince seemed to be going well. Ranu was taking her on holiday for a few days and Leah was sure that it was the only thing that was keeping her going. She wanted to cry when she thought about the amount of work Jenny had put into her rehabilitation. No one would give her a chance.

'Okay, ladies. Let's set to work,' called Giulio.

The spring collection was a huge success, and Carlo had excelled himself this year. Afterwards, the photographers clustered round Leah. As always, Carlo insisted on putting his arms tightly around her and kissing her cheek. Leah squirmed, but it was too late.

'Is the romance still on between the two of you, Miss Thompson?' one gossip columnist shouted above the throng.

Leah turned away.

'Gentlemen. Enough. Leah, as you know, is shy. We are both tired now,' said Carlo.

'What about the young man you were spotted having dinner with in Sardi's?'

Leah sighed. Someone had caught Leah and Brett leaving the restaurant arm in arm, taken a photo and splashed it across every tabloid in America. 'The model and the millionaire's son,' had run the headlines. Leah had not realised the photo would have reached Italy.

Carlo looked at her oddly, then replied, 'Is it not okay for Miss Thompson to go out with a business associate when she is alone in a new city? Okay, ladies and gentlemen. I think you have enough now. *Scusate*.'

He pulled Leah away from the clutch of photographers.

'*Scusa*, I have some people to see, then I wish to take you to dinner.'

Carlo strode away, and Leah knew that she had been issued with an order, not an invitation.

Half an hour later, Carlo came to collect her. They walked outside and Carlo opened the passenger door to his red Lamborghini.

There was an uncomfortable silence as they drove through the quiet streets of Milan and out into open countryside.

'Where are we going, Carlo?'

'I told you. I'm taking you to dinner.'

Having trusted him completely for years, Leah had now accepted that something had changed on the night of her twenty-first birthday. The sense of unease inside her grew as they sped further away from Milan.

Carlo turned left through a large pair of wrought-iron gates and up a sweeping drive. He parked the car in front of a large *palazzo*, which was floodlit and looked like a fairy-tale castle.

'Welcome to my home,' Carlo said.

Leah could not help but suck in her breath. Carlo was always promising to show her his *palazzo*, but her visits to

Milan in the past few years had been busy and she had never managed it.

She got out of the car and followed him up the wide steps to the porticoed front door. It was opened by a butler.

'Good evening, Antonio.'

'Good evening, sir.'

'Is everything arranged?'

'*Sì*, sir. Follow me.'

Leah followed Carlo and the butler through the expanse of exquisite rooms, each one seemingly grander than the last. The high ceilings were delicately painted in pastel shades, depicting religious scenes, and the furniture looked priceless. It reminded Leah more of a museum than a home, and she thought how Brett would appreciate the works of art covering the walls.

At the end of a long marble-floored corridor, lit by count-less chandeliers, Antonio opened the double doors and led them into the room.

Leah gasped. She looked up at the ceiling, which was maybe fifty feet above her. She could barely see the other end of the room, it was so vast.

'The ballroom,' said Carlo. He offered her his arm. 'Come. We will eat.'

The ballroom was completely empty save for one table by the large french windows, which opened onto a floodlit terrace.

Carlo led her across the great expanse of floor to the table, which was set for dinner.

As they sat down, a waiter appeared from nowhere and opened the champagne resting in an ice bucket. He poured it into two glasses, then went onto the terrace and clicked his fingers. Immediately, the sounds of gentle classical music floated in from the terrace and Leah saw the string quartet playing outside.

Carlo smiled at Leah's awestruck face. 'See, I told you I was taking you to dinner. It is beautiful here, is it not?'

Leah nodded. 'Yes. It's a fairytale setting.'

Carlo's smile grew larger. 'I am glad you like it. Come. let's have a toast. I know you do not like drinking, but one will not hurt.'

He raised his glass and Leah reluctantly raised hers.

'To us.'

'To us,' she murmured.

The meal that followed was the most sumptuous Leah had ever tasted. Minestrone, osso buco, a shin of veal on a bed of risotto – delicately spiced with herbs that had been grown on the estate – and zabaglione for dessert.

Leah threw up her hands in despair when a large selection of cheeses was brought by the waiter and placed on the table.

'Really, Carlo. I can't. I'm going to burst. That was the most delicious dinner I have ever had. I'm amazed you ever want to eat out when you have a cook like that at home.'

'Yes. Isabella is a wonder. She has been with our family for years. Now, I think it is time we danced.'

The waiter slid back Leah's chair and she stood up. Carlo led her onto the terrace and bowed formally.

'May I have the pleasure?'

Leah nodded and Carlo put his arms around her. They waltzed slowly to the soft music and Leah felt humbled by the beauty of the scene. She only wished that the arms around her were Brett's.

'Oh *cara*, you look more exquisite tonight than I have ever seen you. Your beauty seems to grow with every passing year. Come, I have something to show you.'

Carlo abruptly stopped dancing and escorted her along the terrace, through another set of french windows.

This room was much smaller and almost looked cosy by comparison to the ballroom. Carlo shut them in.

'Here. Sit by the fire. The autumn breeze is a little chilly.'

Leah sat down in a comfortable red velvet chair and Carlo sat opposite her.

'Would you like a little brandy, *cara*?'

Leah shook her head and watched as Carlo stood up and went to a large gold-inlaid cabinet, on top of which was a selection of heavy crystal decanters. She noticed that Carlo seemed uncharacteristically nervous. He poured himself a large measure of brandy and threw it back in one. He poured another and brought it back to his chair by the fire.

Carlo stared at the burning logs, moving his glass round in his hands.

'You are probably wondering why I have asked you here tonight. The past six weeks without you have been unbearable. The separation has confirmed what I have always known. I love you, Leah. I want you to be my wife.'

He took a small black velvet box out of his top pocket, revealed a shimmering diamond ring and bent down in front of her chair.

'It is only what the fashion world has been expecting. We are meant to be together, you and I. You will live here with me, in the kind of splendour your beauty deserves, and one day you will give me children as beautiful as you.' Carlo took Leah's hand and slipped the ring on her fourth finger.

'Say yes, *cara*, and I will make you the happiest woman alive.'

Leah looked down at the ring on her finger. Suddenly the entire absurdity of the evening hit her and she wanted to laugh.

It was all so perfect. The handsome young prince, proposing to his lady amidst the opulent splendour of his palace. Right from a storybook. The only problem was that she loved another man.

She took a deep breath, shook her head, and removed the exquisite ring from her finger. Leah handed it to him.

'No, Carlo. I can't marry you.'

Carlo looked as though he had been slapped across the face.

'Why not?' His amazement was genuine and Leah realised that not for a second had Carlo contemplated the fact that she might say no.

'Because I'm in love with someone else.'

The amazement turned to horror.

'Who?'

'He's the gentleman you saw me with in the photograph. His name's Brett Cooper and I've known him since I was fifteen.'

'You are telling me that you have been having an affair for all these years, while patient Carlo looked after you, cared for you and never once touched you?' His voice was trembling with anger.

Leah shook her head. 'No, Carlo. I met him again on my twenty-first birthday. He's living in New York and we met up there.'

Carlo stood up and paced around the room.

'*Un momento, per favore!* So this is just a crush. Some little boy who has kept you company while you were lonely in New York. You will get over him, Leah. He cannot offer you what I can, what you deserve. A beautiful home, a title. Do not throw this away. We were made to be together.'

'As a matter of fact, Brett's father is one of the wealthiest men in the world. Not that money matters,' she added. 'Remember, I have my own anyway, and I'd love Brett even if he didn't have a penny.'

'After all I've done for you, this is my reward. I made you what you are and now you repay me by screwing some nasty little boy who is still wet behind the ears.' Carlo's voice was rising.

Leah stood up. 'I'm very grateful for everything you've done for me, Carlo. You've been wonderful and I regard you as one of my closest friends. But I think I'd better leave now.' She calmly walked towards the door.

'All this time you are acting like the Virgin Mary with me and seeing other men. Well –' Carlo rounded on Leah and she saw the glint of triumph in his eyes – 'it is too late. This afternoon I told the press of our engagement and forthcoming marriage.'

Leah stopped in her tracks. 'You did what?'

Carlo said nothing, just smiled at her.

'How dare you say that without my permission? Who the hell do you think you are?'

'The man who turned you from a *goffa*, stupid little kid, to the star you are now.'

'Jenny was right. She said you believed that my success is all down to you. But you don't own me, Carlo, no one does. You'd better ring the press tomorrow and tell them there's been a mistake. If you don't, I will.'

'I cannot do that. It will be in all the papers across the world tomorrow morning. *Cara*, please. Let us not argue. I know you love me. You will forget this other boy.' Carlo reached his arms towards Leah, but she moved away, trembling with anger.

'Don't touch me, Carlo!'

He followed her and pulled her roughly into his arms.

'I think you owe me a kiss at the very least.' He pressed his lips to hers, trying to prise open her mouth.

'Stop it! Stop it!' Leah wriggled free of him, panting. 'As

289

far as I'm concerned, I never want to see you again. Our contract finished at the end of this show and I won't sign another. I want you to call your chauffeur and have him take me back to Milan this instant.'

Carlo's expression changed and his voice softened. '*Cara*, surely you cannot be serious? *Va bene*, maybe I was a little hasty, telling the press before we finalised arrangements ourselves—'

'Carlo, for the last time, I do not love you, I do not want to marry you and what you have done is despicable. Call for a car now! Otherwise it will be me who'll be calling the press.'

'Okay, okay.' Carlo rang a bell. 'We will talk tomorrow when you are calmer.'

The butler appeared and Carlo spoke to him in Italian.

'The car is outside.'

'Goodbye, Carlo. I hope for your sake that the damage you have done can be rectified.'

Leah left the room and followed the butler down the long hall, quivering with fury.

On the journey back to Milan she tried to make sense of what Carlo had done. If he was telling the truth, then it was too late to do anything. The story would be in the papers tomorrow morning.

Brett.

Leah bit her lip. She knew how dreadfully insecure he was about her relationship with Carlo already.

The minute she arrived in her room, she put a call through to Brett's office. Pat said he had just left. She tried the duplex, but only reached the answering machine, so she left a message asking him to call her at the hotel.

She had to try to explain before he saw the papers.

Leah tried to convince herself that Brett would understand, but as morning approached, so did the doubt in her heart.

14

Carlo Porselli, the Italian fashion designer who took the Milan shows by storm this week, yesterday announced his engagement to his muse and top model, Leah Thompson. This is not an unexpected event; the two young lovers have been inseparable for the past four years.

Miss Thompson spent a romantic evening with Carlo at his *palazzo* on the shores of Lake Como last night to celebrate the forthcoming wedding. She was seen slipping back into her suite at the hotel Principe di Savoia as the dawn was breaking.

Miss Thompson flies back to New York today to continue her commitments to Chaval Cosmetics, but Carlo assured me that she will return to Milan to live as soon as her contract is up. Congratulations to the both of them!

Leah studied the photograph of Carlo kissing her outside his salon and sighed. As the taxi taking her to her apartment from Kennedy Airport sped through the streets, Leah read four separate articles in further newspapers. They were almost identical, word for word.

'Oh God.' Leah rubbed her forehead in dismay, knowing that there wasn't a hope in hell of Brett avoiding the news. She wondered whether she should call her lawyer and sue, but what was the point? The papers had every right to print what Carlo had told them . . . so she'd have to sue Carlo. By the time she arrived at the entrance to her apartment, Leah's head was spinning.

'Oh no.' Leah let out a gasp of dismay as she saw the paparazzi surging towards her cab.

'Have you set a date yet, Leah?'

'Congratulations, Miss Thompson!'

'What about Brett Cooper, the man who's been escorting you since you arrived in New York?'

'No comment, no comment.' Leah fought through the crowd of journalists and photographers. She needed to gather herself together before she started making a statement, and Madelaine had always instructed her girls not to talk to the press directly. The first thing she wanted to do was to call Brett.

The apartment was silent. Leah flung her suitcase into her bedroom and walked along the hall to Jenny's room.

The door was shut. Leah tapped on it. 'Jenny, Jenny! I'm back! I need to talk to you.' There was no reply. Leah opened the door and found it in darkness, but could make out the sleeping form in the bed.

'Jenny, wake up. There's a horde of journalists downstairs and . . .' Leah crept to the bed. Jenny was fast asleep. 'Jen, wake up.' She shook her friend gently. Still no response.

Leah pulled back the curtains and light shone onto the pale, immobile face in the bed.

Then she noticed the vodka bottle lying next to the empty bottle of pills on the duvet.

'Jenny, wake up!' Leah shouted and shook her violently, panic rising in her stomach.

'Oh God.'

Leah picked up the telephone by the bed and dialled emergency.

'Hello. Ambulance, please. Yes.' Leah gave the address. 'I think she may have taken an overdose. Please hurry. I can't wake her . . . what? No, I don't know how long ago. Okay, I'll do that.'

Leah put the receiver down and hurried to get her duvet from her bed. She threw it on top of the inert, lifeless form, then sat holding the cold hand.

'Oh Jenny, please don't be dead. Come on, Leah's here now.' Tears plopped down her face as every second seemed to last for ever and all she could do was to sit there uselessly, unable to help. All thoughts of her own problems left her as she prayed that it wasn't too late.

At last she heard the intercom buzz.

She answered and within a minute the paramedics were beside Jenny, testing her vital signs.

'Okay, let's get her to hospital.'

They lifted Jenny onto a stretcher and Leah held the lift as they squeezed in.

'Is she . . . ?'

Leah couldn't bring herself to voice the words.

'She's alive, but only just. She's been unconscious for several hours.'

At the doors of the apartment building, the paparazzi closed in as the medics lifted Jenny into the back of the ambulance and immediately attached an oxygen mask.

'Who is this, Miss Thompson? A friend of yours?' A journalist pushed her way to the front of the pack.

'You coming with us, miss?' said the medic.

Leah nodded gratefully as she was hauled inside the ambulance and the doors shut.

As soon as they arrived at Lenox Hill Hospital, Jenny was taken straight off into emergency, leaving Leah to pace around the deserted waiting room. Tears kept coming to her eyes as she thought of how hard her friend had tried to pull herself back together again, and how no one had been prepared to give her a chance. Jenny was dying from the pressure of having to be perfect.

Eventually a doctor appeared through the swing doors.

'You're the friend of Jennifer Amory?'

Leah looked up slowly, her face turning ashen. 'Yes,' she whispered.

'Well, we think that Miss Amory is going to be all right. She's in intensive care and will be pretty sick for the next few days, but she should pull through.'

'Thank God,' breathed Leah, fresh tears coming to her eyes. 'Was it an overdose?'

The doctor raised his palms. 'Yes. Whether it was intended or not we have yet to discover. But whichever doctor prescribed the diet pills we have just pumped out of her stomach should be shot. Mixed with alcohol, they can be lethal. I doubt very much if Miss Amory had eaten anything for the past two days. We found no evidence of that inside her. Was she on a diet, do you know?'

'Yes. But I had no idea the health spa had prescribed her pills.'

'Health spa? Is that what they call them these days?' The doctor raised an eyebrow. 'I'll be telling Miss Amory not to waste her money on such places in the future. The pills these places prescribe are sometimes untested and unsafe. You can't mess around with your metabolism as if it's a second-hand car, you know.'

'Can I see her?'

The doctor nodded. 'She's sleepy and a little frightened, which is a good sign. Come with me.'

Leah followed the doctor down the corridor and into a small private room.

Jenny was lying in the bed with tubes running from all parts of her body into large monitors. Her eyes were open and they lit up in her pale face when she saw Leah.

'Hello.' Her voice was hoarse and no more than a whisper.

Leah bent over and kissed Jenny's cold cheek, then sat in the chair next to her.

'The doctors say you're going to be just fine.' She smiled.

'I didn't mean to take so many. I . . . I just lost count.'

'Well. No more of those for you in the future. You know what those kinds of pills can do to you now,' Leah said gently.

'Yes, but I was so desperate to keep the weight off. I had an important appointment on Monday and I wanted to look my best. Madelaine said it was my last chance and . . .' Tears came to Jenny's eyes and Leah reached for her hand.

'Shh, I'm going to call Madelaine first thing on Monday morning and we'll get it all sorted out. So don't you worry about that. You just try and get some rest and I'll be back to see you as soon as I can.'

'No!' Jenny grasped her hand. 'I don't want anyone to know. Please, Leah, promise me you won't say a word.'

'Okay, okay. I promise.'

The doctor was beckoning Leah towards the door.

'I have to go now. Try and sleep. Everything's fine. Bye, darling.'

Jenny gave a shadow of a smile as Leah kissed her once more then left the room with the doctor.

'Leave visiting her again until tomorrow. All she needs now is a lot of sleep.'

'She told me just now that she didn't mean to take so many of those pills, so I don't think it was deliberate.'

The doctor shrugged. 'Who knows? Sometimes this kind of thing can be a cry for help. Anyway, we'll make sure our therapist has a good long talk to her before we let her out of here.'

* * *

Leah took a cab back to her apartment, feeling cold despite the relative warmth of the late September weather. The journalists had thankfully dispersed, but her head was reeling from the events of the past twenty-four hours. She let herself into the silent apartment and wearily made her way through to the sitting room where she saw the familiar figure sitting on the sofa.

'Hello, Brett.'

He did not turn to acknowledge her. 'Hope you don't mind. I let myself in with my key. I thought under the circumstances that I'd better return it.'

His voice was flat and cold and his words were slurred. Leah realised he was drunk.

The last thing she felt like was a major confrontation. She was drained and exhausted.

'Took you some time to get home. Been celebrating the good news, have you?'

'No, Brett. As a matter of fact I've been at the hospital. Jenny, she – oh, it doesn't matter.' Jenny had sworn her to secrecy. Leah shook her head weakly and went to sit in the armchair facing Brett.

'I tried to call you last night and—'

'I know. Got your messages. Nice of you to give me prior warning, or was it to ask me to be best man?' Brett spat.

'Look, Brett, please. Give me a chance to explain, before you jump to conclusions. I—'

'Conclusions! Jesus Christ, Leah! The whole of America knows you were seen slipping back into your hotel room at dawn, having spent a cosy evening alone with Carlo. Are you denying that?'

'No, I . . . But they've got it all wrong. I did go with Carlo to his *palazzo*. He invited me for dinner and I didn't realise what he'd got planned and—'

'Ahh, sweet, innocent little Leah, dragged off by big, bad Carlo to his lair. How come it took you until dawn to escape? Was he holding you prisoner, or couldn't you be bothered to drag yourself out of his nice warm bed?'

'Enough!' The tone in Leah's voice was that of white-hot anger. 'I am not prepared for you to sit in my apartment and talk to me like this. I'm guilty before I've been tried and you haven't even given me a chance to explain.' Brett was momentarily stunned by Leah's rage. 'Carlo *did* propose to me at his *palazzo*. I was horrified and disgusted. And I said NO, for God's sake. But he'd already told the press I'd accepted. The stories were ready to run. I have done *nothing* wrong, Brett. Nothing.'

Brett stood up, and swayed a little. His eyes were struggling to fix on Leah. 'That's a convenient little story.'

'You're drunk, Brett. I think we'd better discuss this when you've sobered up.'

Brett took a stumbling step forwards. 'And wouldn't you be drunk if the girl you loved had lied to you, spent a night with another man, and then announced her engagement to the world? Well, you got what you wanted, Leah. You paid me back well and truly for hurting you when you were younger. I hope it makes you feel good.'

Leah watched Brett lurch towards the door. It was pointless trying to explain further. He was too drunk and irrational to listen. Tears pricked the backs of her eyes as she followed him down the hall towards the door.

'Well, goodbye, Leah. It's been nice knowing you. I hope you have many years of happiness with that Italian prick.'

'Brett.' She reached for his arm. 'Go home and when you've calmed down, please call me. And just remember how I believed you and gave you another chance.'

For a second, Leah saw a flicker of comprehension in Brett's eyes. Then wounded pride and anger returned. Brett shook

297

his head, turned and wandered unsteadily down the corridor towards the lift.

Leah banged the door shut, fell to her knees and sobbed her heart out. She knew she had lost him again.

Eventually, she dragged herself wearily into her bathroom and took a shower. Feeling a little recovered, she sat on her bed and called the hospital. Jenny was resting comfortably. Leah took the receiver off the hook and crawled under the cool sheets.

But sleep would not come. Everything was so confused. Carlo, Jenny, Brett . . . Leah gazed at the ceiling and thought how many girls around the world would give anything to be her. Beautiful, successful, rich. But these things came with a very high price. And Leah was unsure whether she was prepared to go on paying it.

15

'Who was that?' the pathetic bundle on the sofa asked quietly.

'Anthony Van Schiele. He wants me to go to lunch with him at his house in Southport tomorrow. He's sending a car at twelve. He's probably got cold feet about this Carlo business and thinks I'm about to throw up the contract to become a *principessa*. I'm going to have to go and provide some reassurance. Will you be okay?'

'I'll be fine, Leah, really.'

Leah walked across the room and sat on the edge of the sofa by Jenny's feet. The pale face and skeletal frame hardly resembled the girl she'd once known.

It had been two weeks since Jenny had been let out of hospital. This had coincided with Leah's work for Chaval coming to an end. She had cancelled all further assignments and nursed Jenny night and day. But, worryingly, she could not detect any improvement. In fact, if anything, Jenny had deteriorated. She seemed to have lost her fighting spirit and every day retreated further into herself.

The doctor had warned Leah that depression was to be expected after an overdose, and that the 'cold turkey' of no diet pills or booze would have a debilitating effect on Jenny's emotional stability.

Having had such a fight to keep her weight down for all these years, Jenny had now gone to the other extreme. Leah was almost having to force-feed whatever she could get down Jenny's throat. She was nothing more than a bag of bones and Leah thought wryly how pleased Madelaine would be.

'If I make you some of that nice soup I bought yesterday, will you eat a little?'

Jenny shook her head. 'I'm not hungry.'

'But you must eat, darling. You're fading away.'

'Everyone has spent the last few years telling me I need to lose weight and now I'm being nagged to eat.'

'At the moment, you couldn't stand up, let alone show that body of yours to a camera. You have to get your strength back, put on a little weight, and then you'll be in the swing of things again.'

'What's the point, Leah? I know you're trying to be nice, but you know as well as I do that my career's finished. No one will touch me with a bargepole,' Jenny said sadly.

Leah bit her lip. After her conversation with Madelaine, she knew what Jenny said was true.

'Well, what about Ranu? He'd hate to see you like this.'

'I haven't heard from him since we got back from our holiday. He doesn't know I've been ill, and I'd prefer it to stay that way. He doesn't give a damn anyway.'

'Of course he does. I thought you said you had a lovely time in Aspen.'

'We did. But I know he doesn't love me, Leah. Besides, he wants a renowned, successful sex symbol to be seen on his arm, not a washed-up old druggie like me.'

'Don't talk like that,' said Leah in despair.

'Why not? It's the truth, isn't it?'

Leah sighed heavily. 'Jenny. You have to pull yourself out of this. You're too young to give up. You have everything to live for. Even if it's not modelling, there are other things in life, things that are much more worthwhile.'

'All I have is my face and my body. I've tried to destroy those and I have nothing left.'

'Jenny, that is the biggest load of crap I've ever heard! It's the photographers and designers that make you feel as though you don't have an inside. You've fallen for it hook, line and sinker.' Leah thought carefully about her next words. 'I'm really disappointed in you.'

'I'm sorry. It's just the way I feel.' Jenny shrugged.

Leah threw up her hands in despair and wandered into the bedroom. It was an autumnal Saturday morning in October, and the trees below her window were turning soft shades of yellow and gold.

For some reason, the beauty of the scene brought tears to Leah's eyes. Perhaps it was because nursing Jenny had given her an excuse to hibernate for the past couple of weeks. She'd needed a break from the camera and the press, to take stock before she re-emerged into the glare of publicity. She'd discussed the Carlo situation with Madelaine, who had been most anxious when Leah had said she might sue.

'No, darling, don't do that. It's bad for your image.'

And your agency's, thought Leah wryly.

'Give it some time, let things calm down. The press will be onto another big story next week. In a couple of months, they'll be pairing you off with someone else.'

'But Madelaine, Carlo shouldn't be allowed to get away with this.'

'I know, darling. He's been a very naughty boy . . . but he did give you your big break.'

'Why do people keep saying this to me, Madelaine? Aren't I in any way responsible? It's my bloody face, after all.' Leah was aware that she had never taken this tone with her agent before.

301

'Yes, darling, yes. But Carlo is a powerful man. I just . . . *feel* as if the right thing to do is to leave it all alone. The story will fizzle out. You and Carlo are tomorrow's chip paper, remember.'

Leah felt her blood pressure rising. 'You don't want me to sue because he and his friends will stop using your models.'

There was a tense pause between the pair. 'You enjoy your life, don't you, Leah?'

'What?'

'The New York apartment, the social status, the money. And all this because you turn up at glamorous locations and have your picture taken. People would kill for your job.'

'What are you saying, Madelaine?'

'That if you want to stay feted and adored by the industry *and* the public, you put on your belt and braces, and carry on as normal. Carlo knows he's made a mistake. Let's use it to our advantage.'

Leah didn't have the strength to fight Madelaine, too. 'Well, you can tell him from me that I don't ever want to work for him again and he's not to try to contact me, otherwise I bloody well will sue!'

The injustice of Carlo's actions ate into Leah night and day. She hated him for destroying her relationship with Brett, who had not called. Even if he did, it would be impossible to build any trust back into the relationship.

All in all, the past two weeks had been dreadful.

'Hello, Leah. My, you look beautiful. Do come in.'

Leah was overwhelmed by the vast house as she followed Anthony through the simple but exquisitely furnished rooms. The mansion was set in a large area of land in leafy Southport, Connecticut.

'What would you like to drink?' Anthony enquired.

'Mineral water, please.'

He gave a nod and prepared the drinks himself, as Leah looked out of the large windows of the elegant sitting room onto the rolling green landscape beyond.

'You really do have a beautiful home, Anthony,' Leah complimented him.

'Thank you. We . . . I designed the place myself. Of course, now that my son is only home for the holidays and since my wife . . . well, it's a bit big for just me. I mostly use the snug and bedroom. I'm thinking of selling it, actually.'

Leah was horrified. 'Don't do that. It's very special. I can hardly believe I'm only a short distance from New York. The view out here reminds me of where I was brought up.'

'And where was that?'

'Yorkshire.'

'Brontë country. I've read all the sisters' books.'

Leah did not hide her surprise. 'Really? So have I. I love them.'

The two of them chatted avidly about their favourite novels, arguing amiably about the different styles of Charlotte, Emily and Anne.

A maid came through to announce lunch, and Leah followed Anthony into the formal dining room, where two places were set at the top of the long table.

'I do feel rather silly having lunch in here, but it's too cold to eat in the conservatory and I thought the kitchen was too informal,' Anthony apologised. 'My son and I always use the kitchen.'

'How old is he?'

'My son? He's just turned eighteen. I packed him off to Yale in September.' Anthony's shoulders dropped a little. 'I have to admit I miss him dreadfully. Anyway, please excuse my indulgence. I have done little else but talk about myself since you arrived.'

'Not at all. I'm really interested,' Leah answered honestly.

After lunch, they sat sipping coffee in the sitting room.

'I must ask you, Leah, whether there is any truth to the story in the press that you're going to marry Carlo Porselli and move back to Italy? I know your work for Chaval is finished for now, but obviously we would like to renew your contract for another year.'

Anthony watched as a cloud crossed Leah's eyes.

'No, Anthony. There is not so much as an ounce of truth in it. I was all for suing, but my agent advised against it.'

'So the story was total fabrication?'

'No . . . Carlo gave the press the story. I know it sounds bizarre, but he was so sure that I was going to marry him that he didn't bother to consult me first. The irony is that all these years, we've never so much as kissed. Anyway –' Leah shrugged – 'Madelaine tells me it'll blow over. I have to say that I'm still inwardly fuming. As a result of Carlo's actions, a very good relationship with someone that I liked immensely has ended.'

Anthony sipped his coffee thoughtfully. 'No chance of a reconciliation?'

'No. But perhaps it's for the best. With my life in the glare of publicity, if it wasn't now, it would be at a later date. I don't think he could have coped with the constant rumours.'

'The media can be very dangerous. Obviously Chaval loves any publicity you get, but not to the detriment of your personal life.'

Leah was on the verge of voicing her disillusionment with her career as a whole, when she stopped herself. This man might be understanding, but he was paying her a fortune to do a job.

Anthony suggested they went for a walk around the grounds to blow away the cobwebs, and they set off. Although it was only a quarter to three, the sky was already darkening. They strolled through the beautifully kept gardens, and the space and peace of nature that Leah missed from her childhood in Yorkshire raised her flagging spirits. As she breathed in the clean, fresh air, Leah began to feel some of her natural optimism return. Suddenly, the city of New York and her problems seemed a very long way away.

'Gosh, I do miss open spaces. I think the city's draining me. It's beautiful here.'

'Thank you, Leah.'

'Although it's a bit too neat for me. I like the rugged, wild quality of moorland,' she quipped.

Anthony chuckled. 'I agree, but here there are all sorts of neighbourhood laws about keeping your gardens tidy. The committee would probably have me thrown out if I didn't keep my grass verges under a quarter of an inch.' Anthony smiled. 'I think you'd like New England. I have a house there. You're welcome to visit any time.'

'I might just take you up on that.'

He looked pleased. 'You were saying earlier that you enjoy the ballet.'

Leah nodded. 'Yes. When I was younger, I wanted to be a dancer. Mind you, I realised when I reached eleven that I'd have to give up all hope of being a prima ballerina. I wouldn't be able to find a leading man taller than me and they'd have a hernia trying to pick me up.' She giggled.

'You may be tall, but I'll bet you're as light as a feather. Anyway, I'm on the board at the Met and there's a gala performance in a couple of weeks. Baryshnikov is dancing. Would you like to come?'

Leah's face lit up. 'Oh, I'd love to, Anthony!'

He looked at her seriously. 'Leah, you must only come if you want to. I was thinking this morning that you may have joined me today because technically I'm your employer and you feel that you can't refuse.' Anthony stopped walking and stared ahead of him. 'I enjoy your company enormously, but I hope you know that I am not the kind of man to bear a grudge if you don't want to spend your free time with an old fuddy-duddy like me.'

'Anthony, believe me, I'd love to. The first time you asked me to dinner I agreed out of obligation, but I really enjoyed – really *enjoy* your company. And there's no way I'm giving up the chance to go to the Met, so I'm afraid you're stuck with me!'

Leah laughed and put her arm companionably through his as they turned and walked back towards the house. Anthony smiled down at her. 'You must have the pick of any man you choose.'

Leah's face clouded. 'No. As a matter of fact, I don't. It's one area of my life that I can't seem to get right, so I've decided that I'm having nothing more to do with relationships in the future. I'm going to keep men as friends. Like yourself.'

Anthony couldn't help the small stab of disappointment that sliced through his heart. He understood the message she was sending him. But maybe in time . . . who knew? Just having her company was better than nothing at all.

Later, as he watched his chauffeur take Leah off back to New York, the feeling of depression, which had not left him for nigh on two years since his wife had died, lifted.

Anthony went into his snug and poured himself a brandy.

He knew that she wasn't ready at the moment, but he was prepared to wait until she was.

An hour later in New York, Leah felt refreshed and happier than she had for a long time. As the car approached East 70th Street, she was determined not to let Jenny and her problems get her down.

When Leah stepped out of the lift and into the apartment, she could hear the rumble of voices from the sitting room. Her mouth dropped open as she walked in.

Miles Delancey was sitting in the armchair by the fire, and Jenny, far from lying in her usual state of lethargy, was sitting up and talking avidly to him.

'Hi, Leah.' She waved. 'You have a visitor.'

'I can see that. What on earth are you doing here, Miles?'

'Hello, Leah.' He smiled at her and stood up to greet her. 'How are you?'

'Just fine,' she replied. 'Are you on holiday here?'

Miles shook his head. 'No. As a matter of fact I've decided to base myself here permanently from now on.'

'But I saw your spread in *Vogue* last month. You've just started to make it in England.'

'I know, but the Big Apple is where the fashion scene is really happening these days. I decided that before I became complacent, I should join the migration across the pond and see what happens.'

'Oh.' Miles's reasons didn't ring true.

'Jenny here has made the most entertaining company for the past two hours.' Miles shot her a winning smile and Jenny blushed. Leah knew that Miles could be exceptionally charming when he wanted to be.

'Miles has been catching me up on all the British fashion gossip,' said Jenny, gazing at him.

Leah could see a light in Jenny's eyes that had been missing for months.

'Yes. Not that there's much to tell. Some wine, Leah?'

'No thanks.'

She watched Miles pour himself a glass and felt uncomfortable about the fact that he had made himself so at home in her apartment.

'Miles wants you to introduce him to anyone you might know who could help him get started over here,' said Jenny.

Miles looked into his glass in embarrassment. 'Jenny, really. You shouldn't have put it like that.' He turned to Leah. 'All I said to Jenny was that any help would not be unappreciated. You know what it's like in this business. It's who you know, not what you know.'

Leah felt the same tiny shiver from years gone by as Miles looked at her with his penetrating eyes.

'He's also staying in some grotty hotel on the Lower East Side. I told him that he could come and lodge here with us until he sorts himself out, as he's an old friend of yours,' said Jenny.

Leah exhaled deeply. Having Miles Delancey stay in her apartment was the last thing she needed. However, he certainly seemed to have provided a tonic for Jenny, and she could hardly say no now.

'Of course. I'm going to take a bath and go to bed. I feel exhausted. Don't keep her up too late, Miles. She's been very sick.'

'I'm fine, Leah. Stop fussing,' said Jenny irritably. 'Sleep tight.' She turned her attention back to Miles.

Leah went off to her room, cross that her peace of mind had once more been disturbed. Having the creepy Miles Delancey in close proximity was something that completely unnerved her.

She climbed into bed and closed her eyes.

That night, she had the dream again. The small voice repeating inside her head . . . 'unnatural things, evil things . . . never mess with nature . . . he will find you . . .'

Leah shot bolt upright and switched on the light. Her heart was pumping against her chest and her body was drenched in sweat.

Leah knew then, with a terrible certainty, that her childhood nightmare was linked to the man in her apartment.

16

'Thanks for letting me know, Roddy. Miranda? No, I haven't heard. I'll think about your suggestion and get back to you as soon as I can. Take care, and I'll see you next week. Bye.'

Rose put the phone down slowly and took a deep breath. She felt exhausted and couldn't remember the last time she'd slept properly. Leaving her studio, she made for the kitchen table and lit up a cigarette. It wasn't even one o'clock, and it was her tenth of the day.

It had been a month since the last telephone call from Miranda. Rose asked herself the same questions over and over as she tried to decide why contact had been so abruptly broken off.

She'd been to the police, who had been most unhelpful. Because Miranda was twenty-one, they said that it was within her rights to disappear without telling anyone where she was, and that it happened all the time. Particularly as Miranda *had* contacted Rose, they'd pointed out that there was no reason for the police to assume she was a missing person, or had been the victim of foul play. Nonetheless, Rose had left a picture of Miranda with West Yorkshire Police, and asked them to send it down to London on the off chance that an officer might spot her. She knew the possibility was one in a million.

Time and again, Rose asked herself if it was her fault that Miranda had gone. She went over and over Miranda's childhood, their numerous arguments haunting her as if they had taken place yesterday. Roddy had told her to stop torturing herself, that Rose had taken Miranda in when she was a baby and loved her as if she were her own.

But Roddy didn't have to look at the pocket version of her missing daughter every day. Chloe's little face lit up the minute she saw Rose, and it broke her heart. Between them, she and Mrs Thompson spoiled Chloe rotten, both of them trying to make up for the fact that the child was little better than an orphan.

Rose only wished that she had told Miranda how she had fought to adopt her . . . how she'd moved heaven and earth for the right to become her mother . . . but it was too late.

She ground her cigarette out harshly in the ashtray and decided to listen to the one o'clock news on the radio.

Mrs Thompson came bustling in.

'Shall I put the kettle on?' she suggested.

Rose nodded. The two of them listened in silence, as had become their routine. Today, the announcer grimly reported that the body of a young woman had been found raped and strangled in her bedsit in King's Cross, north London. Doreen Thompson watched with sympathy as Rose stiffened and reached again for her cigarettes.

'The woman, yet to be identified, is believed to be in her early twenties. She is a known prostitute who has operated out of King's Cross for the past eighteen months. Other prostitutes in the area have been warned to be on their guard after what police describe as a particularly vicious attack. A full-scale investigation is underway to find the killer.'

Rose breathed a sigh of relief. 'Thank God,' she whispered.

'There you go, Mrs Delancey.' Mrs Thompson placed a

steaming mug of coffee in front of her. 'Do you want anything to eat before I pop to the village to collect Chloe from nursery?'

'No thanks, Doreen. I think I'll take this back to my studio.'

'Okay.' Mrs Thompson paused. 'She's still alive, Mrs Delancey. Miranda will come back, I know she will.'

Rose stared out of the kitchen window.

'I hope you're right, Doreen.' She sighed as she stood up. 'Thank you.'

'What for?'

'For all your help with Chloe and for just . . . being here.'

'No need for thanks, Mrs Delancey. I worship that little girl. I'll be back in forty-five minutes or so.'

Rose nodded, then wandered back into her studio and gazed at the painting she was working on. She could see the fear and frustration that had been transmitted from her inner self onto the canvas.

What struck her as particularly cruel was that her career had taken off since the first exhibition – to a point where she had enough commissions to work until she was ninety. Her bank account contained a small fortune, and all her money worries were behind her.

Even her years of anxiety over Miles's future seemed to be over.

In truth, she had always harboured concern for her only son. Although scrupulously polite, he had been such a lonely child. Despite her best efforts to get him to socialise with other boys, Miles had always shunned reality, preferring to live inside his imagination. Even when they spent time alone together, Miles had always seemed distant with his mother. And occasionally, although she tried to ignore it, she saw something in his eyes that was . . . cold. She dare not think about the reason why. No. Better to leave the past behind.

Now it seemed that her son had found his calling, and he had grown into a talented young man. Recently, her conversations with Miles had been as positive as they ever had been.

Frankly, Rose should be feeling better about herself than she had for a long time.

But Miranda was causing her grey hairs and sleepless nights.

Rose stood, picked up a brush and dabbed it into the Hooker's green and yellow ochre oil paint she had mixed earlier. She made a sweeping stroke on the canvas in front of her, and wondered if it was her destiny to live her life without peace.

17

'Miranda, welcome aboard.' Santos smiled and stretched out his hand to help her up the steep steps from the small launch floating alongside the boat.

Miranda grimaced as he kissed her on both cheeks. 'You are looking quite beautiful, as always, my dear. Did you have a pleasant flight?'

'Yes, thank you.'

'Good. Now, I suggest you have a rest in your cabin and join me in the sitting room at eight. We will have drinks, then dinner. Marius will take your luggage down. Follow him.'

Miranda nodded and walked with the burly crewman down some steps into the luxuriously carpeted bowels of the vessel. He stopped in front of her usual room and unlocked it. Once Miranda had stepped inside, Marius, dressed in his smart white uniform, closed the door firmly and returned to the aft deck.

Miranda was no longer impressed by the splendour and opulence of her cabin. She immediately made for the drinks cabinet and poured herself a large vodka and tonic. Then she sank down into one of the comfortable leather armchairs and looked out of the large porthole to the sparkling blue sea beyond.

She took a gulp of her drink. During the flight to Nice, she had decided that the only way she could possibly survive another dreadful weekend with Santos was to become paralytic.

313

The thought of him touching her sent a shudder right down her spine.

He revolted her. That was the only word for it. She had not laid eyes on him for over a month and had spent every night in London terrified that he would ask her to join him on his boat once more. Last time she had spent the weekend with him here, aboard this floating palace with all his lackeys, he had behaved outwardly in the same caring manner that he had always shown when she was with him. But later, when they were alone in his cabin together . . . Miranda felt sick at the things he had asked her . . . ordered her to do.

Ian had taken to popping in to see her on a Friday evening, and Miranda lived for these occasions. It was the only chance she got to talk to another human being during the whole week. He bought her books and presents to keep her occupied, and Miranda could see the sympathy for her plight in his eyes.

He'd stay for a drink and tell her about his week, and relate funny anecdotes to try to bring a smile to her face, but he would have to leave all too soon. He was usually rushing off home to change for a dinner party, or to spend the weekend with friends in the country.

'I wish I could come,' she'd sigh sadly.

'So do I,' Ian would answer as he kissed her chastely on the cheek. 'Take care of yourself, and try not to get too down. I'm sure things will sort themselves out.'

But Miranda was aware that these were empty words of comfort. Ian knew as well as she did that there was little hope of that.

In the past couple of weeks, she had started to fantasise about him. She imagined how it would be if things were different. Ian and she going out to dinner, walking in the park, going to the theatre. She'd begged him to take her out again, but Ian had looked wary and said that it might look suspicious and it was best if he visited her at home.

How could Ian be of any comfort when Miranda knew that he was just as scared of Santos as she was?

He was so kind and gentle, unlike any man she had ever known. Miranda was starting to wonder whether she had fallen in love with him. She'd never believed in such things in the past, certainly not with someone as outwardly ordinary as Ian. But the feeling she experienced when she woke up on Friday morning, knowing she was going to see him in a few hours' time, was quite magical.

He understood how she felt about Chloe, and the guilt she harboured for resenting the way the baby had forced her to be a mother when she was little more than a child herself. Miranda constantly berated herself for those feelings, wishing that there was some way she could contact Rose and tell her how much she loved her little girl, and how sorry she was for ever treating Chloe with anything other than affection. She missed her desperately.

But Ian had warned her time and again that Santos would use the child as a lever. Miranda poured out her pent-up feelings to him each week, and he would sit quietly – listening, never judging. She was finding it harder and harder to watch him leave.

Miranda poured herself another vodka and listened to the hum of the engines as the boat gently pulled out of St Tropez harbour.

She sat down again and thought how sweet Ian had been last night, dropping by on a Thursday evening because he knew she was flying off to the boat for the weekend. When she had heard the key in the lock, she had been sitting on the sofa, tears running down her face, staring blearily at the television screen.

Ian had fixed her a large drink and sat down next to her.

315

'I can't go through with it, Ian. I know what kind of things he'll make me do. Oh God.'

He had taken her gently in his arms and rocked her while she cried. The feeling of being held by him made the weekend ahead of her even more unbearable.

'I'd rather be dead. Please, don't make me go.'

'Shh, come on now, Miranda. It won't be that bad. Some women would give anything to be flying off in a private plane to spend a weekend with a billionaire on his boat.'

Miranda looked up at him. 'But I'm not like that. I used to think I'd do anything to live a life of luxury. I thought I could handle it. All I want now is to live in a little house somewhere with my child and have the freedom to take a walk down the street when I want to.'

Miranda also wanted to add, 'and have you with me every day,' but she could not.

'You have to help me, Ian. I can't take much more of this. Did you know that Santos keeps a gun under his pillow?'

Ian raised his eyebrows. 'No, but I'm not surprised.'

'I swear, Ian, that if he makes me do anything . . . Oh God. I'll kill him.'

Ian looked at the white face and the wild eyes and knew that Miranda was speaking the truth.

'Look. Don't be silly. That wouldn't solve anything. You go through this weekend as best you can, and when you come back next week, we'll have a serious talk. There has to be something we can think of.'

'Do you mean it?' Miranda's face lit up.

Ian nodded. 'Yes. Just promise me you'll be a good girl and do everything Santos tells you.'

Ian had left just before nine, when Santos called, and Miranda had felt able to speak to him normally.

*　*　*

And now here she was on the boat, with Ian hundreds of miles away, and at the mercy of her captor.

'Come on, Miranda. Grit your teeth and think of what Ian said. You'll never have to do this again,' she said, and went to take a long, hot bath with another large vodka.

'Good evening, my dear. You are looking beautiful. Here, I have a small gift for you.' Santos handed her a leather-bound box and the ten guests in the salon stopped talking and watched Miranda open it.

She drew in her breath as she gazed at the glittering diamond necklace, bracelet and earrings. The set was by far the most impressive that Santos had ever given her. She wondered what he would ask for in return later that night.

For the next hour, she listened to Santos as he chatted about where they would sail tomorrow. He commanded the complete attention of everyone around him, and Miranda silently loathed the amount of power that money could provide. The man did not deserve to have his opinions respected. But she had been caught in the trap along with everyone else in the room. And like them, she must pay lip-service.

Miranda's attention was caught by a man who sauntered in through the salon door and took a glass of champagne from one of the stewards. His face looked familiar. Miranda was struck by how handsome he was. He was perhaps in his late forties, with silver creeping into his blond hair, and a pair of piercing eyes whose glance she knew she'd seen somewhere before.

Santos turned and saw him. 'Ah, David. Welcome. I am so glad you could make it.'

'Yes. I apologise for arriving so late. I was held up in New York on business.' David forced a smile. Miranda recognised the same revulsion she herself experienced every time she looked at Santos.

317

'Miranda, this is David Cooper. We have become good friends during the time we have been working on a business project in Rio together. I am most honoured that a man as busy as he has graced us this weekend with his company.'

'It's a pleasure to be here,' David said.

Miranda held her breath as she stared at David Cooper, waiting for him to recall that he had a niece of the same name whom his son had met during his holidays in Yorkshire, years ago.

David did no such thing, just smiled warmly and took her hand to kiss it.

'Delighted, Miranda.'

He turned his attention away from her and started chatting to Santos. Miranda let out her breath slowly, trying to still her pumping heart. Thank God Rose and he had had no contact in the past. Miranda realised rationally that there was no reason for David to know who she was. Brett had probably never even mentioned her. But it was nonetheless disturbing to know that there was a connection between her and this man. If Rose ever discovered that she was a kept mistress who earned her keep through performing lewd acts, she might never let her see Chloe again.

And yet, there was part of her that wanted to confide in her new-found uncle, to tell him what she was going through and ask for his help. After all, he was by all accounts just as powerful as her captor, and the first person she had seen truly command the attention of Santos.

There was a bright flash of light as one of the guests used a small camera to take a photograph of Santos, Miranda and David.

'For my photo album.' He smiled ingratiatingly.

'*No!*' The voice was a terrifying roar and everyone in the salon jumped. 'Take his camera and dispose of it and the film.'

Santos was bright red with anger. One of the crew who had been serving drinks nodded and removed the camera from the hands of the frightened guest.

'I . . . I'm sorry. Please, I apologise.'

Santos's anger evaporated and he became the charming host once more. 'Do not apologise. It is a rule I adhere to as I am wary of becoming a public figure. I enjoy my anonymity and freedom too much. Let us go in to dinner. Miranda, please escort David into the dining room.'

Miranda was studying her uncle's face. He was staring at Santos with an expression that resembled . . . what, triumph? He smiled down at her and offered his arm. They followed Santos, who had taken the arm of a beautiful red-headed girl, through to the dining room.

Miranda was placed between the two men at the table, with the girl, whose name was Kim, on the other side of Santos. Miranda noted that he seemed to be paying her a lot of attention and wondered hopefully if this would get her off the hook tonight.

'Isn't this boat heavenly?' commented David to Miranda with a warm smile. 'I myself have a yacht on the Amalfi Coast, but it's nothing compared to this. Unfortunately, I never seem to have time to go cruising. I was thinking of selling it actually, but maybe I should wait and see how much I enjoy this weekend.'

'Yes,' said Miranda.

'You're English, aren't you?' David asked, as waiters brought in large tureens of soup.

'I am.'

'Where do you hail from?'

'Oh, er, London.'

'Really? I'd read your accent as much further up north. But I've spent most of the last twenty-five years in New York, so

I've probably lost my ear for the native nuances of Britain.' He smiled. 'I love London myself. I spent some of the best years of my life there. What do you do for a living, Miranda?'

Miranda was nonplussed. Didn't David realise what she was?

'Okay. Let me guess.' David looked at her thoughtfully. 'Well, you're pretty enough to be a model, but something tells me you're not. Do you work for Santos?'

Miranda nodded slowly. It was the truth, after all. She didn't understand why he seemed so interested in her.

'He's a fascinating man, isn't he?'

The words sounded genuine enough and Miranda wondered whether she'd imagined the look of revulsion in his eyes when he'd first arrived in the salon.

'Yes.' Miranda knew that her level of conversation was the standard of the average ten-year-old, but she couldn't be trapped into making a mistake.

David, however, did not seem to notice. He chatted away to her about his project with Santos and seemed to take it for granted that she knew all about it. Miranda listened and found that she was relaxing a little. He seemed a very nice man, not at all the power-hungry megalomaniac that Brett had hinted he was. He also treated her with an unspoken respect, which restored her self-confidence a little.

After dinner, they went back to the salon and sat drinking liqueurs.

David sat in a chair next to Miranda. He was fascinated by her. For all her sophisticated outer packaging, she was obviously very young, and determined to give nothing away about herself. He found this refreshing. Once women knew who he was, they would often throw themselves at his feet.

She also reminded him distinctly of someone, but he couldn't place who.

He wondered what her role was here. Surely this girl was not one of Santos's whores. She didn't possess the world-weariness and jaded quality that marked them out so clearly.

'I think it is time for us all to retire. Tomorrow we will dock at Lavandou. Breakfast is at eight.' Santos stood up, and the evening was immediately at an end for the rest of the occupants of the salon.

'Come, Miranda.' Santos held out his arm. She looked at him, hating him for making it obvious to everyone that she was his possession and would be spending the night with him. She stood up slowly and turned to David.

'Goodnight, Mr Cooper.'

David rose, took her hand and kissed it. 'Goodnight, Miranda. It's been a pleasure.' He smiled at her somewhat sadly, as she took Santos's outstretched arm and left the room.

Santos led her down to his stateroom. 'I think Mr Cooper was quite taken with you, Miranda. Well done. He is an important business colleague and I want him to be kept happy. But now, it is time for us.' He opened the door to the room. The lights were dimmed, but to her horror, Miranda could see clearly the naked shape of the red-headed girl lying in the bed. Santos went over to the drinks cabinet and poured a ready-mixed cocktail into a glass, before handing it to Miranda.

Miranda gulped it and closed her eyes, starting to swim in the deep, murky waters of drug-induced drowsiness. Unable to fight any longer, she let herself sink slowly to the bottom.

18

'Are you okay, Leah? You seem awfully quiet lately.' Jenny watched her buttering toast in the kitchen as she stood in her dressing gown, holding two mugs of coffee.

Leah nodded. 'I'm fine, Jenny. I've just been busy, that's all.'

'All work and no play makes Leah a dull girl,' Jenny commented. 'Have you seen Brett recently?' She put the two mugs down on the worktop.

Leah had known that Jenny would ask at some point. Although it had been over a month since their relationship had abruptly terminated, Leah had not mentioned the demise to Jenny. In the past couple of weeks, she had been up to her eyes with work and Jenny had been out most evenings in the company of Miles Delancey. Anyway, it was not something she wished to hold a post-mortem on.

'No. Brett and I are finished, and to be honest, I'd prefer not to talk about it, if you don't mind.'

Jenny looked genuinely upset. 'Oh Leah. I really thought that you two . . .' She stopped as she saw Leah's face harden. 'Okay, I'm sorry. I won't mention another word.'

'You and Miles seem to be getting on well.' Leah looked at her friend and could hardly believe it was the same girl. Miles had achieved in two weeks what she had not been able to in months. Jenny's eyes were sparkling, she had put on

322

weight and the colour had returned to her cheeks. Whatever Leah felt about Miles, she was happy that he seemed to have provided the tonic Jenny needed to set her on the road to physical and mental recovery.

Jenny's face lit up and she smiled coyly. 'We are. He's the best thing that's happened to me in ages. I feel a new woman. Isn't he gorgeous, Leah?'

Leah nodded uncertainly. Although Miles had shown nothing but kindness towards Jenny since he'd been at the apartment, her instincts about him would not be shaken. After all, Miles had seduced her own mother and Rose into believing he was the perfect gentleman. Ever since the night in the barn all those years ago, Leah knew better. She remained convinced it had been Miles who had grabbed her.

'I think I'm in love,' Jenny whispered. 'We just get on so well. We've spent more or less every second together, and he keeps telling me how beautiful I am. I'm actually starting to believe him.' She giggled. 'Anyway, I'd better take his coffee to him before it's stone cold. See you later.'

As Jenny lifted the two mugs from the worktop, the sleeve of her satin dressing gown fell back to her elbow and Leah saw a large purple bruise encircling the circumference of Jenny's arm.

'Ouch! Jenny, how on earth did you hurt yourself so badly?'

Jenny blushed and shook her arm so that the bruise was once more covered by her dressing gown, slopping coffee over the floor at the same time.

'Oh, I fell yesterday. You know how clumsy I am. I don't think I've got my sea-legs back from being sick. I'm fine, really.'

Leah watched Jenny leave the room. Something about the shape of the bruise and the way Jenny had blushed when questioned told Leah that her friend was lying.

* * *

The following evening, Leah let herself wearily into the flat. It was quiet, and she presumed Miles and Jenny were out. It had been another long, hard day, but she was looking forward immensely to the prospect of going to the ballet with Anthony tonight. Leah showered, then dried her hair and tried to decide which gown she would wear. She chose a favourite Lanvin dress, put on a little make-up and slipped into the luxurious garment. She tried on a variety of different necklaces, and finding nothing to suit, remembered that Jenny had a teardrop diamanté one that would look perfect. She went out of her bedroom and down the corridor to knock on Jenny's door, not expecting a reply.

'Leah, I'm busy,' Jenny's voice, unusually harsh, replied from the other side.

'Sorry, Jenny. I was just wondering if I could borrow your diamanté necklace to wear to the ballet tonight?'

There was a pause before Jenny answered. 'I've lost it.'

'But I saw it yesterday on your dressing-table. Can you have a look for me?'

'Please, Leah. Go away. I'm busy.'

Thoughts of vodka bottles and tablets filled Leah's mind. This time she wasn't taking any chances. She tried the door. It was locked.

'Jenny, let me in now, otherwise I'm calling that doctor at the hospital.'

'I'm fine, just leave me alone.'

Leah acknowledged that Jenny did not sound drunk, but God knows what was going on behind that door.

'I mean it. If you don't let me in, I'm calling Lenox Hill now. They told me to if you started acting strangely. Come on, Jenny, open this door.'

'Okay, okay.'

Jenny's face appeared, half hidden by the doorframe.

'See? I'm fine.' She held out the diamanté necklace. 'There you are. Enjoy yourself tonight. I'll see you later.' Jenny moved to close the door, but Leah was too quick for her. She pushed the door wider and marched in, looking for evidence. There was none to be seen. Feeling rotten that she'd obviously been mistaken, she turned to Jenny to apologise.

'Jenny, I'm sorry, I just thought . . . Jesus!'

Jenny was staring at the floor. The right side of her face was bright purple and her eye was half closed.

'What happened? How on earth did you do that?'

Jenny shrugged. 'I did it last night when I went to get a glass of water from the kitchen. I didn't bother to turn the lights on and I tripped over the hall table and fell.'

Leah immediately remembered the bad purple bruise she had seen on Jenny's arm yesterday.

'I don't believe you. Start telling the truth or I'm calling the hospital.'

'Look, Leah. It's none of your damn business and if you don't believe me, I don't care. I am telling the truth. Just stop interfering in my life, will you? It's like having an over-protective mother watching my every move! I can look after myself, thank you.'

Anger rose inside Leah. 'Oh, really? And what would have happened if I hadn't come back from Milan and found you? I don't expect to get thanks for looking after you the way I have done, but Christ, Jenny! Don't treat me like an idiot! I'm not the enemy, I'm your best friend who loves you. Miles did that to you, didn't he? Didn't he?'

Suddenly Jenny crumpled. Tears came to her eyes and she sank down onto the bed. 'Don't shout at me, Leah, please. I'm sorry I've been ungrateful, but I knew you wouldn't understand. Okay, Miles did get a bit rough last night, but he was so apologetic. He's promised never to do it again.'

325

'Really? And what about that bruise I saw on your arm yesterday? This is ridiculous, Jenny. Apart from anything else, how can you expect to start working as a model again when you're covered from head to toe with bruises? Miles is leaving here tonight,' Leah said firmly.

'Oh no, please. Don't make him go. He's helped me so much. I just wanted to die before he arrived and he's been so good and kind. I love him, Leah. I need him. And I believe him when he says he won't hurt me again. He just gets a little too passionate, that's all.'

Leah gave a long sigh. She was in a no-win situation. If she told Miles to leave tonight, Jenny would blame her for it and sink back into the black depression. If she let him stay, well, surely she was putting Jenny in danger of another kind?

'Please, Leah,' Jenny pleaded, 'I promise it'll never happen again. Give him one more chance. I don't know what I'd do without him.'

Leah went to sit on the bed beside Jenny. 'You've only known Miles for a couple of weeks. How can you love anybody who tried to hurt you like that?'

Jenny shrugged. 'He didn't mean it, honestly. He's told me how much he loves me. And he was worried about going for his interview today, that's all. I'm sure that when he gets a job and his green card sorted out, he'll calm down.'

Leah could hardly believe the way Jenny was protecting Miles. For a man to use his physical strength against a woman was a heinous crime. Leah looked at Jenny with pity in her heart and fear in her mind.

'Okay, Jenny. I'll let him stay. Personally, I think you're crazy even to contemplate having him near you again, but as you said, I'm not your keeper. However, this apartment is in my name, and as your landlady, if that man so much as touches you in anything other than a gentle way again, he's out. No more chances, no more excuses. I'm not happy about it at all, but—'

Leah was cut off in mid-sentence as Jenny's arms were flung around her. 'Thank you, Leah. I swear it'll never happen again. I know it looks dreadful, but Miles isn't like that, really.'

'Who's he been to see today?'

'*Vanity Fair*. I gave him the contact and he called and mentioned your name. I hope you don't mind, but I know once he gets started, he'll feel much better.'

The last thing Leah wanted was some brutal maniac who beat up women getting a job on her recommendation. She stood up.

'I've got to go. I'm meeting Anthony at seven and I'm going to be late. For God's sake, look after yourself and inform Miles that from now on, I don't want him to use my name to get him through any more doors, okay?'

Leah left the room, quickly donned the necklace, threw a wrap over her shoulders and went to hail a taxi. She sat in the back feeling frustrated. Couldn't Jenny see that Miles didn't love her if all he wanted to do was to hurt her in that way? He was using both of them for their contacts and a place to stay in New York.

And he had seen an opportunity to prey on someone weak and defenceless.

The cab pulled up outside the Metropolitan Opera House in Lincoln Center. She met Anthony, as arranged, in the bar. He kissed her on both cheeks and then took a step back.

'Are you okay, Leah? You look disturbed about something. Anything I can help you with?'

She shook her head as she accepted a glass of Buck's Fizz from him. 'No, I'm fine, really, Anthony. I can't wait to see the ballet. Thank you so much for inviting me.'

As the overture of *Swan Lake* hummed softly around the

packed auditorium, and Baryshnikov appeared on the huge stage in front of her, Leah relaxed.

Her eyes filled with tears at the ballet's climax, and she could hardly speak as they left the theatre after several standing ovations for the brilliance of the famous male dancer.

'That was absolutely wonderful,' Leah sighed. She felt on a high as they walked out onto Columbus Avenue.

'Hungry, Leah?'

She smiled. 'I can always be persuaded to eat.'

'Then we shall go and find some supper.'

The limousine drove them to the GE Building in Rockefeller Plaza. Leah followed Anthony inside and up in the lift. They entered a spectacular dining room. The aubergine silk walls, green leather chairs and waiters dressed in pastel tails gave the impression of a thirties timewarp, while a band played.

The maître d' greeted Anthony warmly and led them to a table by the window. Leah looked down sixty-five giddy floors to the street, way below.

'Where are we?'

'The Rainbow Room. One of my favourite haunts.'

'I love it,' Leah enthused.

After consulting his dinner partner, Anthony ordered two steaks tartare and a bottle of dry white wine. 'Are you sure there's nothing wrong? You've been very quiet tonight.'

'No, really, it's nothing.'

'You're sure?'

Leah nodded, feeling guilty that Anthony had noticed.

'Okay, Leah, but I hope you've realised by now that I'm your *friend* as well as your boss. Any time you want to talk, feel free. I'll always be there to listen. Actually, I hope you won't think me forward, but I was wondering what you're doing over Christmas?'

'I promised to spend it with Jenny, my flatmate.'

'Oh. Well, you know I told you that I have a house in Vermont?'

'Yes.'

'I'm going up there and my son, Jack, is going to join me. I wondered if you'd like to come along? Jenny would be very welcome too. It's a big house and if it snows, it's quite beautiful.'

'Thank you for the offer. I'll speak to Jenny and ask her.'

An hour and a half later, Anthony dropped Leah at the door of her apartment building. Her lovely evening had cheered her up, but she wondered what she was coming home to in the flat.

Jenny was in the sitting room, calmly sipping coffee alone.

'Hi, Leah, did you have a good evening?'

'Yes, it was lovely. Where's Miles?'

'In the spare room. Honestly, Leah, he was so repentant. He bought me a huge bunch of flowers and I read him the riot act and told him he wasn't coming back into my bed until I said he could. But the good news is, he got a three-page spread from *Vanity Fair* this afternoon. Isn't that great?'

'Yes,' said Leah insincerely. 'Now, I have a suggestion to put to you. Anthony has invited me to spend Christmas with him and his son in Vermont. I want you to come with me.'

Jenny's face dropped. 'Oh. But what about Miles?'

'Jenny, I wouldn't get a moment's sleep if I thought you were here by yourself with Miles. I'm sure he'll be able to fend for himself for a few days and I really do think a break would do you the world of good. Besides, I think it might be fun. Anthony's a really nice chap.'

'I don't know, Leah. I'll have to ask Miles and—'

'I'll make a bargain with you. I'll promise to turn a blind eye to what he's done if you agree to come to Vermont with me. You owe me one, Jenny.'

'Okay, okay.' Jenny sighed. 'Miles won't be happy, though.'

'Tough shit. It's time he realised that you have a mind of your own. I'm going to bed. See you tomorrow. Goodnight.'

'Goodnight. Leah?'

'Yes?'

'Thanks. And really, Miles will never hurt me again.'

'As long as you're sure.'

'I am.'

Leah nodded and went to her room, still unconvinced.

But as she lay in bed, she began to look forward to Christmas. And she had to admit she liked Anthony. In a world full of selfish, aggressive males, his gentleness and sensitivity shone out like a beacon.

He gave her hope for the future.

19

Miranda heard the key in the lock. She sat deadly still on the sofa, twisting a hanky around her fingers. She listened to the footsteps in the hall, her heart a slow thud against her chest. Every time the key turned, she froze with fear, thinking that it might be him, that he might have decided to fly to London and check up on her.

'Hello, Miranda. I thought I'd pop in and see how your weekend with Santos was and . . .'

She was in his arms before he could finish, sobbing pitifully. He placed his hands on her heaving shoulders, desperate to comfort her, but nervous that she was so close.

'Oh God, Ian, I can't face it any more. The things he made me do, I . . . I can't tell you. I'm so ashamed.'

'Come on now, Miranda. It can't have been as bad as all that.'

But she clung on to him. 'It was, it was. Oh God.'

Miranda was becoming hysterical. Ian led her back to the sofa and sat her down. He tried to move away but she would not let him. She stared at him, her eyes pleading.

'You have to help me. I can't stand it any longer. I'll kill myself before I'll see him again. Please, Ian.'

'Okay, okay,' he soothed. 'Let me get us both a drink and we'll talk this through.'

Miranda let go of his arm and he went over to the drinks cabinet to pour them both a stiff whisky.

'Here. This'll calm you down.'

Miranda took the glass from him and sipped the warming liquid.

'There now. Nothing's worth getting in this state about, is it?' He smiled gently. 'Tell me exactly what happened.'

After a lot of coaxing and two more drinks, Ian managed to get the story out of her. The tale of what Santos had forced her to do filled him with loathing and disgust.

'The worst part was that he drugged me with something, but I can remember everything that happened. I can't go through it again, Ian, really.'

As he put his arms around her, a sudden instinctive feeling that he must protect this girl from his monster of an employer surged through him. He'd tried to pretend for the past few months that he was only carrying out his duty by visiting Miranda regularly, but the truth was that he could hardly wait to see her.

Ian could deny his feelings no longer.

· What this meant for his career prospects and his elderly parents he was not prepared to think about, but he could not stand by and watch the woman he loved endure that kind of treatment from Santos again.

'Miranda, darling Miranda. Believe me, I'll do all I can to help you.'

'You will?' The look of gratefulness in her eyes as she stared up at him washed away any doubts he might have had before.

'Yes.'

'Thank you, Ian.' She threw her arms around him and held him tight, murmuring something incoherent into his shoulder.

'Pardon?'

Miranda pulled away from him and looked down at her hands.

'I said, I love you, Ian.' She sighed deeply. 'I don't expect you to feel the same way about me. After all, I'm Santos's prostitute and . . .'

This time it was Ian who took Miranda in his arms.

'Oh darling, that doesn't matter. You don't realise what I went through at the weekend, thinking of you with *him*, imagining what he was making you do. I've tried to stop myself feeling like this, but I can't help myself. I love you too.'

He took her face gently in his hands and kissed her lips timidly, knowing that she might back away in fear. But she did not.

Neither found themselves able to break away from the other. For the first time in her life, Miranda understood how sex could be the ultimate manifestation of love, pure and beautiful, and she knew that never again could she let another man use her body as a vessel for his own pleasure.

Afterwards, exhausted, they lay wrapped naked in each other's arms.

Ian stroked her hair gently. 'I promise you, Miranda, whatever happens, I will never allow that man to touch you again.'

The dreadful fear of the past few months left Miranda for the first time. How wrong she had been to think that the world was about power and money. She would give anything at this moment to transport her life to a little house with Ian and Chloe. They would have love and freedom. And that was all that really mattered.

'I'm going to think of something, darling. I'm going to get you out of here. We'll start again somewhere else, where Santos can't find us and—'

The harsh jangling of the telephone broke into their new-found peace. Both of them jumped and the look of fear appeared on Miranda's face once more.

'Answer it, sweetheart.'

'I can't.' Miranda bit her lip and clung on to him tight. 'Make it stop, Ian, please.'

'Come on, darling. We mustn't let him think anything is wrong. He'll become suspicious and that'll make it even harder for us. You must answer it. I promise you won't have to speak to him for much longer. Go on.' He reached over to the table, picked up the receiver and handed it to her.

'Hello.' The agonised look on Miranda's face was too much for him to bear. Ian stood up, walked out of the room and went along the hallway to the bathroom.

He leaned against the door and wondered if Miranda realised what the consequences of their actions tonight could be.

20

LaGuardia Airport had a holiday atmosphere, the sense of expectation and smiling faces making a change from the usual harassed businessmen anxious to get to their next meeting.

Leah and Jenny made their way through to their departure gate and settled themselves on the plane.

'Tell me more about our host. Are you in any way . . . involved?' asked Jenny.

'Absolutely not. Anthony's just a very good friend of mine. I'm sure you'll like him. His son'll be there too.'

'So you don't think he's got you down for Christmas under false pretences?'

Leah shook her head. 'No, I'm sure of it,' she smiled. 'He lost his wife two years ago and he still misses her dreadfully. He probably wants a full house, that's all.'

When the plane touched down at Lebanon Airport, Anthony was waiting to collect them. His face lit up as he saw Leah, and he came to help with the luggage.

'Goodness. You're only staying for a week. It looks like you've come for months.'

'That's what comes of being Santa Claus, I'm afraid. I haven't brought anything to wear, just lots of presents.' Leah giggled. 'This is my friend Jenny, by the way.'

'Hello, Jenny. Welcome. It's good to meet you.'

The women followed Anthony out to his jeep, taking in the bracing but crisp air. After they had set off, Leah gasped at some of the scenery.

'It's so pretty here, Anthony. It reminds me of England.'

'I guess that's why they named the place after your little country. I thought you'd approve.' The atmosphere was festive as they drove along the country roads to the quaint village of Woodstock, nestling at the foot of the Catskill Mountains. Anthony chatted away about his plans for the week.

'It's anything goes, really. Do what you want, when you want. There is snow up on Suicide Six and plenty more expected, so we can ski if you'd like.'

Leah shook her head. 'I don't ski.'

'Oh, but I do!' enthused Jenny. 'I adore it.'

'Great. So does my son, Jack. I don't ski much myself, so it'll be fun for him to have company on the slopes.' He lifted a hand from the wheel and pointed through the windscreen. 'Here we are, girls. Home sweet home.'

Anthony's house was set in rolling countryside with a view of the mountains beyond. It was painted a bright white, with green shutters framing the leaded windows. A porticoed terrace encircled the entire structure, around which Anthony had hung fairy lights.

'Oh Anthony. It's so . . . picturesque,' Leah uttered softly.

'Thank you. It was my grandparents' house originally. They lived here for fifty years and when my parents died, it was passed to me.' Anthony dragged the suitcases out of the boot and Leah and Jenny followed him up the steps to the front door. As they entered the large hallway and followed him into the sitting room, the first thing they saw was a real ten-foot Christmas tree standing in the corner, lights twinkling and presents piled high underneath. The big fireplace was a blaze of orange warmth and the mantelpiece was decorated with holly. The New England Sheraton mahogany sofa was strewn with patchwork cushions and the stripped-wood floor was covered by a priceless Sarouk rug.

'Oh, it's like something out of a fairy tale,' breathed Jenny.

'It reminds me of a ballet I once saw. *The Nutcracker*. It's beautiful.' Leah smiled.

A young man came bounding down the wide stairs two at a time. He entered the sitting room and smiled warmly at the two girls.

'Now, let me guess. You couldn't possibly be Anthony's son, could you?' Jenny grinned.

'You noticed the resemblance, then? I'd like to say that Dad got his boyish good looks from me, but . . .' The young man shrugged. 'Now who is who? I know you're both superstar models, and I'm gonna brag for the next six months at college about the fact that two of the most beautiful girls in the world came to my house just to spend Christmas with me, but . . .' Jack studied Jenny. 'Are you Leah?'

Jenny shook her head, secretly delighted that Jack thought that she might be the famous model his father employed.

'That shows how well our massive advertising campaign penetrates into the great American public's psyche, doesn't it, girls?' said Anthony, his eyes twinkling.

Jack shook hands with them. 'It's good to meet the both of you.'

'Jack, why don't you take Jenny and Leah upstairs and show them to their rooms while I organise lunch? Half the fun of coming here is that we do everything ourselves.'

Leah followed Jenny and Jack up the stairs.

'Okay, Leah, you're in here.' Jack led her into a large bedroom.

'If you want to wash up and unpack, we'll see you downstairs for lunch in twenty minutes or so. Come on, Jenny, follow me to your quarters.'

They left the room and Leah immediately went to the window. She wondered whether Anthony had purposely arranged for her to have this room, for the view over the rolling green countryside was quite breathtaking and suddenly made her feel very homesick. She wondered what her mum and dad were doing.

She perched on the big window seat, half enjoying the sweet pain of reminiscence. But then Brett leaped into her thoughts, as he always did when she thought of home. She allowed herself to wonder where he was spending Christmas Eve, how he was feeling, and whether he was missing her like she was missing him.

'Here, let me help you with those, Mother Christmas.' Anthony laughed as Leah staggered into the sitting room with her mountain of presents a few minutes later.

Together, they placed the wrapped gifts under the tree.

'Fancy helping me with lunch?' Anthony was wearing a flowered apron over his jeans.

'Of course. I think you could start a new trend in men's fashion in that,' Leah said as she followed him into the big comfortable kitchen that reminded her immediately of the one in Rose's Yorkshire farmhouse. The smell of good home cooking was in the air, and carols were playing softly on the radio. A sense of well-being filled Leah and she started to feel very glad she had come.

'Some mulled wine for you?' Anthony offered. 'Most of the alcohol gets boiled off.'

Leah went to peer inside the big pan simmering on the stove. The smell was delicious.

'Sure, I'll try it.'

'Good. It's my own special recipe. Speaking of which, I have to warn you that Christmas luncheon tomorrow will be prepared, cooked and served by yours truly.' Anthony ladled some mulled wine into two glasses and handed one to Leah. She took a sip and approved of the warm, spicy taste.

'This really is very good. I'm impressed by your proficiency in the kitchen. I'm hopeless.'

'Don't be so modest. I'm quite sure that's untrue.'

Anthony started serving the soup into four bowls, placing them along with freshly baked bread onto the scrubbed-pine table, while Leah called Jenny and Jack.

They bounced into the kitchen, laughing about something, and Leah was thrilled to see Jenny's eyes sparkling.

'Before we tuck in to what I hope is going to be a spectacular repast, I'd just like to say, on behalf of my son and me, how glad we are that the two of you are here. Now, please begin, before the soup gets cold.'

Lunch was a jolly affair, with mulled wine flowing, and the food almost as good as Mrs Thompson's. Clearly, Jenny and Jack had struck up an immediate rapport, and the quick wit that Jenny had been renowned for in the modelling world seemed to have returned to her.

By the time they had finished, it had gone three o'clock and the sky outside was darkening.

'I don't know how anyone else feels, but I could do with a nap before the evening's festivities. It's a tradition that we invite a few long-standing friends in for a drink on Christmas Eve. Then we all walk to the church for midnight mass.'

Everyone agreed that they could use a rest.

Leah lay on the comfortable bed, a sense of peace inside her, the cares of the past few months slipping away in this tranquil atmosphere . . .

'Hello, sleeping beauty.' Jack smiled as she came down the stairs into the sitting room. 'We wondered if you'd ever wake up again.'

339

'I'm sorry, I . . .'

'He's only teasing, Leah. That's what this place does to you. Can I just say how lovely you're looking tonight,' ventured Anthony.

'Yes, you scrub up quite well, don't you, Leah?' Jenny teased.

'Ignore her. Sit down and have a drink.' Jack patted the sofa beside him and handed Leah a glass of champagne. 'Dad says you don't drink very much, but it *is* Christmas.'

'You make me sound so boring, Anthony.' Leah smiled at him across the room. 'I notice you're not wearing your pinny to greet your guests.'

'Er, no. A guy's got to ring the changes and I will be in it all day tomorrow.' Anthony was dressed impeccably in a pair of grey flannels and a beautifully cut blazer.

There was a knock on the door and Jack jumped up to answer it.

An older couple bearing gifts came down the steps into the sitting room. Anthony kissed them, provided them with a glass of champagne and introduced them to Jenny and Leah.

During the next hour, the doorbell rang again and again. Soon the sitting room was full of people.

Leah noted that they all seemed as relaxed as Anthony himself. There was not a businesslike New Yorker among the group, and not once did any of them mention her modelling contract, although they clearly knew who she was.

Leah went to the kitchen for a glass of orange juice and Anthony followed her.

'Are you enjoying yourself, Leah? I hope you don't mind my friends coming round. I know how often you have to stand and make small talk at drinks parties.'

'Not at all. They seem so much more relaxed than other Americans I've met. More real,' she added.

'Yes. Although it might surprise you to know that most of

them have large businesses based in New York. But they all come here for Christmas and it's an unspoken rule that no one talks "shop" when we're in Vermont. Bill, who we were speaking to before, is the head of a big electronics company, and Andy runs a PR firm in Manhattan.'

'I'm amazed,' said Leah genuinely.

'We'll all set off for church in a few minutes, although you don't have to come if you don't want to.'

'Oh, I'd love to come. I haven't been to midnight mass for years.'

'Great. I'm so happy you and Jenny are here. It's made it feel . . . well, almost like a family again.' Leah gave him her warmest smile. 'Come on, you'd better find your coat. It's freezing out there and the forecast said to expect snow.'

The small church was chocolate-box perfect, lit by candles with a choir who were dressed in traditional robes. Everyone sang their hearts out during the familiar carols, and at the end of the service, Leah went forward with Anthony to receive communion. She looked at his bowed head next to her at the altar and felt a wave of affection for him.

As they left the church, tiny flakelets of snow were starting to fall.

The congregation drew in their breath at the magic of the scene. Soon, they kissed one another and went their separate ways with cries of 'Merry Christmas'.

Anthony offered Leah his arm.

'It may look lovely, but snow on ice can be lethal.'

Leah took his arm and they set off, with Jenny and Jack following behind.

'I have to say that this is my favourite night of the year. And this place never fails to provide the perfect setting.'

'I haven't felt this Christmassy for years,' agreed Leah.

'You poor world-weary thing, you. How old did you say

LUCINDA RILEY

you were? Fifty?' Anthony smiled down at her. 'I was only joking, Leah, really,' he added, studying her serious face with concern.

'I know. But you're right. I'm twenty-one and sometimes I do think like I'm fifty. Do you realise that I'm only three years older than Jack?'

'It has crossed my mind, although it's hard to believe. You've just led such different lives.' They had reached the front of the house and Anthony took her hand, pulling her up the rapidly whitening path. 'Come on, let's get inside by the fire and thaw out.'

The four of them sat near the warmth of the flames, drinking cocoa.

After half an hour, first Jenny and then Jack made their way to their respective bedrooms.

Anthony checked his watch. 'A quarter to two. That's enough hours into Christmas Day to open my special bottle of port.'

He stood up and went to the drinks cabinet. He came back and filled two glasses.

'Not for me, Anthony.'

'As a matter of fact, it's not for you anyway.' He placed the glass on the hearth of the fire. 'It's for our merry friend, just in case he should pop down the chimney to visit us. We have a glass of port together every year. Cheers.' Anthony raised his glass to the chimney and sipped the ruby liquid. 'Please, if you're tired, feel free to go to bed. I always stay up into the small hours on this special night.'

Leah did not feel in the least bit tired, just wonderfully relaxed and peaceful. She stared into the fire and thought how good it was to be with a man whom she did not find in the least bit threatening. With whom she could be herself.

'It's sad, isn't it, how we all grow up and stop believing in magic,' she remarked.

'Yes,' said Anthony slowly. 'But there is magic all around us. As we grow up, our minds just become too cluttered with practical thoughts and we lose touch with it. That's why nights like this are special. It's time out from the real world. Time to dream and recapture our lost innocence. When I'm here, I remember that the world is a wonderful place, full of beauty. As you grow up, you have to search harder for that beauty. It's there, but it's hidden.'

Leah nodded in agreement and once more felt a glow of genuine affection for this deep, sensitive man.

They sat by the fire together in companionable silence.

'Right, as I'm only going to get a couple of hours' sleep before I come on duty, I think I ought to go to bed.'

'Mmm.' Leah stretched. 'I feel so relaxed. Couldn't I just curl up by the fire like a cat and go to sleep here?'

'Anything you want, Leah, but you may be a little more comfortable in a bed.'

'You're right.' Leah moved reluctantly and stood up. Anthony did the same.

'Goodnight, Anthony, and thank you for such a lovely day.' She reached up and kissed him on the cheek.

'Don't thank me, Leah. I can't tell you what it means to me that you're here.' He took her hand in his and kissed it.

She smiled, then walked slowly towards the stairs, pausing on the first step. 'Merry Christmas, Anthony.'

'Merry Christmas, Leah.' He watched her lithe perfect body move gracefully up the stairs, then bent down to grasp the extra glass of port. He drank it slowly, savouring the taste.

Leah was an unusual woman. Under that perfect exterior, she had such maturity and depth. In her, he had found the hidden beauty he had just spoken of.

21

Leah woke up six days later with a feeling of foreboding. The thought of going back to New York this afternoon was anathema.

She could hardly believe how wonderful the week had been. No stress, no problems, just good company, a lot of great food and, most important of all, no timetable. She had been able to get up when she liked, eat when she was hungry and sleep when she was tired.

Anthony had made the most cordial host, always full of ideas for things to do, but assuring Leah that if she wanted to lie by the fire all day eating mince pies and reading a novel, then that was fine too. And in fact, while the weather had been so bad, that was how the two of them had whiled away the hours. Jenny and Jack had struck up a great friendship and were usually out before Leah was up, heading for the ski slopes. They would return around four, ready to take on Leah and Anthony in a massive snowball fight.

It warmed Leah's heart to see the way Jenny had blossomed and she thought how much good the break seemed to have done her too. She wondered if Jenny and Jack were having an affair, and hoped that this meant Miles was out of the picture, but their relationship seemed to be that of great buddies rather than anything physical.

As she took her clothes from the wardrobe and started packing them into her suitcase, she knew she would miss

Anthony's constant company when she got back to New York. She had spent some time over the last few days mulling over whether she was attracted to him and decided that . . . yes, she was. Not in the all-consuming passionate way that Brett had inspired, but in a calmer, perhaps more mature sense.

She had little idea how Anthony felt about her. He hadn't ever given the slightest indication that he regarded her as anything other than a very good friend, which, under her present circumstances, was all she wanted.

But as she walked down to breakfast, she felt sad that their holiday together was over.

'Good morning. It's pancakes and maple syrup to set you up for the journey back to the city.' Anthony placed a plate piled high with calories in front of her. For a change, Leah did not feel hungry.

'Don't remind me,' she moaned. 'I have this big ball tomorrow for New Year's Eve that I have to attend for Chaval.'

Anthony sat down and began to make inroads into his plate of pancakes.

'I know. I'm going too. We could both play hookey and stay here instead.'

'Don't tempt me. I love it here. The thought of New York fills me with horror. When are you going back?'

'Tomorrow. I'll spend this evening clearing the place up and catch a flight midmorning. Do you want me to pick you up before the ball tomorrow night?'

'That would be lovely. I hate going to these things by myself, and at least I'll be arriving with the president of the company,' she quipped.

Three hours later there were sad goodbyes at the airport. Jenny and Jack seemed heartbroken to be leaving each other.

'God.' Anthony sighed. 'It's like when you were a kid and

had to say goodbye to your best buddy because you were going off to school.'

Jack smiled and turned to kiss Leah goodbye. 'It's great to meet you. Thank you for coming here. You're so good for Dad. Take care of yourself.'

Leah stared sadly out of the plane window as they left the snow-covered countryside far below.

'Well, I have to say that that was the best Christmas I have ever had,' said Jenny.

'Me too,' agreed Leah. 'Come on then, spill the beans. When's the wedding?'

'Honestly, it wasn't like that at all with Jack and me. He's like the brother I've never had. We just got on so well. Plus, he has a serious girlfriend at college and I have Miles.'

Leah's heart sank. 'Oh.'

'I can't wait to see him. And anyway, what about you? Anthony is charming. I can't believe he's the boss of such a big company. He's so modest.' Jenny gave a sly grin. 'And, boy, is he in love with you.'

Leah swung to face Jenny. 'I don't think he is, you know. It's the same as you and Jack. We just enjoy each other's company. It's odd really, because there's a twenty-year age-gap, but we just click.'

'How do you feel about him?'

'I like him enormously.'

'But you don't fancy him?'

Leah paused. She didn't want to analyse what she felt for Anthony for fear she might spoil it. 'I don't know.'

Jenny shrugged. 'Leah, if I had a lovely man like that who so obviously adored me, I'd never let him go. You two are good together. Very good. Don't dismiss the idea out of hand, Leah.'

Leah looked at Jenny. She shook her head slowly.

'I won't.'

22

Miranda heard the knock on the door and rushed to greet Ian. He picked her up in his arms.

'Happy New Year, my love,' he whispered.

'And to you.' Miranda nestled in his arms, so happy that the interminable hours of the past week were over and Ian was here, holding her.

He put her down. 'Come on, let's go through to the sitting room. I have some presents for you.' He put an arm round her.

Ian was immediately hit with guilt and sorrow as he saw the small Christmas tree that Miranda had erected. She rushed to collect the three presents that were underneath it.

'For you,' she said excitedly.

'Oh darling, I feel so dreadful that I had to leave you alone over Christmas. We just couldn't afford Santos smelling a rat, that's all. You know I missed you dreadfully? I spent every day counting the hours until it was over.'

'So did I,' Miranda breathed. 'Thank God for television. I've watched everything from *It's a Wonderful Life* to *Mickey's Christmas Carol.*'

Miranda did not tell him how she had spent Christmas Day in a haze of tears and alcohol, thinking of what Rose and Chloe were doing in Yorkshire. Only the fact that Ian would be back from his parents' on New Year's Day had pulled her through.

'But the best Christmas present of all is, guess what?' Her eyes sparkled.

'What?'

'Well, Maria came to see me yesterday to tell me that she was going back to Germany for a week to see her family. She left yesterday evening and won't be back until next Tuesday. So, you could stay here tonight if you want. There are no spies.'

Ian already knew, for Maria herself had telephoned him three weeks ago. This had given him time and the perfect opportunity to put his plans into action. He pulled Miranda close and hugged her. 'Of course I want to.'

'There's champagne on ice. I thought we'd have our own Christmas and New Year together.'

'Well, let's have a glass of champagne and we can open the presents.'

'Okay!' said Miranda excitedly. She held him close again, as if unable to lose touch with him for a minute in case he disappeared.

Ian laughed. 'Go on, silly, get the champagne. I've got a surprise for you.'

After Miranda had retrieved the nicest bottle she could find, Ian popped the cork and poured it into the flutes.

'Here's to us,' said Miranda.

'To us.' They clinked glasses. 'I promise you that I will do anything I can to make this New Year better than the last one.'

They soon got down to the serious business of opening presents. Miranda had gone wild on one of her credit cards, finding it a huge pleasure to spend Santos's money on Ian. It was the only way she could think of defying him.

Ian leaned over and kissed her. 'Thank you, darling. They're all wonderful. Now, it's time to open yours.'

Ian handed her a slim envelope wrapped in pretty paper and tied with a bow.

When Miranda saw the contents, tears filled her eyes and she could hardly speak.

'Oh Ian, I . . .' She studied the tickets carefully. Two flights to Hong Kong booked in the names of 'Mr and Mrs Devonshire'. There was also a marriage licence in the same names.

'Oh Ian . . . are you asking me to . . . ?'

'Yes, my love. To marry me, to run away and start afresh together where Santos can't find us. I've got everything lined up. We'll get married in a registry office, then catch a taxi straight to Heathrow. Then we board a plane that afternoon which will take us to Hong Kong. I've a friend in business over there who's offered me a job. I'm afraid I won't be keeping you in the lap of luxury, like you're used to, but we'll be free and far away from Santos. We have to do it this week because Maria's absence will make it much easier for us. I also know that Santos is on his annual Christmas break with his wife and children. He's on his boat until January the tenth, so by the time he gets back, we'll be long gone.'

'But Ian, I'll need a passport and—'

'Hush, Miranda. Tomorrow morning, Roger will be busy helping me at the office. I want you to go out first thing and have your hair dyed a darker colour. Then I want you to have some passport photos taken. I'll call round for them tomorrow night. If you go out in the car with Roger, wear a hat. I'll have new passports for both of us by Friday. All these contacts I've acquired during my years working for Santos have come in very useful.'

'Do I really need to have my hair dyed, Ian?'

'It's an added precaution. I don't want to leave anything to chance. If this goes wrong, well . . .' He shook his head.

Miranda burst into tears. 'Oh God, thank you, Ian. I'm so happy.'

He wiped the tears from her cheeks. 'You look it.' He smiled wryly.

'I'm sorry. They're tears of happiness, I promise. I can't believe that this whole nightmare is going to be over. I love you.' Miranda kissed him with such passion, Ian was almost overwhelmed.

A thought crossed Miranda's mind and her face darkened. 'Ian, what about Chloe?'

'I've thought long and hard about it. There's no way we can get her out of the country with us. But, once we're thousands of miles away, you can contact your mother, let her know you're okay and take it from there. I'm sorry, Miranda, but while you're a virtual prisoner here, you're never going to see Chloe again. At least, if you're free, there's a chance.'

'You're right,' said Miranda quietly. 'Do you think I'll ever see her again, Ian?'

Ian squeezed her hand. 'Of course, my darling.' He pulled her to her feet. 'Come on now, I want to celebrate our engagement.' They walked slowly to the bedroom, arms tightly clasped around each other.

They were still awake when the dawn broke and Ian rose to leave.

'We won't have time to discuss things tomorrow when I call round for the photos so, remember, only one small bag. We want it to look as if I'm just taking you out for lunch. I'll organise some clothes for you, but wear something pretty. After all, it will be your wedding dress.'

'Won't Santos assume that we've gone together, once Roger tells him I was last seen with you?'

'Yes. But there's no simple way around it. I'm the only other person trusted to take you out, so it has to be me.'

Ian walked back towards the bed. He kissed Miranda gently on the lips and turned to leave.

Fear coursed through her veins as she watched Ian go.

'Ian!' she almost shouted.

'What is it?'

'I'm scared. What if something goes wrong?'

'Everything's arranged. Just remember, this time next week we'll be man and wife and all this will seem like a bad dream. I love you, Miranda.'

'I love you too.'

He blew her a kiss as he walked out of the bedroom.

Miranda settled back on her pillows but knew that sleep would not come. She crept to the window and drew back the curtain.

She could see him in the half-light, walking at a brisk pace away from her and the flat, to his car, which he had secreted a few streets away.

'Goodbye, my love,' she whispered quietly as she dropped the curtain back into place.

23

'Hello, Leah. How was the flight?' Anthony kissed her on both cheeks as she got into the back of the limousine and they drove off towards the Museum of Modern Art.

'Absolutely fine. It's hard to believe I left Woodstock only twenty-four hours ago.'

Anthony studied her as she lapsed into silence, looking out of the window.

'Is everything okay? You seem a little quiet.'

'I'm sorry, Anthony. Everything's fine.' Leah smiled at him.

In truth, she did not feel fine at all, but couldn't put her finger on the reason why. Miles had greeted them both pleasantly when they had returned yesterday. He'd kept the apartment spotless and Jenny and he were off to some party in the East Village tonight.

For whatever reason, a sense of impending doom was upon her and she could not shake it off.

The limousine drew to a standstill along Fifth Avenue as a group of cheering New Year revellers, dressed up in outrageous costumes, crossed the road. They were all young, probably the same age as Leah. For a second, she desperately wanted to throw off her elegant evening gown, escape from the restrictive confines of the rarefied, privileged world in which she lived and run to join them.

Anthony sensed this. It made him feel guilty for wanting to take Leah away for ever. But, in some ways, if he asked her the question tonight, wouldn't he be giving her back her freedom? She would never have to stand in front of a camera again and could spend her days however she pleased.

As the car proceeded slowly across West 53rd Street, he gently touched her arm.

'Don't look so sad, sweetheart. The power is yours to change your destiny, if you so wish.'

Leah looked at him carefully. She was amazed that Anthony had understood how she felt.

'I'm being spoiled. After all, who back there wouldn't swap their life for mine? Money, fame, youth . . . I suppose I'm the American dream.'

The limousine pulled up in front of the Museum of Modern Art and Anthony helped Leah out. As they joined the bejewelled throng entering the building, Leah could not help but remember who she had been with the last time she had been inside.

Leah left Anthony to remove her long velvet evening cloak. When she returned to him in the vast downstairs room where the ball was taking place, Anthony was surrounded by people, some of whom she knew from Chaval. All eyes in the group turned as Leah walked towards them.

Even a professional model who graced catwalks and billboards all over the world had nights when her radiance was staggering. And tonight was one of Leah's.

Her hair was coiled in curls upon her head, and she was dressed in a Jean Muir ballgown, its black satin bodice covered in threaded silver. The skirt, made of layer upon layer of black tulle, moved as softly as a ballerina's around her ankles.

Anthony held out his hands to her.

'Leah. What can I say? You look . . . beyond stunning. I think you know most of the people here?'

Anthony introduced the guests she had not met, and they went to take their places at one of the tables, which were laden with crystal and antique china plates.

Once the lovely meal was finished, the band began to play and people started to dance.

'May I have the pleasure?' Anthony asked.

'Of course.' She took his outstretched hand and they walked to the floor.

As they began to move to the steady rhythm, Leah glimpsed David Cooper dancing a few feet away from her. He saw her, waved and smiled. Anthony saw this too, and acknowledged him with a nod.

'I didn't know you knew David,' he said.

'I don't – well, not very well. I've only met him once.'

'He's a strange one. A bit of an enigma in the business community of New York. It's actually quite unusual to see him at a public function such as this. He keeps himself to himself, especially since his wife died a few years ago. Mind you, I know how he feels. You can become very anti-social.'

The band stopped playing and the pair returned to their table. The director of the museum stood up and made a speech about how much good tonight's ball would do for the foundation, and asked everyone to raise their glasses to the New Year, which was fast approaching.

Everyone joined in the countdown and twelve o'clock struck. As the cheers went up, Anthony hugged Leah tightly and kissed her chastely on both cheeks.

'Happy New Year, Leah. I hope it brings you happiness and peace.'

'I wish the same for you, Anthony.'

They went onto the floor to join hands with the rest of the guests and sing the traditional 'Auld Lang Syne'.

Afterwards, the dance band increased the tempo, and sedate ladies picked up the hems of their ballgowns to jive.

'This isn't really my scene,' said Anthony. 'But, please, you carry on.'

Before Anthony could let go of Leah, they were interrupted. 'May I?' It was David Cooper.

'Hello, David. Yes, with pleasure.' Anthony released her into David's arms.

Leah, faced with the choice of being blatantly rude, or dancing with Brett's father, nodded and began to move to the beat.

'How are you?' David asked.

'Fine, thanks.'

'You really do look stunning tonight.'

'Thank you.'

'I thought it was a great pity about Brett and you. I just had a feeling it was serious.' A relationship post-mortem with David Cooper was not how she wanted to welcome in the New Year. 'I was surprised when Brett asked for his trip abroad to be moved forward.'

So, Brett had left the country.

'Yes,' she replied ambiguously.

'Anyway, you're seeing Anthony Van Schiele?' David enquired.

Leah shook her head. 'No. He's my boss and we've become good friends.'

David smiled. 'Honestly, no need to be coy with me. I understand the way the world works. Just because you had a fling with my son doesn't mean you have to enter a convent now it's over.'

Leah wanted to scream. This man had no idea of her feelings for Brett, and the way he was dismissing their love as a 'fling' made her feel sick.

355

LUCINDA RILEY

'I don't intend to enter a convent, I can assure you! Now, if you'll excuse me . . .' Leah extricated herself from his arms and walked towards the powder room.

She washed her hands, which felt clammy, then lingered on, reluctant to go back to the party. She wanted to go home.

Eventually she ventured out into the lobby and found Anthony holding her cape.

'Time to go?' he asked.

Leah nodded gratefully. 'How did you know?'

He led her out of the building to the waiting limousine.

'I watched you with David Cooper. I have to admit I'm intrigued to know your relationship. Do you want to come back to my apartment for a nightcap? You can tell me all about it there.'

'Okay.' Leah realised that it was silly to be coy when they'd spent the past week under the same roof.

Anthony's apartment on the sixty-seventh floor was a comfortable, spacious set of rooms with a lovely view over New York. Like his house in Southport, it was sparsely but elegantly furnished.

'Will you join me? I get embarrassed drinking by myself,' said Anthony, opening the drinks cabinet.

'Okay. You know I'm not anti-alcohol for moral reasons. I just don't particularly like the taste.'

He nodded. 'I'll make you a *crème de menthe frappé*.'

Anthony mixed the drinks and sat down opposite her. 'So, how *do* you know David Cooper?'

Leah rubbed her tired eyes. 'It's a long story.'

'We have all night.' Anthony raised his glass, clinking the ice within.

'Okay. Do you remember when I first came to your house I told you that I'd just ended a relationship?'

356

'Yes.'

'David Cooper is his father.' Leah recounted the whole story, from meeting Brett when she was younger to the final blow that he had left the country without a goodbye.

Anthony sat quietly listening, nodding occasionally.

'The whole thing has really knocked my confidence.'

'I can understand you feeling like that, Leah. When you feel deeply for someone, as you obviously did for Brett, and they let you down, it does odd things to you. I hate to sound patronising, but you will eventually get over it. Take it from one who knows.'

'Yes, but seeing David Cooper tonight has brought the whole thing back.'

Anthony suddenly looked a little nervous. 'Look, Leah, it may be the wrong moment after what you've just told me, but we've always been honest with each other, haven't we?'

'Of course.'

'Well, the thing is . . .' Anthony, usually so eloquent, was struggling to find the right words. 'When I first met you, I thought that you were an exceptionally beautiful woman. Then, as I started to get to know you better, I saw how much more there was to you. Your beauty masks your other qualities very successfully, so it has been a constant pleasure to discover your depth of character, and your genuinely good soul.' Anthony's eyes were drawn into the bottom of his glass as he tried to share his feelings. 'This may sound like a typically American tribute, but what I mean to say is that the past week confirmed what I thought to be true. I've done something I never believed I'd do again after Florence died. I've fallen in love with you.'

Anthony continued to study his brandy as Leah watched him, electing not to speak. She knew he had more to say.

'The thing is, I'm not the type of man who runs around in

the fast lane with lots of different women, and when I first realised I loved you, I felt guilty because of Florence, and also because of the age-gap between us. I tried to convince myself that it could never work, and that you needed someone young.' He met her eye. 'Like Brett.' Anthony gave a sigh. 'But then, after spending time with you, I started to think that, having grown up so fast, you might want someone older.' He swallowed hard. 'In short . . . I want you to marry me, Leah.'

Silence reigned heavy in the apartment as Leah sat, stunned by the revelation.

'Having just heard about Brett, I understand that it will take time for you to get over him. I know what it feels like. Losing someone close is the most painful experience in the world, so take as much time as you wish. I just thought that, before we proceeded any further with our, uh, relationship, you should know about my ulterior motive. But I promise that if you don't feel the same as I do, we can carry on as before.' He put three fingers in the air. 'Scout's honour.'

'Anthony, I . . .'

'It's okay, you don't have to say anything. I'm not looking for answers tonight. I'm sure this has come as a surprise and I want everything to go on as we are. When you feel ready, you give me your answer.'

Leah's eyes were wide. 'Thank you for telling me, I know it must have taken a lot of courage. I feel honoured that you have asked me to marry you . . . I feel . . . Well, I don't know how I feel, because I've never thought about our relationship in those terms before.' She looked deeply into his eyes. 'I promise you I will think about it.'

Anthony looked a little relieved. 'Good. That's all I ask. Now, I have to fly to France tomorrow for a meeting and I shall be away for a couple of days. May I ring you when I get back?'

'Of course.'

'Great. I'll call Malcolm and have him bring the car round to take you home.'

Anthony escorted her to the door of the lift, and kissed her once more on both cheeks.

'Take care, Leah. I'll see you soon. And I mean it, there's no pressure, so don't worry about what I've said to you tonight.'

'I won't. Thank you for a lovely evening.'

The lift door closed and Leah descended to the lobby, where Malcolm was waiting. As she sank into the luxurious leather of the car seat, her mind was whirling. Despite what Jenny had said to her on the flight back from New England, Leah honestly hadn't seen this coming. She and Anthony hadn't even so much as kissed. Their relationship was a friendship. A *wonderful* friendship, but that was it. Wasn't it?

After the thirty-minute drive, Leah turned the key in the lock and stepped into her darkened apartment. She started towards her bedroom, but a noise stopped her. It was very faint, and sounded a little like a wounded animal. She followed the quiet whining to the sitting room, but found it pitch-black. She fumbled for the light-switch and turned it on to its dimmest setting.

There, sitting huddled in the middle of the floor, was Jenny. She was naked, shivering and rocking herself to and fro, emitting small keening cries. As Leah stepped closer and stood just two yards away, she drew in her breath in horror.

Jenny's body was covered in violent purple bruises.

24

Leah stood for a second trying to calm herself. Jenny still seemed unaware of her presence. She knelt down next to her friend, taking care not to startle her.

'Jenny, it's Leah,' she said softly. Jenny jumped as she put a hand on her shoulder.

'Oh God,' Jenny moaned.

Leah took off her velvet cape and wrapped it around the shivering girl's shoulders, before deftly lighting the gas fire.

'Come on, now, let's sit you over here. You'll catch your death otherwise.'

Slowly, Leah manoeuvred Jenny across to the warmth of the flames. She was weeping softly and all Leah could do was to hold her tightly in her arms.

'Oh Jenny, Jenny,' she whispered. 'Why did he do this?'

'I . . . I mentioned what a lovely time we had in Woodstock and how well Jack and I hit it off. He accused me of sleeping around. He . . . he called me a . . . whore . . . he tried to strangle me and . . .' Jenny could go no further. She looked up at Leah, who could see the harsh red marks on the delicate skin of Jenny's neck already turning grey and blue.

'Where is Miles?'

'In my bed, fast asleep. He was very drunk. He probably won't remember anything about it in the morning.'

The thought of the perpetrator of this dreadful crime being

less than a few yards from where they were sitting sent shivers down Leah's spine. Her mind whirled as she thought of what was best to do.

'I'm going to call the police.'

'No! Don't do that!' A look of dreadful anguish came onto Jenny's face. 'Please, Leah,' she begged, 'don't don't *don't*!'

Jenny's voice was rising and she was becoming hysterical. The last thing Leah wanted to do was to wake Miles.

'Okay, okay, shush. I won't call the police. But I think we ought to take you to the hospital to get you checked over.'

'No!' This time there was fear on Jenny's face. 'He didn't hurt me really badly. It's just the shock. I'm fine, honestly.'

'Are you sure you're not in pain?'

'My neck feels sore, but that's all. Please don't make me go to the hospital, Leah. They'll ask who did it and I can't face answering all their questions tonight. If I'm not feeling right tomorrow, I swear I'll go,' she promised pleadingly.

'You know that this can't carry on, don't you? And that Miles has to leave tomorrow?'

Jenny nodded slowly. 'He could have killed me.'

Once more, Leah had ignored her own instincts. Guilt washed over her. She should have thrown Miles out the last time.

'Come on, let's get you into bed. You can sleep with me tonight, then first thing tomorrow morning I want you at the emergency doctor's to get yourself looked at. You're not to come back until after lunch. I have a few things to say to Miles.'

'Oh Leah, why is my life such a mess?' Jenny asked sadly. 'In Woodstock I really felt that I was beginning to win. I felt . . . happy. I was really looking forward to seeing Miles and getting my career on the go again. And now? It's useless. Why, Leah, why?'

Leah shook her head slowly, as she helped Jenny from the floor.

'I don't know, Jenny, I really don't.'

25

The following morning, Leah dispatched a forlorn Jenny to seek medical attention.

Then she made herself a cup of hot, strong coffee and sat in the sitting room to wait for Miles.

At eleven o'clock, she heard Jenny's door open. Her heart beat steadily against her chest as Miles, dressed in Jenny's bathrobe, padded into the sitting room.

'Morning. Want some coffee?'

'I've got some.'

She followed Miles into the kitchen and watched as he calmly filled the kettle and switched it on.

'Happy New Year, by the way.' He smiled. 'Boy, last night was quite a night.'

'You could say that. Sit down, Miles. I need to talk to you.'

He looked vaguely surprised at the stern way Leah spoke to him.

'Okay. Where's Jenny, by the way?'

'Out.'

'Oh. I wouldn't have thought that she'd have been up so early. We both had a little too much to drink last night at the party we went to.' The kettle boiled, and Miles filled his cup before sitting opposite Leah.

The way he could be so nonchalant after his brutal actions the night before unnerved Leah.

'Miles, I found Jenny crying when I got home at three in the morning. She was very distressed. She said that you'd tried to strangle her.'

A look of genuine amazement crossed Miles's face. 'What!' He laughed loudly. 'Well, she obviously had too much dancing juice last night.'

'No, I don't think so. She was covered in bruises, and it's not the first time it's happened. A month ago, she had a badly swollen face and a black eye.'

Miles's face darkened and his penetrating eyes glittered. 'Are you saying it's me who's been inflicting these injuries?'

'Yes. Not only has Jenny herself told me it was you, but it's hardly likely to be anyone else, is it? You were with her all of last night.' Leah thought how ridiculous the conversation was. 'I was all for asking you to leave a month ago, but Jenny wouldn't have it. She said that you always apologise afterwards, and that you'd promised not to do it again. So I let you stay. But, Miles, this can't go on. I want you out of this apartment today.'

He sat silently, staring at Leah. The look on his face was the same one that had made her shiver as a child. It made her feel almost unclean.

'You believe Jenny, then?' he said slowly, his eyes unblinking.

'Yes. Of course I do. I saw the bruises for myself. I have no reason to doubt her. Now, I need you to pack your bags this morning and be gone by lunchtime. You're lucky Jenny has refused to call the police. If you go away and promise never to try and contact her, I won't either, for the sake of your family.'

'My family? What family?'

'Rose, Miranda and Chloe, of course. They'd be devastated if you ended up in court for beating up a woman.'

Miles stood and walked slowly over to Leah, ensuring that he towered above her. For the first time, Leah felt fear course through her veins.

'You'd know all about my family, wouldn't you? You were always trying to get in on the act when we were kids, sucking up to Rose and seducing that pathetic cousin of mine. You've got a nerve, telling other people how to run their lives. Miss Pure, Miss Perfect.'

Miles brought a hand towards her face and, for an instant, Leah thought he was going to hit her. Instead, he gently traced the contours of her face, his fingers moving down her neck towards her breast. This galvanised Leah into action. She jumped up.

'Stop it, Miles! Don't you dare touch me! Get out of here, now! Otherwise I'm calling the police!'

'Okay, I'm going.' Miles sauntered towards the door, but stopped to turn back. His dark eyes glinted as he stared at her.

'You'll regret this, my dearest Leah.'

Ten minutes later, Miles reappeared with his suitcase and threw the front door key onto the floor. 'I'll let myself out. *Ciao.*'

Leah heard the front door slam and listened as the lift descended. She hoped that would be the last she ever saw of Miles Delancey. He inspired a terrible, cold fear inside her, which at present rendered her incapable of moving. She felt as if she was sixteen years old again, and alone with him in Rose's barn.

Come on, Leah. He's gone now. He won't come back. He knows what would happen if he did.

Two hours later, she heard the key in the lock and thought of the struggle she would have in once more convincing her dearest friend that life really was worth living.

Jenny arrived in the sitting room. She looked pale and dreadfully miserable.

'Has he gone?'

'Yes, my darling.'

'Oh.' Jenny promptly burst into tears. Leah stood and put her arms around her friend.

'You know, I really loved him. What will I do now?' Jenny wept.

'Carry on and look to the future. I'm sorry, Jenny, but really, you must see that you're better off without that bastard. I've known Miles a long time and there's always been something about him that makes me uneasy. Any man who could do what he's done to you is rotten to the core.'

'I know. But he gave me a reason to live. I was so depressed before. Now he's gone.'

'Oh Jenny. Look how happy you were in Woodstock. Why not give Jack a ring? He'll cheer you up.'

'No. He's gone away for New Year with his girlfriend. I'm not number one in anyone's book.'

'You're number one in mine. We've got each other. Oh Jenny, please – you have got to fight on. There'll be other men who'll love you and take care of you, not hurt you like Miles did.'

Jenny slumped onto the sofa. 'Is it worth it, Leah?'

Leah wiped the tears from her friend's face. Jenny needed positivity. She chose to be strong.

'Of course it is, silly. You've just had a really rough time, that's all. Things will get better. Trust me.'

Jenny grasped Leah's hand. 'Oh Leah. You're so strong. I wish I was like you. You've been so good to me. I just cause you nothing but problems.'

'That's what friends are for. All I want in return is to see you get over this as quickly as you can. You must try. Promise?'

Jenny shook her head forlornly. 'I can't. Miles was all I had. Everything else has gone.'

'Come on, Jenny, you mustn't think like that.' Leah was desperately trying to think of something she could say to cheer Jenny up. 'What did the doctor say?'

'Not a lot. You know what they're like. He didn't believe that I'd fallen down the stairs, but said there was nothing he could do unless I'd tell him the truth. He checked me out and I'm fine. I've got a prescription for some sleeping tablets and some Valium.'

'Well, give them to me. We don't want to start all that again.'

'I didn't even pick them up,' said Jenny quickly.

'Okay. Well, promise me you won't. Pumping yourself full of drugs won't help, you know that, don't you?'

Jenny nodded.

'Why don't you go and have a lie-down? You must be exhausted. I'll make you a cup of tea and bring it in.'

Jenny gingerly stood up. 'Yes, I am a bit tired.' She squeezed Leah's hand once more. 'Thanks for everything.'

'Any time. Go on. I'll be in in a minute.'

Jenny stood and wandered slowly out of the kitchen. Leah filled the kettle, wondering what she should do. She was not qualified to deal with someone as badly depressed as her friend, and after last time, the responsibility weighed heavily on her shoulders. She decided to ring Jenny's consultant at Lenox Hill.

The receptionist told her that the doctor was on holiday until tomorrow, and advised her to call back then. Leah put the phone down. There was nothing more she could do now, but she would ring first thing tomorrow if Jenny was as unstable as she seemed at present.

'There you go.' Leah handed the hot steaming tea to the pathetic figure in the bed.

'Thanks.'

'Would you like me to stay with you?'

Jenny shook her head. 'I'll be fine. I feel very sleepy. I'm sure I'll nod off.'

'Okay. But call if you need anything. I'll be in my room.'

Leah closed the door behind her, and went into her bedroom to try to catch up on a little sleep herself.

Anthony's proposal last night came into her thoughts for the first time. With Jenny and Miles, she hadn't had a chance to think about it.

Did she love Anthony? She felt comfortable in his presence, cared for and, most rarely of all, completely understood. And yes, she found him attractive.

But marriage? Leah didn't know.

At half past ten that evening, Leah went into Jenny's bedroom. She was sitting upright, eating an apple and watching her portable television. Her hair was brushed and shining, and Leah thought she looked remarkably well under the circumstances. She sat on the bed and took Jenny's hand.

'Hi, Leah. I'm feeling much better.'

'You look it. Do you want to come and sleep in my room tonight?'

'No. I'll be fine in here.'

'Are you sure?'

Jenny gave her a bright smile. 'Absolutely.'

'I'm so proud of you, Jenny,' Leah said warmly. 'You know where I am. Goodnight, and sleep tight.' She stood up.

'Leah?' Jenny reached out her hand and pulled Leah towards her. 'You've been fantastic over the last few months. The best friend I could have hoped for. Thank you so much. I love you.' Jenny flung her arms round Leah and held her tight.

'I love you too. Happy New Year, darling.'

LUCINDA RILEY

'Yes, Happy New Year. You deserve the best of everything. Just hold on to who you are and you'll always be fine.'

As Leah walked out of the room, Jenny waved.

'Goodbye,' she whispered through her tears as the door closed.

At nine o'clock the following morning, Leah took a steaming mug of coffee into Jenny's room.

Before she saw anything, the strong, alcoholic fumes told her the worst had happened.

Leah switched on the light and moved towards the still, pale body of her friend. She removed the empty bourbon bottles and Valium packets from the duvet, before checking Jenny's pulse.

Leah gathered the girl into her arms and held her tightly.

'Oh Jenny, my darling Jenny.'

Leah wept.

26

Miranda stood in front of the mirror, checking her appearance for the last time. After much deliberation, she had decided on a simple Zandra Rhodes suit of cream silk, trimmed with ermine.

She had spent the last night sleepless, eventually risen at five and spent hours fixing her new dark hair.

Miranda looked at her watch. Five to ten. Ian should be here at any minute to take her and her small overnight bag out of this nightmare and on to a new life together.

Yesterday, she had called Roger and had him drive her to the bank. There, she had drawn out every penny that was in the account Santos had opened for her. She had taken five thousand in cash, and the other twenty thousand on a cheque made out to the new name on her passport. Ian would worry if he knew what she had done, but by the time Santos found out, they would be hundreds of miles away, and the money would give them a start.

Miranda went through to the sitting room and sat down. Her hands were clasped nervously together and she could not help but watch the small clock on the mantelpiece, the seconds ticking away.

'Please don't be late, Ian,' she murmured. Since agreeing to the plan she had woken in cold sweats from vivid dreams of

Santos turning up at the airport, trying to stop them getting on the plane.

The clock ticked past ten o'clock as Miranda sat still, in an agony of waiting. She remembered Ian's words.

'If I don't arrive by half past ten, pick up your bag, get out of the flat, and run like hell until you can find a taxi. We'll meet at the registry office. Failing that, get a taxi to Heathrow and I'll see you in the departure lounge.'

Miranda knew Ian had arranged for Roger to go off on some kind of job this morning, and the chauffeur had told her yesterday that he wouldn't be available until lunchtime. The coast was as clear as it would ever be.

For the hundredth time, Miranda checked inside her small clutch bag for the address of the registry office. She knew it off by heart now anyway.

The clock ticked on to quarter past and Miranda could stand it no longer. She got up and poured herself a good measure of vodka. The tasteless liquid flowed down her throat.

At twenty-five past ten, Miranda was in such a dreadful state of trepidation that she had taken to pacing the floor.

'Oh God, please come, please come,' she repeated again and again.

The silence in the room was deafening, and she switched on the television, hoping that it would give her something else to concentrate on. She would wait until twenty to eleven and then do as Ian had asked and take a taxi to the registry office.

She stared blankly at the ten-thirty news bulletin.

Then she saw Ian's face appear on the screen.

Miranda wondered whether she was hallucinating. She moved forwards and listened intently to what the newscaster was saying.

'. . . killed in a hit and run accident at eight o'clock yesterday evening. Police are appealing for any witnesses who might have seen the driver of the car. And now, on to the weather. The cold snap is set to . . .'

Ian's face disappeared. Miranda sank to the floor, believing she was going to faint.

'No, no, oh God, no . . .'

She rocked to and fro, her mind unable to absorb what she had just seen.

Her fingers and toes were tingling as her heart raced dangerously inside her chest. She took deep breaths, trying to control herself.

The faintness passed. Miranda stood up unsteadily and reached for the vodka bottle. She took a huge swig and returned to the sofa.

Something inside of her told her that it was vital she stay in control. She forced herself to think about her next steps.

Ian was dead. Had it been an accident? Miranda could not accept that it was.

Santos must have found out about them.

Everything that Ian had told her about Santos came rushing back into her mind. He had warned her that the man was evil enough to kill.

Miranda was in mortal danger and there wasn't a second to lose. In a giant effort, she put her grief and anger to the back of her mind. This was survival. If she didn't move quickly, there was every chance that she could end up dead.

Instinct took over. Miranda grabbed her overnight bag and headed for the front door. She opened it to see a familiar face.

'Nooo!!' She tried to push past the chauffeur, beating her knuckles into his chest, but he simply picked her up and carried her kicking and screaming back inside the flat.

'Shut up! Shut up!' Roger slapped her repeatedly across her face as Miranda screamed hysterically.

'Murderer! Murderer!'

'Do you think we're all blind and stupid? I'm warning you, madam. If we have any more trouble, that little brat of yours in Yorkshire is dead! Do you understand me?'

Roger threw an envelope into Miranda's lap.

'I'm leaving you here to calm down. Look inside the envelope and don't forget what I've told you. Mr Santos isn't happy, not happy at all. And we all know what happens then.'

Miranda heard the front door slam.

She opened the brown envelope.

Inside were pictures of her daughter, Chloe. She was standing outside her nursery school in Oxenhope village, holding tightly to Mrs Thompson's hand, wearing a dress that Miranda had bought just before she left.

The sight of her beautiful daughter and the happy scene made the tears fall once more.

They could hurt her at any time. Chloe was in danger because of her selfishness.

She ran to the telephone and picked up the receiver. The line was dead.

She tried the front door. It was locked from the outside.

She was a prisoner.

Miranda finished off the rest of the vodka, then started on the whisky. Three hours later her mind was numbed.

The answer was simple. Miranda went into the kitchen and drew out the biggest bread knife. If she was dead, Chloe would be safe, and Santos would move on to another victim.

Miranda positioned the knife at her wrists. She touched the skin and drew a little blood.

The sight made her throw the bread knife to the floor. No. That was a coward's way out. She was the only person alive who could make Santos pay for destroying her and killing Ian.

A sudden strength surged into Miranda's body. She picked up a priceless antique figurine that rested on the countertop.

She hurled it towards the door. It shattered into hundreds of small pieces.

'Bastard! I'll find a way to make you pay, Santos. For both of us,' she added quietly.

27

'Ashes to ashes, dust to dust . . .' The vicar intoned quietly.

Leah watched the older couple, holding on to each other for support, move towards the open grave. The woman threw a pink rose on the top of the coffin, then turned into the comfort of her husband's arms and began to weep softly.

The grey January morning seemed to reflect the couple's grief. As Jenny's mother passed Leah, she grasped her hand. Leah found herself looking into the same beautiful blue eyes that had made her friend so striking.

'Thank you again, Leah. I know you did everything you could. Jenny loved you like a sister. She was always telling us about how good you were to her.' The woman stared into space for a moment, squeezed Leah's hand, then moved away.

The crowd began to disperse as Leah moved forwards, steeling herself to look down into Jenny's grave.

'Goodbye, Jenny. Love you,' she whispered.

Tears stung the back of her eyes, but she was unable to let them fall. The whole thing was too surreal. She could not imagine that the oak casket strewn with flowers had anything to do with her young, beautiful friend.

Others at the funeral had wept copiously, Madelaine in particular.

Leah moved away from the grave and felt an arm on her shoulder.

'You okay?'

The voice was strong and comforting, and she turned her eyes up to Anthony. Jack was standing next to him, his eyes full of sadness.

'Yes. We'd better get back to the apartment. I think I've spoken to most people to give them directions.'

Anthony nodded and put his arm around her. They followed the last few mourners out of the graveyard.

Leah was silent on the short journey back in Anthony's limousine. All conversation seemed banal in the light of what had just taken place.

When she opened the door to the apartment, the sitting room was already filled with guests, and caterers were handing out glasses of sherry and soft drinks.

As Leah moved through the crowd, she felt faintly sick as she heard snatches of conversation. They were talking about the latest young British modelling sensation and last month's issue of *Vogue*.

It was as if Jenny had never existed.

'Darling, what can I say? This is so, so tragic. Jenny was one of the best I've ever had.' Madelaine, the picture of elegant grief in her black Lanvin suit with veiled pillbox hat to match, stood in front of her.

Leah wanted to scream. Madelaine hadn't given a *damn* about Jenny when she was in trouble. All she'd cared about was making sure that her 'product' didn't screw up her commission by going off the rails. This woman, along with all the other hypocrites in the room, was as responsible for her friend's death as Jenny herself. They had all been happy to make as much money as they could out of her when things were going well, but had dropped her like a hot potato as soon as she ran into problems.

Leah fought to control her anger. 'Anthony, this is Madelaine. She runs Femmes.'

Anthony held out his hand and Madelaine took it. 'It's good to meet you, Mr Van Schiele. Leah has told me so much about you. Her campaign for Chaval seems to be going very well. I hear that sales have increased by a quarter since Leah began. Well worth the little fee I negotiated, don't you think?'

Madelaine batted her eyelashes flirtatiously. Leah felt real loathing.

In the past week, numb from grief, shock and guilt at being unable to prevent her friend's death, Leah had paced around the eerily quiet apartment, trying to make sense of it all. She had come up with no answers, but had made a decision. The false world in which she lived had destroyed a young, beautiful girl who should have only been starting out in life, not lying in a box six feet under. It was a corrupt world, and although Leah guessed that it was probably no worse than any other type of business, she needed breathing space to try to recapture the simple joy of being young and alive. At twenty-one she felt like an embittered old woman. She wanted out.

You two are good together, very good. Jenny's words came back to her.

As Leah stared at Madelaine, she realised that she had at her fingertips the only weapon that could genuinely hurt this hard, cold woman who had treated Jenny so cruelly. Remembering the white-hot rage that had erupted inside her when Madelaine had prevented her from suing Carlo – the man who had *destroyed* her relationship with Brett – she knew what she had to do.

A great rush of satisfaction rose inside her and she reached for Anthony's hand.

'I have something to tell you, Madelaine. When I've

finished the assignments I'm booked for, I'm giving up modelling for good.'

A look of horror replaced the smile on Madelaine's face. The money she had earned from Miss Thompson had bought her a very nice house in Cap d'Antibes and a Porsche 924.

'I . . . but . . . why, Leah?'

Leah had never seen Madelaine lost for words, and she relished the pain on the woman's face. She just hoped that Jenny was here somewhere, watching and enjoying. She looked up at Anthony. A flicker of surprise was in his eyes, but it disappeared quickly.

Madelaine repeated the question. 'Why?'

Leah was still staring up at Anthony. She grasped his hand tighter and smiled at him.

'Because Anthony and I are to be married as soon as possible.'

Part Three

March to August 1984

1

New York, March 1984

Leah woke to the soft chirping of the birds hailing the coming spring. She kept her eyes closed, enjoying the few peaceful moments between sleep and wakefulness, when every muscle in her body felt relaxed and refreshed.

Reluctantly, she opened her eyes and glanced at the clock positioned on the bedside cabinet. Half past eight. She hadn't even heard Anthony leave this morning.

Exhaustion had consumed her during the first three months of her two previous unsuccessful pregnancies, and again, at ten weeks, she was feeling weary and washed out.

Leah rose slowly from the big comfortable bed and entered the en suite bathroom. She filled the large round tub with water and bath essence and climbed in, putting her flannel over her face. She breathed deeply, wondering what she would do with the day that stretched before her.

Anthony and Dr Adams, her gynaecologist, were insistent that she moved as little as possible. No riding, no swimming in the beautiful indoor pool . . . In fact, nothing that would tax her above turning the page of a book.

Leah stepped out of the bath, wrapped herself in a big towel and padded into her dressing room to find something to wear.

381

She stood in front of the full-length mirror. Her body was still as firm and toned as it had been when she'd graced the covers of magazines across the globe.

Leah sighed deeply as she put on a soft all-in-one cashmere jumpsuit. Although she could never admit it to Anthony, sometimes she missed those days. She used to be needed. If she was late for a booking, it would cause countless problems for the assembled crew hired on the shoot.

For the past two years she could have spent every day in bed and no one in the world except Anthony would have noticed.

'Come on, Leah, stop it, you sound so spoiled,' she said to her reflection. She left her dressing room, walked along the heavily carpeted corridor, down the sweeping staircase and across the large hall.

A light breakfast of croissants, fruit and decaffeinated coffee was waiting for her in the conservatory where she liked to sit in the morning and observe the beautiful gardens. This morning, the view was more exquisite than usual. The last of the snow had been washed away by a light March rainfall, and the first proper sunshine of the year was in evidence, heralding the rebirth of nature. Leah sat down at the table, poured her coffee and hoped this was a good omen for her own baby's birth.

There were only four weeks left until she passed danger point. The previous two pregnancies had miscarried at twelve and fourteen weeks respectively. Dr Adams was sure that if she could get past that, she would carry the baby full-term.

Leah hated the unfairness of it. She, who had never smoked, hardly drunk alcohol in her life and kept incredibly fit, didn't seem to be able to produce what millions of other women accomplished with ease. Although she'd had stringent tests after both miscarriages, the specialists seemed unable to pinpoint the reason. They told her that she was in good health and there were no problems at all with her insides. Rather than making her feel better, this news made her feel worse, for she had no excuse for her problem.

They both wanted a baby so badly. Anthony, in his mid-forties, was aware that the years were passing all too quickly. And yet, he was producing his side of things with no problems at all, whereas, at twenty-three, Leah was struggling to do the same.

If she lost this baby, she knew that she could not go through it again. The mental agony of every twinge, any sudden slight pain, which under normal circumstances she wouldn't have noticed, now threw her into a panic.

Leah knew objectively that she'd become unhealthily obsessive about her problem. It had completely taken over the past year and put a strain on her otherwise happy marriage. Anthony had shown nothing but kindness, love and understanding, whereas she had become irrational and short-tempered.

If only she could produce one baby . . . Leah was sure it would stop her feeling so terribly depressed. After all, she had everything else a woman could want. Her marriage was successful, she had a beautiful home and enough money to do whatever she wanted.

Anthony had insisted that her earnings from her days as a model were not to be touched, as he had enough for both of them, so the money had been invested and was making a small fortune.

Oftentimes, Leah berated herself for her selfishness. She had become so caught up in her problem that her dreams of doing some good in the world with her money had been lost. She would sit alone, blushing guiltily as she watched the newscaster describing another disaster in some far-flung corner of the world; of starvation and bloodshed which left thousands homeless and dying; and she would tell herself how lucky she was and that she must do something to help. Then she would feel a pain in her stomach and become caught up once more in her own troubles.

Once this baby's born, she told herself, as she cut a kiwi fruit into neat little pieces, *I'll set about doing something worthwhile with my life*.

The post was sitting neatly on a silver tray. Leah leafed through it, taking out the letters addressed to the couple and leaving Anthony's to one side. All of them were invitations to charity functions, gallery openings and official dinners. They depressed her, as she knew that until the baby was born, she wouldn't be going anywhere.

Leah's heart lifted as she saw her mother's familiar writing. She opened the envelope eagerly. They spoke every week, but it had been over two years since she had last been to England. With the miscarriages, the depression that followed, then the new pregnancy, there never seemed to be the opportunity. And now it would be at least eight or nine months before she could return. That was, of course, if she managed to have the baby.

Her mum kept her up to date on the gossip in Oxenhope. She still worked part-time for Rose Delancey – although she didn't need to any more, since Leah had provided her parents with a comfortable yearly income – but her mum said it got her out of the bungalow and she enjoyed it. Leah was fascinated by the mysterious disappearance of Miranda. Apparently, she'd not been seen since Leah's twenty-first birthday party in London. She'd gone off, leaving little Chloe all alone, and hadn't been heard of since. The things that her mum called her were not kind, but Leah knew that Miranda had never done much to endear herself to anyone. Still, leaving her only child was about as low as you could sink.

Leah could hear in her mother's voice how she adored Chloe. It sounded as though Mrs Thompson had stepped in as surrogate mother to the seven-year-old child, while Rose locked herself in her studio to paint.

As for Miles, her mother was always asking Leah if she had seen him lately in New York. Now that he was such a successful photographer, Doreen was sure that they would be mixing in the same circles. Leah would say no, then quickly change the subject. She had told nobody about the way he had treated Jenny, just watched with horror as his name began to appear in the credits of large spreads in American *Vogue, Vanity Fair* and *Harper's Bazaar*. She prayed that Jenny had been a one-off, and that by staying silent she had not endangered the lives of other women that crossed his path.

And Carlo? Well, she'd heard nothing from him since the night he'd asked her to marry him. Leah supposed that he had heeded Madelaine's warnings to leave her well alone. She'd read in the papers that Maria Malgasa was once again his muse and top model. The whole incident had left a horrid taste in her mouth, souring what should have been pleasant memories.

Leah read her mother's letter slowly, biting her lip when she discovered that her dad was due to go into hospital for a hip replacement. His own had crumbled because of his arthritis, and although her mum was cheerful about it, Leah could sense her underlying current of anxiety.

If only she could go over and be with her parents for the operation.

Leah decided she needed a walk. She let herself out of the conservatory and stepped into the biting air, trying to put all unpleasant thoughts out of her head. Stress was bad for the baby, and the tiny creature inside her was the most important thing in her life.

2

Although it was four o'clock in the morning, David was wide awake. Delphine Airways flight DA412 had left Kennedy Airport five hours ago to begin the long journey east towards Nice.

He rose and went upstairs to the 747's deserted bubble to have a drink. He sat in one of the comfortable chairs and nursed a brandy.

Tension engulfed him, making every nerve-ending quiver with a gut-wrenching anticipation. He wouldn't call it fear. No, fear was what he had experienced in Treblinka. It was more that he was experiencing a sense of destiny, as if his whole life had been guiding him towards this journey across the world to take revenge on the man who had murdered his parents and abused his beloved sister. And, of course, for all that came later.

Everything was in place. There had been a flurry of calls between himself and the organisation in the past week. All David had to do was join Franzen at his St Tropez villa as planned. There was already a member of the organisation posing as one of his staff.

David had been issued with a gun, which he had been taught to fire with accuracy. It was to be used only in an emergency, to protect his own life. The organisation wanted Franzen alive.

They had devised this plan so that their target could be extradited by his government and forced to stand trial in Europe
for his crimes against humanity.

David had to get through an evening exhibiting perfectly
normal behaviour, then once Franzen had put pen to paper
– to sign the warrant for his own arrest – David would be
removed from the villa and it would all finally be over. He
would have his vengeance.

He thought of the effect that events would have on Rose.
He could only hope that her revitalised artistic career would
pull her through. He knew that the exhibition at the gallery
he had purchased in London had proved a phenomenal launch
pad for her return to the scene.

David checked the time. He needed to sleep, to relax.

He went back downstairs to his seat. He closed his eyes
and sent up a prayer.

As the private helicopter hovered above the villa's landing
pad, David was able to take in Franzen's palatial residence.
It was positioned high up in the Var hills and boasted a
magnificent view of St Tropez's Pamplonne Beach. The property itself was modern, clearly crafted with the owner's
security concerns in mind. Half a dozen closed-circuit cameras
adorned the whitewashed walls, and an imposing metal fence
ran around the perimeter – save for the front of the villa,
where the immaculate lawn turned into scrubland and gave
way to a cliff edge.

When the helicopter touched down, Franzen was waiting
to greet him.

'Mr Cooper, it's a pleasure to see you again.' He shook his
hand warmly. 'You know Miranda, of course.'

He stared at the emaciated girl standing just behind
Franzen. He remembered her from three years ago as being

387

lively and blonde. The woman now had lank brunette hair and seemed to have aged dramatically.

'It's good to see you again, Mr Santos. And of course I remember Miranda – although I think you've changed your hair colour.'

'She has. A female whim, but I think it rather suits her, don't you? I asked her to leave it that colour, didn't I, dear?' He smiled at Miranda, who nodded sullenly.

David smiled. 'Well, it's good to see you again, Miranda.' He looked for a reaction behind the dull, expressionless blue eyes and wondered what on earth had happened to the girl to effect such a change in her. He thought, with a sickening horror, of the way Franzen had treated the women in his life. He was momentarily thankful that *she* hadn't stuck around long enough to suffer the fate of this poor soul before him . . .

'I thought we could go onto the terrace with a bottle of champagne,' said Franzen. 'We can take in the view.'

He turned and began to follow a stone path away from the helipad towards the sparkling azure swimming pool. David felt the helicopter re-engage its engine, and turned to see it taking off. Within seconds, it was a speck in the vast sky. He felt his stomach turn.

'Are we alone this weekend?' David enquired.

'Yes, well, sometimes a man needs a little solitude when there is business to attend to. I felt it was better to keep the party small. Others may join us tomorrow when the deal has been completed, but for the present, it is just the three of us and my butler.'

The trio stepped onto the lavish marble terrace, where a man in a white tailcoat was standing waiting with champagne. He offered a flute to Franzen, and then his guests.

'Let us toast to an enjoyable and fruitful weekend, shall we?' Franzen raised his glass.

A warning bell rang in David's head, but he put it down to his own neuroses. The butler had to be the man from the organisation.

Half an hour later, it was becoming breezy and there was a chill in the air.

'It is time to go in. Dinner will be at eight, after which we shall get to work. Please, relax and enjoy the villa. I'm sure you would like a shower after your long flight, Mr Cooper?'

'Thank you, that would be great.'

'Towels have been prepared for you in the upstairs bathroom. You will find it at the end of the corridor.' Franzen waved as he walked through some sliding glass doors and disappeared inside.

'So, my dear, would you mind if you left us men to work out a little business? I am sorry, but once it is done we can spend the rest of the weekend enjoying ourselves.'

Miranda shook her head. David did not miss the look of relief on her face.

'Goodnight, David.' She rose from the table and walked towards the staircase.

'Now. I suggest we go into the study, and I shall pour some liqueurs while you prepare the papers for signature. Yes?'

David nodded in acquiescence. He stood up and followed Franzen through the open-plan living room and into the study.

He tried to steady his hands as he unlocked his briefcase and drew out the papers. As he did this, he pressed a knob to start the tape recorder, hidden in the bottom of the case. He had practised this move many times and performed it fluently now. David placed the case on the floor. The reassuring steel pressing into his right-hand side underneath his jacket comforted him.

LUCINDA RILEY

Not long now, David. Just keep calm. Everything is going according to plan.

He handed the papers to Franzen, who put them on the mahogany desk and raised his brandy glass.

'We must have a toast before we proceed. To our continued co-operation and fruitful partnership.' Franzen knocked back the brandy in one.

'Indeed.' David sipped his brandy slowly. He needed a clear head.

'I have to tell you, David, that I was a little surprised when you put this proposal to me. You were the last person I would have expected to be involved with, how can I put it, a rather shady group of militants in South America. By approaching me and asking me to supply arms to this group – sworn enemies of my own country – it would mean immediate arrest and then expulsion if the Argentinian government discovered my involvement. So obviously my people went to a great deal of trouble to make sure that you were all you seemed.' Franzen eyed him.

David's body turned to ice. 'And what did they discover?' he asked slowly.

Franzen paused for a long time. Then he smiled. 'That you were indeed all you seemed. A clean-cut rich businessman. My men could find nothing to mar your record.'

David relaxed and chuckled with Franzen.

Franzen leaned forward towards David, the expression in his eyes changing instantly. 'But then, they do not share the *personal* connection that we do.'

David's mind travelled back to the last time he'd seen that expression in Franzen's eyes. They glinted evil.

'I knew who you were, of course. How immature to think that I would not.' He leaned back in his chair, crossed his arms and laughed.

David's body was rigid as he listened to his slow, hypnotic words. Franzen knew his identity. There was nothing left.

'Oh dear, perhaps I should not make fun of you. After all, your experience in Nazi hunting is limited, is it not, David?'

Years of work had been ruined.

'How?' Was the only word David could manage.

'I have kept a watchful eye, for obvious reasons. I have to admit, when you first approached me, I was in disbelief. Surely your little friends wouldn't have selected such an obvious candidate for my capture. I had your apartment searched, just to be certain.' Franzen threw his hands in the air. 'Under the circumstances, was it not a little stupid to have a Rose Delancey painting entitled *Treblinka* hanging in your study?' Franzen took a deep, satisfied breath. 'David Delanski. Brother of the delightful Rosa. Well, how could I ever forget her? After that, it was easy. Your merry band of intrepid hunters have been known to me for years. But I have to say that it was a clever plan. It would have worked . . . with a different leading man.'

'You bastard,' David breathed.

Franzen chuckled. 'Come now, David. Your kind believe yourselves to be so clever. You think you deserve to rule the world. But this arrogance is stupid. You will never achieve the power you long for.'

David stood. 'There's another in this house, you know. Any minute he'll—'

Franzen lifted his hand. 'Of course. My faithful butler. He has worked for me for two years. And then I discovered his links to your little friends. Very impressive. But he is tied up in the wine cellar and shall not be coming to your aid. I will dispose of him later.' Franzen brushed a piece of fluff from his jacket. 'I decided that it was best to get rid

391

of you both at the same time. Neat and tidy, like the old days. You may have escaped from Treblinka, but I will make amends.'

David realised that Franzen was still living in the days where he could murder someone on a whim. 'So, how are you going to dispose of me? I presume that's why you've gone to the trouble of getting me here and emptying your household?' he asked as calmly as he could.

Franzen nodded. 'Yes, you are right. One of my men could have picked you off long before now, but I felt that it was only right that I completed the job I began forty years ago. And I didn't want to ruin your little plan.' Franzen smirked. 'A nice, simple fall is what is needed.' Franzen gestured to the window, and the end of the garden. 'The poor, drunken tycoon that went over the cliff while enjoying a pleasant break at his friend Santos's villa. I imagine it will make headlines. Congratulations!'

Something inside David burst, a well of hatred opening itself. He swiftly reached inside his jacket, just as he had been taught, and pulled the gun on Franzen.

'Enough! It has to finish, Franzen! I was sent here to make sure that you paid for what you did in Treblinka in front of the world, but now I see that it is my destiny to kill you myself. I promised vengeance when I left Treblinka. Stand up! Now!'

David trained the gun on Franzen, who smiled, shrugged, then did as David had asked. He stood up slowly.

'As you wish, David Delanski. You're in charge.'

'Turn around! Move forward!' David roared. With one hand pressing the gun into the small of Franzen's back, he steered his enemy towards the sliding glass doors of the living room and forced him onto the terrace by the pool. He knew he should lock Franzen in one of the bedrooms and radio for help, but pictures of Rosa's terrified face after their father's death were scudding through his mind.

They reached the edge of the garden, and David forced Franzen to step over a small manicured bush, onto the scrubland. For the first time, he could see the sheer drop down to the water. The villa was positioned on an outcrop, and David's eyes widened at the uneven serrated rock that overhung the choppy Mediterranean Sea five hundred feet below.

'Stand in front of me,' he instructed his captive.

'As you wish.' Franzen moved precariously close to the edge.

'Jump,' David said.

Franzen snorted. 'As if I would make it so easy. You'll have to shoot me, Delanski. Though I doubt you have the stomach.' David raised the gun and held it inches from the back of Franzen's skull. Adrenalin pumped through his veins, making him light-headed and nauseous. His breathing was coming in short, sharp bursts.

'I've waited a long time for this moment.' David was trembling with emotion. 'I swore that I would take revenge for what you did. This is for Mama, Papa, Rosa and all the others. May God show mercy on your soul!'

David fired. And fired again. Two hollow clicks cut through the breeze and echoed around the clifftop. David pulled the trigger again and again, but there was no explosion. Then he heard something more frightening. The sound of laughter. Hysterical, victorious laughter.

The big hand was around his throat and a gun pointed to his head before David had time to move. His own, empty weapon dropped out of his hand and fell behind him as he was forced into the position that Franzen had occupied only seconds before. Now Franzen had him by the scruff of his shirt, and were it not for his tight grip, David would have tumbled to his death.

'You foolish, pitiful little man. While you showered, I emptied your gun. My old friend, it is not I who am destined to die tonight, but you, David Delanski.'

'One question before you dispose of me. Did you ever feel any remorse for murdering thousands of innocent people?'

'Never. You may say a prayer if you wish. Jews usually like to pray before they die.'

The gun was pressing harder into his neck, and Franzen's face was only an inch away from his.

'No? Then so be it. It is a pity that you will not have an opportunity to give my best wishes to Rosa. I miss her so.' Franzen chuckled. 'As I *know* she misses me. How did you react when you found out about our little reunion?' David grimaced. 'I thought as much. I like seeing you in pain, David. It makes me feel good.'

'Bastard,' David whispered.

'I'm not done yet, Delanski. As you know, I've been on to you since we first started our business dialogue. I wanted to make you suffer for this sad attempt at vengeance. Just as before, I've played a long game.'

'What do you mean?'

'The girl. Miranda. I have kept her like a pet. Treated her like a dog.'

'I don't doubt it. But what does it have to do with me?'

Franzen's lips curled into a grin that sent a shiver down David's spine. 'She's Rosa's daughter. I had my people find her.'

David was stunned. 'It . . . can't be . . . I . . .'

'I have made your precious Rosa suffer terribly for the sins of her brother . . . again!' Franzen tutted and increased the pressure on the gun. 'I win, Delanski. As always. And, in case you were wondering . . . Miranda isn't as good in bed as your sister.'

David used every remaining ounce of strength to lash out

at Franzen, but it was no use. Franzen chuckled again. 'Goodbye, David. It has been interesting reacquainting myself with you.'

Forgive me, Rosa, I tried. But lost, like all the others before me.

There was a sickening thud from behind Franzen. He let out a scream and the gun fell from his grip as he let go of David, who lurched forwards, throwing himself to the ground. There followed a crack, which he recognised as the sound of bone splintering. Franzen groaned and fell backwards on top of David. Summoning all his might, he heaved Franzen off him, sending him towards the cliff edge. Franzen's legs disappeared from view, leaving him desperately clutching at the scrub, hanging on for dear life.

David watched as a pair of red high heels came into view. A right foot gave a swift, firm stamp to her captor's face, and David watched as Kurt Franzen toppled over the cliff.

David lay gasping for air.

Eventually, he looked up and saw the figure silhouetted against the sunset. She was holding his empty gun and staring straight ahead of her.

'Thank you, thank you.' David panted. 'Are you all right?'

The figure nodded. 'Do you think I killed him? I hit him very hard on the back of his head.'

'I don't know, but I doubt anyone could survive that fall.'

'I wanted to kill him, David. I didn't do it to save you, you know. I did it for myself.' *And for Ian,* Miranda thought to herself.

The calmness with which she spoke frightened him. The girl was obviously in shock.

David stood up. 'Miranda, why don't you go back inside? I think we ought to get help as soon as possible. I'm going to the cellar to see the butler.'

'Okay. I feel tired. And cold.' Miranda held out her arms. 'Please help me.'

David walked towards her as Miranda began shivering violently. He folded the girl into his arms.

'It's okay, it's all over now.'

She looked up at him. 'Yes. Take me home to Rose, David.'

David made his way to the wine cellar and found the butler gagged and tied to a chair. He released him quickly.

'The plan has gone wrong. He was on to us months ago. Franzen will never be brought to trial. He is either dead or dying in the water at the bottom of the cliff.'

The butler put a hand on his shoulder. 'David, you did all you could. I will radio the team to arrange a rendezvous. We will leave immediately.'

David nodded and slumped into a chair, not able even to begin thinking about Franzen's most recent revelation.

Miranda . . . Oh Miranda . . .

3

Rose put down the telephone and sank to the floor. The shock of hearing David's voice again was as much of a revelation as discovering Miranda was safe.

She closed her eyes and took five long, deep breaths.

She was going to see her brother again after all these years. He'd been brief on the telephone, promising to explain all when Rose arrived. He was sending his private plane to Leeds Bradford Airport to pick her up and fly her to France. She had been assured that Miranda was alive and well, but he thought it best if they met in St Tropez without Chloe so that they could all talk.

Rose knew she could not begin to put together how David had found her daughter in a St Tropez villa. Surmising was pointless and in less than twenty-four hours she would know the full truth.

Just before the Learjet landed at Nice, Rose applied a new coat of lipstick and brushed her thick titian hair.

As she emerged from customs, she saw him. He looked older, of course, the grey streaking his blond hair.

Her feet were carrying her towards him, nearer and nearer.

He saw her and his eyes lit up.

'Hello, David.'

'Hello, Rose.'

'Good flight?'

'Not bad.'

'You must be tired.'

The banal conversation continued as Rose followed him through the airport and out to the car park. David unlocked the passenger door of a Mercedes and helped her in.

'You look beautiful. You've hardly changed at all.' David was staring at her.

'You look well too.'

'Thank you.'

David got into the car and started the engine. They drove in silence, neither of them knowing how to bridge the gap between where they were now and where they had left off twenty-eight years ago. Anything they could think of to say was either too lightweight or far too heavy for them to handle. Rose looked out of the car window at the breathtaking view of the Mediterranean.

Fifteen minutes later, David pulled the car over into a small parking area. There was a deserted bay below.

'Let's go for a walk. I have things to tell you that you need to know before you see Miranda.'

Rose nodded and stepped out of the car.

The windswept figures spent two hours on the beach. As the grey March day sent the waves skidding into the shore, they walked along, side by side, keeping their distance. Then the woman stopped, sank to her knees and put her head in her hands. The man reached down to comfort her, cradling her in his arms.

Eventually, they stood, and continued walking, his arm around her shoulders.

*   *   *

The light was growing dim as Rose and David returned to the car.

Rose was shivering, not only from cold, but from shock and emotion. David helped her in and she sat staring in front of her. He walked round to the other door and climbed in behind the wheel.

'So you see, it's all my fault, Rose. Franzen hunted her down because of me.'

Rose shook her head. 'I don't blame you, David. How could I? You were trying to bring about some justice. We both know that you never would have tried any of this if I hadn't . . .' Rose swallowed hard. 'I should have worked harder to find her.'

David shook his head. 'It was an impossible task. Miranda used her real mother's surname, mainly because she didn't want you finding out where she was.'

Rose turned to David, her face ashen.

'Did she tell you what her real mother's surname was?'

David shook his head. 'No. Does it matter? At least Miranda is not tied to any of this by blood.'

Rose's eyes filled with tears. 'Oh David, that is where you are so wrong.'

'Rose, oh Rose!' Miranda flung herself into her mother's arms, crying piteously. Rose stroked her daughter's brunette hair, her heart breaking. She knew that it wasn't over for her daughter yet.

The three of them ascended the tiled stairs of David's rented villa and entered the salon. David poured them all a stiff drink and sat down on one of the comfortable sofas.

'We have a lot to tell you, Miranda, about your past, and about ours. I wanted Rose to be here before I began.'

'You start, David.' Rose sat down next to Miranda and held the shivering girl tightly in her arms.

'Do you have any idea why I was at Santos's villa this weekend?'

'Business?'

'You could call it that. Frank Santos's real name was Kurt Franzen. He was deputy commandant at Treblinka, a death camp for the Jews in Poland during the war. He murdered our mother, our father and countless others. He did unspeakable things to Rose. But, then . . . Rose . . . it wasn't her fault, but . . .' David paused before he began to tell the full story. The pain of doing so, of speaking it aloud, was almost more than he could bear.

Miranda grabbed Rose's hand as David recounted the atrocities of the man she had just killed. He told her of Anya, who'd helped them escape, and how she'd been raped by Franzen and other SS officers.

'But once Anya, Rose and I escaped from Treblinka, we realised the battle for survival was not yet over,' David continued. 'We lived on our wits, hiding in forests, using the money I had stolen from Treblinka to buy what food we could find. Anya gave birth to her baby in a barn near the Polish border. She was very sick afterwards, but eventually she recovered.' David looked at Rose and knew that she too was reliving the terror. 'The war came to an end and we managed to make our way to Austria. Do you remember Peggetz, Rose?'

Rose nodded. 'Yes. A terrible place, a terrible time . . .'

4

Peggetz Camp, Austria, 1945

Hundreds of men, women and children were making their way towards the displaced persons camp run by the British army, all of them nursing the hope that this would be their way home. Alongside the masses, convoys of army trucks filled with soldiers advanced across the mountainous countryside around Lienz.

Rosa and Anya were dropping with exhaustion and Anya's toddler, Tonia, grizzled ceaselessly as she was bumped up and down in the makeshift baby carrier slung round Anya's back. Approaching three years old, the hardship of the past few years had delayed her growth.

Peggetz camp stretched endlessly along the Drau Valley. It had been a German barracks and was now filled to the brim with refugees of all nationalities, and surrounded by thousands of Cossack soldiers. Their horses could be observed grazing for miles in the green countryside.

'David, it looks like Treblinka,' Rosa said uncertainly as they followed the others through the wooden gates.

'Hush now, Rosa. We won't be here for long. All we have to do is find a British officer and tell him we are half English. They will help us.'

The four of them spent their first night in Peggetz under the stars, as there was no room for them inside the dormitories.

The next morning, David left Anya and Rosa chatting with a young Cossack soldier, and located a uniformed British officer.

'Excuse me, sir.' David had not spoken English for many months and struggled to recall his former fluency. 'My sister and I have family in Britain. We want to go there as soon as possible. See.' David showed the officer his mother's British passport.

The officer, surprised at the dishevelled boy's good English, studied the passport.

'You say this is your mother?'

'Yes, sir. I have the address of my grandparents. Is there a train we can catch to England from here?'

'I'm afraid it doesn't work quite like that, my boy. There are hundreds in this camp who wish to leave, and many who would like to go to England. The Red Cross is in that hut over there. If you go and see the officer in charge, he might be able to help you.'

David's heart sank as the man turned away. He knew that his mama had run away with his papa and hadn't spoken to her parents since. They were not even aware of their grand-children's existence.

He wandered miserably over to the hut that the officer had indicated, joining a line of people waiting to see the Red Cross official. Eventually, it was David's turn.

'Name.'

'David Delanski. And Rosa Delanski, my sister. We want to go to Britain to our grandparents.'

'Do you indeed?' The official looked sceptical.

David explained as best he could about their situation. The official's expression, hardened by hundreds of similar stories, didn't change.

'All I can do is to write to your grandparents in Britain to see if they can corroborate your story. Then there might be a chance for you. Do you have any identity documents?'

'Yes. My mother's passport.'

'Anything else?'

David remembered the locket, now back round his neck. He unclasped it carefully.

'Here. Send that. My grandmother gave it to my mother.'

The official looked pleased. 'Good, that will be helpful. Although it may be some time before we hear anything. Post is still struggling to get through, and we have a lot of cases to deal with.'

'What about our friend, Anya? She has no home and she wants to come to England too.'

'What nationality is your friend?'

'Ukrainian.'

'Ah. What did you say her name was?'

'Anya. I don't know her second name.'

'All right. I'll see what I can do. In the meantime, please remain in the camp.' The officer watched as the boy left the room. For him and his sister, there was a slim chance, but for the Ukrainian girl . . . none. They had just received orders that all Soviet citizens were to be repatriated, by force if necessary. The thousands of Cossacks and other Russian refugees would be moved out in a few weeks' time, back to their homeland to face an unknown fate.

David discovered, while he was waiting in the queue to see the Red Cross official, that in the village of Lienz it was possible to buy bread and fresh milk, albeit at extortionate prices. He returned to Rosa and Anya, who were still sitting where he'd left them with the Cossack.

'When are we going to England?' Rosa asked him.

'Soon, I promise.' David did not let Rosa see the fearful doubts that were in his mind.

His sister stood up and hugged him. 'Good. I don't like it here.'

'I know. We just have to wait until they contact our grand-parents. Then we'll be off.'

Anya indicated the Cossack. 'David, this is Sergei. He says there is a tent near his that has just been vacated, but we must go now before someone else finds it.'

David shook his hand. 'Thank you, Sergei. If you would take the girls with you to the tent, I will go into Lienz and find some supper.'

Anya translated into Russian and Sergei nodded.

That night, the two men built a fire over which they cooked the large sausage that David had purchased earlier. It was a warm night, and after the sun had set, some of the Cossacks began singing and dancing with the women. David was persuaded to accompany them on his violin. Anya danced with Sergei, while Rosa looked after little Tonia. Her mother didn't come back to the tent until dawn was breaking.

'David, there is a rumour among the Cossacks that there is to be forcible repatriation for Russians and Ukrainians. Can it be true?'

David shrugged. 'I don't know, Anya.'

Her eyes were filled with fear. 'My family fled ten years ago to escape the Communist regime. I couldn't bear to go back there. Sergei says we would all be punished.'

'But why, Anya? You have done nothing.'

'I know, David, but Stalin; he is a . . .' Anya pulled at a blade of grass. 'Anyway, the Cossacks are going tomorrow for a meeting with Field Marshal Alexander. I think they will explain everything then.' Anya turned and looked into David's eyes. 'I cannot go back to Russia. I would rather die.'

David nodded. 'If there is a problem, we will leave here immediately,' he said simply.

'Thank you. But if anything did happen . . . I . . . would you take care of Tonia for me?'

'Of course, Anya.' David did not hesitate. 'But I think you're worrying for nothing.'

'Maybe.' Anya left the tent and observed the beautiful Austrian countryside, a rock of fear in place of her heart.

The following day, David watched with Anya as the Cossack officers were loaded into trucks.

That evening, the trucks came back empty.

The following day, Major Davies, the officer in charge of the camp, announced that the rumours were true. Forcible repatriation had been agreed between Stalin, Churchill and Roosevelt. People were to be moved back to Russia as from tomorrow.

All hell broke loose following the revelation. Thousands of Russian refugees – men, women and children – started to pick up their meagre possessions and walk, like automatons, away from the camp.

Later, a makeshift platform was erected in the main square. The priest was going to hold a service of prayer before the loading began the next morning.

David searched through the milling, wailing crowds for Anya. She was nowhere to be seen.

He didn't understand. He knew that the Cossacks would be considered enemies of the Soviet Union for fighting with the Germans, but surely innocent women and children wouldn't be punished?

David returned to the tent, where he found Tonia fast asleep, wrapped up in a blanket. There was a piece of paper pinned to her.

Dear David,

Sergei and I have left the camp. We face certain death if we stay. You may not understand, but believe me, it is true. We are going to Switzerland, where we hope we can find asylum. The journey will be perilous, and that is why I ask you, please, David, to take care of Tonia until I send for her.

I will find you in England.

Thank you, my dearest friend.

Good luck and goodbye.

Anya.

The following day, David watched through a window of one of the now empty dormitories as people were loaded, screaming and kicking, into trucks. Shots rang out time and again. It was like revisiting his worst memories of Treblinka. He had foolishly believed the war was at an end. David thanked God that Anya had left.

'May God go with you,' he whispered, as he hugged Rosa and Tonia to his chest.

David Cooper had to shake himself to return his mind to the present day. Miranda was staring at him in stunned silence. It was a while before she turned to Rose. 'Why did you never tell Miles and me about your past? I know that it doesn't have much to do with me, because I'm adopted, but surely . . . ?'

'Darling.' Rose gripped Miranda's hand. 'Forgive me, for that is where you are wrong. David, please continue.'

David nodded. 'After Anya left, and the rest of the Russians were repatriated, news came from England that our grandparents were willing to take Rose and me in. But Tonia, Anya's child, was unable to join us. The authorities at the camp told us not to worry, that the baby would be adopted.' David ran a hand through his hair. 'What choice did we have? Before we left the camp, we wrote a letter to baby Tonia, explaining how her mother had escaped repatriation. We told her that Anya had sworn to find her once she was settled, and how we both loved her, and wished she could come with us to England. We wrote down our full names, plus our grandparents' address in London, and asked the Red Cross to put the letter in Tonia's file for safe-keeping until she was old enough to understand. Then we left for London and a new life.'

'What happened to Anya?' asked Miranda, quietly.

David studied Rose's guilty face.

'We don't know, Miranda. We think that she and Sergei were probably caught and shipped back to a labour camp in Siberia. Not many escaped.'

'And Tonia? The baby?' She looked up at Rose, who was deathly pale. Rose looked at David, who nodded imperceptibly.

'Rose has something else to tell you, Miranda. Then you might understand why this has so much to do with you. I'll be in my bedroom. Call me if you need me.'

Rose nodded as David left the room. Rose looked at her daughter. The time had come.

'Darling, I want you to be very brave, like you have been so far. I'm going to tell you about your real mother.'

5

Yorkshire, October 1960

The writing on the envelope was strange, penned in an unfamiliar hand. Rose picked it up from the mat and saw that it had been readdressed from her grandmother's house in London and sent on to her old London address. It had then been redirected, along with the rest of her post, to her new home in Yorkshire.

Miles was crying in the kitchen, so she took the letter with her and opened it with one hand, while spoon-feeding her three-year-old son with the other.

The English was broken and badly spelled. It took her a long time to decipher the first sentence.

'*Deer Miss Delanski . . .*'

Just the use of the name made her shudder. As far as she was concerned, Rosa Delanski had not existed for many years.

My name is Tonia Rosstoff. I am locking for you or David Delanski. My Mother was Anya Rosstoff. You knew her at Peggetz. Please, very urgent I meet with you. Please to come to address at top of page. Quickly pleese.

Tonia Rosstoff.

Miles began to scream as the hand holding his apple sauce stopped inches away from his mouth as Rose read the letter.

The address at the top of the letter was somewhere in east London.

First things first.

She concentrated on feeding her hungry son, then cleaned him up and put him in the makeshift playpen she had erected in the corner of the kitchen. Miles sat happily playing with a toy truck and Rose sat down to read the letter again.

The content sent shivers up her spine. Her first instinct was to call David, but . . . no. That was impossible. Not after what she had done. Rose would have to deal with this by herself.

The thought of having to travel back to London was bad enough, but to meet the little baby whom they had abandoned to her own fate made her heart palpitate. On the other hand, the girl was obviously desperate to see her. She checked the original postmark and saw that the letter had taken over three weeks to reach her in Yorkshire.

Her conscience would not let her ignore it. She would have to go.

She couldn't take Miles but, even though she had lived here in Oxenhope for over three years, she still knew no one. The community was very tight-knit, and because she was a single woman with a baby, who had bought the big farmhouse on top of the hill, the locals eyed her with obvious suspicion.

Rose decided to take a walk down to the village and enquire in the post office if there was anyone who would like to earn a bit of extra cash childminding.

As she expected, Mrs Heaton, who ran not only the tiny post office in the centre of the village but the local gossip grapevine too, was unforthcoming.

'Childminding, you say . . . hmm.'

The woman was obviously dying to enquire where the boy's father was, and Rose fought her irritation. After all, she wanted to live here for the rest of her life. She gave Mrs Heaton a smile.

'Yes. I have to go to London tomorrow and I don't want to take Miles with me. I'll be back in the evening. It really is quite urgent.'

'Poor mite. No one to look after you, eh?' Mrs Heaton clucked disapprovingly. 'Well, I might know someone,' she said slowly.

Rose's face lit up. 'Wonderful, who?'

'Doreen Thompson. She's got a two-month-old baby. She's a good lass, is Doreen. She stays at home *all* the time, to look after Leah,' hinted Mrs Heaton.

'Can I ask where she lives?'

''Cross the road and off the square. Number eight. She'll be in. Say I sent you'

'Thank you, Mrs Heaton.'

Number eight was a small end-of-terrace house, with a line of white nappies hanging on the line in the tiny yard outside. Chickens complained and scattered as Rose unlocked the wooden gate and pushed Miles through the narrow opening.

She knocked on the door and a woman holding a baby peered at her through the kitchen window.

'Mrs Heaton from the post office sent me,' she called through the glass pane.

The frown lines on the face of the woman disappeared and she opened the door.

'Mrs Thompson?'

'Yes.'

'Mrs Heaton told me that you might be interested in a spot of childminding, seeing as you have one of your own. Hello, sweetheart.' Rose extended a finger to the baby opposite, who happily curled her small fat hand round it and locked it in a vice-like grip.

'Oh, I'm not entirely sure . . .'

'The thing is, Mrs Thompson, that I have to go urgently to London tomorrow and the journey is too long for Miles. I'd only be gone a day. I should be back from London by seven, but I'll have to catch the first train tomorrow morning. I really am quite desperate, Mrs Thompson. And Miles is a good baby. He won't cause you any problems, will you, darling?'

Miles was fascinated by a chicken that was hovering near his pushchair. He reached out his arms to grab it, but it smartly ran away.

'Well, I ought to ask my husband, but . . .' Mrs Thompson's face softened as she looked down at the beautiful little boy in the pushchair. '. . . I'm sure it won't harm just this once.'

'I'll pay you, of course. Would two pounds be enough?'

Mrs Thompson looked as if she might faint. Then she shook her head. 'No, I couldn't take that. After all, he'll cause me no extra work, seeing as I'm here with Leah any road. Ten bob'll do fine.'

'No . . .' Rose was delving into her handbag to find her purse. 'I want to pay two pounds because I'll have to bring Miles here early tomorrow morning and you've been so good to help out at such short notice. Here.' Rose handed the amazed woman two crumpled notes. 'Thank you. I'll be round tomorrow at six, equipped with everything he'll need. Bye.'

Rose smiled to herself as she wheeled Miles through the gate and started on the long walk up the hill. She instinctively knew that her son would be fine in the capable, motherly hands of Mrs Thompson.

* * *

411

As the train pulled into King's Cross at a quarter past eleven the following day, Rose felt physically sick at the mass of people.

After making her way along the crowded platform, she climbed into a taxi and gave the driver the address from the top of Tonia's letter. She just wanted to get this over and done with.

Half an hour later, the car drew up in front of a rundown block in Tower Hamlets.

'The flat you want is in that building over there, but I'm not taking you any further. It's not a nice area, this, miss.'

Rose could see that perfectly well for herself.

She walked across the courtyard and looked up at the small crumbling balconies draped with grey washing. There was an echo of children's voices, but they were unseen.

She opened the door to the block the driver had indicated and started up the stone steps. Cold filled Rose's bones, and she winced at the acrid smell of rotting rubbish. She remembered the scent well.

The peeling door to the flat was scuffed with black boot marks, and part of the pane was missing.

Rose took a deep breath and rang the bell, which didn't work, so she knocked on the letterbox.

There was no reply. She knocked again, louder this time.

Still nothing.

The door on the other side of the landing opened and a pair of brown eyes peeped out.

'Gone away.'

'Sorry?'

The woman studied Rose, and opened the door further.

'Gone. In ambulance. Two weeks. Very sick. Maybe dead now.' The haggard-looking woman gestured helplessly.

'Do you know which hospital?'

'Probably Whitechapel. Very near.'

'Thank you very much. I'll try it.'

Rose started down the steps. She knew where Whitechapel was and decided it was faster to take the brisk ten-minute walk than get a cab. She prayed that she wasn't going to be too late.

On arrival, Rose asked about Tonia at the information desk, hardly daring to breathe as the woman looked down her lists.

'Here we are. Tonia Rosstoff. Ward 8.'

The woman gave Rose directions, and Rose traipsed along the pale green corridors, trying not to inhale the scent of sickness and disinfectant.

Rose asked the sister behind the desk which bed Tonia was in.

The sister looked grim. 'Are you a relative?'

'No.'

'Oh.' The sister thought for a moment. 'I was hoping you might be. It seems that Tonia doesn't have any family. Unfortunately, she came in too late. She's really very sick.' She gave a sad shrug.

'Is she going to be all right?'

The sister shook her head. 'I'm afraid not. She has tuberculosis, but at a very advanced stage. All we can do is keep her comfortable. Poor thing. Nurses aren't meant to get attached to our patients, but Tonia, well . . . you'll see what I mean in a minute. She has so much sadness in those young eyes.' The nurse sighed. 'And her poor child. She was brought into the hospital with Tonia, suffering from malnutrition.' Rose's heart jumped. 'She's fine now, and ready to leave the ward, but God knows what will happen to her when her mother dies. She'll be taken into care, I suppose. Anyway, follow me.' The sister began to whisper as they walked into a small side ward. 'I'm afraid her English is not good and she's very weak.'

413

The pathetic sight that lay in the bed brought tears to Rose's eyes. Tonia seemed dwarfed by the life-preserving paraphernalia surrounding her.

Rose edged closer and saw that Tonia was asleep. She was tiny and dreadfully thin. Her cheekbones stuck out of her hollow white face, and there were huge black marks around her eyes.

Lying there, with her blonde hair spread across the pillow, she looked no older than a twelve-year-old child, although Rose knew the girl must be eighteen.

'I'll leave you,' whispered the sister and quietly closed the door.

Rose sat down in the uncomfortable wooden chair by the bed.

'Tonia,' she whispered. 'It's Rosa. Rosa Delanski.'

There was no response. Rose took the girl's hand and squeezed it. She tried some Polish.

'Tonia, *kochana*, Tonia, darling.'

The eyelids fluttered, then parted. Tonia looked up to the ceiling, as though she was having a dream.

Rose squeezed her hand gently.

'Tonia, *kochana*, do you understand Polish?'

Tonia turned very slightly, as though the movement might bring about great pain. She looked at Rose, then nodded.

It was a long time since Rose had used her native tongue, and she began carefully.

'I am Rosa Delanski. You wrote me a letter asking me to come and see you.'

'Yes.' The voice was no more than a whisper. 'I never believed you would come. Thank you.'

'What was it that you needed to see me about?'

The pressure on Rose's hand tightened and Tonia heaved herself upright.

414

'I have a baby. Three months old. In ward in hospital. Please, look after her when I . . .' This effort seemed to have exhausted Tonia and she fell back onto the pillows. '. . . die.'

'Oh Tonia, what has happened to you? There are so many things I want to ask. When we left Peggetz, the Red Cross assured us you would be adopted and . . .'

Tonia shook her head violently. 'No. Orphanage. Terrible. Please, not my child. Please. I have written a letter . . . in the cabinet –' Tonia inclined her head slightly – 'Look inside.'

Rose did so. There was an envelope and nothing else.

'In case you came. It asks for you to look after Miranda. A request from her mother, see?'

Tonia struggled to speak, which did not help Rosa's confusion.

'Can I open it?'

Tonia nodded.

The letter was written in bad English, but it informed the reader that either David or Rosa Delanski should have custody of Miranda Rosstoff if Tonia died.

'I would kill my baby rather than leave her. I was left to grow up alone in a terrible place. No love, only hunger, unhappiness.' Tears were spitting out of Tonia's eyes as passion gave her strength to speak.

Rose's heart was breaking. Tears fell down her cheeks too.

'Oh Tonia, why did you not contact us sooner? If only we'd known, I . . .'

'I did not know about you before. Only twelve months ago. I was in prison – I had to steal and take men to earn money to eat – and a social worker asked me about family. I said I had none. She got my file from the authorities and in it was your letter. I wrote, but got no reply. I came to England to find you. Then got pregnant. Then got sick. Had my baby, then this.'

415

Tonia was panting hard.

'Shh. Take it easy, Tonia. You have time to rest.'

Tonia's wide eyes gazed at Rose, full of fear.

'No. I think I will die soon. I'm frightened . . . oh dear Lord, I'm frightened.'

Rose leaned over and gathered the girl up in her arms, feeling the fragility and the lifeforce ebbing away. She stroked her hair, her tears dampening Tonia's head. Never had she felt so utterly helpless. The effects of the past and the futility of life were never more apparent than now.

'I'm here now, *kochana*, Rosa is here and she'll look after your baby for you, I promise. Oh my darling.'

Tonia pulled away and stared at Rose, her eyes full of relief. 'Thank God you came before it was too late. Miranda will have family. Please call the sister.'

Rose gently lay Tonia back on the pillow and alerted the sister, who came running down the corridor.

'Is she all right?' Her face was a picture of concern.

'I don't know. She said she wants to see you.'

The sister moved to Tonia's bedside and leaned near her patient. Tonia whispered to her for a long time, struggling with the words. Eventually, the sister nodded and raised her head.

'I think she said I'm to promise that I'll let you take her baby home . . . that you are the only family she has.' The sister inhaled deeply, ordering her thoughts. 'That you loved her mother, and she wants you to be Miranda's mother. Can you ask her in Polish if I've got that right?'

Rose did so, and Tonia nodded. 'Yes. Not orphanage, please, promise.'

The sister's eyes too were full of tears.

'Why don't I go and get Miranda now?'

A smile broke on Tonia's face and the sister hurried out of the room.

Rose sat down once more and took Tonia's hand. 'There, now, *kochana*. You see? You're not to worry. Miranda is coming here now and I swear she will leave with me. I'll love her and look after her as if she is my own. You just concentrate on trying to get better.'

The sister brought in a white woollen bundle. Tonia signalled that Rose was to hold her.

Rose could not help letting out a small cry as the baby was placed gently in her arms.

'She is beautiful, isn't she?' whispered Tonia, studying the two of them.

'Yes. Just like her mother. And grandmother.'

The sister watched the dying mother holding the fingers of her tiny baby she had so bravely handed on to another. She did not think she had ever witnessed a more heartrending scene.

Tonia's eyes were closing.

'It's time to leave now. Tonia must be exhausted.'

Rose nodded.

'Goodbye, Tonia. I'm going to come back in a couple of hours' time and we can talk again.'

Tonia opened her arms for the baby. Rose placed Miranda in them and Tonia held her tight.

'*Do widzenia, kochana.* Goodbye, my darling.' She gently kissed the top of Miranda's head, then handed the baby to Rose.

'She is yours now, Rosa. I thank you from the bottom of my heart.'

'You can see her again later, my love,' said the sister.

Rose kissed Tonia.

'Goodbye, Tonia. I'll keep my promise, I swear. You rest now.'

Tonia nodded. Her eyes followed Rose and her baby out of the door. She blew a small kiss, then lay back and closed her eyes.

When Rose came back to the hospital two hours later, the tear-stained sister shook her head sadly.

6

Rose opened her eyes. She had closed them to shut out the present and take herself back to that bleak hospital room. The entire event was etched so clearly on her memory and she wanted, at the very least, to be able to tell her daughter everything her mother had said before she died.

Miranda was sitting very still. Rose wanted to continue to the end.

'I have to say that I was not able to take you straight home to Yorkshire as I promised Tonia. Both that dear sister and I knew when we made our promise that the world didn't work like that. But at least your mother died happy, believing that you wouldn't have to suffer the fate she herself had endured. After Tonia died, you were placed in the care of foster parents. I applied immediately to adopt you, but because I was unmarried, I was thought unsuitable. It took me three years and numerous court hearings before I finally brought you home with me. And that sister kept her vow. It was her statement and Tonia's letter that finally convinced the court to let me adopt you. I'll never forget the day I finally held you in my arms and knew you were mine.' Rose gave a sob. 'Oh Miranda, I swear that I loved you as my own, and yet

419

you always felt you were second best to Miles. Sometimes I wanted to tell you how I'd fought for the right to adopt you tooth and nail, just to prove to you how much I cared.'

Miranda stared into space. 'When I killed Santos – I mean Franzen – I took revenge for my real mother and my grand-mother.' She looked ashen. 'From what you say, there's a possibility that he was my grandfather.'

Rose hugged her daughter tightly. 'Anya, your grandmother, was forced to have relations with other SS officers. We will never know for certain.'

'Oh God,' Miranda whispered.

The women sat in silence for a long while, both contem-plating the stomach-churning truth.

Eventually, Miranda looked up at Rose. 'He deserved to die, didn't he?'

'Oh my darling, yes, yes.'

'He threatened Chloe. He took pictures of her and said he'd hurt her if I tried to contact her. I . . . love her . . . so much. And he killed Ian. For the past two years he's kept me locked up, like . . . an animal in a cage, because I'd tried to run away. I –' Miranda's voice broke and she could not continue.

'He knew you were my daughter. He did this to hurt me, and to hurt David. He was a twisted, diabolical, evil man. His cruelty did not end at Treblinka. It would never have ended. But you should never have suffered. It was my fault.'

Miranda shook her head. 'No. It wasn't. You saved me from life as an orphan. You took me in and loved me. I don't blame you.' Rose fought back tears at Miranda's assertion. 'I'm scared, Rose. Will they send me to prison?'

'No, darling. David and his organisation are making sure that will never happen. As far as the authorities are concerned, you were not at that villa. David has told the French police that Franzen was missing when he and the butler awoke in the morning. The body was lacerated and mangled by the rocks. Trust me, the case will be taken no further. There are hundreds who wished Franzen dead.'

'But they wanted him alive so he could be extradited and stand trial. I ruined all those years of planning.'

'I believe it's for the best. I, for one, would not have been able to go to court to give evidence against him. The thought of seeing that man ever again . . .' Rose shuddered.

'He made me do some terrible things, Rose. I . . . can't tell you.' Miranda gripped Rose's arm.

'Oh my darling. I, too, suffered in the same way. And then made some terrible mistakes. I'd blocked it all out in order to survive, but the pain is still there. Miranda, we have to help each other through now. We both have to try and start again, for Chloe's sake, if not ours.'

'How is she?'

Tears came to Rose's eyes. 'Beautiful.'

'I'm desperate to see her, but I'm so scared she may have forgotten me.'

'Darling, not a day has passed when we didn't talk of you. Miranda, you've no idea how terrified I've been. I haven't slept properly since you disappeared. The things I imagined . . .'

As Miranda saw the agonised look on Rose's face, a ray of sunshine streamed into her mind, clearing out the deep cobwebs of insecurity, hate and anger. She saw with clarity that all through her childhood, Rose had shown her nothing but patience and love. Only now was she able to recognise it.

Miranda felt an enormous sense of guilt for the pain she had caused not just Chloe, but Rose too.

'I can't deny that I put you and Chloe through such a terrible time because of my own selfishness, but I believe that I have been punished,' she said tearfully, and Rose gripped her daughter's hand tightly. 'I fell in love with someone who was neither rich nor handsome, and he was taken from me. Through him, I began to understand the true values in life, and I know now that I can be a good mother to Chloe.' Miranda paused. 'I'm going to need your help in the next few months.'

Rose stretched out her arms.

'And I yours, darling. And I yours.'

Mother and daughter talked through the night, and only as dawn was breaking did Miranda rise.

'A couple of days ago, I felt my life was over, but you've helped me to see things about myself and my past that I needed to understand.' Miranda sighed. 'I'm so dreadfully tired now.'

'Go and sleep. I am here now. The nightmare is over,' said Rose.

'Yes. Goodnight, Mother. I love you.'

Miranda left the salon.

Rose sat in contemplation for a long time, before heading to the terrace to watch the breaking dawn heralding another day.

There were so many things that, like Miranda, she had to consider now.

'How did she take the news that Franzen could be her grandfather?' A gentle hand was placed on Rose's shoulder.

'What was there to say? It's a cruel, gruesome thought. But she's already been through terrible things. It went as well as could be expected. There is so much for her to take in, to understand. It seems unfair, history repeating itself.'

David sighed. 'We are not here to question why. The older I get, the more I believe that our destiny is mapped out for us before we give our first scream of existence.' He paused. 'I've missed you, Rose. I'm sorry that I shunned you. I should never have . . .'

Rose moved away.

'Miranda and I will return home to Yorkshire as soon as possible.'

'Please, Rose. Stay a little longer. Surely Miranda needs more time to adjust? Have you told her about who Miles is?'

Rose swallowed hard. 'No. I couldn't.'

David nodded. 'I understand. Perhaps that's something I could help you with.' Rose nearly laughed out loud. Her son had been the reason David had cut off all contact with her so many years ago. 'And there is something I wish to talk to you about,' he added.

'What's that?'

'Brett. I have tried to protect him in the same manner you have protected your own children. He knows nothing of the past. Oh Rose, I fear that I've been a dreadful father . . . selfishly dissuading him from his obvious artistic talent because I couldn't handle it. But now I have to fix it, and make sure my past doesn't damage my son's future any further. I need your help.'

'How can I help?'

'Well, this is what I plan to do . . .'

7

Industrialist Frank Santos, who was reported missing from his villa during a short holiday in the South of France, is believed to have fallen off a cliff while intoxicated. A body has been retrieved, and the French police do not suspect foul play. The alarm was raised by Mr David Cooper, a close friend and business associate of Santos, who was the only other person at the villa apart from the butler. Although Mr Santos owned companies across the world, he shunned the limelight, preferring to live a quiet life in . . .

Brett caught the bulletin in the early hours of the morning, just as he was leaving his apartment for Kennedy Airport, and the news confused him further. He'd received a call from his father last night, asking him to catch the next flight to Nice, where David would meet him.

Eleven hours later, when Brett emerged from Arrivals, there was David, looking dapper in a pair of casual trousers and designer sunglasses.

'Hello, Brett.' His father put an arm around him. 'Thanks for coming at such short notice. Let's get off, shall we? We're meeting Rose and Miranda in St Tropez for dinner.'

'Rose and Miranda? Why?'

David walked swiftly to his hired Mercedes, threw Brett's

holdall in the back and opened the passenger door. He started the engine and the pair set off out of the airport.

'Brett, I have about two hours to put you in the picture. I feel dreadful for never telling you any of this, guilty for being such a bad father, and a complete shit for never listening to anything you tried to say to me.'

David concentrated on a difficult right turn as Brett's mouth dropped open.

His father continued to speak in a completely calm manner.

'An enormous number of things have just happened which you have a right to know about. I'm going to start from the beginning and I suggest you hear me out. Save any questions for when I've finished. You'll be shocked, amazed and sickened, but I have to tell you everything.'

So, as they drove through the magnificent scenery along the coast of the South of France, David told him his story, beginning in Poland and finishing with the events a few days ago at Santos's villa.

'I know it's an outrageous amount to ask anyone to take in at one go, but I think it was best to get it all out. I'm sure you have a list of questions and I shall do my best to answer them.'

'Oh Dad,' Brett's voice broke with emotion. 'Why didn't you tell me? If only I'd known. I would have helped, you know. You shouldn't have shouldered all this alone. I'm sorry if I'm not responding to it very well. But it is a revelation . . . and part of me too. You shouldn't have protected me. I had a right to know my heritage.'

'I know that now. But if I had told you, then I could never have escaped. It would have been part of my future, and yours.'

'But the whole point is, Dad, that it has been. It's had a huge effect on you, and therefore on me . . . and Mum,' Brett said sadly.

'I did what I thought was right, for all of us. Maybe I was wrong. I'm very sorry, Brett, for being so blind. It's difficult to explain how I've felt. I . . .' David shook his head.

'Try, Dad. I might understand better than you think.'

'Okay.' David thought for a minute. 'Making money was almost an obsession for me. It was an unemotional currency, and yet so powerful. I was able to block off all the confusion and hate that was the legacy of my past, and to concentrate on that. It couldn't hurt me; I was in control of it and it made me feel safe.' He exhaled deeply. 'I was also very good at it.'

'Poor Mum,' whispered Brett, almost to himself.

'Yes.'

'Did you love her?'

'Sorry?' David was deep in his own thoughts.

'Did you love her?'

'Yes, Brett. And like you, she tried very hard to reach me. It was entirely my fault that she wasn't able to.' David wished to go no further and changed the subject. 'Look, obviously I brought you over here to tell you all this, but there's another reason. How happy are you working for Cooper Industries?'

Brett shrugged. 'I enjoy it.'

David eyed his son. 'I've been honest with you, Brett, so please be honest with me.'

'Okay, Dad,' his son replied slowly. 'When I first came into the company, I hated it. I felt resentful that you'd never considered what I actually wanted to do with my future, and that you'd always assumed I would follow in your footsteps. My business acumen has never, and *will* never match yours. I don't thrive on making mega-deals. But over the years, I suppose I've learned to accept it better.' Brett began to fiddle with the electric window control. 'I've settled down and tried to forget all those dreams I had of being an artist. Am I happy? I'd

426

have to say, no, not really. But I feel ashamed, because of all the millions of people who would swap their poverty-stricken lives to be me.'

'Hmm,' pondered David. 'The thing is, Brett, most of this is my fault. After all, if you had been poverty-stricken, then nobody would have cared if you'd gone off to France and spent the rest of your life painting. So, in fact, having a wealthy family has hemmed you in, not helped you.'

Brett nodded slowly. 'Maybe.' He looked out across the Mediterranean, which lapped at the Côte d'Azur. 'I have one last question. Was it because of your need to break from the past that you didn't see Rose for all those years?'

This was a question David had been dreading, but his answer was prepared.

'Partly. We also had a very bad . . . disagreement over something. Both of us were too proud to say sorry. So stupid, really. We wasted twenty-eight years. Anyway, it's all mended now. Speaking of which, your Aunt Rose and I have cooked up a plan for you. It was her idea and I want you to know it has my full blessing.' David pulled the car to a halt. He reached over and squeezed Brett's hand. 'Forgive me, son. I hope I'm going to be able to make amends.'

Brett saw the tears in his father's eyes.

The moment was gone quickly as David jumped out of the car, but it was the first time in his life that Brett had seen his father show any true emotion towards him.

'So that's the plan. What do you think?' Rose's eyes were shining in anticipation.

The seafront restaurant was empty, with the first of the tourists not expected until April when the weather began to improve. Rose had been waiting for them when they arrived, a bottle of white wine on the table.

Brett was stunned at the proposal his aunt had just put to him. He eyed his father nervously.

David smiled at him. 'Brett, I told you that I gave this plan my full blessing. If it doesn't work out, there will always be a place for you at Cooper Industries.'

'We thought that it was the perfect way for you to find out if it's what you want,' Rose continued. 'There'll be no pressure, and rather than sailing straight into art school, you'll be able to work at your own pace.'

'You'll also have one of the best teachers there is to guide and help you.' David smiled. 'Well? What do you say?'

Brett looked from one to the other. He was overwhelmed. Rose had suggested that he come to England with her and work alongside her in her studio for a few months. After that, he'd be free either to continue painting and go to art school, or to slip back into Cooper Industries in his present situation.

'I . . . Dad . . . what about my work at Cooper Industries? I can't just walk out and leave you in the lurch?'

'We'll cope, just.' David's eyes were gentle. 'It is what you want, isn't it, Brett?'

'Well . . . yes. Oh God, yes!' Brett laughed.

'Miranda and I are flying back to England in a week,' Rose said. 'We want to spend some time together before we go back to Yorkshire and see Chloe, her little girl. You're welcome any time after that.'

'Well, I have some things to tidy up at work, but . . .'

David brushed Brett's remonstrations away with a flick of his wrist. 'Nothing that can't be sorted out.'

Brett clapped his hands together. 'Okay then. You've got yourself a deal!' His eyes were shining and he looked as if an enormous weight had been lifted from his shoulders.

'I'm just sorry it's taken this long. How I could have ignored my own son's talent, coming from the background he does, I'll never know,' said David sadly.

'Hold on a minute, Dad. I haven't put brush to canvas in years. I may not be able to do it any more.'

'Believe me, Brett, you will. I didn't paint for almost twenty years. It never leaves you,' Rose assured him.

Brett was interested to see his aunt and his father together for the first time in his life. There was an intimacy, a warmth between them, that belied any rift that had separated them for so long. He felt overjoyed. For the first time in his life, he felt as though he was part of a united family.

A figure was standing just outside the restaurant, searching the tables with her eyes.

'Miranda! Over here!' David waved.

She smiled at him shyly and walked over. David stood up and pulled out the spare chair.

Brett studied the thin, dark-haired girl with astonishment. He could hardly believe it was Miranda. David had told him that she had been through a tough time, but the retiring shadow of the girl he had once hated produced a wave of sympathy in him. 'Hello, Miranda. How are you feeling?' he asked gently.

She raised her eyes and looked at him nervously. 'I . . . better, thank you.'

'Good. I can't even begin to imagine what you've been through. I think you're an incredibly brave person.' Miranda didn't know what to say. 'Actually, it looks as if I'll be joining you in England in a couple of weeks. You must be looking forward to seeing your daughter,' he said kindly.

Miranda's face lit up and her expression cleared. As she looked at Brett, her eyes were filled with an unspoken gratefulness.

'Yes,' she said simply.

How she wished that Brett *had* been the father of her child.

8

Rose wanted to weep as she watched Miranda nervously fiddling with the buttons on her coat while the taxi drove up the hill towards the farmhouse. Her daughter grasped her hand.

'What if she doesn't remember me? I look so different.'

'She will,' Rose replied, exuding a confidence she didn't feel.

Brett waved the two women away and said he'd help the driver with the luggage and pay him.

Miranda, still holding tightly on to Rose's hand, walked towards the front door.

It opened before Rose had time to insert the key.

Mrs Thompson's face appeared from behind it.

'Is everything all right, Doreen? Chloe?' she asked as calmly as she could.

'Chloe's fine,' said Mrs Thompson. 'Here you go, love. I told you your mum was coming home today, didn't I?'

A beautiful seven-year-old child appeared shyly from behind Mrs Thompson. She looked nervously at the two women standing on the doorstep. For one dreadful moment, Rose thought Chloe was going to run to her.

'Hello, Granny.' She smiled sedately.

Then she turned her eyes to Miranda, who was standing stock-still, staring at her.

'Hello, Mummy,' she said and reached out her arms.

With a cry, Miranda swept Chloe up in her arms and hugged her, never wanting to let her go.

The two older women's eyes were misty as they watched. Rose felt a hand on her shoulder. She turned and saw that Brett's eyes were too. They watched as Miranda carried her child inside and into the sitting room.

'Oh my darling, my baby,' she wept. 'Mummy's home now, Mummy's home.'

9

Leah woke up and saw that the sun was shining through the cracks in the curtains. She lifted herself from the bed and opened them. It was a beautiful April morning and her spirits rose.

After all, she had every reason to be happy. She was past the danger point by three weeks and was feeling good. Her gynaecologist had confirmed that the baby was fine and that there was absolutely no reason why she shouldn't be optimistic about carrying this one to term.

As she climbed out of bed, a slight pain in her side made her wince. Leah ignored it, knowing that it was perfectly natural to get the occasional pain. It soon passed, and she decided to go next door and look at the nursery. She hadn't done this for the past four months, scared stiff that it might be a bad omen, but today she felt relaxed and positive about her pregnancy.

The nursery had been fitted out two years ago when Leah was pregnant for the first time. The cradle was swathed in dust sheets, which she quickly removed, and the cupboard was filled to the brim with all manner of expensive baby clothing.

'What a lucky little baby you're going to be,' she said to the lump in her stomach.

She left the nursery and went to take a shower.

By the time she arrived in the conservatory for breakfast, she was starving.

She made short shrift of the orange juice and croissants, then tucked into a bowl of fruit as she leafed through the mail. There were three letters for her this morning. Two she recognised as charity circulars, and the third was in an unfamiliar hand.

She opened it, and gasped in horror when she saw the contents.

It was a photo of her, in one of Carlo's dresses, taken at the spring collections in Milan. The photo had been torn out of a four-year-old April edition of *Vogue*.

Her face had been slashed lengthways and across with a knife.

Leah held the photo with shaking hands, unable to tear her eyes away.

She checked inside the envelope. There was nothing else.

'Oh my God,' she breathed.

Carlo.

Things had been too quiet on that front. She had not heard a word from him in the past two years, although there had been rumours that his business had taken a nosedive since Leah had left.

A pain in her side made Leah wince. Tension. She mustn't worry or get uptight. She needed to call Anthony and tell him. He would know what to do.

Leah stood up and walked through the sitting room towards the telephone.

Another pain made her cry out as she doubled over.

'No! Oh no!'

Betty, the housekeeper, came rushing in, having heard Leah's cries. She found her mistress crouched on the floor, her face a picture of agony.

'Call an ambulance, Betty. And Anthony. I'm losing the baby. No!' she groaned, then passed out.

433

10

Leah lay back on her pillows, having hardly touched the breakfast tray that Betty had brought her. She hadn't been hungry since she'd arrived home a week ago.

Anthony had suggested they fly to the house in Woodstock where they'd spent the most idyllic Christmases. Leah had shrugged and said that if that was what Anthony wanted, it was fine by her.

Anthony was urging her to see Dr Simons, a psychiatrist, but Leah did not want to be told that she was depressed. She already knew that.

A small tear caught in the corner of her eye when she thought of the little white bundle that in five months' time she would have been holding. She didn't want to talk to anyone about these thoughts.

Leah opened her post without enthusiasm.

There was another one, her face and body slashed to ribbons, this time taken from Carlo's autumn collections a year later.

Her eyes filling with tears, Leah rolled the photo into a tight ball and threw it into the wastepaper basket. She knew she ought to tell Anthony, but she wasn't up to interviews with the police, or dealing with threats.

At present, she didn't really give a damn if she died.

* * *

Betty brought the slashed magazine page to Anthony after she had cleaned their bedroom.

'I think you ought to see this, sir.' She was very fond of the sweet young girl who treated her and the other staff so gently, and she was as worried about Leah's present state of mind as Anthony was.

He took the tatty piece of paper, looked at it and sighed.

'Oh dear.'

'I found it in the wastepaper basket after breakfast. She could have done it with her fruit knife, sir.'

'Thank you, Betty, for bringing this to me.'

'That's all right. I'm concerned for her, sir. That lovely picture of madam, it looks as though she was thinking of . . .'

'Yes, Betty. Thank you.'

'Very good, sir. Madam will be down in a few minutes. Her luggage is just being brought downstairs.'

Betty left the room.

Anthony folded up the piece of paper and stuffed it in his pocket. This was the wrong moment to deal with it. Maybe when they had relaxed for a couple of days at the house in Woodstock, he would ask her.

Leah came into the sitting room. She was looking thin and pale, but quite beautiful in a Donna Karan soft woollen trouser suit.

'Ahh.' He went to her and kissed her on the cheek. 'Stunning as always. Ready to go, darling?'

Leah nodded silently.

'Come on, then. We don't want to miss that plane, do we?'

She shook her head.

'Sweetheart, I promise you that these few days will do you the world of good. You love the house and we don't have to move beyond the front door if you don't want to. Could you manage a small smile for me, darling?'

Leah tried, but it was a pretty rotten attempt.

'Pathetic.' Anthony chuckled. 'Well, let's go.'

He steered her out of the room and five minutes later they were in the car heading for the airport.

Anthony set down the tray of orange juice, coffee and croissants at the bottom of the bed.

'How are you feeling this morning?'

'Okay,' came a muffled voice.

'Shall I open the curtains? It's a beautiful day.'

'If you want.'

Anthony sighed in sad frustration. He felt wounded that Leah had insisted on separate bedrooms when they'd arrived at the house. Of course, he had acquiesced. After all, he couldn't imagine the physical and emotional toll all this was taking on his precious wife. He only prayed that after a couple of days of complete rest and relaxation, Leah would move back into their shared quarters.

So far, that had not proved to be the case. Day after day he'd suggested nice things to do, places to visit, restaurants he knew she loved, but there had been little response and no enthusiasm. All he wanted was to be there for her, but at present, she was refusing his support. Leah seemed a million miles away from him, and now she refused to share his bed.

He sensed the beginning of the end.

Anthony kept telling himself that it was just depression, that the change that had been wrought in Leah would pass, that it was not because her feelings towards him had altered. Every day, however, as she cold-shouldered him, it was getting harder to hang on to that belief.

Anthony knew he mustn't give in. If he did, he was certain he would lose her completely.

He took a deep breath to steel himself against her frostiness and opened the curtains.

'There. Look at that.'

Anthony came and sat down on the bed as the sun streamed in through the windows. 'Anything you'd like to do today, sweetheart?'

Leah sat up slowly, pushing her magnificent hair away from her face and shielding her eyes against the bright sunlight.

Anthony had rarely seen her look more beautiful.

'Not particularly,' she shrugged.

'I was thinking we might take a drive into Woodstock, do some shopping at that little boutique you love, then have some lunch at the Woodstock Inn. What do you think?'

'I'd prefer to stay here, to be honest. But if you want to go, then . . .'

Something inside Anthony broke. He stood up.

'It's okay, Leah. You just stay here and feel sorry for yourself. You know, most women . . .' Anthony stopped himself as he looked into her eyes. The expression there had not changed. He ran a hand through his hair distractedly.

'Look, I'm sorry. I'm doing my best to understand how you're feeling, but . . . I'm going out for a walk. I won't be long.'

Leah watched as Anthony left the bedroom. She knew she should feel something about Anthony's reaction, but she couldn't. There was only the same, aching numbness that prevented her from reacting, as though reality itself had deserted her.

She heard the door slam and supposed she should worry.

Anthony marched out of the house and down the long driveway, berating himself for ever mentioning that he would like another child. So far as he was concerned, he loved Leah to distraction, and although having a baby would cement their

437

union, Anthony was only anxious that Leah should not lose out for marrying an older man.

He had prayed for Leah's sake that this pregnancy would be successful and he'd been equally devastated for the same reason when it was not.

The doctor had explained time and again the clinical reasons for Leah's change of personality, that it was a state of mind she could not help. He had implored Anthony to show patience and understanding, but he was only human. The deterioration since her first miscarriage had been a gradual but noticeable process, and Anthony longed for the return of the bright, happy girl that he'd married.

Anthony sometimes pondered the theory that Leah was bored and that was why she had focussed her energies on having a baby. Her quick, enquiring mind needed more than the daily routine of being a businessman's wife, especially after the hectic life she had led before she married. He had asked her time and time again if she'd like to go back to modelling, or indeed choose some other career that enabled her to put her brain to good use. Leah had always refused.

As he strolled down the wooded avenue, listening to the calling of the cuckoos in the evergreens high above him, Anthony found himself wondering once again why Leah had so suddenly decided to marry him. At the time, he had been so overjoyed that she had agreed, he had not paused to think too deeply. But now, as he witnessed their relationship deteriorating before his eyes, he had to ask whether Leah had ever really loved him to begin with.

Anthony was scared. Losing Leah was a nightmare he couldn't handle. A wedge was forcing them apart, and he didn't know how to bring them back together.

*　　*　　*

Later, they sat together on the terrace. Anthony had returned full of apologies and Leah had tried to be pleasant.

He stood up and went to her. 'Why don't we go out for a nice romantic dinner? You could put on the new Christian Dior dress I bought you last week. What do you say, darling?' He put his arms round her neck and kissed her lightly on the cheek.

Leah struggled out of his arms and shook her head. 'I'm too tired to go out. You go if you want. I'm going to have a lie-down.'

She disappeared inside.

Anthony shivered, even though the May night was warm. He sighed and picked up a copy of *The New York Times* to try to take his mind off his problems.

His attention was caught by a photograph on page fourteen. It was of the model Maria Malgasa in her heyday, looking stunning in one of Carlo Porselli's designer gowns.

Anthony read the paragraph below.

Maria Malgasa, known to millions in the mid-seventies as the world's highest-paid model, has been found strangled in her hotel room in Milan, where she was on a shoot for *Vanity Fair*. The crew discovered her body when she did not appear at the airport for the flight back to New York. Her long-term lover, Carlo Porselli, is helping police with their enquiries. Details are still vague, but it is believed that there was evidence of sexual intercourse.

Later, Anthony showed Leah the article.

'You knew her, didn't you?'

Leah nodded as she observed the photograph. Anthony watched as her face turned deathly pale.

'Oh . . . God. Anthony, I've been receiving pictures of myself through the post, slashed.'

LUCINDA RILEY

'Oh darling, we thought that was your doing . . . We found the one you received on the day you lost the baby, and Betty showed me one that she fished out of the bin.'

Leah shook her head. 'In the photographs, I'm always wearing Carlo's clothes at Carlo's shows. The postmark on the envelope was Milan. If he's doing this to me, don't you think it's possible that he . . . Maria?' Leah could not voice the words.

'I don't know. But I'm calling the police now.'

11

'*Per favore*, please believe me. I left Maria straight after dinner. She said she was tired and wanted an early night.' Carlo swept a hand through his dishevelled hair as he gazed across the desk at the police officer.

'But, Signor Porselli, your fingerprints are on her personal effects, and all over the room.'

'But I've told you!' Carlo banged his fist down on the desk in frustration. 'Maria and I made love before we went out to dinner that evening, not afterwards. I said goodnight to her by the hotel lift and returned to my apartment alone.'

'It is a pity that nobody in the hotel lobby can verify that. The porter swears he saw a dark-haired man who fits your description accompanying Miss Malgasa up to her room, fifteen minutes after you say you left. And that he saw the same man leave at half past four in the morning.'

Carlo sighed deeply. '*Non lo so*, I don't know who that man was. It was not me. I loved Maria! She was my top model! Why would I wish to kill her? I have no track record of violence, do I? Ask any of the models I have worked with over the years.'

'We have, Signor Porselli.' The officer threw a clear plastic wallet across the desk. 'Take a look at those.'

Carlo drew out the shredded photos of Leah.

441

'Attch! These are *nauseanti*! Depraved!'

'We think so too, and so does Mrs Van Schiele, who has been receiving them through the post. The last one carried a Milan postmark.'

Carlo opened his mouth to speak, but stopped himself. He knew by the way the officer was looking at him that he believed he was guilty of both crimes.

'Was she to be your next victim, Signor Porselli?'

Carlo felt tears of self-pity and indignation pricking at his eyelids. To think that he, Carlo Porselli, the great designer, was being held in this pigsty of a Milanese police cell, suspected of murder.

'I shall leave you now to think about what I have just said, *signore*. We have enough evidence to charge you as it is.'

'When my friends hear of this, you will suffer!' Carlo shouted as the officer moved towards the door of the cell.

The officer smiled. 'I think, *signore*, that you don't have as many friends as you thought. *Buonanotte*.'

The cell door banged shut.

Carlo put his head in his hands and wept.

The two-hour flight from Linate Airport arrived on time at Heathrow. The passengers made their way through passport control, customs and out into the fresh May air.

He bought a newspaper while he waited in the queue for a taxi. As the cab sped away from the airport, he smiled as he read the headlines. Carlo Porselli had been charged with Maria Malgasa's murder.

He'd planned it that way, to pay Carlo back for the way he'd stolen Leah from him and turned her into an arrogant, self-serving whore who'd treated him like scum.

Maria and the others had satisfied his need for a short

while, but now it was time to claim the woman who had always been his. He'd sent her warnings and now all he had to do was wait. He knew she'd come to him.

The cab took an hour to reach King's Cross station. He boarded the train and settled down for the long journey north.

12

Brett awoke to the chirping of a family of dunnocks, who were nesting under the eaves of the farmhouse outside his bedroom. He squinted in the morning light at the clock and saw that it had just gone six. He bounded out of bed, donned an old sweatshirt and jeans, and slipped downstairs to his studio. He smiled as he entered the room. It had been Rose's before she had converted one of the barns, and she had passed it on to him. He stood for a second, glorying in the smell of paints and clutter that had been of his own making.

He studied the painting on his easel carefully.

Brett knew that this was by far the best of anything he had painted up to now. The colours were so subtle, blending into each other in a perfect, natural harmony.

This was not just Brett Cooper apeing another artist. It had an individuality and uniqueness of its own. It had identity.

It had taken nine paintings and three months of solid work to get him to this point. The rest, scattered around the studio, were good, but lacked singularity. Rose had been very encouraging, telling him that he must continue and that, eventually, his own personal style would start to blossom. She told him that he had a natural talent that needed to be cultivated, worked on and given freedom to express itself.

Brett knew that, at last, he had done just that.

In his formative years, he had taken an object or landscape and emphasised it at its full beauty. But since he had started painting again, he felt he wanted to say something on the canvas, give the painting a meaning. The one he had just completed was of a beautiful young girl, reaching for the heavens. The top half of the painting was full of glorious colour; the sky was blue, the sun was shining, the apple trees around the girl's head were in full bloom, and Brett had used romantic expressionism to the full. But for the bottom half of the painting, he had used much darker colours. There were male hands grasping at the girl's ankles, and the ground below her was cold and black. One of the male arms was stretching up towards her barely covered midriff.

Brett stared at it for a moment. 'Woman in Chains,' he murmured.

He would bring Rose in to see it today. Half the joy of living here were the long conversations over a bottle of wine that went on deep into the night. Rose would tell him of her days at the Royal College, and they would discuss the works of Freud, Bacon and Sutherland, plus her contemporaries in the fifties, taking hours over each painting from Rose's huge collection of catalogues.

But as Brett looked at his new painting, he knew the time had come to move on. There was no question of his returning to work for his father in New York. He needed to be in an institution full of young artists, to grow alongside them. His Aunt Rose was keen on his following her into the Royal College, but Brett knew where he wanted to go – Paris, where his grandfather Jacob had lived and learned his craft. It was beckoning to him; he dreamed of it at night so vividly that he awoke in the morning questioning the reality of the new day.

He decided that the time had come to discuss his future

with Rose, to tell her that he wanted to go to study at the Beaux-Arts de Paris. Brett took his palette and a brush and began to put the finishing touches to the new painting. As always when he worked, his mind turned to Leah.

He had read of Carlo's arrest for the murder of Maria Malgasa with a large degree of horror and a small amount of satisfaction. Brett had often wondered why Leah had never married Carlo, after the announcement in the papers. He had presumed that they had fallen out in some way, but now this had happened, doubt was beginning to creep into his mind. He'd been so drunk and angry when he'd confronted Leah, in no state to listen to her explanation. What if she had been telling the truth? After all, the man had just been charged with the brutal murder of another model.

Brett sighed. It was pointless torturing himself. Leah was happily married to another man. The relationship was not meant to be. He was destined to spend the rest of his life dreaming of a woman who could never be his.

Brett put his paintbrush down and realised that he was hungry. He opened the door to his studio, walked down the hall and paused to pick up the post.

Miranda and Chloe were already in the kitchen, eating breakfast. The little girl's face lit up when she saw Brett.

'Hello, Uncle Brett. Have you been painting more pictures?'

Brett nodded. He often experienced a feeling of *déjà vu* when they were sitting at the table at breakfast. Mrs Thompson bustled round the kitchen and Brett would let his mind wander back to that first holiday he had spent here. So much time had passed, so much water under the bridge.

Rose arrived in the kitchen.

'Morning, everyone.' She looked exhausted.

'Sleep well?' enquired Brett politely.

'No. I suddenly had a major panic about the New York

exhibition at three o'clock in the morning. I've been in my studio ever since.'

'Honestly, Rose. I know you've never shown over there before, but your work is superb, really,' comforted Brett.

'Thanks, dear, but it's less than two months away and I've still got another four paintings to complete.'

'We'll be there to support you, Mother,' said Miranda gently.

'I know you will, darling. I'm sorry if I'm being neurotic, but it matters so much that I'm a success over there.'

'You will be, promise. Come on, Chloe. Let's go and get you dressed, sweetheart,' said Miranda.

'Okay, Mummy.'

The two of them left the room.

Rose sighed. 'Miranda worries me, Brett. She's so up and down. I'm hoping the trip to New York will do her good, although I'm not going to have much time to spend with her. It's a shame she and Chloe can't stay over with me for the whole month, but Chloe has to be back to start school.'

'I'm sure they'll have a wonderful time. Dad's duplex is stunning and right in the centre of everything. He told me he's going to take some time off work while you're staying with him to show Miranda and Chloe around.'

Rose smiled. 'That'll be nice.'

Brett rose. 'I'd better get back to work. Could you come to my studio later, when you have a moment? I have something to show you, and I want to have a chat.'

'Of course.'

Rose sat at the table and yawned.

If she went to New York, she wondered if she would ever return home.

13

Leah mooched around the beautiful sunny garden, viciously cutting dead heads off roses.

She checked her watch. Ten past ten. An entire day stretched before her, culminating in an interminable evening of strained conversation over supper when Anthony arrived home.

She could not believe the way she was feeling inside. Dead, numb, with not the slightest flicker of interest in anything.

Even when the police had interviewed her and she had shown them the slashed pages sent to her through the post, she had not really felt anything. It was as if she were a bystander, watching her life take place from a distance. She had felt nothing when Carlo had been charged, her evidence only compounding the fingerprints found in Maria's hotel room. The police said they might ask her to go to court as a witness for the prosecution, but Leah didn't want to think about that.

She was sure that she didn't love Anthony any more. Though it still pained her to watch how she could so easily wound him with a word.

They had not slept in the same bed for over three months. The thought of sex with him repulsed her, only reminding her of her inadequacies and the deaths of her three babies. She had known it was pointless to keep trying. So she had decided to stop.

She often pondered whether Anthony was having an affair. It was only natural that he should take comfort with another woman. But he was never late in and he called her constantly when he went away on a business trip.

In some ways, she thought it would be better if he had got someone else. It would halt the guilt. She wished that he would show some anger, like that time in Woodstock when he had snapped at her, but instead he accepted the way she was towards him with resignation.

Anthony had suggested that they tried again for a child, and when Leah had refused point-blank, had suggested adoption. She had still refused. To adopt a child would be a public confirmation of her inadequacies.

So, she went from day to day, just waiting until it was time for bed and she could slide into sleep and have her wonderful dream. It was recurring: a baby in her arms, small and soft and dependent; Brett standing proudly by, looking with love in his eyes at both of them.

She wouldn't think of him for weeks at a time, then she'd have the dream and would spend the following day remembering how she had felt about him, how perfect their love had been. It stirred in her sexual feelings that she thought long since dead, and she guiltily thought of Anthony and how he would feel if he knew.

But then there was the other dream; the one she'd had since she was a child. The dark figure, chasing her across the moors until she could run no further . . . and hearing Megan's voice over and over, warning her . . .

Leah shook her head and tried to bring herself back to the present. Instinctively, she knew that she was wasting precious time, that her life had fallen badly off course and she wasn't doing a thing to help put it back on track.

It was as if she was in limbo, waiting for an event that she *knew* would come to save her from herself.

Until then, life must go on.

Leah picked up the fallen dead roses from the ground and made her way back towards the house.

The telephone was ringing. She picked it up.

'Hello.'

'Oh Leah. It's Mum. I . . .'

There was a choking sound from the other end of the line.

'Mum? Are you all right? What's wrong?'

'I . . . I'm sorry. Leah, it's your dad. As you know, he's been recovering fine from his hip operation, but last night, the hospital called me. He's had a heart attack, Leah, a bad one. They don't know whether he'll pull through. Oh Leah, I'm so frightened. I don't know what to do.'

'Mum, listen to me. I'm going to catch the next Concorde to England. I'll fly to Leeds from Heathrow. Is Dad in Airedale Hospital?'

'Yes.'

'I'll meet you there as soon as I can. Mum, hang on, and tell Dad to do the same. I'm on my way.'

'Thank you, Leah. I . . . we need you.'

'Keep calm, Mum. I'll call you from the airport when I know what time I'll be arriving at Leeds.'

Leah put down the phone and immediately dialled British Airways reservations. She got the last seat on the lunchtime Concorde to London. It arrived at half past ten in the evening, missing the connecting flight to Leeds. She'd have to hire a car and drive through the night up to Yorkshire.

She ran upstairs to throw some things into a suitcase and wrote a note to Anthony:

Family crisis in England. Dad has had heart attack.

Call you when I get there. L.

Malcolm drove her to the airport and she rushed through passport control as she heard the last call for her flight.

As the plane took off, Leah experienced a rush of emotion. It almost took her breath away with its power. There was deep pain, yes, but something else too.

For the first time in months, she felt needed.

Leah arrived at Airedale Hospital at four in the morning. The nurse directed her to the intensive care ward. Doreen Thompson was sitting in the waiting room, staring into space. Leah bit her lip as she saw how her mother had aged since she'd last seen her. Small patches of grey had spread through her hair and her face was tired and haggard.

Leah threw her arms around her. They held each other for a long time as Mrs Thompson wept quietly.

'Thank you for coming, Leah. I was going mad with no one to talk to.'

'How is he?'

Mrs Thompson gestured helplessly. 'They say he's the same. No better, no worse. He looks dreadful. So pale . . . He's wired up to all these machines. He opens his eyes sometimes, but he can't talk.'

'I'll go and see him.'

'Do you want me to come with you?'

Leah shook her head. 'You stay here and try and get some rest. You look all in.'

Leah walked slowly up the quiet corridor. She saw other relatives sitting by their loved ones, even though it was the middle of the night. There were no set visiting hours in intensive care.

The nurse pointed to the room in which her father was lying. Leah took a deep breath and walked in.

She choked back a sob, nothing preparing her for the sight of the father she worshipped looking so frail and still. He was lying flat on his back, with monitors and drips attached to him.

'Dad. Dad,' she whispered softly. 'It's Leah.' She leaned right over so that if he opened his eyes, he'd see her. But he didn't.

Leah sat down heavily in the chair placed by his bed. She reached for his claw-like hand, misshapen after many years of steroids and other drugs. His poor body had taken so much suffering and Leah had never heard so much as a word of complaint from him. He was in his forties, but looked sixty-five.

'Dad, Leah's here now. I want you to concentrate on getting better very soon, so Mum and I can take you home and we can be a family like we used to be.' Tears rolled down Leah's face as she thought of all the times she could have flown back home to see them. She berated herself for being so wrapped up in her own problems. And now it might be too late.

'Dad, do you remember when I was a little girl, and we used to look out onto the moors and you'd tell me the names of all the different birds as they flew above us? And my first day at school when I cried and wouldn't go in? You told me that you'd stay the whole day outside and if I didn't like it, I could come out and you'd be waiting to take me home. Of course, once I got in there, I was okay, but you were waiting for me at hometime. I've often wondered whether you did really stay outside for the whole day.' Leah smiled through her tears, as she watched her father's eyes flicker open and a slight smile appear on his face.

Leah sat there for two hours, before going to find her mother, looking a little brighter, in the waiting area.

'The doctor makes his rounds shortly. Why don't we pop along to the canteen and have some breakfast? You must be starving after your journey.'

The last thing Leah was thinking about was her stomach, but she probably did need to eat.

The canteen was bustling with the changeover from night to day staff. Leah and her mother managed to force down a cooked breakfast.

'How long before the doctors know whether . . . well, the danger is passed?'

Mrs Thompson shrugged. 'They don't, really. On top of everything else, Dad's running a high temperature and is weak anyway from the hip operation. That's what did it, Leah. It was too much for his poor heart to cope with. They don't know at the moment how badly the heart attack has affected him. I've never been one for prayer, Leah, but I've sent a few up in the past couple of days. Me and your dad, well, he's the only man I've ever known. We married when I was so young. Twenty-five years. I know I sometimes get irritable with him, but he's my two eyes, Leah. I couldn't live without him.'

Leah held her hand as her mother sobbed, then quickly dried her tears with her sodden hanky. 'Anyway, no time for tears,' she said briskly. 'We've got to be strong for your dad now. Keep believing he's going to pull through. He's got to,' she said simply.

For the following two days, Leah and her mother kept a constant vigil by his bed. They talked to him, read to him, held his hand and stroked his forehead. The nurses suggested they went home and got some sleep, but neither mother nor daughter would hear of it. 'We want him to know we're always here,' said Mrs Thompson firmly.

On the third morning since Leah had flown in from the States, the doctor called them both into his office.

'Good news. We're taking Mr Thompson out of intensive care this morning.'

'Oh, thank God, thank God,' Mrs Thompson wept.

'But he's going to be in hospital for another three weeks or so, and after that he'll need careful nursing. Now, as we know he's out of danger, I suggest you two go home and get some rest. We don't want another couple of patients, do we?'

'Thank you, doctor, thank you.' Leah led her mother down the corridor, and they popped their heads round the door of her father's room. A nurse was removing the electrodes from his chest.

They walked to the bed. Her father's eyes were open and alert. He mouthed hello.

'We're just nipping home to get some shut-eye for a few hours, love. Prepare ourselves for your return.' Mrs Thompson raised her eyebrows and Leah was thrilled to see her mother's normal banter was back.

Mrs Thompson leaned over her husband and kissed him on the forehead. 'If you ever do that to me again, Yorkshire puddings are off the menu for good.'

Mr Thompson smiled and nodded. He mouthed, 'See you later.'

Mother and daughter left the hospital with a spring in their step, drove back to Oxenhope in Leah's rented Escort, and slept like babies for the rest of the day.

14

A week before Mr Thompson was due to come out of hospital, Leah made an appointment to see his doctor.

He ushered her inside and she sat in a chair in front of his desk.

'How is my father?'

'Making very good progress, Leah. As I said, he will need careful nursing for some time to come. We can provide help – the district nurse will check on him every other day – but I'm afraid the majority of work will fall into your mother's hands.'

'This is what worries me, doctor. She's completely exhausted. Mum's looked after Dad for twenty years now. I can stay for a few more days, but eventually I will have to return home to the States. I thought of hiring a nurse, but the bungalow is small and Mum's useless at delegating. So I've come up with an idea. What if I sent them both away to a convalescent home for a few weeks? It would mean Mum would be with Dad, but she'd be able to have twenty-four-hour nursing backup to do all the things that have to be done, and at the same time have a break herself. She needs the rest as much as Dad does. I've rung a few private homes and I've found one near Skipton that looks lovely in the brochure and takes couples. It would get Mum off to a flying start and stop me worrying quite so much.'

The doctor nodded. 'I think it would be splendid. But they're very pricey.'

'That doesn't matter. I just wanted to know whether you thought it was a good idea.'

'Definitely. For both of them.'

'Good. That's settled then. I wonder if you'd tell Mum, doctor? If I tell her, she'll go on about the money and tell me that she doesn't want a fuss made.'

'Of course.' The doctor smiled understandingly.

'Now, you two. Go away and don't worry about anything. Dad, try and make Mum relax, will you?'

'I'll do my best, lass.' Mr Thompson was lifted into the back of the ambulance taking them to the convalescent home twenty miles from the hospital.

'Good. Bye, Mum. Have a rest. That's the whole point of your going.'

'Yes, Leah, but really, me and your dad would have been fine at home.'

'Shut up, Mum!' Leah hugged her tight. 'I'll be flying over to see you when you get home.'

'If you get a chance, tell Chloe I miss her and I'll be back soon.'

'Yes, Mum.' Leah blew them both a kiss as the ambulance doors were closed. She watched it drive out of the hospital grounds and sauntered to her car.

As she let herself into the bungalow, depression hit her. The past two weeks had been completely taken up with worrying about her father and supporting her mother. She had not had time to think about her own problems. But now, with the bungalow so empty and quiet, her mind moved to Anthony and her troubled marriage. She'd rung him a couple of times to let him know how things were going. He'd been as sweet as always, saying that of course she must stay for as long as she wanted, that she only had to ask and he'd be over to England and by her side in an instant. Leah had said she wanted to spend a week or so tidying up loose ends before she flew back and Anthony had accepted this without question. She'd reckoned some time alone was exactly what she needed to sort herself out.

Leah mooched around the bungalow, putting the cups on the drainer away and straightening the already perfectly placed sofa cushions. Eventually, she sat down and gave a long sigh. Maybe it was a reaction from the past two weeks, but today was not the day to start down a path of soul searching.

She grabbed the keys to her car and left the bungalow. She knew where she wanted to go.

The Parsonage had had a new coat of paint since she was last here. An extension had been added, containing a souvenir shop and extra space for exhibits.

The queue to get in was enormous, but Leah stood happily in the sunshine, listening to the coach party of Americans, bedecked with video cameras, chattering loudly in front of her. She found it odd to think that she had spent the past three years among them; they seemed so foreign out of their own country.

Inside, the Parsonage was exactly how she remembered it. She wandered round slowly, soaking in the atmosphere she'd loved as a young girl. The last time she had been here . . . was that why she had come? To evoke memories that were so pleasant, yet so painful still?

She pondered this as she walked down the cobbled main street, stopping at the Old Apothecary to buy herself some mustard-seed bath powder.

457

She paused in front of the Stirrup Café. To hell with it. If she was going to wallow in past memories, she could at least do it properly.

Leah sat down at a table by the window so she could watch the world go by, and ordered a shepherd's pie.

Just as she was about to take a sip of coffee, she glanced out of the window and saw a tall figure with a familiar head of titian hair walking up the street. Was she seeing things? He seemed to glance in her direction, but then continued walking until he was out of view.

The most dreadful disappointment swamped Leah. She slurped her coffee, deep in thought.

The little bell by the door tinkled, but she didn't look up.

'My God. It *was* you. I wasn't sure at first, but . . .'

He was standing in front of her, smiling nervously.

'Hello, Brett.'

'I . . . hello.'

'What are you doing here?'

Brett looked surprised. 'I live with Rose up at the farmhouse. Didn't your mother mention it?'

'No. But she has had other things on her mind recently.'

'Yes. I was dreadfully sorry to hear about your father. Rose told me. But he's recovering well, isn't he?'

Leah smiled. 'Yes. It was pretty touch and go for a while, though.'

Brett hesitated. Then he said, 'Would you mind if I sat down?'

Leah shrugged nonchalantly. 'Sure.'

Brett put a bag containing two loaves of bread on the floor by his chair. 'Rose loves the bread from the baker up the street. I come into Haworth to get it for her.' Brett wondered why he was apologising for being here when this part of the world was now his home.

'I'm starving. Are you eating?'

'Yes.'

'I'll have whatever you're having.' Brett caught the eye of the waitress.

'Yes?' said the waitress, pad at the ready.

Leah blushed. 'Another shepherd's pie, please.'

'Right you are.'

Leah looked at Brett and knew immediately that he remembered too.

'How long are you in England for?' he asked.

'Another week. I'm staying at the bungalow. So, you don't work for your father any more?'

'No. It was his suggestion that I come over here for a few months to paint. Then if I was sure it was still what I wanted, I could apply to art schools. As a matter of fact, I had some good news this morning.' Brett fiddled in the pocket of his jeans and drew out a creased letter. 'The paintings I submitted to the Beaux-Arts de Paris have got me an interview in ten days' time. Oh God, Leah, I want to go and study there so badly. It was where my grandfather went, you know.'

The waitress arrived with the food.

'No, I didn't. But I'm thrilled for you. I can't believe that last time I saw you, you were so sure that your father would never let you leave his business.'

'I've done this with his full blessing, Leah.' Brett sighed as he lifted his fork and began to eat. 'So much has happened to our family in the past year. It's too complicated to explain, but Dad was hiding all sorts of wounds which made him the way he was. He's been through a pretty gruelling time and the experience has changed him completely. He's a different man.' Brett paused. 'And so am I.

'Leah, you must come up to the farmhouse for a drink. I know Rose would love to see you. She's off with Miranda and Chloe to New York for her first American exhibition in three weeks' time.'

'Really? And how is Miranda? Back from her mysterious absence, then?'

'Yes. And, like my father, a changed person. As a matter of fact, she and I get on like a house on fire these days. And that little girl of hers is adorable.'

Leah did not know how to reply. Brett ranting on about how wonderful Miranda was still stung.

'You know, I've got to make tracks, Brett.'

'Look, Leah. I really do think we should talk. I behaved like a first-class idiot last time you saw me. Could I ask you to join me for dinner tonight?'

'Not tonight.'

'Oh.' Brett looked disappointed. 'Tomorrow, then?'

'Okay.' It was out before she could stop it.

'We'll go to Steeton Hall. Rose says the food is terrific. I'll pick you up at eight from the bungalow.'

'Fine. See you then, Brett.' She took some money out of her purse and placed it on the table. 'Bye.'

Brett watched her as she left the restaurant. Ten minutes later, he strolled up the High Street, hands shoved deep in his pockets.

Leah, Leah. She was here. He had just spoken to her, not fifteen minutes ago.

Brett made for the moors at the back of the Parsonage where he had first kissed her. He sank down into the sweet-smelling grass. The sun was still high in the sky and he closed his eyes.

Was it over? Instinct told him not.

But to start it up all over again . . . Brett felt scared. Scared of the pain of throwing himself open to his emotions after closing them off for so many years.

His father had locked up his heart and thrown away the key. It was safer that way, it brought no surprises, no suffering. On the other hand, thought Brett, it made life flat, like one of his charcoal sketches that hadn't been filled with the living, breathing beauty of colour.

He still loved her.

The past was the past. And he wanted a future.

The following evening, Leah was reminded of the first time she had been due to meet Brett in New York. She tried on every outfit that she had brought with her, and for the life of her could not decide what to wear. Usually, she was able to go straight to her wardrobe and pull something out, knowing instinctively that it was right.

She felt like a teenager again, and mused how she never had these problems when she was going out for dinner with Anthony.

But then, Brett had always made her feel like this: self-conscious and as nervous as a kitten.

She had spent a sleepless night at the bungalow and decided that it was a mixture of being alone for the first time, and struggling with her conscience over seeing Brett tomorrow.

A couple of times, as the dawn broke over the moors, she thought of calling Anthony, but she didn't. He might hear the guilt in her voice.

For goodness' sake, Leah, you're only going out to dinner with an old friend, that's all.

But her heart wouldn't agree.

Brett drove down into Oxenhope village. He turned onto the new estate and the bungalow appeared before him, the sight of it bringing a wave of apprehension.

Leah had seemed so calm yesterday, as if their meeting had not affected her at all. He'd been a bag of nerves and had talked

461

far too much, he thought. He'd been in such a state that Rose had nearly murdered him when he admitted he'd left her bread somewhere in Haworth.

Every sense tingled with anticipation as he drove up to the front door. He switched off the engine.

Come on, Brett – she's a married woman, his head told him . . . *This is a pleasant dinner for two, to apologise for past misdemeanours.*

They were both sensible, mature adults now.

His heart told him otherwise.

'Hello, Leah. You look very nice.'

'Thank you, Brett.'

He stood on the doorstep, unsure whether he should go in, or whether Leah had plans to go straight to the restaurant. He took the plunge and decided to ask.

'Shall we make our way straight there? It's a nice drive and we can have a drink before we eat.'

'That's fine.' Leah shut the door behind her and they walked towards the car.

The journey to Steeton took under twenty minutes. Rose had donated her battered Range Rover to Brett for the duration of his stay and Leah enjoyed the distinctive smell of old car: a mixture of leather and petrol.

They managed small talk successfully for most of the journey, arrived at the restaurant and made themselves comfortable in the bar. Brett ordered a pint for himself and a white wine for Leah.

'You drink these days, then?' he asked.

'Only on special occasions.'

'I am truly honoured, ma'am,' replied Brett, wondering whether he should launch into his explanation immediately, or wait until dinner. He decided the latter.

'So, why did you give up modelling?' he asked.

'I'd had enough. And when my friend Jenny died, it was the last straw.'

Brett looked genuinely upset. 'I'm sorry, Leah. I had no idea.' He swallowed hard. 'What was it? Booze, drugs?'

'She attempted suicide twice, the second time successfully,' replied Leah.

'That's tragic. I . . .' Brett knew he didn't have the words. 'So, how long have you been married?'

'Over two years.'

'Happily?'

Leah inhaled deeply. 'We've had our problems, but, mostly, yes. Anthony is a very good and kind man.'

'I'm glad. Am I right in thinking he's older?'

'Yes, by twenty-two years. He's only forty-six, no age at all these days.'

'No.' Brett saw the maître d' beckoning them. 'Shall we go through?'

Leah followed Brett into a candlelit conservatory. A table for two was laid by the window.

'This is charming,' said Leah, as she picked up her fork to make headway into her avocado and prawns.

All through dinner, Brett kept finding the right moment to begin his speech, then losing courage and talking of something else.

In the end, he ordered two coffees and a cognac, and steeled himself.

'Look, Leah. I want to apologise for the way I behaved that night in New York. I was dreadfully drunk, angry and upset. I didn't accept your explanation.'

Leah shook her head. 'No. You didn't, did you?'

'I was so devastated when I read all the newspapers telling me the girl I loved was about to marry someone else. I flipped.'

Leah surveyed Brett calmly. 'Just for the record, Brett, I was telling you the truth. I had never had an affair with Carlo, and I was livid when he told me he'd informed the media that we were getting married. I wanted to sue, but Madelaine, my agent, stopped me.' Leah shrugged. 'Anyway, it's all water under the bridge now. I can understand why you were so upset.'

Brett sighed. 'When Carlo was arrested for Maria Malgasa's murder, I suddenly thought that he probably did take you to his *palazzo* that night under false pretences.'

'Yes, he did, as a matter of fact. Just as I told you.' Leah shook her head. 'I don't know, Brett. Carlo was a lot of things: spoiled, selfish, arrogant, but I can hardly believe he is a murderer. But on the other hand, he was sending me photos of myself through the post slashed with a knife. I went to the police and I think that helped corroborate the evidence against him. His trial's later this year. Anyway –' Leah shuddered – 'let's talk of happier things. Where did you go when you disappeared into the blue yonder?'

Brett told Leah of his travels around the world, visiting his father's properties, until he noticed that they were the only couple left in the restaurant.

'I think we'd better let the poor staff go home to bed.'

He paid the bill and they wandered out to the car.

Brett pulled the Range Rover out of the car park and drove down the long path. Using the darkness to hide his embarrassment, he said, 'Look, I have to ask you. Can you forgive me and could we start again?'

'Yes, Brett. I'm sure we can become friends. It was all a long time ago.'

It was not the reply he'd wanted.

They lapsed into silence as Brett drew up to the front of the bungalow.

'Thanks for dinner,' Leah said, and Brett turned off the engine.

'Anytime. I can't tell you what a load it is off my mind to be able to explain everything to you after all this time.'

'I'm glad you did.'

Leah opened the door.

'Goodnight, Brett.'

'Goodnight, Leah.'

She closed the car door and walked towards the bungalow.

She unlocked the door and walked inside, shutting it behind her.

Leah sank onto the floor, a mixture of relief and thwarted anticipation making her feel quite faint. Oh God, she had wanted to invite him in so badly, but . . . no, the relationship had ended in New York, and whatever the reasons, he was her past, not her future.

She picked herself up, threw off her shoes and walked down the passage to the kitchen.

Leah filled the kettle and turned on the radio to fill the quiet. She sat down at the table, feeling enormously proud of her self-restraint.

She made herself a cup of coffee and padded down to the sitting room.

The coffee cup smashed with a crash to the floor, spilling its boiling contents everywhere as she saw a face silhouetted at the window.

It took all of her self-control to prevent a scream leaving her lips as her hand went to her mouth.

'It's me, Leah! Brett! My car won't start!'

15

As Leah lay in Brett's arms the next morning, she knew that it had been inevitable the minute she had opened the door to let him in.

Neither of them had been strong enough to fight it.

They had tried, Brett insisting that he would walk home, then drinking gallons of coffee to put off the moment when the decision had to be taken.

Dropping from weariness, yet every part of her alive with suppressed desire, Leah had at last stood up and suggested Brett could sleep on the sofa, as she was in the bungalow's spare room, rather than make the long walk home.

He'd apologised profusely for the inconvenience and accepted the duvet that Leah handed him with thanks and a promise to call the nearest garage first thing in the morning.

'Goodnight, then,' she had said, as she turned to leave the room.

He'd caught her hand. 'I love you, Leah. I've never stopped loving you.'

Then he'd pulled her close and kissed her as she had dreamed of him doing so many times over the past years.

They had made love there on the floor, unable to draw apart for even a short time and find the bedroom.

He had been everything she'd known he'd be: tender, loving,

passionate; words she'd almost forgotten the meaning of. And she had responded in a way that amazed and frightened her. She wanted to explore, touch and caress every single part of his body.

'Oh God, Leah. Oh God.' He looked down at her with tears in his eyes. 'It's you, it's always been you right from that first summer. And there'll never be anyone else. I know it. I feel it so deeply. Oh my love.'

And she had lain there, unable to feel guilt or sadness, only suffused by the pure joy of being loved by him once more.

Later, when they had climbed into bed and made love again, Leah reached for Brett's hand in the darkness.

'I have to go back, you know.'

He couldn't expect any more than she had given him. 'I know.' He squeezed her hand. 'Then let's make the most of the time we have.'

Never had Leah known the days to fly by so fast.

Because they both realised that each second they spent together was precious, they made every moment special and filled to the brim with love. Leah had put away thoughts of the future and had decided she must pay the price of the time she spent with Brett at a later date.

Rose knew immediately, of course, when Brett arrived home the following afternoon, explaining embarrassedly that the Range Rover was still broken down in front of the bungalow. The happiness in Brett's eyes was unmistakable and she could not help but be glad for him. She did not preach to her nephew about the consequences of what he was doing; she knew that he was fully aware and had decided to accept them.

Leah, only fleetingly feeling a pang of guilt, revelled with Brett as they took an unashamedly romantic trip back into the past. Hand in hand, they went back to the Parsonage, they strolled up onto Haworth Moor and kissed where they had first kissed; they lay in the grass by the farmhouse and made love under the burning blue sky. At night, they drove to Haworth and joined the tourists eating at any one of the cosy pubs or good restaurants, before making their way back to the bungalow for a night of love.

All was as it had been. And the figure watched them now, as he had watched them then.

Four days, three days, two days . . . Leah woke next to Brett on the morning before her flight back to New York and was sick in the bathroom.

Brett found her, pale and miserable, staring into space at the kitchen table.

'What is it, Leah?' He hoped he knew.

'Nothing,' she replied.

'You look ill.'

'I'm not feeling too clever. It must have been that chilli we ate last night.'

Brett was desperate to persuade her to admit the truth. He sat down next to her.

'Is it because you have to go back to America tomorrow?'

He had said it, voiced what they had both tried not to think about for the past six heavenly days.

The spell was broken and Leah burst into tears. Brett let her cry, unsure of what to do or say.

'I'm sorry.' Leah fumbled in her dressing-gown pocket for a tissue and blew her nose. She stood up, a surge of strength replacing vulnerability, and walked out of the kitchen and back into the bathroom.

As she showered, the full consequences of what she had done hit her. Tomorrow, she had to fly back to her husband and try to pretend that nothing unusual had happened, when she was certain her feelings for Brett were written all over her.

Anthony wasn't a stupid man. Surely he'd guess. Waves of shame filled Leah as she thought how Anthony had only ever shown her love and affection, and she had repaid him by having an affair the minute she was out of his sight.

Leah sat naked on the bathroom floor, head in her hands. If Brett asked her – which so far he hadn't – to stay, would she?

Oh God, she didn't know. Having thought that the time alone in Yorkshire would give her space and time to think about the state of her marriage, all it had done was to complicate things beyond logical thinking.

There was no doubt in her mind that she loved Brett, but then she saw Anthony's dear face, looking down at her. A knocking broke into her thoughts.

'Are you okay, Leah?'

'Yes. I'm just coming out.'

Leah unlocked the door. She walked straight into Brett's arms and, five minutes later, into bed.

Their last evening together had been planned down to the finest detail. Champagne at the bungalow, then to Old Haworth Hall for dinner.

It was a disaster. The sight of Leah's half-packed suitcase in the bedroom was enough to ruin the evening before it had begun. Brett had booked a flight to Paris for his interview at the Beaux-Arts, so that the two of them could travel to Heathrow together. They were leaving in Leah's rented car at five tomorrow morning, which meant that goodbyes, and last-minute advice for Brett from Rose, had taken place earlier that afternoon. He returned to the bungalow utterly miserable.

Neither of them touched their food at the restaurant and they made a last, silent journey back to the bungalow in the newly repaired Range Rover.

Leah made coffee and they sat in the sitting room, deep in their own thoughts.

This is the last night I'll ever spend with her.

How can I bear the thought of leaving him?

'We ought to go to bed. We have an early start tomorrow,' she murmured.

'Leah, I . . .'

'Shh,' Leah put a finger to his lips. 'Don't say anything.' She led him into the bedroom and they made love for the last time. There was a desperation and a tenderness in the physical act that mirrored feelings neither could voice. But they both knew they would never forget it for as long as they lived.

They did not sleep, but arose at four and made a final check of the bungalow. Leah closed the front door and posted the keys through the letterbox, then they set off in her rented car.

Leeds Bradford Airport at seven in the morning was a depressing place. Thankfully for them both, the shuttle to Heathrow was on time.

An hour later, they made their way through to the check-in desks for Leah's ten-thirty Concorde flight to New York. Leah watched her luggage disappear on the moving belt. The next time she saw her suitcase, she would be minutes away from seeing Anthony too.

Brett was chalk white and his eyes were bloodshot.

'Coffee?'

She shook her head, knowing she was causing herself more pain by prolonging the inevitable.

'I think I'd better go. My flight will be called soon.'

'Okay.' Brett checked himself. The lump in his throat was threatening to spill over into his eyes.

He walked alongside her, the distance to passport control agonisingly short.

She stopped, only feet away from the divide that would swallow her up and make her disappear for ever.

'Goodbye, Brett.' Her eyes were lowered.

He could hold out no longer. The tears ran down his face and he didn't care who saw.

'I love you,' he whispered.

She turned and walked towards the desk.

Brett watched her as if life had suddenly wound to slow motion. She gave her ticket to the security girl.

'*No!*' Brett hardly knew it was his voice. She had passed the desk and was about to disappear behind the screen.

He was galvanised into action. '*Leah! No!*' He ran towards her, bypassing the astonished security girl, and grabbed hold of her.

Shaking, he stood and turned her to face him.

'You can't go, you can't do this to me. I know you love me. Please, please, Leah. We were always destined to be together. Admit it!' He almost shook her. 'You love me, Leah, you love me.'

She looked at him, at the tears pouring from his eyes.

At that moment she chose her future, for better for worse.

'Yes, I love you.'

Two hours later, as Air France flight A300 left the ground heading for Paris, Brett smiled at the beautiful woman sitting next to him.

'You won't regret this, my darling. I promise.'

Leah smiled back. Then she turned and looked out of the window and shook her head slowly.

16

Anthony put down the telephone slowly. He stood in the magnificent hall, the chandelier above him glittering even more brightly as he looked at it through the tears in his eyes.

He willed his body to move, to take him into the sitting room where he could pour himself a large brandy.

She wasn't coming back.

The thought repeated itself over and over in his head, and still his brain would not register it as a plausible event that was going to happen. Surely, in a few hours' time, he would drive down to the airport and greet his wife on her return from England. He would bring her back to their home, and life would continue as normal.

No. Leah was never going to be inside these four walls again. She had fallen in love with another man and had left him.

It happened all the time: to his friends, neighbours, to people all over the world, every single day. And now it had happened to him.

Anthony felt as if he'd had a severe physical blow. His legs were no more than two sticks of quivering muscle and he grabbed a brandy glass and poured a large measure before they deserted him altogether.

He sat down heavily, spilling a little of the brandy on the cream sofa.

The Fabergé clock ticked as usual on the marble mantelpiece.

Silence. The silence that would be Leah's legacy to him; his only companion.

The sense of devastation that filled him was total. Even when his first wife had been so ill, he had not felt like this. But then he'd had time to come to terms with losing her, as he'd watched the life seep slowly out of her.

It was the shock. Never once during Leah's extended time away from him had he considered she wouldn't return. Thinking back, Anthony knew that it shouldn't come as a surprise. She'd been so desperately unhappy for so long. It was obvious now that this had been because she no longer loved him.

In her telephone calls from Yorkshire she'd sounded much brighter, and Anthony had been happy to let her have as much time as she needed if it would return to him the old Leah.

But he now realised the reason she'd sounded so happy was because she had fallen in love with someone else.

The pain was terrible. Anthony felt physically sick when he glimpsed in his mind's eye Leah making love to another man.

He should have known when he first married her that she was too young to be tied down to an older man such as himself. Brett was the same age as she was. Strong and fit; Anthony was sure Leah would have no problems bearing a child with him.

He refused to believe, however, that any man could love a woman more than he loved Leah.

He loved her totally, unselfishly and to the exclusion of all others. Anthony wept.

17

'Are you happy, my darling?'

She nodded slowly. She was in the most romantic city in the world, planning her future with the man that she had loved for all these years.

Yet she couldn't rid herself of a terrible sadness. The freedom and joy that she had found with Brett in Yorkshire had vanished the second she'd made the collect call to Anthony from Heathrow Airport.

He had sounded heartbroken, devastated. But he had not begged her to return. He had said that he loved her, that he would always love her, that he wouldn't stand in the way of her happiness.

Leah wished he'd ranted and raved and then she wouldn't be feeling quite so guilty.

Leah had kissed Brett goodbye outside the Beaux-Arts de Paris yesterday. His interview had taken most of the morning, so she had spent the time visiting old friends in their designer salons along Avenue Montaigne. Her luggage was presumably still at Kennedy Airport and she had only the dress she stood up in. The designers had welcomed her into their sanctums with open arms, and when she had told them that she might be moving to Paris permanently, they had begged her to return to her old profession and work for them. She had protested that surely she was too old now, and they had laughed and said that twenty-four was nothing these days – look at Jerry and Christie and Marie!

She'd left feeling gratified, but confused. The realisation of what she had done hit her. She went to sit in a cafe and had a *citron pressé* and a Brie baguette.

Leah had celebrated with Brett on the evening of his interview. He had been told he had been accepted at the Beaux-Arts. They had dined at Maxim's and Brett had asked her how she felt about living in Paris for the next few years. She had said that tonight was not the moment to start planning the finer details, but that she was sure she wouldn't mind at all.

The offer of modelling work was tempting in one sense – after all, she would have to have something to do while Brett was studying – but Leah was convinced that there were other things she could do that she would prefer.

Brett's face had lit up when she had told him she had the option of modelling again.

'That's fantastic, Leah. Me at the Beaux-Arts de Paris, you working again. After all, you've told me that you've been bored with nothing to do save weed the garden for the past few years. Are you going to think about it?'

Leah nodded. 'Oh yes.'

Brett wouldn't be able to understand how she felt about returning to modelling, about how deep Jenny's death had cut . . . and Leah knew she couldn't expect him to.

Leah kissed Brett and rose from the big comfortable hotel bed. She went to the bathroom and turned on the shower.

One day left in Paris before they returned to Yorkshire and the start of her new life.

Maybe when they arrived back at the place that held all their memories, she would feel more secure and positive about the future.

The hot water ran over her body.

Once the pain and guilt of leaving Anthony had lessened with the passage of time, she would be able to appreciate once more what she had with Brett.

18

'The thing is, Rose, that I was wondering whether you'd be able to put up an extra person for the next few weeks, just until we fly off to Paris.'

Brett was standing in the kitchen at the farmhouse, looking at the floor. He felt terribly embarrassed.

Rose sighed. 'Where is she now?'

'At her parents', breaking the news. They arrived back from the convalescent home yesterday and she thought it was better to get it over and done with immediately. We would rent something just for the next three weeks or so, but everything is chock-a-block. It's right in the middle of the tourist season.'

Rose nodded slowly. 'Of course Leah can stay here. Presumably, I won't have to make up an extra bed?' Her eyes twinkled.

Brett blushed. 'No.'

'Well, you and Leah will be here by yourselves, then, because Miranda, Chloe and I fly to America in a week's time. The farmhouse will be empty. Goodness knows what Doreen Thompson's going to make of all this. Leah has told her husband, hasn't she? I'm not going to have him turning up here with a couple of heavies and destroying the place, am I?'

'No. Apparently he took it reasonably well. I don't think they've been happy for quite some time.'

Rose looked at Brett's sparkling eyes and felt glad for him. 'Leah's okay about moving to Paris with you?'

'Well, we haven't discussed it seriously, but I think so. I'll probably leave for Paris in a couple of weeks to give me time to find an apartment before term starts. Leah will join me as soon as I've got somewhere. She wants to spend a bit more time with her parents and make sure they can manage on their own.'

Rose's face became serious. 'Leah must love you a hell of a lot to do what she's done. Even if the relationship with her husband wasn't the happiest, she's given up everything for you. Don't let her down again, Brett.'

'I won't, Rose. You know how I feel about her. I'm so lucky to have been given another chance. I want to marry her the minute she's free.'

'Good.' Rose smiled. 'I have to pop into Leeds this afternoon to buy some clothes for America. Anything you want?'

'No, thanks. I think I'll go into my studio until Leah arrives. My fingers are itching after five days of rest.'

Brett walked over to Rose and put his arms round her. 'Thank you, Rose. I knew you'd understand.' He kissed her and went out of the room.

Rose watched him go. She hoped that nothing would happen to stop her still idealistic nephew finding happiness with the woman he loved.

'Leah! I thought you were safely back in America with Anthony! What are you doing here?' Mrs Thompson's face was filled with happiness as she ushered Leah inside the bungalow.

'I'll tell you in a minute. First of all, I want to hear about you two.' Leah followed her mother into the sitting room and hugged her father. 'I must say, you both look like new people.' Leah squeezed her father's hand, feeling dreadful at having to impart such upsetting news when they were both looking so well. Leah drank a cup of tea slowly and listened to her mother expound the wonders of the convalescent home.

'So. Now we've told you our news, tell your dad and me why you're still here.'

Leah took a deep breath and did so. She wanted to weep at the shock on both of their faces.

'I'm sorry.' It was all she could think of to say.

After a long silence, Mrs Thompson spoke. 'Are you absolutely sure you're not making a terrible mistake? Anthony's such a nice, kind man. He's been so good to you.'

Leah wanted to cover her ears. Her mother was right, but it was more than she could bear to hear.

'I've been unhappy for a long while, Mum. And Brett, well . . .' Leah wrung her hands. 'I love him.'

'He let you down before, Leah. He can do it again. No sense of responsibility, that young man. His head's up in the clouds, like his aunt.'

'He won't let me down, Mum. He's changed, grown up. He's not a boy any more. He's a man.'

'I knew that young man was going to be nothing but trouble the first minute I set eyes on him all those years ago,' ruminated Mrs Thompson. 'So where are the two of you going to live?'

'Brett's asking Rose if she wouldn't mind putting me up at the farmhouse until Brett and I go to Paris in September.'

'Paris, is it? And what will you do with yourself there while Brett's involved with his paintings?'

'I've been offered jobs with two of the fashion houses.'

Mrs Thompson's eyes glinted. 'Now, who was it that told me not so many years ago that she would never step on another catwalk for as long as she lived?'

'I haven't decided yet,' Leah answered, irritated that her

mother had picked up on this. 'I've just been bored silly doing nothing for these past years . . .'

'Don't you think you're going to find it a bit difficult living with a student after Anthony? After all, that's what Brett will be. He's going over there to work, night and day. How much time will he have left for you?'

'Enough. I love him, Mum, and I've made my choice. Anyway, I need my own life, free from depending totally on a man. That's what went wrong with me and Anthony.'

She turned to her father, who sat silently in his chair.

'What do you think, Dad?' Leah looked desperately at him. He stared at her for a moment, then he shrugged.

'The main thing is that our Leah's happy. Are you happy, love?'

'Oh yes,' answered Leah, looking him straight in the eye. 'Very.'

19

The night before Rose, Miranda and Chloe were due to leave for America, Leah and Brett joined them for an uproarious supper at the kitchen table.

'May I propose a toast to Rose Delancey, who I know will take America by storm. To Rose.' Brett lifted his glass.

'To Rose,' chorused Miranda, Chloe and Leah.

'Thank you for that tribute, Brett, dear. And here's to you and Leah and your new life together in Paris. I hope one day to be wheeled round the Tate in my bath chair to study your paintings. You'd better not become more famous than me, mind you! Cheers!' Rose laughed.

Leah stood up. 'And I'd like to say thank you, all of you, for making me feel so welcome here. I'm very grateful.' Leah glanced down at Miranda, who smiled shyly back at her.

'Right. Well, what do you say that we all lend a hand with the washing-up?' suggested Rose.

Miranda shook her head. 'No, Mother, you go into the sitting room. I know you want to have a chat with Brett. Leah and I will do the dishes, won't we?'

Leah nodded. 'You wash, I'll dry.'

'I'll help you, Auntie Leah.'

'Okay, Chloe.'

Leah studied the dark head bent over the sink and decided that being a brunette suited Miranda now. Subtler, deeper and much more interesting. Leah could sense a sadness in her, and understood why Brett had found her so much easier to get on with. Miranda had shown Leah nothing but kindness since she had moved into the farmhouse, although they had not had much of a chance to talk.

'Are you looking forward to America, Chloe?' Leah asked, as the little girl conscientiously wiped a plate.

'Oh yes. We can see Mickey Mouse.' She nodded.

'Well, Chloe, Uncle David's said we might be able to if you're a good girl,' Miranda answered, winking at Leah over Chloe's head.

'Do you like my dungarees, Auntie Leah? Auntie Doreen bought them for me today as a present.'

'They're very smart, Chloe.' Leah smiled. There had been a tearful farewell between Doreen and Chloe earlier. The little girl seemed more attached to Mrs Thompson than she was to her own mother or Rose, which was not surprising.

The washing-up done, Miranda hung the tea towel over the radiator. 'Chloe, why don't you go upstairs and get into your pyjamas? Mummy will be up in a minute.'

'Okay. Will you come and tell me my bedtime story, Auntie Leah?'

'Of course.'

Chloe's eyes lit up and she skipped happily out of the kitchen.

'Chloe seems to have taken a real shine to you, Leah. And your mum's been so good. Chloe thinks the world of her.'

'She's a lovely little girl, Miranda. You must be very proud of her.'

Miranda smiled. 'I am. Leah, I . . .' She fiddled embarrassedly with a clean coffee cup. 'In case I don't get a chance before you and Brett go off to Paris, I just wanted to apologise for what I said on the night of my sixteenth birthday. I was so jealous of you and Brett and . . . the things I said were a pack of lies. Brett and I did little more than kiss, and that was under duress on Brett's part. I knew he loved you then, and I hated him for it. I'm so sorry. You two would have been together ages ago if it hadn't been for me.'

Leah sat down at the kitchen table. 'Miranda, please, forget it. I have. Okay, so I was devastated at the time, especially when I thought that Brett might be Chloe's father . . .'

Miranda's face darkened. 'He wasn't. I mean, he isn't. I swear, Leah.'

'Well, I just presumed he was when you kept so quiet about her father.'

Miranda nodded slowly and looked up at Leah. For a second, Leah recognised in Miranda's eyes a desperate need to unburden herself, but the look passed in an instant.

'I'm so glad that you and Brett are together. I'm not the person I was when I was younger and I loathe the way I behaved. I was hoping that maybe in the future we could be friends.'

'I'd like that very much, Miranda.' Leah smiled. 'You have a wonderful time in New York. It's a marvellous place and I'm sure you'll love it. When you come home, maybe we could go for lunch in Haworth before I go to Paris. Now, I'd better go up and see Chloe.'

'Yes. Thank you, Leah.'

Miranda sat in the kitchen staring into space. There were tears in her eyes as she struggled to bury the memories that had haunted her since she was no more than a child.

'Are you okay, darling?' Brett moved close to her in the bed the next night and nuzzled the side of Leah's face. 'You seemed a bit quiet tonight.'

483

Leah stared up at the blackness.

'Yes, fine. Just a bit tired, that's all. I've not been sleeping too well recently.'

'It's been a long day. We were up at five driving Rose, Miranda and Chloe to the airport. They'll be in New York by now. I can't believe that this time last year, I was living there too. Isn't it strange the way life has turned out?'

'What do you mean?'

Brett sighed in the darkness. 'Well, last night I sat at the kitchen table thinking how we're all so different, each one of us, and yet we're back here, together again. It's as if that first summer affected us all, our lives and our futures. There was a sense of destiny in the air.'

'There was,' said Leah quietly.

'Goodnight, darling.' Brett kissed her and wrapped his arms around her.

Leah closed her eyes.

And it came again. Every night now, she had the dream; every night it was the same. Only tonight, for the first time, she saw his face.

'*No!*'

Leah sat bolt upright and reached for the lamp switch.

'Darling, what is it?' Brett sat up next to her, alarmed.

She could sense him, so near that she could still hear his breathing.

'I'm sorry. I had . . . a nightmare.'

'Oh sweetheart. You've been having a lot recently. Come here. I'll look after you, Brett's here.'

He rocked her in his arms gently, his hand caressing her hair.

Even surrounded by his love, she knew with a certainty what prevented her sleeping for the rest of the night: that no one could protect her from the man who had haunted her dreams since she was eleven years old.

Fate ... Megan ... evil ... Fear ground in her stomach until the dawn broke.

She was back here of her own free will. She had fulfilled her side of destiny and she knew that it would not be long before he fulfilled his.

20

'Are you sure you'll be okay by yourself, darling? I hate to leave you all alone in this big house.'

Brett's suitcases were packed and standing ready in the hallway. The two of them were in the sitting room, watching for the taxi.

Leah smiled reassuringly. 'Of course I'll be okay. Mum and Dad are only down the road if I get lonely. And Miranda and Chloe will be back soon.'

Brett pulled her closer to him. 'I'll start apartment hunting tomorrow. I reckon I should be able to find something in the next couple of days. You'll probably be on a flight to Paris by the end of the week.'

'Yes.'

'Will you promise to speak to Rose's solicitor about getting a separation from Anthony? The longer you leave it, the longer it will be before you're free.'

'Yes, I promise,' Leah replied definitively.

Brett tipped her chin up towards him and kissed her gently on the lips. 'You don't know how much I'm going to miss you.'

'Me too,' replied Leah.

They saw a car climbing slowly up the hill.

Brett stood up. 'Well, darling, this is it.'

Leah followed him into the hallway and picked up a suitcase.

'I love you, darling. Take care and I'll call you when I reach the hotel.'

Brett hugged her.

'Goodbye, Brett.'

He opened the front door and the taxi driver took the suitcases. Leah watched the car make its way down the hill, and waved until it was out of sight.

She turned and went back into the house.

It was strangely eerie being all alone. Leah pondered whether she should go to her parents', then decided against it.

She went into the kitchen to fix herself something for supper. Soup and bread sufficed.

She checked the clock. Half past six. A whole evening alone.

Leah made her way into the sitting room, admiring once more how Rose had managed to turn the rundown house into a cosy, comfortable haven.

Sinking down onto one of the deep sofas, she picked up the remote control and switched on the television. Leah flicked from channel to channel, and seeing there was nothing that took her fancy, turned it back off again.

There was a pile of magazines on a coffee table. She heaped them onto her lap and turned over the pages without registering anything in them.

Ten to seven. Leah was appalled at how bad she was at being alone. She used to be able to keep herself amused for hours when she was younger, and the days spent by herself at Anthony's house had been regimented, following a strict routine. Most of the time she'd been so preoccupied with thinking about the babies, or the loss of them, that she hadn't noticed much else.

It suddenly struck Leah that she had no idea who she was any more.

Her life was in a dreadful mess and that sensible, centred girl she'd been when she was younger had slipped out of her grasp without her realising it.

What about that dream of doing some good with her money, making the world a better place? She'd let that disappear the minute she encountered problems of her own.

Leah moved from the sofa and walked tentatively towards the well-stocked drinks cabinet. She took out a bottle of gin and stared at it thoughtfully.

It was her decision to take and she wanted a drink.

She poured herself an inexperienced measure of gin and added some tonic.

The bitter taste caught in her throat and she spluttered helplessly. She added a little more tonic and went and sat back down again.

Men. They had ruled her life since she was fifteen. First Brett, then Carlo, then Anthony. Even though she'd had such a successful career, her entire life had centred around what was happening in her personal life.

As she thirstily sipped her drink, she remembered about the happiest time she could recall – when she and Jenny had shared the apartment in New York. She missed the nights they would stay up until dawn, telling stories and laughing about the bizarre universe which they had found themselves inhabiting.

Too much time to brood had made her problems with having a child grow out of all proportion.

Leah got up and poured herself another gin.

She thought she'd been so in charge of her own destiny, when in fact she'd been as much manipulated by others as her dead friend had been. She cried because the world was so difficult and beautiful and cruel and wonderful and because for the first time tonight she could see herself so clearly.

Leah got through half the bottle of gin, but she didn't feel drunk. The startling clarity with which her life came into focus made any hangover worthwhile. Leah knew that she needed to make her own choices, with nothing other than her own well-being in mind.

She loved Brett more than anything.

In spite of their tumultuous journey, he made her feel safe. But did she want to live with him in Paris? Leah had to accept that she wasn't fully convinced. She was even less certain about returning to the world of modelling. Reminiscing about Jenny tonight had made her question how she could even attend those meetings in Paris.

Put simply, she would tell Brett about her concerns. If it was true love, then what were a few flights every now and then? If Brett disagreed, he had a choice to make about their future together. Regardless of the outcome, Leah would make sure that she was all right.

Her mind turned to her parents, and their opinions. Her father's voice echoed in her head.

The main thing is that our Leah's happy. Are you happy, love?

'I know I can be, Dad. I *choose* to be,' she whispered to herself.

Leah was resolute that she would be solely responsible for the direction of her life. No one else would have a say.

Her recurring nightmares? They were manifestations of her unsettled state – a way of telling her that things weren't right. Relief flooded through her. Yes, that was it.

Five days at most, before Miranda and Chloe came back. Five days without Brett to sort herself out. An oasis that she was sure she'd been granted for a reason.

Leah went upstairs later, knowing that physically she would suffer tomorrow, but mentally she had a sense of freedom that she relished.

She knew she would find the answers now.

Peaceful, for the first time in months, Leah crept into her bedroom, crawled under the duvet and fell into a dreamless sleep.

He saw the lights go out.

An owl hooted from somewhere in the barn.

No, not tonight. It was too risky. The others had been gone for about ten days now, but Brett might come back.

He knew the moment wasn't right.

He would wait.

21

Anthony's lunch was disturbed by his doorbell ringing incessantly. Who the hell wanted him this badly on a Sunday?

'All right, all right, I'm on my way,' he mumbled, as he met Betty approaching the front door.

'It's okay, Betty. I'll deal with this.'

Betty shrugged and disappeared down the corridor.

Anthony looked through the eyehole and saw the familiar uniform of a policeman. A plain-clothes man was standing next to him. The man flashed an ID card through the eyehole. Anthony nodded, switched the alarm system off and unlocked the door.

'Can I help you?'

'Detective Cunningham, FBI. Sorry to bother you, sir, but is Mrs Van Schiele at home?'

'No, I'm afraid she's, er . . .' Anthony could not bring himself to say it. 'She's on holiday.'

'I'm sorry, sir, but could I ask you where exactly she's gone?'

'England. Yorkshire, actually. To visit her parents.'

Cunningham gave a frown of concern. 'In that case, sir, I think we'd better come in.'

'She's all right, isn't she?'

'As far as we're aware at present.'

Anthony guided them to the sitting room.

'What exactly do you want to speak to my wife about?'

'These, sir.'

The detective took a thick polythene envelope from his briefcase. He handed it to Anthony.

Anthony took the envelope and studied the contents. There were back copies of American *Vogue*, *Vanity Fair* and a couple of English editions of *Harpers & Queen*.

He looked nonplussed at the detective. 'I don't understand why you're showing me these.'

'Shall we sit down, Mr Van Schiele?'

Cunningham patted the seat next to him on the sofa and the officer positioned himself in a chair opposite.

'Has your wife received any more odd mail recently?'

Anthony shook his head, thinking through the pile of post still waiting for Leah in the hall, unopened.

'No, I don't think so. I haven't opened it since she's been away, though. But anyway, Carlo Porselli is locked away in an Italian jail awaiting trial.'

Cunningham nodded. 'Unfortunately, this is our fundamental problem. We don't believe that it was Mr Porselli who sent your wife those slashed pages.' Cunningham waved the magazines at Anthony. 'We found these during the course of another investigation, and other things besides.'

'I . . . I'm sorry. I'm terribly confused. Could you explain?' said Anthony.

'Sure. A couple of days ago, the police were called to an apartment in New York. The downstairs neighbours were complaining of a noxious smell coming from the apartment above them. The police broke in and discovered the rotting corpse of a young woman under the floorboards. We reckon she'd been there for a good while. I was called to the scene. In a room in the apartment, we discovered hundreds of photos of your wife pinned to the walls. They had been slashed violently with a knife and defaced. There was also a charcoal sketch of your wife from when she was younger that had been ripped to shreds. We also found these.' Cunningham picked up one of the magazines and opened it at a previously marked page. 'In all four of them, there is a page torn out. We thought nothing of it at first, but having asked the magazines in question to send us identical copies, we noted a link. In each magazine, the page that had been torn out was a photo of your wife, Mr Van Schiele. And when we checked with those slashed photos you handed in to us several months ago, we discovered they were the missing pages.'

Cunningham surveyed Anthony's pale face silently. 'There is no doubt that it was this man who sent the pages to your wife. We are also pretty sure now that the wrong man is being held for the murder of Maria Malgasa. The young woman found under the floorboards was killed in an identical way to Malgasa. We've got on to forensics and confirmed that there were other unidentified fingerprints found in the Milan hotel room in which she was murdered. They match not only with those on the New York victim's effects, but also with another unsolved, identical murder of a prostitute in Britain, committed three years ago.' Anthony was horrified. 'There is another connection, too. The man who rents the New York apartment in which we found the body is also known to have been in Milan at the time of Malgasa's death. In fact, he was the photographer on the shoot.'

Anthony could stand it no longer. 'Who is this man?'

'Miles Delancey. The fashion photographer. Unfortunately, he's gone missing. He hasn't returned to his New York apartment since he was in Milan on the photo shoot with Maria Malgasa. We believe he flew straight to Britain. And we're almost sure his next intended victim is your wife.'

22

'The telephone rang a while ago, love. I was asleep when I first heard it and it stopped before I could get it. When it rang again, I picked it up with my claw, but I'm afraid I dropped it.' Mr Thompson pointed to the receiver, lying on the floor by his chair and giving out a monotonous bleep.

Mrs Thompson picked up the instrument and replaced it on the set. She raised her eyebrows. 'I wonder who it could have been? I've just left Leah up at the farmhouse, and the telephone there hasn't been working for a couple of days, so it couldn't have been her. Never mind, I'm sure they'll try again if it's urgent.'

Mr Thompson nodded, once again feeling embarrassed by his frailty.

'I'm going to go and make your dinner, love. It's your favourite: Yorkshire puddings and beef stew.' Mrs Thompson smiled at her husband and went into the kitchen.

He was awoken by the sound of a car in the distance.

He listened intently, as the noise receded. He had no idea how long he'd been asleep, but the barn was in blackness. He found his torch and shone it on his watch. Ten to ten.

He'd been having a dream, about her.

He couldn't hold out any longer.

It had to be tonight. He'd watched the house for four days and no one except her mother had visited. She was alone now and he must make his move before anyone came back.

Another hour, and he would go to her.

He relished the thought of what he would do to her, slowly caressing himself.

Once he'd loved her, worshipped her. She was so perfect, too perfect to be touched physically by a man.

But then she had thrown him out of her apartment, onto the streets. She'd threatened him and treated him like scum.

And three weeks ago he'd watched her screwing that bastard, Brett, on the moors.

Then he'd known for sure that she was no better than the rest.

She was his. She always had been.

And now it was time.

He went to the edge of the barn and peered round. The upstairs lights had gone out.

There was no need to break in. After all, this was his home and he had the key.

There were no exterior lights and he crept stealthily along the outside of the barn, the half-moon silhouetting him against the sky.

He ran swiftly to the front door, put the key in the lock and opened it slowly.

The hall was in complete blackness. He closed the door and stood behind it, trying to make out his surroundings.

As his eyes adjusted he saw a figure in a long robe coming down the stairs. He slunk back into the shadows and allowed himself a smile.

She was coming to him.

His body pulsated as he watched her descend the stairs, long dark hair falling over her shoulders.

She reached the bottom and crossed the hall.

Miles made his move. His hand went over her mouth as he grabbed her and dragged her along the corridor and into the sitting room.

She struggled, but was helpless against his brute strength.

He threw her on the floor, face-down.

'You know who I am. And you knew I'd come for you, didn't you?'

'Miles—'

'Shut up! If you make another sound, or move, I'll kill you.'

It was so important that she didn't talk, didn't ruin the moment he'd been waiting for.

He bent down and ripped the robe from her. Yes, he would take her as she lay.

She was emitting small kittenish noises as he savagely tore into her, but he couldn't hear them any longer. Soon enough, his hands moved to her slender neck and closed round it. He squeezed, laying the full weight of his body on top of her.

'You bitch! You've wanted this since you were a little girl. You've always been mine, always. And I thought you were so perfect, so pure, and all along you were screwing that bastard!'

Miles squeezed harder, until the life had left his prize.

He stood up quickly. The guilt would soon consume him, as it always did. He would have to get out of here as soon as possible. He could take Rose's Range Rover. She kept the keys in the bureau by the sitting-room door.

'Mummy!'

Miles turned to face the doorway he had bundled Leah through.

A small figure was standing there. A hand reached for the light by the door on the wall.

Miles blinked.

The figure looked past him to the body on the floor.

She emitted a small cry.
'Mummy!'
The blue eyes looked up at him.
'What have you done to Mummy?'

23

The little girl ran past Miles and knelt by the body on the floor. She shook her and began screaming at a piercing level when she could elicit no response from it.

Miles stood there, paralysed. He didn't understand, he . . . 'Chloe, what on earth?'

Miles swung round to see Leah standing behind him in the doorway. She clapped her hand over her mouth as she stared into his eyes. Then she looked beyond him to the scene on the floor.

Miles shook his head, trying to make sense of the situation. He had just taken the girl standing in the doorway. She was lying dead on the floor.

'Chloe, come to Leah. Come on. Mummy will be okay. Come to Leah.'

Miles's hair had grown long and was unkempt and greasy. His face was dirty and he smelled odorous.

But it was his dark eyes that shocked her. She saw they were full of madness.

He seemed confused. He had come for her, as she'd dreamed he would. Instead he had found Miranda, returned early from America.

Her only thought was to get Chloe out of this house, away from him. There was nothing she could do now to help Miranda.

And she had to do it while Miles was caught off balance.

'Chloe, come on, darling.' She beckoned to the child, unable to focus on the naked body on the floor, dark hair covering the face.

'Let's go to the kitchen and get a drink, sweetheart.' Her eyes never left Miles's.

She steered Chloe out of the room, very slowly, then turned and walked towards the kitchen. She closed the door behind her with a slam and locked it. Leah knew her only option was to flee. The telephone had been broken for a couple of days, so contacting the police or an ambulance was out of the question. She bent down to talk to the hysterical little girl.

'Now, Chloe. I want you to do everything Auntie Leah says and be a very grown-up girl. We have to run as fast as we can to get help from the village for Mummy. Okay?'

Chloe nodded.

Galvanised into action, Leah stood up and pulled Chloe across the kitchen to the back door. With trembling fingers, she unlocked it, grabbed Chloe's hand and fled out into the night.

Miles stood immobile, staring at the body on the floor. He walked across to her and knelt down. Heart pumping against his chest, he smoothed the thick hair back from her face and rolled her over.

The piercing blue eyes stared up at him, lifeless.

An animal howl left him as he pulled her close to him and held her to his chest.

'Nooo! Please, No!'

Not Miranda.

She had understood him, had taken him into her bed since they were small children and comforted him when he was having one of his terrible dreams. He rocked the motionless body in his arms, caressing the dark hair that had led him to murder her. Tears streamed down his face. He kissed her, willing life back into her.

A fleeting movement outside caught his attention. He sat up, dropping Miranda's body onto the floor. Two figures were fleeing down the hill.

Immediately, he was filled with hatred. This was her fault. She had caused Miranda's death and she had to be punished for it.

He stood up and ran to the front door.

'Come on, darling. You can do it. Keep going.'

Leah was panting and dragging Chloe behind her.

'Please, can we stop, Auntie Leah? I can't run any more.'

'You have to, Chloe, you have to for Mummy.'

Leah was trying to formulate a plan. The most important thing was to get away from Miles. He was insane, he would kill them both. She would run down to her mum and dad's and get help from there.

'Ow!' Chloe screamed as one of her slippers flew off her foot and the harsh gravel cut into her tender skin. She stopped and ran back for the slipper, and as she did so, two headlights came over the hill and began bearing down on her at a frighteningly fast pace.

'Quick! Onto the moors!' Leah turned left onto the grassland. She would have to go across country to the village, down past the reservoir. He couldn't follow them that way.

She heard the noise of the car slowing down, then the rumble as it turned and started across the moors.

'Oh God, oh no!'

Chloe was screaming now at the top of her voice. All Leah could think of was getting to her parents, to safety, to help.

Please, don't let him catch us. Please, God, help us!

She pulled Chloe down and across towards the reservoir. The car was getting nearer and she could almost feel the white light of the headlamps boring into her back.

There was nowhere to hide and Chloe's little legs were unable to keep up with her own.

Then an idea flashed through Leah's mind. It was not Chloe he was after, but herself.

She looked behind her. The car was no more than five hundred yards away. There was no escape. He would catch them and kill them both.

At least she could give Chloe a chance.

With a surge of strength that Leah did not know her exhausted body could give her, she hurled Chloe away from her and down the hill to her side, praying that the child would make a safe landing. She checked behind her and saw that the car had not stopped, but was continuing after its prey.

Then she kept on running. Running across the moors, running for her life, as she had in the dream time and again.

She saw a low wall two hundred yards away from her and for the first time, a ray of hope entered her head. He could not follow her in the car, he'd have to get out.

Her chest heaving painfully now, she begged her legs to go faster as she ran towards the wall.

He was so close now. She could not look behind.

She reached the wall and heaved herself up onto it. The reservoir shimmered below the steep incline of the moors, and on the other side, the lights of Oxenhope twinkled.

She jumped off the wall and landed, screaming in pain as her weight fell on her ankle and there was a sickening crack.

No, please, don't let me pass out, I'll die, I'll die.

She hauled herself onto her haunches and stood up, the pain from her ankle so dreadful that she felt dizzy and sick.

Must keep going, must keep going. Tears were falling freely down her face as she heard the car screech to a halt behind her. Then the sound of a door opening.

Hobbling as fast as she could, she saw blue flashing lights against the sky, and willed herself once more not to pass out from the pain.

'It's no good, Leah. I'm coming for you. I'm so close behind you, inches away. Give up now.'

'No! No!'

A tufted hillock sent her flying headlong to the ground.

It winded her. She tried desperately to move, but she could not.

She lay there, waiting.

Now there was no escape.

She heard his breathing behind her. She closed her eyes and said a prayer as she heard the scrub crackle and he knelt behind her.

Hands went round her neck and squeezed. She could not fight any longer.

This was her destiny.

She felt her breath draining from her.

Then a shot rang out.

The pressure round her neck stopped instantly. Leah knew she should try and move, but she could not.

'Stand up, arms in the air, and you will not be harmed.'

Woozy from lack of oxygen, Leah thought she was dreaming as the male voice rang out across the moors.

Miles knelt upright, looking above him.

'Give yourself up and we will not harm you,' the voice repeated. 'Move away from the girl.'

Miles blinked as a spotlight was switched on, bathing the moors in light.

'Never, never. She's mine.'

The hands went back round her neck.

Oh God, no. Please, no!

Then another shot sounded. Miles jumped and screamed in pain. He rolled off Leah and lay, clutching his leg.

'Come on! Come on! Get up!' he screamed to himself.

Miles stood, blood soaking the trouser covering his shin. He pulled Leah to her feet. He put his arms around her chest and dragged her towards the wall.

'Let the girl go now, Miles.'

The foul stench of his breath washed across Leah's face. 'They won't shoot while I've got you to protect me, see?'

They reached the wall and he heaved them up onto the top of it and they rolled down together onto the other side.

'We're going to get in the car and you're going to drive.'

'I . . . I can't. My ankle.'

He was dragging her towards the car. He opened the driver's side and lifted her into it. Then he crawled across her and landed in a heap in the passenger seat.

'Drive! Drive!'

Leah fumbled with the keys in the ignition. The car started and she gingerly put her foot down on the clutch, and yelled in pain as her ankle took the strain.

'Shut up, you stupid bitch! Drive! Downwards. Away from those bastards!'

Leah put her foot on the accelerator. The car jolted forwards. Miles was struggling to roll his trousers up to see if he could stem the blood running from his leg.

'We're heading towards the reservoir, Miles. We have to go back up to reach the road.' The steep incline below Leah with the shimmering pool of water at the bottom filled her with terror.

'No! Drive downwards and we'll cut across country when we reach the reservoir.'

'But Miles, it's too steep, we'll—'

'Just do it!' he roared.

'Okay, okay.'

She could see in the mirror that there were headlights following her down the hill.

'Faster! Faster! They're catching up!'

'I can't! We'll crash.'

'For Christ's sake!'

Miles pushed her foot off the accelerator and placed his own on it. His hands went round the steering wheel.

'Stop! Please stop! We're going to go into the reservoir!'

But Miles wouldn't listen. The car went careering at great speed down the hill, the water coming closer and closer.

Leah knew they faced certain death at the bottom.

'Oh God, oh God!' she wept. She moved her foot away from the pedals, her entire weight pressing against the door.

There was only one thing she could do. She fumbled behind her and found the handle.

Using all of her strength, she tugged at it and it opened.

She tumbled out of the car and was thrown to the ground.

There was an explosion not yards from her as a bullet from a marksman hit one of the tyres.

She managed to lift her head and watch as the car toppled over and over, burst into a ball of orange flames and plunged into the water below.

Then she passed out.

24

Rose's face was ashen as she watched the coffin being lowered into the ground. Her eyes were red from crying.

There was very little left to bury of Miles.

Anyway, what member of the clergy would give a service for a man who had murdered his sister, and others?

Rose felt faint as she listened to the vicar intone the blessing on Miranda's soul.

Others around her placed wreaths beside the grave and began to walk away.

'Come, Rose. It's time to leave.' Brett put an arm around her shoulders.

She shook her head. 'No, Brett. I want to stay a while longer. Would you mind seeing to the guests at the farmhouse until I get back?'

'Of course not.' Brett shrugged uneasily. 'Don't stay too long.'

'I won't.'

Rose watched the others walking off into the distance. The drone of the cars died away and all she could hear on the balmy September afternoon was the twittering of the birds in the trees.

She walked towards the grave and knelt down.

'Miranda, sweetheart. I don't know whether you can hear me. If you can, I ask you to listen to what I have to tell you.

I must tell someone, explain why it is my fault that you are lying down there. I pray you'll understand and forgive me.'

Rose wiped the tears from her face and took a deep breath.

25

David and Rosa spent their first night in London huddled close together under a hedge in Hyde Park.

David had never felt such sheer hopelessness. He knew that it was because he'd been fooled into believing that they had at last found sanctuary.

No one had been more surprised than he when the Red Cross official had informed him of the letter from his grandmother, Victoria. He had started to think that a reply would never come, as the days turned into weeks, and those into months. But at last, an official had called David into his hut and informed him that his grandmother had written saying that she was happy to give them a home once they arrived in London. She had enclosed some money to arrange a berth on a ship as soon as possible.

David's one regret was having to leave baby Tonia at the camp. She was not family and even if she was allowed to travel to England, he could hardly ask his grandparents to take her in too. But the Red Cross official had assured him that Tonia would be well cared for and adopted as soon as a home could be found for her.

The ship had docked at Tilbury, and they had been put on a bus to King's Cross station. There they had been met by a

507

small, beautifully attired woman, and a tall imposing man in a suit, who looked at the gaunt teenagers with thunder in his eyes. This was Robert, Lord Brown, their maternal grandfather.

As Victoria and the rest of the British nation had listened in horror to the reports of the atrocities that the Germans had committed against the Jews, her husband had sat unmoved.

He was anti-Semitic, anti-German, anti-everything but the British. His years in India had made him the worst sort of patriot, and his views were narrow and arrogant in their certainty.

When Beatrice had called from Paris to say that Adele was missing, and it had then become obvious that she was never going to return, Robert had completely cut her from his mind and his life. He had told all his friends that she had died in a tragic car accident near the Arc de Triomphe. He had even insisted on going away to their house in Somerset the week that the funeral was meant to be taking place.

Victoria had begged him to help her search for their daughter, but he had, with some aggression, ordered that Adele's name was never to be mentioned in his house again. That she was dead.

Consequently, he had read the letter from the Red Cross with a face like thunder, almost exploding when he saw that his daughter had married a Jewish man. He had thrown it on the fire and told his wife never to mention the subject again. The answer was absolutely and utterly no.

'Let them rot like their mother,' he had growled.

'I cannot believe what you're saying to me, Robert! For pity's sake! These are your grandchildren, your family!' Victoria wrung her hands in despair.

The heavy-set, balding man put his hands on the mantelpiece and shook his head. Victoria sat down heavily in a chair. It was hopeless.

'So, what do you want me to do? If we refuse to take them in, they will be deported as illegal aliens and sent back to a displaced persons camp in Poland. They have suffered so much already. I cannot believe that even you would wish that on anyone, least of all your own flesh and blood.'

'They are not my own flesh and blood! My daughter is dead. She died twenty years ago. These persons are obviously imposters.'

Victoria felt the bile rise in her throat as she listened to him. He was sick, cruel, but worst of all, he was a hypocrite. He could stand at the Cenotaph, publicly paying tribute to all those English war dead, and yet he would turn his grandchildren out of the house, onto the street, because they were half Jewish.

Victoria had defied him, writing to the Red Cross to assure them she and Robert would give them a happy home. To *hell* with that man. If it came to it, she would take them and leave. Victoria's plan had only unravelled when Robert had intercepted the reply detailing the Delanskis' arrival at the station. He had descended into a vile rage, threatening to deport them and turn his wife out on the street with nothing.

After hours of begging and persuading, Victoria had agreed with her husband that their grandchildren should remain in England, on the proviso that they were told firmly by Robert that they were never to attempt to contact him or his wife again.

At the station, Victoria's heart had shattered into a million pieces as her husband declared that David and Rosa were no grandchildren of his.

David thought the offer of a home in England had sounded too good to be true.

Curiously, he found himself grateful to Lord Brown. He would not contest their being in the country. Being deported back to the living hell of further incarceration in Poland was not an option David could risk. Rosa might not even survive the return journey. He watched her sleeping, nestled into him against the bitter cold under the leafy hedge.

She'd had such a terrible life so far, more than anyone should have to endure. She had seen dreadful pain and suffering and she did not remember what comfort, love and security were.

As David looked down at her, a little strength seeped into his bones. He had promised Mama he would take care of Rosa, and he would.

He had to find a way of making a life for both of them. He now knew for certain that the only person he could rely on was himself.

He gingerly opened his violin case, his hands almost completely numb from the cold. He felt under the lining and drew out the remaining coins.

Four left. And they were a mixture of German and Polish currency. He knew he could not use these here; it would arouse too much suspicion.

Then he would have to sell his violin. There was no choice. The Stradivarius was hugely valuable and if he could get a good price, it would provide food and shelter and give the two of them a chance.

Having held on to it for this long, David felt guilty that all else had failed.

Once the dawn broke, David woke Rosa and they crossed a big roundabout into a road called Oxford Street.

'I'm so hungry, David. Do we have any money for something to eat?'

David shook his head. 'No, Rosa, but we will have by lunchtime.'

'How?'

'Never you mind. Come on, let's go down there. It's a subway of some kind. It'll be warmer.'

They walked down the steps at Oxford Circus tube station. There was a bench in the corner and David led Rosa to it and sat down.

'What are we going to do, David? What if the police come after us?'

'We'll make sure they don't find us, sweetheart.'

He checked the clock on the other side of the station. Ten to eight.

He stood up and went across to the ticket office.

'Excuse me,' he enquired to the sleepy clerk. 'Could you tell me how I get to Suddeby's? I believe it is an antique shop in Bomb Street.'

The clerk chuckled. 'I think you mean Sotheby's in New Bond Street. Yes. It's not far from here at all. It's just up the road.'

David listened to the clerk's directions. 'Thank you, sir.' David went back to Rosa and held out his hand. 'Come on, Rosa. We're going to find some breakfast.'

'Come in, come in.' The man ushered David and Rosa into a small room, crammed with valuable and beautiful objects.

'My name is Mr Slamon. My assistant tells me that you have a rare object you would like to sell. Can I see it?'

David nodded and placed his case on the man's desk. He removed the instrument and handed it to him.

Slamon's eyes lit up as he fingered the delicate spruce wood of the front of the instrument. He turned it over and surveyed the unmarked maple back. The workmanship on the violin was exquisite. He checked the facsimile label as his excitement mounted.

'Beautiful, quite beautiful. Where did you get it?'

'My mama and papa bought it for me for my tenth birthday. We lived in Warsaw.'

'You are a very lucky young man to have parents who would buy you such a treasure. Did your parents ever tell you if the violin has a name?'

'Yes. The Ludwig.'

Slamon studied the young man opposite him carefully. It was highly unlikely that if he had stolen the violin, he would know its name.

'Of course, we will have to check that it is authentic, which will take a couple of days . . .'

'No!' said David. 'I want to sell it now.'

Slamon coughed. 'I see. Umm, have you any proof that the instrument is yours? I mean, Sotheby's could never be seen to handle stolen goods.'

David's eyes lit up with anger and he grabbed the violin from Slamon.

'If that is how you feel, then I shall take my violin elsewhere.'

'Now, now, calm down. I do apologise, but since the war, we've had all manner of individuals offering us possessions that couldn't possibly be theirs.'

'Play, David,' Rosa said quietly. 'That will convince him.'

David felt deeply hurt at having to prove that he was no thief, but then he saw the hunger in his sister's eyes and nodded.

'All right. I will play for you.'

He nestled the violin lovingly under his chin and placed the bow across the strings. He closed his eyes and played.

Slamon was finally convinced. The familiarity between instrument and player was ineffable – something that could only be built up over a number of years. The boy played exquisitely. And the sound was that of a rare and beautiful violin, fashioned by the great master himself.

'Thank you. That was very beautiful. And I do apologise for doubting you. Obviously, I will still have to have a second opinion from my colleague, but having heard you play, I am convinced that it is indeed authentic. May I take the instrument, please?'

David handed it to him, his eyes wary.

'You may accompany me if you wish, or I could ask my assistant to bring some tea and biscuits in here while you wait.'

Rosa's eyes lit up.

'We'll wait here,' he said grudgingly.

Half an hour later, Slamon was back, smiling.

'My colleague agrees with me. It is indeed the Ludwig, made by Stradivarius in 1730.' Slamon sat behind his desk. 'Now, we conduct auctions every Wednesday and Sotheby's would take a ten per cent handling fee, of course. I reckon something like this could fetch—'

'Please, sir. I told you, I'd like the money today.'

'I see. Well, what we could do is give you an advance of some kind, until we have a purchaser. As a matter of fact, there is one particular gentleman who I know will be very interested. How say you I give you a two-hundred-pound advance, with a receipt stating that the remainder will follow as soon as we have sold the violin?'

'And how much will you sell it for?'

Slamon tapped his fingers on top of his desk. 'Mmm. Now let me see. I reckon we'd put a reserve price of twelve hundred pounds, so that would be the minimum you would receive, less our handling fee. But with a piece as rare as this, it could go for up to two or three times the amount.'

'I'm sorry, sir, but how much is that in zlotys, Polish money?'

'I couldn't tell you off hand. What about French francs? Could you calculate, er, zlotys from them?'

David nodded.

Slamon did some figures and related them to David.

David quickly did some sums in his mind. His eyes lit up. The amount was a fortune, enough for Rosa and him to live on for years.

'All right. I shall take the two hundred pounds, but I wish you to sell the instrument as soon as possible.'

'Fine. I'll just have the cheque made out to . . . ?'

David shook his head. 'Cash, please.'

Slamon shrugged. 'All right. It will take a little longer, though. More tea?'

An hour later Rosa and David emerged into the watery October sunlight.

He swung Rosa round and hugged her tight.

'See? I told you David would sort it out. Right, let's go and find a cafe and have the most enormous breakfast you've ever seen!'

They spent the next two nights at a small hotel just off the Bayswater Road. David bought himself a suit and went to see letting agencies to find a place they could rent.

The first office he visited asked him to fill in a form.

At the top, he had to put his name.

David thought quickly. He did not want to write his real name down there, just in case the police were after him. What was it that the man in the cafe had called policemen? Co . . . Coo . . . Coopers! That was it.

He wrote his new name in the box and smiled. David Cooper. It sounded good and very English. David and Rosa Delanski were dead from this moment on.

He told the secretary at the letting agency that he was looking for a small flat for himself and his wife, thinking that a young brother and sister looking for somewhere to live might arouse suspicion.

She gave him the address of two places to visit and he bought a map of London and hopped onto a red bus. The first flat, in a place called Notting Hill, was small and poky and the landlady was nosy.

The second, a stone's throw away from the hotel in the Bayswater Road where they were staying, was much more pleasant.

The only problem was that there was only one bedroom, with a big double bed in it.

Never mind, thought David. He would sleep on the sofa in the living room.

The flat was on the top floor, with a landlord who lived off the premises. It was small, but spotlessly clean, and would do them well to begin with.

David said he'd take it and move in immediately. He got round the problem of providing references by giving the landlord six months' payment in advance. In the grim days of post-war recession, that sort of hard cash softened anyone's rules.

Rosa loved it. She danced around the flat, as pleased as punch.

Later, they went off in search of food for supper. With rationing still in force in London, David and Rosa had to part with a fistful of money as the shopkeepers surreptitiously produced hidden wares from under the counter.

But it was worth it as they tasted Rosa's wonderful meal of chicken rissoles and 'little hoofs', a tasty potato dish that their mama used to make. They washed it down with a bottle of wine that went straight to their heads.

'A toast to the Coopers! Speaking of which, I've been thinking. Perhaps we should adapt your name. David doesn't stand out, but Rosa is a little more unusual. How would you feel about becoming *Rose* Cooper?'

Rosa thought for a moment, before raising her glass.

'I like it! It's very . . . English.'

26

David and Rose lived happily together in the flat for almost two years. The Ludwig had sold for two and a half thousand pounds and financially they were secure. David had never known such sheer joy. They had no friends, no one they knew in London, but David did not miss that. He had Rose. His confidante, his sister, his genius. They spent twenty-four hours a day together, revelling in exploring London, exulting in the security of their tiny flat. After so much terror, pain and uncertainty, the sanctuary of their small home and each other became their rock.

David would lie on the couch, content to watch Rose as she stood at the easel he'd bought her and sketched him and anything else she could find.

Slowly, her paintings began to change from the purely representational work she had always done.

Sometimes, she would throw the brush down and hurl herself on the bed in frustration.

'Oh David, I've a thought that wants to come out, but I can't transfer it.'

David took Rose to as many galleries and exhibitions as he could find. They went to the National Gallery and the Tate, and wandered down Cork Street to study the *Miserere* series by Georges Rouault at the Redfern Gallery. But the exhibition that fascinated Rose most was that of Graham Sutherland's work at the Hanover Gallery.

'It's so . . . brutal.' Rose turned to David. 'I want to go home and paint.'

Later that week, David studied a painting that Rose had just finished. He shuddered as he looked at it. There was something dark and bleak about it: distorted faces and eyes staring at him from behind bars at strange angles.

'Rose, what have you called this?'

'Treblinka,' she answered lightly.

David knew it was time for Rose to move on. She needed to have her talent fostered.

It scared him: the thought of Rose knowing other people, going off and leaving him for hours while she was at art school. But very soon he would have to find work anyway, especially if he was to pay for Rose's tuition.

They discussed it that night over dinner.

'Oh David, do you really think they'd accept me at the Royal College?'

'I'm sure they will, once they've seen your work.'

The following day, David hailed a taxi and stacked four of Rose's canvases on the back seat.

'Exhibition Row, please, driver.'

The taxi pulled up in front of the grand entrance to the Royal College of Art, and David heaved the paintings inside.

'Well, Mr Cooper, this isn't really the way we do things around here,' said the flustered receptionist. 'You need an application form and—'

'Could you ask someone to look at these, please, and contact us if he thinks my sister might have talent?' David wrote down his name and address on a piece of paper.

'Good day to you.' David nodded at the startled woman

and walked out of the building, supremely confident that someone would spot the genius he knew Rose possessed.

He was right. Ten days later, Rose received a letter asking her to come to the college the following Monday. She would have to spend two days at the college doing life drawing and attend numerous interviews.

Rose was in a frenzy of nerves the night before.

'You'll pass with flying colours, I promise you.' David hugged her tightly.

Three months later, in the September of 1948, Rose began her diploma course at the Royal College of Art. Although she was only seventeen, the school had recognised her talent and accepted her.

The first day without her was unbearable. David mooched round the empty, silent flat, not knowing how to occupy himself. He felt desolate without her.

But he had things to do, plans to make. He had to start thinking about his own future. They still had money to live on for the next couple of years, but Rose's college course was going to take a big slice out of it.

David found a pencil and a pad and sat down at the kitchen table. He made a list of various jobs that he thought he might be suitable for, then crossed each one off.

None of the things on the list appealed to him in the least. He wanted to be his own man, start his own business where the sky could be the limit. He was so different to others of his age that he knew he could never fit into an everyday office environment.

He wandered round the flat, hands in his pockets, thinking.

At half past three, he gave up. He had just made a cup of tea when the doorbell rang.

David opened the door and saw that it was his landlord.

'Come in, Mr Chesney. I have the rent for you.'

'Thank you, Mr Cooper. I like my tenants to be on time with their payments.'

'Do you have many?' asked David, handing him an envelope.

'Oh yes. About twenty-five. I own seven houses. Bought them for a song after the war and converted them. Best thing I ever did. Goodbye, Mr Cooper.' Mr Chesney tipped his cap and disappeared down the stairs.

David closed the door and went back to the table to drink his tea. He mulled over what Chesney had said. The man had given him an idea.

The following day, David went to visit a number of local estate agents. He was astonished to see how cheap an average terraced house was. He took details on a cross-section of the properties back home and sat down and worked out some figures.

David checked and rechecked them, to make sure he had not made a mistake.

He hadn't. The money to be made was excellent, if he was prepared to risk the initial capital. He suspected it was a growth market, with more and more young people preferring to move and have a place of their own. Many could not afford to buy or rent houses, but they could afford flats.

David made detailed notes and drew up cashflow projections. Then he went into the City of London to try to find a bank to help finance his project. Each one said no. David came home disheartened but not prepared to give up.

He knew he had to make a decision. The only way he could do it was to take the rest of the money from the sale of the Stradivarius, leaving enough for Rose and him to live on for the next six months. With that, he could afford to buy either two small houses or one large one and turn them into self-contained units.

He went home with a bottle of champagne and celebrated with an ecstatic Rose, still overwhelmed by her first week at college. He did not tell her about the gamble he was taking.

'Here's to us.' David raised his glass. 'To the property tycoon and the greatest painter of the next half of the century.'

27

In the following three years, David's business went from strength to strength. With the onset of the fifties, David found that demand was outstripping supply. He acquired a reputation for providing quality conversions at a very reasonable rent. His tenants were happy and word spread.

By 1951, David owned fifteen houses around London. He started looking at land that had been bombed which he could buy cheaply to build office blocks in the City. The banks were now falling over themselves to lend him money.

Everything was perfect. Except for one thing.

Rose. During her first year at the college, nothing much had changed. David had worked hard at his business during the day and they had spent the evenings together as usual. Then during the second year, Rose had started staying out late. She'd come in after midnight, talking avidly of the Colony Room in Dean Street, where she and other students from the college had drunk with Muriel, the proprietor, and artists such as Bacon and Freud.

She started going to part-time evening classes at Borough Polytechnic, along with others from the Royal College.

'Oh David, Bomberg's techniques are so exciting. He rejects anything that's artificial or concocted. He's teaching me so much.'

David listened patiently and nodded and smiled in the right places. He was happy that Rose was developing her talent, and tried not to mind that she had little time or energy left for him.

But during the third year, David hardly saw her. Rose blamed it on her workload at college, that she had to stay late to get paintings finished, but often there was alcohol on her breath and sometimes she wouldn't appear until the early hours of the following morning.

And during her last term, Rose often did not come home at all.

David wondered if she had a man.

She was a young girl; she deserved a normal life and he must not prevent it.

On the night after Rose's graduation from the Royal College, David took her out to dinner. She had just been granted her first showing at the Redfern Gallery. She was tingling with excitement.

'Can you believe it, David? Me, having an exhibition! And it's all thanks to you.'

'No, Rose. It's your great gift. And to celebrate, here.' He handed her an envelope.

'Can I open it?' she said excitedly. David nodded, knowing how she loved surprises.

She read the enclosed document and her face dropped.

'What's wrong?'

'Oh David, I'm so sorry.'

David was filled with trepidation.

'Why? What do you mean? I thought you'd be thrilled to move to a new apartment in Chelsea. I own it, Rose. We own our own home.'

Rose looked at him across the table. Then she dropped her eyes.

'I . . . I wanted to speak to you about this before, David.'

'What? For God's sake, tell me, Rose.'

'I think it's best if we don't live together any more. There's someone I've met . . .' Rose shifted uncomfortably in her chair.

David nodded. He had been preparing for this moment. 'It's all right, Rose. I understand.'

She put her face in her hands. 'No . . . I'm afraid you don't.'

Her brother managed a chuckle. 'Whoever he is, as long as he looks after you, and has good personal hygiene, then I'm looking forward to meeting him.'

'You don't realise—'

'What's his name?' David took a swig of his wine. 'Is he English?'

Rose shook her head. 'No.'

'Oh. Polish?'

'German,' Rose whispered.

David tensed a little, but wanted to assure Rose that he bore no grudges. 'Please don't worry about that. Did you meet at the Royal College?'

Rose had turned pale. 'Sort of. He . . . was an admirer of my work. He bought one of my paintings.'

'Did he? Really, Rose, you don't need to be nervous.' He reached across the table and put a comforting hand on hers. 'I'm happy for you.'

Rose shut her eyes. 'You'll never forgive me, David.'

David furrowed his brow. 'What needs forgiving? You still haven't told me his name.'

Rose took a deep breath. 'His name is Frank.'

'And what does Frank do?'

Rose's eyes darted about the room. 'He's a businessman. He does deals all over the world. Something to do with security.'

'Ah, so he's a little older, is he?' David suddenly understood his sister's reticence.

'Yes.'

'Well, as long as he treats you properly, I have no problem with it.'

Rose put a hand to her mouth. David was alarmed to see her eyes filling with tears.

'He *does* treat you properly, doesn't he?'

'He's changed, I swear.'

David frowned. '"Changed?" So, this is someone from the past?'

Rose looked as if she might be sick. 'Yes,' she managed.

'Rose, what are you talking about?'

'He says he always tried to protect me . . .'

David's blood had turned to ice. 'Protect you?'

'From the horrors of Treblinka.'

David tried to speak, but found he could not.

'He said that he'd resolved to watch over me during the last few years. That he cared about me more than anyone he had ever met . . .'

'Rose . . .' David's eyes were wide with fear. 'You don't . . . you can't . . .'

Rose was weeping now. 'I know it's impossible for you to understand. But I love him.'

Her words cut through David's heart like a knife.

'Franzen? Kurt Franzen?'

His sister nodded solemnly.

'The monster who killed our father?'

'He didn't want to, David. He had no choice. If he didn't show strength, he would have been killed himself.'

David felt as if he was in some sort of nightmare from which he could not awake.

'You don't really believe that, do you, Rose? For God's sake, he was one of the commandants of the camp!'

'Everyone was answerable to someone.'

'He *abused* you!'

'Because he loved me. He has apologised to the ends of the earth. He knows what he did was wrong when I was so young.'

'Rose! Have you gone mad? I – I . . .' The world in front of David began to blur and swim.

'Oh David, I'm so sorry.'

'How is he here?'

'He has some powerful friends who are helping him start afresh. That's all he wants. It's all *I* want.'

'I – I will contact the authorities. He cannot be allowed to . . .' David went to stand up, but found that his quivering legs were no use to him.

'I know, David, *I know*. I can't explain it. But I just don't think I can live without him. He—'

'He's tracked you down! Hunted you! Can't you see that?'

'It only proves to me how much he cares . . . He risked everything when he contacted me after buying the painting.'

'I can't comprehend what I'm hearing, Rose! He killed thousands. He killed our . . . our . . .' David was breathless. 'You're sick. This is a sickness, that is all. You can be cured.'

Rose slowly shook her head. 'I was so scared of telling you, but you deserved to hear. I'm going to leave now.'

Rose stood up from the table, tears tumbling down her face. David mustered the little strength he had, and grabbed her hand.

'You don't really love him. He's tricked you, Rose. He's using you! Don't you see?'

'No, please, David. I can't listen. I'm sorry, I'm truly sorry.'

She ran from the restaurant and out into the night. David found he was unable to follow her.

She did not come home that evening, or the night after. David's attempts to contact her proved futile. None of her friendship circle would provide him with her whereabouts.

He went to the police, of course, but had little information to give them. He knew it was important that they did not examine him or his sister too closely. After all, following their grandparents' refusal to adopt them, they technically had no right to live in Britain.

Two weeks later, David realised that Rose was never coming back.

28

London, 1950

Kurt Franzen inhaled deeply on his cigarette as he stood on London's Victoria Embankment, staring into the flowing River Thames. It was a dirty, dirty river that ran through the heart of this grand city. What a ripe metaphor for such a hypocritical country. They had banded together to stop the German war machine under the guise of decency and democracy. But no one in the history of the world had conquered and enslaved as the British had done.

Perhaps that was why he found the defeat particularly galling.

Franzen had convinced himself that it had all started with that rat, David Delanski. The escape from Treblinka that day had done something far worse than wound Franzen's pride. It had inspired others. From that moment on, the prisoners knew that there was a *chance* for them.

On the second of August 1943, there had been an uprising at the camp. With a duplicate key to Treblinka's arsenal, conspirators had managed to steal thirty rifles, twenty hand grenades and several pistols, along with tanks of petrol. Some had set buildings ablaze while a group of armed Jews attacked the main gate, allowing others to climb the fence. Two hundred prisoners escaped that day, with fewer than half recaptured.

That had been the beginning of the end for Kurt Franzen. He knew what the consequences would be. As a humiliated failure, he would be sent by Nazi High Command to the front line to be disposed of. Franzen wouldn't let that happen, of course. He had ensured that he had an escape plan in place, should he ever need one. The deputy commandant did not wait for his seniors to arrive; he fled Treblinka that night.

It was well known to him that several Catholic leaders were sympathetic to the Nazi cause, fearing the common enemy of Bolshevism. No doubt he could convince some bishop that he was a scapegoat – a victim who was to be persecuted for something he did not want to do in the first place.

Franzen had heard some of the Catholic Ukrainians talk about a path to South America via a community in Genoa. For months, he had mapped out the route he would take across Hungary and Yugoslavia, should it be necessary. With the use of counterfeit papers he had kept handy in case of such an event, Franzen made his way to Italy. Sure enough, some old fool helped him with an Argentine visa and a falsified Red Cross passport.

He'd got out long before the others had started to use the so-called 'rat lines' at the end of the war. The extra two years had given him time to establish himself in Buenos Aires, and when the hunt for escaped Nazis had begun, Kurt Franzen had been all but forgotten. The lack of red tape and prying eyes meant that Argentina was a playground to him. Using his charm and intellect, he built trust, gained connections, grew his businesses . . . and if anyone ever questioned who he was, he would ensure that they did not last long.

Frank Santos, as he had become, had outgrown suspicion, and now travelled the world as a free Argentinian citizen.

Even here. Had he felt nervous coming to England, one of the Allied powers that had brought Germany to its knees?

Perhaps, a little. But he knew that the revenge would be worth it.

He could kill David Delanski, of course. But that seemed so . . . inelegant. He wanted to make David suffer a humiliation similar to his own.

Franzen knew the key.

With his efficient network and amassed wealth, it had been relatively simple to track them down. Now would come the more difficult part of his plan.

After he had purchased Rosa's painting – or Rose Cooper's painting, as she was calling herself – he had written to her. The letter was immaculately crafted, showering praise on her artistic ability, suggesting that a gift had been given to her by the gods. He had provided the address of his rented London flat to write back to, and the correspondence had continued for a number of weeks. Franzen had always prided himself on his ability to turn a phrase, and enjoyed the game of manipulation immensely. He had told Rose that although he was an international businessman, his real passion lay in the arts, that her work had unlocked something in him which had been hidden . . . he was lonely . . . she was special . . .

Franzen was acutely aware of just how vulnerable this young woman was, and he made sure to exploit this weakness at every possible opportunity. As per his plan, Rose's heart opened further with each letter he sent.

He had calculated that, after what she had been through in her short life, she would be craving a sense of security. This was Franzen's way in. In his final piece of correspondence, he had offered to become a benevolent benefactor, financially supporting her so that she could focus solely on her art.

As he had anticipated, it was Rose who had suggested a meeting after this.

His lips curled into a smile. The strategy was bearing fruit. She was beginning to feel wooed and cared for.

The meeting was set for the following week in the River Restaurant at the Savoy. Franzen had chosen the location carefully. Although he did not anticipate a scene, the up-and-coming artist would not cause a ruckus among the high society whom she hoped would be her clients.

When Rose walked in, he recognised her instantly. Her thick, titian hair and moonlike eyes transported him back to another time. She was as beautiful as he remembered. This would not be a chore.

He stood up and raised an arm. When she saw him, her face broke into an enormous, beaming smile. Clearly, the recognition was not reciprocated, just as Franzen had hoped. For obvious reasons, these days he sported a different hairstyle, and used make-up to cover his definable moles and blemishes.

Franzen knew the name of the game today was humility and generosity. During the first two courses, the conversation flowed like wine, allowing him to weave his web of compliments and reassurances, before talk turned to money.

'Really, I'd like to support you through the remainder of your studies and beyond.'

'Honestly, Frank – you've been so kind already. I could never ask you to—'

He waved his hand. 'Imagine what Monet could have achieved if he did not have to worry about bills, my dear!' Rose giggled, as he topped up her champagne. 'Plus, I'm ever so rich and have no one to spend it on.' Franzen noted the look of sympathy in her eyes, and knew he was winning.

'Well, I . . .'

'No need to force a decision before dessert, my dear. Tell me more about your love for Van Gogh. I adore hearing you talk so passionately.'

By the end of the lunch, all of Rose's defences were well and truly down. She was within his grasp. After settling the enormous bill, Franzen was waiting for his moment. As Rose reached for her water glass, he smoothly put his hand on hers. To his delight, far from pulling away, Rose held him tightly.

'I have loved meeting you in person, Rose.'

She blushed. 'And I you, Frank. Thank you for lunch.'

'My pleasure. Are we agreed that I will cover your expenses while you paint?'

'How could I refuse? Thank you.' The pair spent a moment gazing at each other, before Franzen leaned over the table and gave her a gentle kiss on the lips. After, Rose smiled widely and cast her eyes to the ground.

'I'm sorry. I could not resist. I hope that I have not offended you.'

'No, not at all!' Rose's reply was emphatic.

Perfect. Franzen inhaled deeply and allowed a pregnant pause. 'I'm so glad that you have had an opportunity to see the real me.' This performance had to be faultless.

'I'm sorry?'

Franzen put his head in his hands, subtly using his fingers to poke his eyes and produce tears.

'Frank? Are you all right?'

'No, my dear, I'm afraid I am not. I was so scared that you would recognise me and run away.'

Rose looked concerned. 'What are you talking about?'

Franzen slowly removed his hands from his face, presenting a facade of sorrow and regret. 'I think you know, in your heart of hearts, that this is not our first meeting.' He took her hand again and looked at her intently. 'I had no choice, you must understand. It was kill, or be killed. It doesn't excuse anything I did, but . . . Oh God!' Franzen forced out a few sobs.

'I don't understand, Frank.'

'I tried so hard to protect you. I always knew you were special. And your brother, of course.' Franzen noted the shift in Rose's expression.

'My brother?'

'Yes. It's why I put him in the orchestra. I knew it would keep him safe.'

'What . . . ?' Rose's voice was a whisper.

'The truth is, I loved you. I was positive that you would amount to something special. That's why –' this had to be the most convincing part of his lie – 'I gave Anya the matches that day. Without them, David could not have lit the fire which allowed you both to escape. I knew about your entire plan. I helped you.' He was particularly proud of this fabrication.

Rose sat in silence, tears filling her eyes. 'Franzen . . .'

'Please! Never call me that. Kurt Franzen was a creation, a toxic, putrid, *hateful* consequence of the Nazi regime.' He mustered all his sincerity. 'That was *not* me.'

Rose remained frozen. 'I . . .'

'You *know* it wasn't me. The real me tried to keep you from harm. My special artist. My *Rosa*.'

She stood up hurriedly. That was all right, this moment was inevitable. He grabbed her hand.

'I understand, my dearest, that you must go. But please, try to remember that I ensured you lived, when so many others died.' Rose went to leave, but he gripped her a little tighter. 'Remember me. The *real* me, not Kurt Franzen. You have my address. And know that you must be careful who you tell about this.' Franzen looked pitiful. 'I do not care what happens to me, of course. But I am aware you and your brother are in this country on false pretences.' He shook his head. 'I would hate for any further ill fate to befall you two because of me.' He gave Rose one final, lingering look, before dropping her hand.

He watched as she made her way hurriedly across the River Restaurant.

The meeting had gone even better than he had hoped. Franzen sat back in his chair and glugged the remaining champagne. If he understood one thing, it was how to break people. He sensed that Rose was close to cracking.

Sure enough, Franzen received a letter from her not two weeks later.

When the pair met again, Franzen continued his narrative: Treblinka was *hell*, and he had been the Delanskis' guardian angel. Shooting her father had been a *kindness*, for he had suffered for too long. Franzen was a *good* man, and a *victim* of his country's evil regime. All he longed for was an opportunity to prove it to her.

As the weeks progressed, Franzen began to deposit money into Rose's bank account. As the weeks turned into months, he had opened doors for her, arranging meetings with wealthy art dealers and potential clients.

Rose's fame slowly started to grow, and she could not deny the help she had received from her 'protector'. It was six months before she kissed him again. Franzen had feigned tears, and insisted that they should only proceed if she truly desired it. This was a long game.

After another three months, they slept together for the first time. Franzen's satisfaction was exquisite. This was his ultimate goal. And as soon as his task was complete, he would leave her for good.

In the summer of 1951, Rose arrived at Franzen's apartment in a state of distress, saying that she had told her brother about their involvement over dinner. As always, Franzen was prepared. He consoled her, told her that he understood, and that everything would be all right.

'He'll never forgive me!' she had sobbed.

'Of course he will. Just give him time,' Franzen lied.

It was his cue to leave the city. The 'relationship' was solid enough that he could make frequent visits, but not have to remain and risk being found by David.

Franzen did everything he could to keep Rose invested in him, continuing to support her financially and making certain that her career was flourishing. He had suggested she change her name to Delancey. That was a subtle way of stealing her away from David. But there would be worse pain to come. Every few months, he would fly to London to visit her and, on occasion, he would fly her out to Buenos Aires. Franzen would ensure they slept together often on these occasions.

It was taking longer than he anticipated. What if she was unable?

But then, over dinner at the River Restaurant, Franzen got the news he wanted. It had taken nearly four years of his life, but the task was complete.

'How far along are you?' he asked

'It would be three months, since we . . .'

Franzen paid for dinner, left, and never contacted Rosa Delanski again.

His work was done.

29

David drank, finding the bottom of every bottle in the city. Once he had confirmed that his sorrows could be drowned, but not extinguished, he turned his efforts to finding Franzen. David poured vast sums of money into private investigators, but none of them were ever able to deliver anything beyond whispers and theories. They found Rose, of course, who was living with her friend Roddy. His attempts to contact her were fruitless. Whether it was by post, telephone or doorstepping, his sister simply could not face him.

Although he had not physically seen her, David observed her fame as an artist steadily grow during the following four years. Every paper he opened was full of the work of the young 'Rose Delancey'. David noted the subtle change of surname.

By 1955, his twenty-four-year-old sister was the toast of London. The art critics embraced her strong individual work, John Russell of *The Sunday Times* highlighting the similarity to Bacon. The undertones of her life during the war were present in all her paintings. Columnists loved her. She had everything: beauty, talent, intelligence and an unknown past.

David had once seen a photograph of Rose and an unidentifiable man in Regent's Park. He was wearing a hat, and his face was turned towards his sister. Perhaps it was Franzen. Perhaps not.

The stories David read only mentioned a 'mystery man'.
Had the whole thing been some sort of fever dream?

As usual, he spent his time concentrating his emotions on his business empire, which was fast moving him towards paper millionaire status.

Then, late one summer night, the telephone rang.

'David Cooper.'

'Hello, David. It's Rose.'

He gulped. Just the sound of her voice was enough to turn him to jelly.

'Hello, Rose.'

'I . . . I was wondering whether I could come and see you tonight? Are you busy?'

David looked at the mountains of paperwork in front of him and said, 'No, not at all. Come round.'

'I'll be there in half an hour.'

The radiance she emitted when she walked into the room was staggering. David understood why the tabloids took such an interest in her.

Rose pulled a cigarette and a holder out of her clutch bag, but after a moment she returned both. She paused by the window to see the view from his apartment and David thought how sophisticated she had become.

'Would you like a drink?'

'Water's fine, thanks.'

'Right. You don't mind if I . . . ?'

'Not at all.'

David took a large gulp from the bottle as he poured the wine into a glass in his kitchen, and returned to the sitting room with the two drinks.

'Thanks.' She took the glass.

'Why did you want to see me?'

'I . . . I wanted to apologise for not contacting you during the last few years. I . . . couldn't.'

She looked up at him and David saw the pain in her eyes. 'Do you understand, David?'

The atmosphere between them was heavy.

'No.'

Rose took a deep breath. 'Before I go any further, I need you to know that Frank . . . *Franzen* and I are no more.'

David's heart thumped in his chest. 'Where has he been for the last few years? I couldn't find a trace of him.'

Rose sipped her water delicately. 'Buenos Aires, mainly. But he moves around a lot.'

The ensuing silence was intolerable.

'I'm so sorry, David. I can see everything clearly now.'

'All right.' Monosyllabic answers were all he could manage as he blinked back the tears.

'I've tried to rationalise it. I've spoken to people. Psychologists, doctors.'

He tried his best to remain calm. 'What do they say?'

'There is a theory about a condition that can develop in the brain. When someone is in an abusive relationship, and there's a power imbalance, sometimes emotional bonds can be formed.' Rose's delivery was pragmatic and clinical.

'I see.'

'The bonds are totally irrational, of course. Paradoxical. The sympathy that the victim feels for their abuser is the opposite of what any sane person would perceive.' He noted that she was finding this very difficult. 'It can be particularly powerful if the relationship begins when the victim is a child.'

David nodded slowly. 'I can understand that.'

'He was nice enough at first, apologising for the past and promising me the world.' Rose swallowed hard.

David reached for a copy of *The Sunday Times* from the

coffee table and held it in front of his sister. 'You've become famous.'

'Yes. He always liked my art. He introduced me to dealers and wealthy collectors. My work has . . . sold well.'

'I know, Rose. I read about it often.'

'Yes. I . . .' She didn't know what to say.

David downed his glass of wine and clenched his fists. He could contain himself no longer. 'What the *hell* were you thinking, Rose?!'

His sister cast her eyes to the floor. 'You were right. I was sick.' She looked at him. 'But I'm better now, I swear. David, I'm so sorry.'

'Sorry? Am I supposed to *forgive* you?'

'Of course not. But I was hoping you might understand . . .'

'What is there to understand? That my sister fell in love with the man who killed our father? The man who exterminated thousands of our own people?'

'I thought he—'

'You thought he *protected* you. I remember what you told me. But he didn't, Rose. I did. I DID!' David threw the newspaper to the floor.

Rose sighed. 'It was wrong, David. I began to realise it as I grew up. My brain was warped. I was so dependent on him in Treblinka. I can see the reasons why it happened, but that doesn't make what I did right.'

'Of course it fucking doesn't! What would Papa say to you? Mama?' David was blazing.

'David—'

'No! Four years, Rose. Four years in which I have had to accept that you chose that *thing* over me. I swore to Mama that I would care for you. I risked my own life to save yours, and this is how you repay me. How you repay our family. How could you? How *dare* you?'

'I'm . . . I'm so . . .' Rose was unable to utter another word before dropping her glass. Her hands clasped her face, and she sobbed deeply.

David took deep breaths, sitting in the rage that had welled up inside him. In spite of his anger, the sight of his sister shaking uncontrollably elicited an automatic response. He was transported back to their sorry life in Warsaw, when she had been a hungry, scared child.

No matter what had happened, Rose was the person he loved more than anyone else in this world. His fury began to diffuse, and he walked over to his sister to envelop her in his arms.

'I'm so sorry, David . . . I'm so sorry.'

He held her tightly for a long time, until her sobs turned to sniffs.

During the long evening that followed, Rose told her brother the details of her relationship with Franzen.

By the end of Rose's story, David was convinced that his sister was little more than a victim of her own awful circumstances. Her family had been cruelly ripped from her in the most inhumane of ways. The vulnerable little girl had come to see Franzen – the sole constant during her time in Treblinka – as a guardian of sorts. Franzen had calculated on this, and, like the deadliest of predators, refused to give up on his prey.

David and Rose had escaped from his clutches, embarrassed him.

He had sought to exact revenge.

'Where is he now?' David asked softly.

'Argentina, I assume. But he had places all over South America. I wouldn't be surprised if he's relocated.'

'Is there any way we can get to him? Via the authorities, I mean.'

Rose shook her head. 'I seriously doubt it. He's so well connected, and there's so much corruption there . . . Oh God, I know it's not what you want to hear.'

David raised his hand. 'It's all right. You're here. You're safe.' He took Rose by the shoulders. 'But I need you to swear to me, Rosa Delanski, that the nightmare is over. You will never see Franzen again. No . . . you will never even *mention* his name.'

David observed the honest fear in his sister's eyes. 'I swear.'

David stood and helped his sister to her feet, then pulled her close to him. As he did so, he noticed that she instinctively protected her stomach by curving her back forwards.

David took a step back, and eyed his sister. A horrific thought entered his mind.

'Are you sure I can't get you a glass of wine?'

Rose shook her head. 'Thank you, but I'm fine.'

'Is there any reason you're not drinking at the moment?'

Rose's face reddened. 'No. I just don't fancy anything tonight.'

He stared hard at his sister's stomach, as she awkwardly tried to hide the slight bulge with her hands.

'Oh Rose.'

'What?'

David felt as though someone had slapped him across his face. As though he were drowning, and couldn't get his breath.

He couldn't let her see.

'I've just remembered that I'm off to America next week. I'm sailing over there and won't be back for six months. I'm thinking of expanding my business in the States.' David was proud of his control. Now he wanted her to leave, so that he could let his grief out alone.

'Oh. Well, I hope to see you when you get back.'

'Yes.' David didn't know what to say to Rose, but he was

confident that this would be their last interaction. 'I'll look out for your paintings while I'm abroad.'

Rose sighed. 'Thank you, but to be honest I'm a bit wrung out at the moment. I feel as if I'm on a production line. I could use a break.'

David sensed his sister's exhaustion.

'Well, you have been a very busy young lady in the past few years. I must congratulate you again on your success.'

'Thank you. It's Papa, really, giving me his gift.' Rose looked up at the wall. 'You have *Treblinka* up there. I hate that painting. Why have you hung it?'

David could have said that it was because it reminded him of the glorious days that the two of them had lived in their cocoon, the happiest time of his life.

Instead, he shrugged. 'I like it, that's all.'

Rose checked her watch nervously. 'I must go, David. I'm meeting Roddy at half past eight.' She stood. 'It's nice to see you again.'

Rose walked towards the door and he followed her.

She turned with her hand on the handle.

'Goodbye, David.' She pecked him lightly on the cheek.

David closed the door behind his sister. In that moment, he forgave her, but vowed that he would never see Rose or her child again.

Rose stood in the corridor, held herself together for a moment, then allowed her cries to burst forth. Although unspoken, she knew that David had realised she was pregnant. It was inevitable. There had been no opportunity to slip in any false explanation about who the father might be. Even if there had been, her brother never would have believed her.

Rose was suffocating. She needed to get away from this city.

'Goodbye, David,' she whispered. 'I'm sorry.'

30

Rose realised that the sky was getting dark. She checked her watch. She'd been sitting by Miranda's grave for over two hours. She wiped away the tears with the back of her hand.

'So you see, Miranda, David could never see me again. It was too painful for him. He went off to America a week later. Oh God, I was so confused, so exhausted from the past few years. That was when I decided to come up here to Yorkshire. The press would have had a field day if I had stayed in London and produced a child. I couldn't have handled that.

'I needed to be alone. At twenty-four, I was washed out, emotionally and mentally. I knew I could never see David again, that he could never accept I had that man's child.

'Miles. Kurt Franzen's baby.'

Rose voiced the words for the first time.

'That is why you are lying down there, Miranda. Because I was too weak to stop myself from falling in love with my own captor. I produced a child who was doomed from the start. I prayed he'd be all right, watched him for any tell-tale signs and found few. Miles was so clever. He was always so charming towards me.

'I was blinded by love. I should have seen long ago what I'd created. A monster.

'So you mustn't blame Miles,' Rose whispered. 'What he became was no one's fault but mine. Oh Miranda. I'm so, so sorry for what I've done. Please, if you can hear me, forgive me, please forgive me.'

Rose sobbed again. Then she looked up as she saw a line of birds settle in the tree above Miranda's grave. The wind rustled and then the birds started twittering, until there was a rousing chorus of life.

It was almost dark.

Rose smiled.

'Thank you, Miranda,' she whispered. 'It's over now, isn't it?'

'No, Rose. It has only just begun.'

A male voice made her jump.

She turned and saw David standing behind her. He took her gently by the shoulders and pulled her upright.

'Come with me, Rose.'

She looked up at him. 'Yes.'

He hugged her tightly.

The two of them walked slowly off down the path, arms wrapped around each other. From the trees above the grave, the birds watched the pair until they were but specks in the distance.

Epilogue

Paris, 1992

'My lords, ladies and gentlemen. I welcome you all here tonight. Thank you from the bottom of my heart for coming to this evening's fashion show, here in the Grand Ballroom of the Ritz. I would like to thank the manager for loaning us this magnificent room free of charge.

'As I'm sure most of you are aware, the Delanski Foundation was set up four years ago. It is a charity with a difference, because it does not discriminate between the different forms of human suffering.

'Suffering can come in many guises; whether it is a young man dying from AIDS, or a war veteran whose pension is not enough to give him even the simple comforts that every person deserves.

'In the past four years, we have helped over one thousand causes, some of them disasters on a national scale, some a single human being.

'Tonight, however, we are helping the Holocaust Foundation to continue their good work. They are a group of men and women who have elected to make sure the murder of six million citizens is not forgotten and will never be repeated in history again. They also counsel victims and relatives who have lost loved ones, to help them come to terms with what has happened to them.'

There was heartfelt applause from the audience.

'I should like to introduce you to my father-in-law, David Cooper, a man I'm sure you all have heard of, who is the president of the Holocaust Foundation. Please welcome him to the stage.'

David came up onto the dais beside Leah. He kissed her on each cheek, and she sat down to listen to what he had to say.

'Good evening, ladies and gentlemen. Thank you for being with us tonight. Leah has steered brilliantly at the helm of an organisation which, when it was launched, took up one room in her home. Now, it commands an entire floor of my block in New York, and she has a larger office than I do.'

There was muffled laughter and more applause at this.

He waited until the audience was quiet.

As David began his speech, Leah slipped off the platform and joined her husband.

'Is she here?' she asked him anxiously.

Brett nodded. 'She's here. Her flight from Moscow was delayed, that's all.'

The star-studded audience bid almost fifty thousand pounds for the sumptuous range of clothes in the new Carlo collection. Carlo himself, a humbled, much more likeable man since his spell in jail awaiting trial for murder, embraced Leah warmly. He had apologised long ago for his misdemeanours, and Leah, knowing what he had suffered, and feeling partly responsible for putting the wrong man behind bars, had been glad to accept.

Rose, David, Chloe, Brett and Leah sat round the table, chatting and enjoying the excellent dinner.

Leah looked round with happiness, musing how strange it

was to see all the people who had had such an effect on her life reunited once more.

After the tragedy eight years ago, Rose had left Yorkshire to go to New York, fleeing the terrible memories that the farmhouse held for her. She had never returned, staying with David at his duplex ever since. Tonight, Leah thought how content brother and sister looked.

Chloe had elected to stay with Mrs Thompson in Yorkshire, flying to stay with Rose in America for the school holidays. Leah couldn't help but be glad that her parents had Chloe to keep them company. With her hectic schedule, Leah's own visits to Yorkshire were less regular than they should be.

She'd regained consciousness that terrible night on the moors and found herself in Brett's arms. After desperately trying to phone Leah and her parents in Yorkshire, Anthony had gallantly managed to contact Brett in Paris, and he had chartered a private jet to fly back immediately. Brett had flown her to New York a couple of days after the incident, once Rose had returned to Yorkshire, and taken Chloe to stay with Mrs Thompson. Leah and Brett had sought refuge in David's apartment.

It had taken her many months to recover from the shock of that night in Yorkshire. With Brett's love and understanding, she had done so. During the past eight years, their relationship had only grown stronger. Brett had listened to her concerns about Paris, and enlisted in New York's School of Visual Arts instead. Under Rose's guidance, his career was really beginning to take off, and she was immensely proud of his dedication. There was no baby, but they were looking into adoption. And who knew what tomorrow might bring? For the present, Brett and the foundation gave Leah all the joy she needed.

And tonight, her work and her personal life were married together.

One year ago, Brett had come to his wife with a request.

'Leah, I need your organisation's help,' he'd said. Then he had told her his idea.

It had taken an enormous amount of effort; leads that led frustratingly to brick walls, bureaucracy and red tape thwarting them time and again.

Then they had found her.

And, finally, she was here.

Brett was tingling with excitement.

He put his hand on Leah's. 'Thank you, Leah. For everything. You don't know what this means to me.'

She rose from her seat. 'David, Rose, Chloe. I wonder if you can come with me. I have someone whom you might like to meet waiting for you.'

Leah left the table, and the others, bewilderment on their faces, followed her through a side door and out of the ball-room.

She led them along the corridor and knocked on a door.

A faint voice answered.

Leah opened the door and went in. David followed.

He stared at the frail lady sitting in an armchair. The face, it was so familiar, and yet he couldn't place it.

She spoke. 'Hello, David.'

Tears filled his eyes as he ran to her, held her, covered her with kisses. As Rose joined her brother, Chloe stood watching in fascination.

'Anya, Anya . . . I thought you were dead. Oh God . . .'

Leah quietly closed the door and left them alone.

Outside, Brett was waiting. He saw her eyes were filled with tears.

'Darling, I have something for you.' He handed Leah a heavy square parcel, wrapped in brown paper. Leah tore off the paper and gasped as she saw the painting.

'It's based on the original charcoal sketch from when you were fifteen. It's a thank-you present for all you've done to help find Anya. It's called *The Hidden Girl*.'

'I don't deserve this.'

'Yes you do, darling. And a lot of people here tonight agree with me. I was so anxious to trace Anya for Dad's sake. Bringing the past into the present will help him finally come to terms with what happened to him and Rose. They suffered so much together and now life has come full circle for all three of them. You've done something wonderful by getting Anya out of Russia and bringing her here. I love you, Leah.'

He lifted her face to his and kissed her gently on the lips.

Inside the hotel suite, a camera flashed.

'Not now, Chloe. You can take photos of your great-grandmother later.'

The pretty sixteen-year-old glanced up at Rose and smiled.

'Sorry, Granny.'

Rose shuddered.

She'd seen that cold, distant look before.

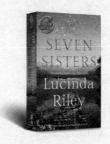

Their future is written in the stars.

The Seven Sisters tells the stories of the D'Aplièse sisters, all adopted as babies by the enigmatic billionaire they affectionately call Pa Salt.

When Pa Salt dies suddenly, the bereaved sisters gather together at their childhood home, a spectacular secluded castle on the shores of Lake Geneva. Each of them is handed a tantalising clue to their heritage, and eldest sister Maia finds herself on a journey across the world to a crumbling mansion in Rio de Janeiro, Brazil.

Eighty years earlier, Izabela Bonifacio's father has aspirations for her to marry into the aristocracy. But Izabela longs for adventure, and convinces him to allow her to first travel to Paris. In the heady, vibrant streets of the city, Izabela meets an ambitious young sculptor, and knows at once that her life will never be the same again.

What links these two young women? In the beautiful city of Rio, will Maia find the answers she needs to understand who she truly is?

Read on for an extract of this epic tale of love and loss . . .

Maia

June 2007

First Quarter

13; 16; 21

1

I will always remember exactly where I was and what I was doing when I heard that my father had died.

I was sitting in the pretty garden of my old schoolfriend's townhouse in London, a copy of *The Penelopiad* open but unread in my lap, enjoying the June sun while Jenny collected her little boy from nursery.

I felt calm and appreciated what a good idea it had been to get away. I was studying the burgeoning clematis, encouraged by its sunny midwife to give birth to a riot of colour, when my mobile phone rang. I glanced at the screen and saw it was Marina.

'Hello, Ma, how are you?' I said, hoping she could hear the warmth in my voice too.

'Maia, I . . .'

Marina paused, and in that instant I knew something was dreadfully wrong. 'What is it?'

'Maia, there's no easy way to tell you this, but your father had a heart attack here at home yesterday afternoon, and in the early hours of this morning, he . . . passed away.'

I remained silent, as a million different and ridiculous thoughts raced through my mind. The first one being that

Marina, for some unknown reason, had decided to play some form of tasteless joke on me.

'You're the first of the sisters I've told, Maia, as you're the eldest. And I wanted to ask you whether you would prefer to tell the rest of your sisters yourself, or leave it to me.'

'I . . .'

Still no words would form coherently on my lips, as I began to realise that Marina, dear, beloved Marina, the woman who had been the closest thing to a mother I'd ever known, would never tell me this if it *wasn't* true. So it had to be. And at that moment, my entire world shifted on its axis.

'Maia, please, tell me you're all right. This really is the most dreadful call I've ever had to make, but what else could I do? God only knows how the other girls are going to take it.'

It was then that I heard the suffering in *her* voice and understood she'd needed to tell me as much for her own sake as mine. So I switched into my normal comfort zone, which was to comfort others.

'Of course I'll tell my sisters if you'd prefer, Ma, although I'm not positive where they all are. Isn't Ally away training for a regatta?'

And as we continued to discuss where each of my younger sisters was, as though we needed to get them together for a birthday party rather than to mourn the death of our father, the entire conversation took on a sense of the surreal.

'When should we plan on having the funeral, do you think? What with Electra being in Los Angeles and Ally somewhere on the high seas, surely we can't think about it until next week at the earliest?' I said.

'Well . . .' I heard the hesitation in Marina's voice. 'Perhaps the best thing is for you and I to discuss it when you arrive back home. There really is no rush now, Maia, so if you'd prefer to continue the last couple of days of your holiday in London, that would be fine. There's nothing more to be done for him here . . .' Her voice trailed off miserably.

'Ma, of *course* I'll be on the next flight to Geneva I can get! I'll call the airline immediately, and then I'll do my best to get in touch with everyone.'

'I'm so terribly sorry, *chérie*,' Marina said sadly. 'I know how you adored him.'

'Yes,' I said, the strange calm that I had felt while we discussed arrangements suddenly deserting me like the stillness before a violent thunderstorm. 'I'll call you later, when I know what time I'll be arriving.'

'Please take care of yourself, Maia. You've had a terrible shock.'

I pressed the button to end the call, and before the storm clouds in my heart opened up and drowned me, I went upstairs to my bedroom to retrieve my flight documents and contact the airline. As I waited in the calling queue, I glanced at the bed where I'd woken up this morning to Simply Another Day. And I thanked God that human beings don't have the power to see into the future.

The officious woman who eventually answered wasn't helpful and I knew, as she spoke of full flights, financial penalties and credit card details, that my emotional dam was ready to burst. Finally, once I'd grudgingly been granted a seat on the four o'clock flight to Geneva, which would mean throwing everything into my holdall immediately and taking a taxi to Heathrow, I sat down on the bed and stared for so long at the sprigged wallpaper that the pattern began to dance in front of my eyes.

'He's gone,' I whispered, 'gone for ever. I'll never see him again.'

Expecting the spoken words to provoke a raging torrent of tears, I was surprised that nothing actually happened. Instead, I sat there numbly, my head still full of practicalities. The thought of telling my sisters – all five of them – was horrendous, and I searched through my emotional filing system for the one I would call first. Inevitably, it was Tiggy, the second youngest of the six of us girls and the sibling to whom I'd always felt closest.

With trembling fingers, I scrolled down to find her number and dialled it. When her voicemail answered, I didn't know what to say, other than a few garbled words asking her to call me back urgently. She was currently somewhere in the Scottish Highlands working at a centre for orphaned and sick wild deer.

As for the other sisters . . . I knew their reactions would vary, outwardly at least, from indifference to a dramatic out-pouring of emotion.

Given that I wasn't currently sure quite which way I would go on the scale of grief when I did speak to any of them, I decided to take the coward's way out and texted them all, asking them to call me as soon as they could. Then I hurriedly packed my holdall and walked down the narrow stairs to the kitchen to write a note for Jenny explaining why I'd had to leave in such a hurry.

Deciding to take my chances hailing a black cab on the London streets, I left the house, walking briskly around the leafy Chelsea crescent just as any normal person would do on any normal day. I believe I actually said hello to someone walking a dog when I passed him in the street and managed a smile.

No one would know what had just happened to me, I thought, as I managed to find a taxi on the busy King's Road and climbed inside, directing the driver to Heathrow.

No one would know.

Five hours later, just as the sun was making its leisurely descent over Lake Geneva, I arrived at our private pontoon on the shore, from where I would make the last leg of my journey home.

Christian was already waiting for me in our sleek Riva motor launch. And from the look on his face, I could see he'd heard the news.

'How are you, Mademoiselle Maia?' he asked, sympathy in his blue eyes as he helped me aboard.

'I'm . . . glad I'm here,' I answered neutrally as I walked to the back of the boat and sat down on the cushioned cream leather bench that curved around the stern. Usually, I would sit with Christian in the passenger seat at the front as we sped across the calm waters on the twenty-minute journey home. But today, I felt a need for privacy. As Christian started the powerful engine, the sun glinted off the windows of the fabulous houses that lined Lake Geneva's shores. I'd often felt when I made this journey that it was the entrance to an ethereal world disconnected from reality.

The world of Pa Salt.

I noticed the first vague evidence of tears pricking at my

eyes as I thought of my father's pet name, which I'd coined when I was young. He'd always loved sailing and often when he returned to me at our lakeside home, he had smelt of fresh air and of the sea. Somehow, the name had stuck, and as my younger siblings had joined me, they'd called him that too.

As the launch picked up speed, the warm wind streaming through my hair, I thought of the hundreds of previous journeys I'd made to Atlantis, Pa Salt's fairy-tale castle. Inaccessible by land, due to its position on a private promontory with a crescent of mountainous terrain rising up steeply behind it, the only method of reaching it was by boat. The nearest neighbours were miles away along the lake, so Atlantis was our own private kingdom, set apart from the rest of the world. Everything it contained was magical . . . as if Pa Salt and we – his daughters – had lived there under an enchantment.

Each one of us had been chosen by Pa Salt as a baby, adopted from the four corners of the globe and brought home to live under his protection. And each one of us, as Pa always liked to say, was special, different . . . we were *his* girls. He'd named us all after The Seven Sisters, his favourite star cluster. Maia being the first and eldest.

When I was young, he'd take me up to his glass-domed observatory perched on top of the house, lift me up with his big, strong hands and have me look through his telescope at the night sky.

'There it is,' he'd say as he aligned the lens. 'Look, Maia, that's the beautiful shining star you're named after.'

And I *would* see. As he explained the legends that were the source of my own and my sisters' names, I'd hardly listen, but simply enjoy his arms tight around me, fully aware of this rare, special moment when I had him all to myself.

I'd realised eventually that Marina, who I'd presumed as I grew up was my mother – I'd even shortened her name to 'Ma' – was a glorified nursemaid, employed by Pa to take care of me because he was away such a lot. But of course, Marina was so much more than that to all of us girls. She was the one who had wiped our tears, berated us for sloppy table manners and steered us calmly through the difficult transition from childhood to womanhood.

She had always been there, and I could not have loved Ma any more if she had given birth to me.

During the first three years of my childhood, Marina and I had lived alone together in our magical castle on the shores of Lake Geneva as Pa Salt travelled the seven seas to conduct his business. And then, one by one, my sisters began to arrive.

Usually, Pa would bring me a present when he returned home. I'd hear the motor launch arriving, run across the sweeping lawns and through the trees to the jetty to greet him. Like any child, I'd want to see what he had hidden inside his magical pockets to delight me. On one particular occasion, however, after he'd presented me with an exquisitely carved wooden reindeer, which he assured me came from St Nicholas's workshop at the North Pole itself, a uniformed woman had stepped out from behind him, and in her arms was a bundle wrapped in a shawl. And the bundle was moving.

'This time, Maia, I've brought you back the most special gift. You have a new sister.' He'd smiled at me as he lifted me into his arms. 'Now you'll no longer be lonely when I have to go away.'

After that, life had changed. The maternity nurse that Pa had brought with him disappeared after a few weeks and Marina took over the care of my baby sister. I couldn't understand how the red, squalling thing which often smelt and diverted attention from me could possibly be a gift. Until one morning, when Alcyone – named after the second star of The Seven Sisters – smiled at me from her high chair over breakfast.

'She knows who I am,' I said in wonder to Marina, who was feeding her.

'Of course she does, Maia, dear. You're her big sister, the one she'll look up to. It'll be up to you to teach her lots of things that you know and she doesn't.'

And as she grew, she became my shadow, following me everywhere, which pleased and irritated me in equal measure.

'Maia, wait me!' she'd demand loudly as she tottered along behind me.

Even though Ally – as I'd nicknamed her – had originally been an unwanted addition to my dreamlike existence at Atlantis, I could not have asked for a sweeter, more loveable companion. She rarely, if ever, cried and there were none of the temper-tantrums associated with toddlers of her age. With her tumbling red-gold curls and her big blue eyes, Ally had a natural charm that drew people to her, including our father. On the occasions Pa Salt was home from one of his long trips abroad, I'd watch how his eyes lit up when he saw her, in a way I was sure they didn't for me. And whereas I was shy and reticent with strangers, Ally had an openness and a readiness to trust that endeared her to everyone.

She was also one of those children who seemed to excel at everything – particularly music, and any sport to do with water. I remember Pa teaching her to swim in our vast pool and, whereas I had struggled to stay afloat and hated being underwater, my little sister took to it like a mermaid. And while I couldn't find my sea legs even on the *Titan*, Pa's huge and beautiful ocean-going yacht, when we were at home Ally would beg him to take her out in the small Laser he kept moored on our private lakeside jetty. I'd crouch in the cramped stern of the boat while Pa and Ally took control as we sped across the glassy waters. Their joint passion for sailing bonded them in a way I felt I could never replicate.

Although Ally had studied music at the Conservatoire de Musique de Genève and was a highly talented flautist who could have pursued a career with a professional orchestra, since leaving music school she had chosen the life of a full-time sailor. She now competed regularly in regattas, and had represented Switzerland on a number of occasions.

When Ally was almost three, Pa arrived home with our next sibling, whom he named Asterope, after the third of The Seven Sisters.

'But we will call her Star,' Pa had said, smiling at Marina, Ally and me as we studied the newest addition to the family lying in the bassinet.

By now I was attending lessons every morning with a private tutor, so my newest sister's arrival affected me less than Ally's had. Then, only six months later, another baby joined us, a twelve-week-old girl named Celaeno, whose name Ally immediately shortened to CeCe.

There was only three months' age difference between Star and CeCe, and from as far back as I can remember, the two of them forged a close bond. They were akin to twins, talking in their own private baby language, some of which the two of them still used to communicate to this day. They inhabited their own private world, to the exclusion of us other sisters. And even now in their twenties, nothing had changed. CeCe, the younger of the two, was always the boss, her stocky body and nut-brown skin in direct contrast to the pale, whippet-thin Star.

The following year, another baby arrived – Taygete, whom I nicknamed 'Tiggy' because her short dark hair sprouted out at strange angles on her tiny head and reminded me of the hedgehog in Beatrix Potter's famous story.

I was by now seven years old, and I'd bonded with Tiggy from the first moment I set eyes on her. She was the most delicate of us all, suffering one childhood illness after another, but even as an infant, she was stoic and undemanding. When yet another baby girl, named Electra, was brought home by Pa a few months later, an exhausted Marina would often ask me if I would mind sitting with Tiggy, who continually had a fever or croup. Eventually diagnosed as asthmatic, she rarely left the nursery to be wheeled outside in the pram, in case the cold air and heavy fog of a Geneva winter affected her chest.

Electra was the youngest of my siblings and her name suited her perfectly. By now, I was used to little babies and their demands, but my youngest sister was without doubt the most challenging of them all. Everything about her *was* electric; her innate ability to switch in an instant from dark to light and vice versa meant that our previously calm home rang daily with high-pitched screams. Her temper-tantrums resonated through my childhood consciousness and as she grew older, her fiery personality did not mellow.

Privately, Ally, Tiggy and I had our own nickname for her; she was known among the three of us as 'Tricky'. We all walked on eggshells around her, wishing to do nothing to set off a lightning change of mood. I can honestly say there were moments when I loathed her for the disruption she brought to Atlantis.

And yet, when Electra knew one of us was in trouble, she was the first to offer help and support. Just as she was capable of huge selfishness, her generosity on other occasions was equally pronounced.

After Electra, the entire household was expecting the arrival of the Seventh Sister. After all, we'd been named after Pa Salt's favourite star cluster and we wouldn't be complete without her. We even knew her name – Merope – and wondered who she would be. But a year went past, and then another, and another, and no more babies arrived home with our father.

I remember vividly standing with him once in his observatory. I was fourteen years old and just on the brink of womanhood. We were waiting for an eclipse, which he'd told me was a seminal moment for humankind and usually brought change with it.

'Pa,' I said, 'will you ever bring home our seventh sister?'

At this, his strong, protective bulk had seemed to freeze for a few seconds. He'd looked suddenly as though he carried the weight of the world on his shoulders. Although he didn't turn around, for he was still concentrating on training the telescope on the coming eclipse, I knew instinctively that what I'd said had distressed him.

'No, Maia, I won't. Because I have never found her.'

As the familiar thick hedge of spruce trees, which shielded our waterside home from prying eyes, came into view, I saw Marina standing on the jetty and the dreadful truth of losing Pa finally began to sink in.

And I realised that the man who had created the kingdom in which we had all been his princesses was no longer present to hold the enchantment in place.

The
SEVEN
SISTERS

The Seven Sisters series is the multimillion-copy
bestselling phenomenon by Lucinda Riley, inspired by
the mythology of the famous star constellation.

Discover the full series at panmacmillan.com

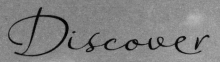

Discover

more spellbending novels from
Lucinda Riley at **panmacmillan.com**

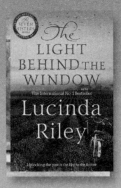

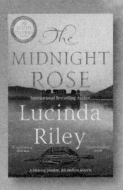

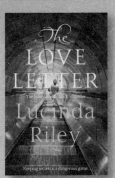

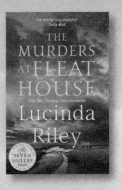